*THE ...*

"A compellingly dark ...
and passion. Alexa Egan promises to be a star of the genre."

—Kathryne Kennedy, author of The Elven Lords series

"Complex world-building and compelling characters. Egan's creatures are sexy, soulful, and dangerous."

—Molly Harper, author of the Nice Girls series

"Replete with dark, sensuous, and honorable characters and a fast-paced, intricate plot, this highly romantic and exciting story is a winner."

—*RT Book Reviews* (4½ stars)

"Sexy shifters, ancient blood feuds, and a heroine who won't quit her man."

—*USA Today* bestselling author Caridad Piñeiro

"Brilliant and inventive storytelling."

—*VampChix*

"A series to keep an eye on."

—*All About Romance*

"You will be pulled into the magical parallel reality created by Alexa Egan and not want to leave."

—*Bitten By Romance*

## Also by ALEXA EGAN

*Demon's Curse*

*Shadow's Curse*

**Available from Pocket Books**

*Awaken the Curse*

*Unleash the Curse*

*Vanquish the Curse*

**Available from Pocket Star Books**

# *Warrior's Curse*

### Book Three in the
### Imnada Brotherhood Series

## ALEXA EGAN

Pocket Books

New York   London   Toronto   Sydney   New Delhi

Pocket Books
A Division of Simon & Schuster, Inc.
1230 Avenue of the Americas
New York, NY 10020

This book is a work of fiction. Any references to historical events, real people, or real places are used fictitiously. Other names, characters, places, and events are products of the author's imagination, and any resemblance to actual events or places or persons, living or dead, is entirely coincidental.

First Pocket Books paperback edition May 2014

POCKET and colophon are registered trademarks of Simon & Schuster, Inc.

For information about special discounts for bulk purchases, please contact Simon & Schuster Special Sales at 1-866-506-1949 or business@simonandschuster.com.

The Simon & Schuster Speakers Bureau can bring authors to your live event. For more information or to book an event contact the Simon & Schuster Speakers Bureau at 1-866-248-3049 or visit our website at www.simonspeakers.com.

Cover illustration by Craig White

Manufactured in the United States of America

10   9   8   7   6   5   4   3   2   1

ISBN 978-1-4516-7293-0
ISBN 978-1-4516-7296-1 (ebook)

# Warrior's Curse

# Prologue

DEEPINGS, CORNWALL—
THE PRIMARY SEAT OF THE DUKE OF MORIEUX
SUMMER 1815

No matter what, they would not see him weep.

Instead Gray bit his lower lip until blood dripped hot down his chin to mix with the streaks already smearing his bruised and battered chest. He twisted against the silver fetters clamped around his wrists and ankles, his torn flesh mottled a sickly shade of green from the metal's poisonous touch, but the struggle served only to sap him of the little strength he had left.

"Just get it over with," he shouted, despising the weakness cracking his voice and the tremors shaking his knees.

The old man merely stared with milky pale eyes upon his only surviving grandson. An aura of disappointment carved long lines in the duke's aged and solemn face. His heir had let him down—again.

Gray's gaze widened to take in the Gather elders ringing the duke like hounds round a carcass. The ruddy-faced, corpulent Lord Carteret, down from his lonesome highland holding. Owen Glynjohns from

Wales, with his bold good looks and bard's clever tongue. The Skaarsgard, who'd traveled from the ocean-sprayed Orkney cliffs, where the basking seals and the rugged fishermen considered each other kin. Each of the men looked on impassively, their duty done if not enjoyed.

The fourth elder watched the proceedings with a face pale as bone and eyes hollow with mute rage, his hands clamped against the arms of his chair like claws. No doubt Sir Desmond Flannery was imagining his own son's sentence, due to be carried out on the morrow. Mac would never snivel or flinch in fear. He was the consummate soldier, unlike Gray, once his senior officer.

Sir Desmond leaned forward, his mouth twisted in disgust. "Enough dallying. Let's have it done then. The sun'll be down in another wee bit and he'll"—he seemed to choke on his words—"he'll shift. The chains aren't intended to hold a bird on the wing."

The elder was right. Already Gray felt the queasy slide of Fey blood magic stealing over him, flames burning blue and silver at the edges of his vision. The sun would set soon, and the curse would take him over, twisting his unwilling body from man to beast for the hours of night. His eyes flashed wildly toward his grandfather before darting away again, his bowels churning ominously.

"Of course." A nondescript little gentleman with a clerk's fastidiousness stepped forward in response. The Arch Ossine—Sir Dromon Pryor—had eyes that missed nothing and a mouth trained for truth-twisting. "Mr. Copper. Whenever you're ready."

Gray tried meeting Pryor's triumphant stare but

faltered when the enforcer stepped to the scaffold, a red-hot iron brand held in one brutish fist.

The restless audience whispered, feet shuffling against the benches, but no one called out or came to his defense. They knew the laws that had governed the Imnada's existence for a hundred generations. Understood that the weak and the sick and those no longer able to serve the bloodlines must be excised like a cancer lest the whole pack be brought low. Lowest peasant or heir to the Duke of Morieux himself, it made no difference when it came to preserving the safety of the five clans.

Gray found himself scanning the crowd for one particular face—though he knew she wouldn't be there. The duke had sent her north months ago. Still, Gray found himself repeating her name in his head like a mantra, a way to hold himself together in these final horrific moments.

What would she have done had she been here to witness his sentence? Would she have turned her back like the rest of them? Or would she have leapt to his defense as she had so many times over the years? He'd never know, and for that he was almost glad.

The brand's heat could be felt from three feet away. Gray clamped his jaw lest he embarrass himself with last-minute pleas for mercy. Still, two rasping words leaked from his bloody mouth as he stood bowed and shaking beneath the weight of his fear.

"Grandfather. Please."

The duke's chin lifted from the sagging folds of his neck while his hands fluttered for a moment. Then Sir Dromon leaned close to the aging leader of the five clans of Imnada, whispering his poison like silver into the old man's ear. The duke nodded. His hands relaxed into his lap. His mouth pursed and his eyes hardened once more, pale and uncaring as stones in a pool.

The enforcer laid the brand to Gray's back, singeing through the skin to the muscles and tendons below. The charred stench of roasting flesh filled his nose. Screams ripped from his body and tore up his throat. They bounced off the stone circle of the Deepings Hall, echoing back to him in waves of anguish. His knees buckled as he arched away from the pain, every nerve aflame, every drop of blood in his veins on fire, his very soul cleaving from his body.

Squeezing his eyes shut, he escaped to the darkest corner of his mind as a hunted creature burrows away from even the hope of light, but the desolate keening sounds of his disgrace followed him as his clan mark was burned away in a stripping of all he was or would ever hope to be. He retched until his ribs cracked and piss leaked into his boots.

But not one tear fell.

They never saw him weep.

She never saw him weep.

# 1

The bells were ringing nine in the morning when Major Gray de Coursy stepped from the hackney at Tower Hill. Despite the hour, fog cloaked the streets in a thick, choking darkness. It swirled in the alleys and gathered in the parks, bringing with it the stench of dead fish, river mud, and chimney soot. Lanterns threw dim greasy pools of light over the cobbles while footsteps and voices echoed eerily in the green-gray miasma. A link boy offered Gray his services but was waved away. His keen vision cut the gloom like a knife, and he wanted no witnesses to his destination.

He passed through a narrow, dingy lane, coming out near the disused waterstairs south of the Tower and St. Katherine's, stopping finally in front of a door set deep into a stone wall—part of an ancient chapter-house, though the wall and yard beyond were all that remained. He knocked once, then twice more.

A key turned. A bolt slid clear and the door swung open on the hunched figure of a man. "She awaits you, my lord."

"It's simply Major de Coursy, Breg. Lord Halvossa was my father's title and would have been my brother's after. Never mine."

"Yes, my lord . . . er . . . Major, sir. As you say." The porter bowed him in, throwing the bolt behind him. "I offered her breakfast but she refused."

"You did as you should." Gray approached a low, columned outbuilding, Breg following. At the entrance, the old man paused, shuffling foot to foot.

"Out with it," Gray said sternly.

The porter licked his lips and gave a quick breath as if steeling himself. "It's an enforcer, my lord. Prowling the streets near Cheapside last night."

"How could you tell it was an Ossine?"

Breg huffed. "I may be rogue and cast from my holding, same as yourself, but I can still sense a member of the five clans right enough. And I know a shaman when I cast my peepers on one. They're different, ain't they?"

"What was he doing?"

"Asking questions. I was afraid to get too close. Didn't want him catching wind of me following. No clansman would sob to hear old Breg had ended as food for the grubs with a stake through his heart, that's for sure."

Gray's mouth curved in a faint smile. "This clansman would. If you see him again, send word. But don't go sniffing around on your own. I can't afford to lose you."

"They're growing bolder, ain't they, my lord . . . Major, sir? I heard tell of a rogue near Clapham disappeared and turned up dead. Another one up north off Islington Road by the Quaker workhouse. It's not safe to be unmarked no more."

Gray's hand tightened around the head of his cane. "Things will change. They must, or the clans are doomed."

"Hope you're right, Major. I surely do."

Gray left Breg and entered the outbuilding, placing his worry over the man's revelations aside to be mulled over later. This morning's meeting was too important for distractions.

Lady Delia Swann rose from her chair to meet him, the lamplight gilding her golden hair and flushing her rose and cream skin. "It's been a long time, Gray."

Her serene beauty hid many secrets, as Gray well knew; her Fey-blood magic, her alliance with his rebels, and her sexual activities with a prince of the realm, two generals, and an archbishop. She assumed she knew all his secrets as well, but there were some things he did not speak aloud. Some fears he refused to name.

"I've been busy." He bowed over the hand she held out, ignoring the glitter of conquest in her eyes.

"As have I, but that doesn't mean we can't be busy together from time to time." Her gaze traveled sensuously over him, lifting the hairs at the back of his neck. "By the looks of you, I'd guess you haven't been to bed yet. Was it that little Nicholls girl? She practically leapt into your arms last night at the Praters' ball. I wouldn't think virgins were to your taste, but then you've always been full of surprises. And she comes with an ample dowry."

"I'm old enough to be her father."

Lady Delia laughed. "Only if you'd sired her at the ripe old age of eleven."

"I should have said I feel old enough to be her father."

"That I would believe. But if it wasn't the Nicholls girl, it must have been Lady Bute." She laid a finger against her full lips, gold-flecked eyes lifted in thought. "Then there's that opera dancer they say tried to drown herself in the Thames for love of the mysterious Ghost Earl. Hmm . . . so many choices . . ."

"Whoever came up with that damned sobriquet should have their heads boiled in oil."

She crossed to his side. "You should be flattered. It makes you seem dashing and dangerous and passionately gallant. A hero in a swashbuckling romance." She cupped his face in her hands. "If they only knew the half of it, am I right?"

He stepped back, out of her reach. "Can we move on with the reason for this meeting?"

She gave a little half shrug. "Of course. Have you made the arrangements we spoke of? If I'm to disappear, I want to be sure all my affairs are in order, and that includes the boy."

His hand tightened around the head of his cane, lips pinched tight. "It's been done just as you asked."

"And my personal payment for services rendered?"

Gray took a leather pouch from his coat and tossed it on a nearby table. "You can disappear quite thoroughly with what's there. Make a new life on the Continent or in the Americas. You'll be safe. You'll be free."

"I like the sound of that. I've already booked passage on the packet to Calais. From there, the world is my playground."

"You leave so soon?"

"You sound disappointed"—she offered him a sly

smile which he did not return—"but now that you've done as I asked, there's nothing more holding me here."

"The boy is here."

"A boy no longer. He'll miss me for a short while, but life will rectify that quickly enough." She shrugged, though he knew she cared more than she let on. "I've been asked politely by Lord Burrell to vacate my town house in favor of his latest *affaire du coeur*, and the family pile in Devonshire was never a home to me." She shivered. "Too full of ghosts for my taste. My sister is welcome to it." The leather pouch disappeared inside her voluminous cloak, and a narrow flat jeweler's box, designs etched into its surface with an artist's skill, was laid on the table in its place. "The last missing Key of Gylferion, as promised. I believe you have the other three already?"

"I might." Gray opened the lid to reveal a notched copper disk, dulled green with age and bent at one corner. On one side, the crescent of the Imnada; on the other, two vertical opposing arrows within a diamond. "How did you get hold of it?"

"Best not to ask. You might not like the answer." She cocked her head, watching him. A frown drew her lips into a pout. "You know, I could take your money and still sell you out to the highest bidder, Gray. The Ossine would be on your doorstep by nightfall. And if they didn't kill you, the Other would. Your enemies are mounting."

He closed the box and slid it into his coat pocket. "You could, but you won't."

"What makes you so certain? I'd sell my own soul if it gained me a profit."

This time it was he who reached out and touched

her cheek. "You say these things, but I know you better."

"You always did." She sighed. "Probably why we never got along." Her eyes grew troubled. "Be careful, Gray. In my line of work, I hear the whispers. You're being watched by my kind as well as yours. There are wagers about who'll move first to eliminate you. Perhaps you should think of joining me in Calais."

He rubbed a thumb across his scarred palm, the myriad pale lines crisscrossing the roughened skin like a tangled skein of threads. Each day brought a new cut and a new scar as he worked the magic that kept him whole and the black curse at bay. A magic that had become an addiction. He could not stop. He could not continue. Either choice brought sickness and then death. "If I can't break the Fey-blood's curse, neither side will have to worry over me for long. I'll be dead and the Ghost Earl shall be ghost in truth."

The mouse squeezed its way into the narrow crack between street and foundation, glancing back once to make sure it had not been followed. No sign of pursuit. The way was clear. Wriggling through the maze of lathing and plaster, it followed its clever rodent nose past the kitchens, which were quiet this late at night, and upward to the ground floor. The study was dark; the dining room, empty, but the mouse expected that. The hour was late. It was the perfect time to explore unseen, and the perfect form in which to do so unnoticed. What was one mouse among a colony of such? A nuisance, but hardly worth more than a stiff whisk with a broom. Better that than a sword in the gut, which might be the reaction should Gray discover the real identity of the rodent creeping along his wainscoting.

Sliding under a broken slat, the mouse moved through the walls with purpose, assessing the town house's layout should quick escape be necessary, searching rooms as it went. No guests resided in the empty chambers. Only half a handful of servants lay sleeping in the attics. Of guards, it saw no sign. He was alone and unprotected. Didn't he understand the danger?

Reaching a small room at the back of the second floor, the mouse paused at the flicker of candlelight coming through a gap in the chair rail. Following the dim glow, it sniffed and pushed its beady-eyed head out through the hole. A bedchamber. *His* bedchamber, by the lived-in, cluttered look of it.

A shocking thought followed close upon this observation. A shocking, unnerving thought that had the mouse shoving its way out through the hole into the room to rise on its hind legs, whiskers twitching. Did that heap of blankets in the bed move? Was someone sleeping? Was it two someones and were they sleeping at all? What if they were in the middle of . . .

So focused on determining whether the four-poster in the corner contained one or two people, it missed the quick descent of a crystal glass that trapped it, held in place by an enormous hand.

A face leaned close, studying the mouse, searching for answers. Older now. Harder. The gentle rounded features and sweet innocence of youth had been stripped bare and scraped raw until it seemed honed like a knife blade, no softness to dull the glittering edge. No tenderness to moderate the harsh austerity. But the same icy blue eyes shone from beneath dark winged brows, the same tiny scar remained at the edge of a strong uncompromising mouth. The same long aristocratic nose flared now with suspicion and doubt.

Scooping up glass and mouse both, the man lifted them to eye level. "Eagles eat mice, you know."

Meeryn Munro was the last person Gray had expected to visit him—in his bedchamber—in the middle of the night . . . alone. Yet here she was, shed of her mouse's skin and seated on the edge of his bed in nothing but his borrowed robe. At this point, he would have preferred her covered in fur. It was far less revealing. Far less apt to make his thoughts wander away from what her unexpected arrival meant.

"You've changed—grown up." A trite and point-less comment. Of course she'd changed since he'd seen her last.

"Age happens to the best of us, I'm told," she answered with a wry smile.

"Yes, but . . ." He waved a hand in her general direction. "The curls are gone"—replaced by soft waves of honey-colored hair—"and your figure has matured"—the gawky, flat-chested girl of his memories was now a woman of luscious feminine curves and long elegant limbs—"and you used to have . . . I mean there were the . . . the . . ."

She wrinkled her nose. "Spots. I know, they were positively horrid, but thankfully long gone. Lemon juice and oil of talc every evening before bed. But surely, I haven't changed that much."

"No, not exactly." His gaze traveled over her from head to foot and back. The ghost of the old Meeryn lingered in the narrow elfin face, pert chin, and full coral lips, but there was a shrewdness in her eyes and a severity to her jaw that had never been present in the laughing playmate of his youth. "And then again—yes."

"Well, you haven't. You look just as you always did."

His smile came laced with bitterness. "That's the first lie I've caught you in tonight."

"It's true. You do look the same. A bit longer in the tooth and leaner in the face, of course, but that's to be expected after . . . well . . . after all you've been through."

She couldn't say the words. He didn't blame her. It had taken months before he could speak of his banishment without vomiting his guts until his throat and stomach were raw and even then he'd not been able to say the word. A sensibility he'd overcome as he had so many others. There was no room in his life for sentiment. He rubbed his scarred palm without even thinking. Dropped his hand to his side when he caught her watching him.

"I heard rumors that you'd lifted the curse," she said.

"Contained . . . not lifted."

"But it's night"—her gaze cut to the window—"the sun is down and you're still . . . they said when the sun left the sky, you were forced to become your animal aspect. Forced from man to beast against your will. That's what I was told."

"There are ways to hold the spell at bay and keep to the form I choose, but it comes at a price." He poured and handed her a glass of brandy from the decanter permanently set beside his bed for those nights he couldn't sleep.

"Things never change, do they, Professor Gray? Still got your nose caught in a dusty old book," she commented with a nod of her head toward his cluttered desk.

"That's where the answers are," he answered. He cleared away the various manuscripts he'd been studying, arranging his pencils in a row, pocketing the four ancient metal disks, being careful to return the Krylesos Pryth, the silver disk of the Gylferion, to its leather drawstring bag. The draught made him sick enough. He needn't add silver's poison to his list of illnesses.

Laughter danced in her eyes. "Your response hasn't changed either. How long has it been—ten years? It's hard to believe."

Ten years—the blink of an eye. An eternity. They'd grown up together; duke's grandson and duke's ward. Close as siblings—closer even. His brother had been eight years his senior and barely noticed Gray except as a nuisance to be shed at the first possible opportunity. Meeryn had filled that slot, becoming his boon companion in all things, from illicit raids on the Deepings kitchens and nasty pranks on the string of tutors and governesses when they were young, to illicit raids on the Deepings wine cellar and midnight forays beyond the protections of Deepings' walls as they grew older.

As a child, he'd foolishly imagined their friendship would last forever. First school, then university, and finally the army ended that dream. Yet, she'd remained a bright memory among so much he'd tried to put behind him when he'd been condemned to exile. Was that remembrance, like so many other things in his life, about to be irrevocably shattered?

"Why are you here, Meeryn? And why sneak in?"

She offered him a flippant roll of her eyes. "Would you have welcomed me if I'd knocked and presented my calling card?"

"Not while Pryor and his enforcers scour London, hunting those they believe to be in league with me." He poured himself a brandy.

"But, you see, it was Pryor who sent me."

He froze with the glass halfway to his lips, but there was no hint of mockery in her placid expression. She was dead serious. "Did he? Interesting."

"I know what you're thinking, Gray, but you can relax. I'm not here to kill you. I'm here to bring you home."

"I *am* home," he replied just as solemnly, placing his still-full glass on a nearby table. This conversation called for stone-cold sobriety.

"Don't be clever. You know what I mean—home to Deepings."

"Why would I do that?"

"To prevent more bloodshed? To broker peace between your rebels and the Ossine?" She paused. "To save the Imnada?"

"Dromon was clever in sending you as his emissary. Anyone else would have been shown the door . . . or the end of my sword. Meeryn, you have five minutes to explain, then you leave."

Defiance lit her unflinching stare. "The duke is dying."

Gray closed his eyes briefly on a silent prayer, though for what he couldn't say. For some reason, he'd always just assumed the old man would live forever; a craggy irascible rock upon which the world crashed and broke. His presence solid and eternal as the cliffs below Deepings.

"He's been ill since you . . . since the summer you were sent away," Meeryn continued. "Then this past spring he took a turn for the worse. It's his heart. They don't expect him to last more than a few weeks."

"And if I said good riddance to the old bastard?"

Candlelight flickered over her face, glinting in her auburn hair, as flames were reflected in her deep brown eyes. "You don't mean that. He's the only family you have left. When he dies, you'll be—"

"Duke of Morieux," he finished her sentence.

"Leader of the five clans," she amended.

Neither role had been his by birth—a fact his grandfather had never ceased to remind him of, even as Gray struggled to fill his dead brother's shoes. He'd finally escaped into the military, unsure by then whether he hoped to win honor in battle or a quick death. There, he'd finally found the praise he'd sought in the letters that arrived from home. A pride that ended in the Gather's circle with the flames charring the clan mark from his back.

"Sir Dromon Pryor is leader in all but name." He stood at the hearth, a hand upon the mantel as he stared into the cold expanse, wishing he might glimpse the future, but seeing only the past.

"His grip isn't as secure as he wants you to believe, and it will only worsen if the duke dies without an heir in place," Meeryn explained. "Rumors spread as your rebellious Imnada grow in numbers. The Gather elders chafe under his heavy-handed authority, and the brutality of his Ossine enforcers only make things worse. Summary executions of clansmen on the mere suspicion of sedition are becoming common."

Gray had known there would be problems once the

Imnada made their existence known to the Fey-bloods. Not for nothing had the shapechangers hidden after King Arthur's murder sparked the savage purges of the Fealla Mhòr, and those born with the blood and power of the Fey sought to wipe the offending Imnada off the map. Only the great N'thuil Aneavala wielding the power of Jai Idrish had saved the shapechangers from extinction a thousand years ago by calling upon the sphere's power to erect the Palings, the great walls of mist that hid and protected their holdings from a dangerous world.

For centuries this had been enough and the clans had continued on untroubled by outside threats. But as the clans numbers declined, so too did the power of the Palings. It would be only a matter of time before the Fey-bloods discovered a way through the wards. Would they come extending an open hand of friendship or the closed fist of war? The years of seclusion and secrecy had hardened the prejudices on both sides until now every encounter was fraught with peril and salted with misinformation.

Gray's rebellious Imnada and open-minded Other sought to fight these ancient perceptions, but for every step forward there seemed to be ten steps backward. Every inch of this battlefield had been won with blood and tears and the bodies of fallen companions. The strife within the clans only added to a body count the Imnada could ill afford.

As if reading his mind, Meeryn added, "The clans won't survive an attack from without while they are beset from within." Tension strained her gaze. "Pryor concedes this and wants to talk."

"Pryor's tongue is as crooked as his brain. Why should I trust him?" Gray asked coolly.

"Don't trust him. Trust me." She smiled, her eyes alight with mischief. "As N'thuil, I can guarantee you safe passage on holding lands. So long as you're with me, you're protected."

She spoke. He saw her lips move, but he heard nothing after the bit about Meeryn being named N'thuil. Voice of Jai Idrish. Living vessel of the Mother Goddess.

Idrin the Traveler, the father of their race and the founder of his house, had brought the clans safely through the Gateway guided by the crystal sphere of Jai Idrish—the Imnada's most sacred relic. He had been the first of a long and distinguished line of N'thuil, bearers of the awesome power and grave responsibility that went along with the mental bond between stone and flesh.

None knew how or why the sphere selected any particular host, but all acknowledged that those the crystal selected stood equal to the wisest of Ossine shamans and the strongest of clan leaders in a strange triad that had served the Imnada since the first comers arrived in their new home—or had at one time.

Jai Idrish had remained stubbornly silent since before Gray's grandfather's grandfather had been born. For the last hundred and fifty years, the Arch Ossines had taken it upon themselves to select the N'thuils, each one more subservient and useless than the last. The respect for the office of vessel and voice eroded with each passing year and each pointless placeholder, until these days it was barely more than a figurehead.

"Sir Dromon selected you to take Tidwell's place? He's never chosen anyone not shaman-trained."

"Sir Dromon did not do the choosing."

"Then who . . . ?" His words trailed off as the truth

dawned. "Jai Idrish chose its N'thuil? That's impossible."

There must be a mistake . . . perhaps he'd misunderstood . . . perhaps she teased him. She'd always been a devilish hoyden . . .

The anointed keepers of Jai Idrish were wizened and learned men with years of experience and acumen to draw on as they guided the clans through tumultuous times. They were *not* curvaceous honeyblondes with clever smiles and secretive brown eyes who smelled of cold seas and warm sun and tempted him with memories of home.

She dragged the robe from her shoulders and twisted around so her back faced him. There, high upon her shoulder blade, was the crescent of the Imnada, a whorl of black against her golden skin. And just to the right of it, still pink at the edges, was the smaller circlet that signified her ascension to the seat of N'thuil.

No mistake.

Unthinking, his fingers traced the needle's narrow marking as it curved up over her shoulder blade to the base of her neck. She shivered and cast him an arch look, the laughter dying in her eyes to be replaced with something uncertain and almost shy. His finger became his hand. The skin of her back was like silk beneath his palm as he caressed downward along her spine to the point where her hips flared and the robe and his own self-control stopped him from descending farther. Her lips parted, and he sensed the suspension of her breath, the tremors running beneath her skin. Her eyes darkened within the thick fringe of her lashes. Was it longing he saw? Excitement?

His heart thrashed against his ribs, and sweat splashed hot and cold over his skin. He wanted to tempt Meeryn further; an inch lower, a breath nearer. Then a breeze teased the candle's thin flame. Her look vanished as if it had never been, and he surfaced from the lecherous swirl of his desire just before he made an utter ass of himself.

"When was your ascension to N'thuil?" Thankfully, his voice emerged only slightly raspy.

Meeryn yanked the robe up to her neck, her body rigid, her gaze fierce. "A month ago. I'm surprised you didn't hear." Her voice trembled, though the emotion behind it was difficult to decipher. "Sir Dromon claims you have spies in every household and know our secrets before we speak them."

"I'm flattered, but unfortunately, my network isn't quite that extensive or well informed."

She opened her mouth as if to respond, her gaze swimming with thoughts left unspoken. Gave an almost imperceptible shake of her head before continuing on. "Muncy Tidwell died unexpectedly a few weeks ago."

Somehow he doubted that was what she'd originally intended to say, but if she wasn't going to remark on his boorish behavior, he sure as hell wasn't. And so the awkwardness dissipated ever so slowly.

"A more useless N'thuil the world has never seen," Gray replied. "But enough about him. Tell me of your choosing. How did it happen?"

She ducked her head, looking almost shy . . . or ashamed. "It wasn't my fault, Gray. Honestly. I woke one night as if someone had called to me. I walked out into the corridor, thinking I was being summoned; that His Grace needed me. I don't remember much after that, bits and pieces, but the next thing I knew I was standing in the tower sanctuary, the crystal glowing warm beneath my fingers. It was as if a piece I never knew was missing had suddenly slotted itself into place and I was whole."

"The clans must be in a tumult over Jai Idrish's waking."

"Hardly. I'm not exactly the N'thuil they were expecting. Nor has the sphere spoken to me since the night of my choosing. I've tried everything, and it remains as cold as the grave under my hand."

"What was Sir Dromon's reaction?"

"The Arch Ossine wasn't happy, but there was nothing he could do once Jai Idrish had chosen its Voice. The laws are clear, and if Sir Dromon is a stickler about anything, it's following clan law."

"Hoisted with his own petard." A smile quirked Gray's lips as the implications of this news sank in. "He must have been furious after so many years with a compliant toady like Tidwell serving as mouthpiece and cover for his crimes. Perhaps that's why Jai Idrish chose you. You've never been compliant in your life."

A fact he just might be able to use to his advantage.


The old man slept—finally. For hours he'd tossed and turned in his bed, whimpering and mewling like an infant searching for his mother. The once massive, bearlike leader of the Imnada clans who'd inspired equal parts awe and fear in friend and enemy alike had shrunken to a palsied shell of himself, his shock of white hair yellowed and sparse, his piercing blue eyes faded to a watery gray with age and pain.

Sir Dromon had sat with him, murmuring pap in hopes of keeping him quiet. Soothed him with stories of the golden days before the duke's son, daughter-in-law, and eldest grandson had died in the stormy seas, only the youngest and weakest of the brood spared from the drowning drag of the waves. Major de Coursy he called himself . . . as if denying his courtesy title of Earl of Halvossa could erase the events of that lost summer day and his guilt in the tragedy.

"Deepings used to ring with laughter, Pryor. Do you remember? The parties and the picnics, the dances and the dinners. Such good times we had then."

"I remember, Your Grace."

"Never again, Pryor. Such a little boat it was. I warned them not to take it out, warned them of the storm. Do you suppose they suffered long?"

"I don't suppose so, Your Grace."

"The boy is all that's left. Why would the Mother spare me the mewling runt and take the others? Is there a lesson in that?"

"Only the goddess knows, Your Grace."

"None left of my house, Pryor. None but a weakling who bears a Fey-blood's curse. A cast-out, unmarked *emnil*."

*And a treasonous, slime-riddled bastard rebel.* But Sir Dromon hadn't poisoned the duke's ears with that truth. He hadn't needed to—not anymore.

The conversation had quickly dwindled to self-pitying complaints, unintelligible babbling, and finally, ragged weeping before the duke drifted into a restless sleep.

Sir Dromon tossed one last contemptuous glance toward the draped tester bed where the duke whuffled and snored. Each day, his grip weakened. Each night his strength failed a little more. Time ran short. If the duke died and Major de Coursy inherited the title, all

Sir Dromon had worked toward over his lifetime could be thrown in jeopardy. The whispers second-guessing de Coursy's exile and the blame surrounding his own part in it grew daily. If he didn't put an end to it, the Gather elders might seek to overturn de Coursy's sentence and place him on his grandfather's throne.

No, it couldn't happen. Sir Dromon wouldn't let it. He'd worked too hard to have that prize snatched from his fingers. While de Coursy remained alive, he remained a threat; a rallying point for all disaffected Imnada. Yet, killing the last son of Idrin's house outright held equal risks. Wavering allies might balk at assassination. Sympathetic clansmen might be swayed to join de Coursy's growing rebellion. No, the traitor must be discredited first. Accused of a crime so heinous that all Imnada would see his death as justice—not murder.

"His Grace is sleeping. I want none to disturb him," Sir Dromon ordered the footman standing watch outside the bedchamber. "But come to me if there is any change. I want to know immediately, day or night."

"Yes, my lord."

Pryor retreated to his bedchamber a floor and a wing away. He'd moved into the duke's residence two summers ago, ostensibly to assist His Grace during his time of grief following the exile of his heir. But after two years he'd firmly established himself as master of the house with unquestioned authority. Or would have, but for one upstart female with delusions of grandeur—the duke's ward, Meeryn Munro. She'd always been a nuisance, but her recent ascension to N'thuil had transformed the irritating thorn in his side to a dangerous dagger at his throat.

He placed his candle on a cabinet, took a seat, and pulled his *krythos* from his coat pocket. Balancing the far-seeing disk on the palm of his hand, he spoke the words that unlocked its powers. The notched glass disk glowed softly, a crackle of energy washing over his hand and up his arm into his brain as he reached out with his mind, using the disk to amplify his telepathy over miles of countryside. The pathing unrolled in his head like a diffuse ribbon of sound and light, but strength and concentration and years of training focused the power of the *krythos* like a spear point: a blade aimed from this tiny corner of England straight to the heart of London and a town house on elegant Audley Street.

*Have you convinced him? Is he coming home?*

The answer erupted in his mind with the blunt strength of an oxen's kick. No finesse. No subtlety. Brute power. Wild power. *Not yet but soon. I've guaranteed his safety as N'thuil.*

The woman grew insufferable in her supposed authority. Did she really believe the title of N'thuil meant anything in these days? Jai Idrish was a useless relic. Its Voice a charlatan who served at his whim. He gritted his teeth. *Whatever you need to do, my lady. The future of the clans depends upon your success.*

*I understand.*

Doubtful. But that was all to the better. Perhaps if he played his cards carefully, he might kill two birds with the same stone; or, more specifically, one accursed eagle and a rather annoying little sparrow.

# 2

<hr/>

"Conal?" Meeryn murmured, dazed and half-asleep.

The sound came again, a gasp broken off, a moan caught behind clenched teeth. Meeryn's eyes snapped open on a room heavy with shadows, but this was not Deepings, and her lover was long dead. His was not the cry that woke her.

It must be Gray.

She rose, grabbing up her borrowed dressing gown, the scents of sandalwood and brandy caught in the folds. A masculine, virile smell to remind her—as if she needed it—that the Gray she'd barged in on last night was not the scrawny, thin-skinned, bookworm she'd known so well. This man was harder, angrier, unpredictable.

She opened the door of her bedchamber, listening for any sign of approaching servants, but the only sound was the low drone of a city on the verge of waking. A roar like the surf pressing against her eardrums. Just when she decided she'd imagined it, the cry came again, but this time the groan ended in a violent smash of glass and a heavy thud.

She hurried down the corridor, only to hesitate in front of Gray's closed door. What if it was naught more than a nightmare? She'd feel an idiot barging into his room for a bad dream. And what if he assumed she'd come for some other reason? That she desired . . . wanted . . . yearned for . . . the thought was completely mortifying.

A thump and muffled oath drained the last of her uncertainty away. She lifted the latch. "Hello?"

The stench nearly buckled her knees. A horrible odor of sickness overlaid by a vinegary sulphur smell that burned her eyes and stung her nose until it ran. Curtains had been pulled across the windows and no candle or fire leavened the gloom, but her heightened animal eyesight pierced the dark easily. A humped pile of blankets and pillows lay beside the bed. A chair rested on its side. But it was the hunched figure of a man in the corner that sent her hurrying across the room, glass crunching beneath her bare feet.

"Gray?" She knelt at his side, a hand on his shoulder, searching for blood or a wound. "What's happened? Did you fall? What's wrong?"

"Curse . . ." he whispered through chattering teeth, his body shuddering, sweat pouring off him in waves. "Left it too long . . ." His eyes burned like blue flames, his face drawn with pain and sickness. "Can't see . . ."

She clasped his hand, blood slicking her palm. "You're bleeding."

"Draught on my desk . . . medicine . . . bring it to me." He curled into a tighter ball, shoulders braced for pain, jaw clamped. "Need it . . . now . . ."

She rose, scanning the room. There on the desk, just as he instructed; a glass vial full of a green greasy brew. She poured it into a cup, wrinkling her nose at the thick rotten-egg smell. "What is this godawful stuff?"

"Sanity," he said, reaching for it. "Survival."

She closed his fingers around the cup. "Drink it."

"Need the blood . . ." With an effort that left him breathless and retching, he struggled upright. Held his palm above the cup as three drops of blood slid into the viscous potion. Immediately, the slimy, slick burn of Fey-blood magic hardened like knives against her mind.

Meeryn felt her stomach rise into her throat just watching him. "Are you sure that's wise?"

He swirled it around before gulping it down in one swig. "Swallow . . . or die . . ." he murmured, closing his eyes and leaning back against the wall with a sigh.

Minutes passed as she watched the sky brighten behind the curtain and the shadows retreat to pools in the corners. Gray's face lost the stretched chalky pallor of the deathly ill, his shoulders relaxed, his hands uncurled to lie flat upon his knees, his shaking stopped.

"It grows worse every day," he said quietly.

"What does? What was that you took?"

"The draught keeps the curse in check, but the trade-off is my life. The potion is eating it away."

"Then stop, for heaven's sake."

He shook his head. "Can't. To go without for more than a few days is to end as you saw me. Slipping toward a horrible and painful death. I need to stay alive a little longer. I haven't finished my work . . . things I must do for the good of the clans. Then I can let go. Gladly let go."

"The Fey-bloods did this to you, didn't they? I can

feel their foul stench all over this. Those soul-feeding, back-stabbing, treacherous—"

"Meeryn." His voice, quiet but firm, pulled her up short. When had he learned that little trick? "The Fey offered the four of us hope. They'd no idea of the consequences. It's their magic reacting with our bodies. We warp the energy, taint it. They would heal us if they could, but there's nothing to be done."

"I don't believe it. They must have known. It was a trick."

"Poison four outcast Imnada? To what purpose?"

"You're the heir to the five clans. They must have known. This was their way of ridding themselves of an enemy leader."

"I'm heir to nothing. Not since the Ossine stripped me of my mark and cast me out. The Fey gain nothing with my death. The Imnada, on the other hand, would be more than happy to have me gone."

"Is there nothing you can do?"

"I may have found an answer. I just need time." He closed his eyes. "A commodity fast running out. A few months—give or take—is all I have."

"Don't be silly," she said, frightened at the resignation in his voice. "We'll figure it out. You and me together. Just like when we were little."

He reached up to push her hair off her face and trace the line of her cheek. His hand was cold and moist to the touch with illness, but his eyes were as brilliant as blue ice. "I've missed you, Meeryn."

Her heart tumbled in her chest. "Fine way of showing it. I came back from the islands all those years ago to find you gone off to the army and nothing but one miserable note shoved under my door as farewell. Do you know how that felt?" She snapped her jaw shut on words she'd never expected to speak aloud. Glanced away on an awkward silence.

"I'm sorry. I knew I should have waited, but . . ." He dipped a shoulder in dismissal and whatever he'd been about to say was left unspoken. "Grandfather was so proud. You'd have thought I'd taken on Napoleon single-handed. After Waterloo and those final days, it was horrid to see him look at me . . . through me . . . as if I was nothing . . . as if I no longer existed."

"I know that look."

"Do you? What on earth could the duke's favorite have done to warrant such harshness? The man thought the sun rose and set in you."

"It doesn't matter anymore. Just remember that being a favorite only means you have farther to fall." She crossed to the window, pushing back the curtains to look down upon the street. "I've missed you too, Gray. For years, Deepings has been a ghost of its former self, but since your exile, it's become a tomb. A tomb for the living."

"Grandfather's really dying?"

"A breath of air could blow his soul through the Gateway. It might be your last chance to make peace with him . . . and with yourself." She turned to see Gray pull himself to his feet and take a few shaky steps toward his bed. Tremors quivered his body, every muscle taut with lingering pain. He leaned against the post, dark head bowed.

"What would I say to him?" he asked.

"Tell him you love him," she answered.

"And if that's a lie?"

"He's only a few weeks left. He'll never know."

He lifted his head, eyes cold as steel in a bleak and brutal face. "I'll know."


Gray rubbed at his bandaged hand in an attempt to alleviate the infuriating itch of healing across his scarred palm. It helped, but not much, and he finally jammed his hand into a pocket, hoping out of sight would mean out of mind. Glancing up, he was just in time to catch David St. Leger holding the one and only copy in existence of Cathal Du's *States of Mirage* by a dog-eared corner. "Bloody hell, David. That book's a priceless historical artifact. Don't dangle it like something the dog hawked up."

David dropped the book in a flutter of dusty pages. "Calm down. It's fine. If it's lasted a thousand years, I don't think one dangling will do it any harm."

Gray rubbed his temples. "Can you restrain him, Mac? My brain feels mushy as an egg; the last thing I need this morning is David's brand of humor."

Mac Flannery looked up from the sheaf of pages in his hand long enough to cock a dubious eyebrow in question. "What would you have me do? Tie him to a chair and gag him?"

"If need be," Gray barked, immediately regretting it as pain radiated from his tender skull all the way down into his toes.

"Why did you even bother asking me here if all you're going to do is threaten and insult?" David crossed his arms as he settled deeper into his chair and put his boots up on the tea table.

"I ask myself that very question." Gray had an almost overwhelming urge to wipe off the offending look with his fists. Hardly the first time he'd wanted to pummel David senseless. Doubtless it wouldn't be the last. But it was clear by the annoying smirk that St. Leger goaded him. Gray refused to give him the satisfaction. It would only encourage him.

"I think command has gone to your head." David eyed him over his steepled fingers. "You're not that much older than I am, yet you treat me like an addled child."

"That's because you act like an addled child more often than not."

David breezed past this criticism unabated. "What of Mac? You don't treat him with such a lack of respect."

Gray's headache was now oozing down his spine into his boots. Even his eyebrows hurt. "I doubt Mac acted like a child even when he was one."

"Good point," David muttered.

"Here, St. Leger." Mac poured him a tall glass of whisky. "Sip it very very slowly."

For five years, Adam Kinloch, David St. Leger, Mac Flannery, and Gray had served together as military scouts. From Lisbon, through Spain, over the Pyrenees into France, they'd prowled, slunk, stalked, and soared, gathering intelligence where no mere mortals could. Until the chaotic days before Waterloo, when a Fey-blood had cursed them with his dying breath.

Exile caused their friendship to unravel. Adam's murder brought them together again. And now treason bound them fast in a dangerous alliance.

Mac's strict sense of honor, devotion to duty, and raw courage made him a valuable asset to the rebel's cause. But David possessed more cunning, street smarts, and savage battle prowess than any man Gray had ever known. He trusted the two of them with his life. He loved them like brothers. Even when, in the case of David, he wanted to bash him over the head.

"Where's your bride, St. Leger? Maybe she can control you."

"Callista likes to try." David tossed back his whisky and held out the glass for another. "If I know my wife, she's babbling nonsense at Mac's son and wishing for one of her own." He shuddered. "Frightening thought."

Mac's wife, Bianca, had recently given birth, the boy barely over a month old. Gray had watched Mac with Declan; seen a father's pride warring with the pain of knowing he'd not live to see his son grow to manhood.

"I believe Bianca and the other ladies headed out into the garden," Mac volunteered. "Your . . . house guest . . . was quite taken with Declan."

"Her name is Meeryn." He paused. "Meeryn Munro."

"I still can't believe she asked you to return to Deepings."

"Pryor seeks to parlay."

"You believe that?" David was on his third whisky by now, loosening years of bitter resentment and a simmering anger that was never far from the surface.

Gray managed to topple into a chair before he doubled over and collapsed. It would do his dignity no good to retch all over the floor or faint dead away. "I have no reason to doubt her, but Pryor's request comes at the perfect time and gives me the perfect entrée into the holding."

"To do what exactly?" David asked cautiously.

Pause for dramatic effect, then . . . "Lift the Fey-blood curse once and for all."

Mac's eyes seemed to take on a hungry desperate gleam. "How?"

"With these." He spread four disks out on the table: silver, gold, copper, bronze.

"The Keys of Gylferion—you found them all."

Four disks forged by the Fey to imprison the traitorous warlord Lucan after the Battle of Camlann and Arthur's fall. Scattered and lost for centuries, only to be brought together again on a snowy mountaintop in Wales three years ago when the Imnada warlord was inadvertently released from his eternal torment. Then scattered again, this time deliberately, in a last attempt to keep them from the hands of the Imnada's enemies. Gray had moved heaven and earth to discover their whereabouts. Offered any price. Committed any crime.

His determination had paid off in these bits of dented, discolored metal laid before them.

"Lady Delia brought me the last one a few days ago," he said.

"How did she lay hands on it?" Mac asked. "It was supposedly locked up tighter than the crown jewels in an Amhas-draoi vault."

"Knowing Lady Delia, she seduced it away from its owner," David said caustically. "That woman could make a dead man stiff, and she damn well knows it. I've seen her reduce the most hard-bitten misogynist to a dancing puppet on a string."

"You speak from experience?" Mac asked, barely hiding his smirk.

David held up his hands palm out as if fending off

an attacker. "Not me. I'm all about self-preservation. You won't see me placing my head in the lioness's mouth."

"Lady Delia risked her life to bring me the last disk," Gray said quietly. "A bit more respect should be owing."

"What was her price?" David folded his arms across his chest matter-of-factly, eyebrows raised in wary cynicism. "Lady Delia doesn't do anything out of the goodness of her heart. She's all about the advantage, the going rate."

"She needed to escape the country. I agreed to assist her."

"Finally diddled the wrong man, did she?"

Gray clamped his jaw so hard he thought his teeth would crack. Yes, she had. And paid for it a hundred times over. He owed her any price she named.

"Lady Delia's a loose cannon, Gray," Mac said with a grim twist to his mouth. "Always has been. Her name is at the edge of every Fey-blood conspiracy, her face hovering just beyond the reach of our informants."

"She may not hold to any particular cause, but she's loyal . . . to me."

Mac and David exchanged looks that spoke paragraphs, but it was David—naturally—who took the bull by the horns. "Care to enlighten two old friends as to the origin of this constancy?"

"No," Gray replied coolly, hoping they would take the hint. He'd not the stamina to fight off their gadflying much longer.

"Your discretion does you credit. I just hope you're not placing trust in the wrong woman."

Gray accepted Mac's warning, but it was far too

late for half measures and faint hearts. His association with Lady Delia was necessary. He'd not second-guess himself now.

"If you have the disks, why travel to Deepings?" Mac asked, injecting reason back into the conversation.

"The Fey-blood sorcerer D'espe meant to kill us outright for the Charleroi massacre. Instead our Imnada blood twisted his magic into a corrosive twining of disparate powers that became the curse we suffer. Only by bringing those two forces back together can we unravel the separate threads until they fall away, leaving us free. The Keys of Gylferion, wrought to imprison Lucan in the Unseelie between, are the same twist of Fey and Imnada powers. Bring them together, strike a spark, and the curse will explode."

"And the spark lies in Deepings?" David asked.

"Jai Idrish." Mac's eyes widened in sudden understanding.

Gray nodded. "Just so. Jai Idrish is the only thing that even comes close to possessing as much innate power as the true Fey. If I can harness the forces locked within the crystal, I should be able to not only separate but completely sever the knotted threads of Fey and Imnada magic binding us to the curse."

"Right, so two years hunting down this knowledge, and the moment you discover this gem of a revelation, the new N'thuil shows up on your doorstep in the middle of the night inviting you to Deepings. What a bleeding coincidence!"

"Do I sense sarcasm, St. Leger?"

"I hope you sense a damned trap."

"Is that what you think?"

"Think? Hell, I fucking know it's one."

"And Meeryn? Where does she fall in this setup of yours?" Gray asked. He'd known from the outset that David would be the hardest to convince. He'd always been a suspicious cynic with a scoundrel's heart and a killer's instincts.

He gave a disbelieving snort and poured himself another whisky. "I don't know—Dromon's patsy or Dromon's stooge. Does her guilt or innocence matter when you're facing a stake to the heart? You'll be dead either way."

"It matters to me," Gray replied.

"No, *she* matters to you. You still think of her as the girl you played Knights and Maidens with when you were children, but ten years is a hell of a long time. People change in such a span. Hell, we're prime examples, aren't we?"

He couldn't argue with David's logic. The same questions had occurred to him in an endless loop of what-ifs, leaving him with no clear answers and a head that pounded like a drum. But one question had overridden them all: What happened if he didn't go? And the answer was as obvious as Mac's haggard features and David's continuing bitterness. The curse—and the dark Fey-blood who'd cast it—would win. They'd be dead. And the clans would fail.

Both were only a matter of time.

He caught himself scratching his bandaged palm once again. Turned it into a slow running of his finger over the seam of the cloth, tracing the latest slide of his knife, the turning of the screw. "I can take care of myself, David. And there are those within the Palings I can call on if need be."

"You're going back no matter what we say, aren't you?"

"I don't have a choice. This could be our last chance. To break the curse. To unite the clans. To broker a peace that will allow the Imnada not just to exist, but to thrive."

David threw up his hands. "Fine. Go. But be careful."

"That's usually my line." Gray tried to laugh off his worry, but David remained tight-lipped, his shoulders braced as if preparing for a fight.

"You're right, and that alone should be enough to give you pause."

Gray took a breath, let it out slowly, and nodded. "I'll be with Meeryn."

Mac's face hardened, lines grooved deep to either side of his moth, brows low. "So you shall. But in this rare instance I agree with David—be very careful."

"The boy never sleeps. I'm fortunate if I can get forty-five minutes together before he's up and squalling. Mac fell asleep putting on his boots last week, and I spooned salt in my tea this morning. We're both exhausted."

"What of the nurse you hired?"

"We let her go. I came home from the theater to find Declan screaming in his cot while Nurse Buntless read a Minerva horror with rags stuck in her ears."

"Oh dear."

"I love him dearly, but what I wouldn't give for eight full hours unconscious in my bed."

"Just what every husband wants to hear."

"Sad to say, but Mac's as desperate for sleep as I am. Last week, we both dozed off halfway through . . . I woke up later with his . . . and he . . . let's just say it wasn't my finest performance."

Meeryn watched the two women sitting on a bench beneath a spreading chestnut tree, blond head and dark bent close together as they chatted. Bianca Flannery's regal beauty was as awe-inspiring as her cool blue stare, while Callista St. Leger's dark sparkling eyes and kindly features invited sisterly confidences and bright laughter. Or would have, had she been anything but Fey-blood. Instead her magic tingled cold against Meeryn's skin and prickled at the base of her brain like a static charge. At least Bianca Flannery seemed no more than human, though even that unmagical race possessed the potential for danger through sheer numbers alone. They'd squeeze the Imnada out of existence and never even realize they were doing it.

But it was the baby lying on a blanket on the grass that drew Meeryn's attention like a lodestone upon a string. He wore a gown of white muslin, a bonnet covering his black curls. Tiny fists pumped the air as he squirmed, his face purpling with frustration.

"How old is he?"

Bianca looked up with a tired smile. "Seven weeks."

"I thought Gray said you were married in February."

"Yes, well . . . don't count too closely."

"At least you were married in time for your confinement."

"Only after some heavy persuading, and the threat of a fry pan to the head. Still, it's all come right in the end, I suppose." Bianca's eyes held a strain she sought to hide behind a sunny expression. "Mac says it's different among the clans. That relations between men and women are . . . more open."

"In some ways. Marriage is controlled completely by the Ossine who oversee the bloodline scrolls. The shamans find the most advantageous pairing for each clan member, and unsanctioned unions are forbidden. But beyond marriage, we're free to take our pleasure where we find it, and Imnada women are adept at avoiding unwanted consequences."

"A handy trait, that."

"It can be unless you . . . slip up."

"Come into the family way?"

"No. Think oneself in love."

She shook off her memories. Shoved Conal's face back down in the dark where it had lived for six perfectly comfortable years. Unfortunately, this visit had dislodged all sorts of disconcerting insights. She'd felt so sophisticated taking Conal McIlroy into her bed, seen it as a mark of her blossoming adulthood and a way to finally prove her maturity to those (namely the duke) who would keep her a child forever. Their time together had been brief but glorious. Sweet memories made while painful ones faded. When the young Viyachne clansman had ridden out of Deepings three years later in disgrace, she'd assumed that her life would end and her heart would break.

Surprisingly enough, neither event occurred.

She'd neither seen nor heard from Conal again, and only learned of his death by chance. By then her youthful adoration had faded, but her grief had been real, and his face and his kiss she carried with her to this day. His knife she carried strapped to her thigh.

"May I?" she asked with a nod toward the baby.

"Of course. He's building to a crescendo, though, so feel free to hand him off if he becomes too much."

Meeryn scooped up the sturdy little boy. She breathed in the clean powdery scent of his skin and nuzzled the downy softness of his hair. Immediately, she felt her shoulders uncurl from around her ears, her muscles relax, and her heart rate slow.

Cooing a favorite lullaby, Meeryn cradled young Flannery as his fingers curled around her thumb and held tight. Thick black lashes fringed deep blue eyes, and his bow of a mouth pursed in a bubbly grimace.

His eyes shut, and an ear-shattering wail sent birds scattering from the trees and a rabbit dodging for cover under a log. Instinctively, Meeryn reached out with the lightest of mental touches, wrapping the little boy in soothing waves of calming energy. Found herself recoiling with a small cry of shock at the Imnada power dancing across the surface of the child's mind like flickers from a thousand stars. Unless she'd interpreted the signs incorrectly, this child would grow up with the ability to shift and the talent to path like other Imnada.

But how? Every Ossine teaching asserted that this was impossible; that only by exact and approved pairings would the Imnada race continue. She reached out once more, easing her way along the child's consciousness, feeling the innate pathways and nascent connections. Every sense bristled with the rightness of what she was feeling. It might be years before his power manifested himself, but even now it shone bright as a flame in the night, a promise for the future.

She should be appalled by this unmarked half-breed and furious with Captain Flannery for marrying an out-clan. Instead affection oozed its way through her insides for this sweet innocent whose very mixed-race existence was an impossibility. And a hope.

"You have the motherly touch," Bianca said. "I wish I could hire you."

Meeryn realized that the boy's eyes had fluttered closed, his body limp as he drifted into sleep. "He's beautiful."

"He is, isn't he? He'll be handsome as his father when he's grown."

*And bear the heart of the panther like his father as well*, Meeryn thought, though she didn't say it. She needed to look into this further before she spoke her discovery aloud, and she knew exactly with whom she needed to speak. It would be the first thing she did upon returning to Deepings.

"Gray says the two of you grew up together." Callista St. Leger broke into the whirlwind of Meeryn's thoughts, her gold-flecked gaze curious. "Was he always so solemn?"

"Not solemn exactly." Meeryn knelt slowly onto the blanket, trying not to wake Declan, enjoying the sweet weight of his body as he nestled against her. "But thoughtful. Quiet. Gray was a dreamer. He'd go off for days alone in the wilds around Deepings or closet himself in the library poring over books until his eyes crossed. His vagueness drove the duke mad."

"Poor Gray. It sounds like his grandfather and he never saw eye to eye, not even when he was small."

"His Grace wanted Gray to be strong, to know how to fight, to be able to defend himself, to be able to defend the clans. Instructors were brought in to train him in all the manly arts. They worked him until he dropped from exhaustion. He hated every minute of it, but he did all his grandfather asked without complaint. I suppose I wouldn't call him solemn so much as stoic."

"It must have done the trick. David says Gray's the best marksman he's ever seen and one of the dirtiest fighters with dirk and sword."

"Second best." Meeryn smirked.

Gray paused in the bedchamber doorway, taking a moment to watch Meeryn as she packed a few last stray items into her valise. She paused, stretched, pushed her hair from her face, and fanned herself. It *was* bloody hot up here. No breeze stirred the curtains or blew clear the rancid odors of London in late summer, and the air hung stale with heat. Wilted curls escaped Meeryn's chignon, while her light muslin gown clung damp and revealing against every feminine curve. A bead of sweat trickled down her neck, following the ridge of her spine as it slid into the collar of her gown. Gray found himself staring, nerves jumping, throat dry.

At least she'd changed out of his dressing robe and into proper attire once the footman fetched her bag early this morning. Now, perfectly buttoned, pinned, primped, and coiffed, she could be mistaken for any affluent London gentlewoman. Nothing to distinguish her Imnada blood but the sinuous grace of her movements, the porcelain delicacy of her features . . .

"I can feel your eyes drilling into my back, Gray. Have you come to assure yourself I'm not stuffing de Coursy valuables down my dress before you shove me out the door?"

. . . and her preternaturally acute senses.

She spun on her heel, eyes glittering with bravado. "Care to check?"

A part of him imagined calling her bluff. Pushing her back against the wall to skim his hand deep into the collar of her gown, cupping the firm weight of her breasts, caressing the buds of her nipples until they hardened with arousal and he smelled the musky scent of desire on her skin.

Another part of him imagined her taking a knee to his groin, a fist to his jaw, and a knife to his ribs. A far more likely outcome. She'd never been one to suffer fools gladly, and that would be about the most foolish thing he could do, for more reasons than he could count.

Straightening from his perch against the door, he strolled into the room, eyes carefully shuttered, pose perfectly controlled. "Tempting, but I like my nose just where it is, thank you. And I already bear a scar with your name on it." He touched a finger to a faded reminder of her wrath at the edge of his mouth.

He needed to get a grip. Despite Lady Delia's outrageous claims of women falling all over themselves for his favors, he'd been sadly lacking in that regard for longer than he cared to admit. Mistresses took proper care and feeding, and he'd never had the patience such neediness required. On the other hand, indulging in a quick back-alley coupling for the price of a few coins and his self-respect didn't appeal either.

"Besides," he added, "you're just being dramatic. It's not like I'm packing you off to Outer Mongolia. You'll be comfortable with David and Callista."

"I was comfortable here."

"This is a bachelor household. You can't stay and you know it."

"You sound just like your grandfather. He spent so much time among the humans, he began to think like them. The Imnada might live within the human world, but we will never be part of it." Her expression dared him to argue.

He chose a middle course. "We may not be a part of it, but a large element of hiding is blending into your surroundings. In our case, it means single females do not stay with single males."

"I spent last night in this den of male iniquity and lightning didn't strike me down."

"Last night was an exception. I couldn't very well throw you out in naught but a robe and tell you to fend for yourself."

"No? You sound as if you contemplated it."

Actually, he'd spent half the night lying awake and staring at the ceiling until frustration and disgust had dragged him from his bed, drenched with sweat and hard as a rock, to spend himself with the help of his right hand and a convenient chamber pot. The debilitating pain of the draught's withdrawal had almost been a relief. At least it gave him something else to focus on besides his out-of-control libido. He had left Deepings . . . and Meeryn . . . behind for sound reasons. Reasons that remained despite the years that had passed. Now, if he could just convince his undisciplined body of his mind's estimable logic, he might be able to pass five minutes without the wild need to drag her against the wall and pleasure her senseless.

She lifted her chin in typical Meeryn challenge. A chin he desperately wanted to kiss right now. "If you must know, it's been a long time since I was a simpering maiden who needed her virginity protected."

By now he'd reclaimed a mantle of gentlemanly detachment and was able to react with barely the flicker of an eyelid, though his gut cramped and he had to work to keep his hands from fisting at his side. "I can't imagine you ever simpered. But the rest doesn't surprise me. You're what . . . twenty-six . . . twenty-seven . . . a bit old to remain untouched, though I find it hard to believe the Ossine have let you continue so long unwed. The ward of the Morieux and close kin to The Skaarsgard would be a coup for any man."

She gave a flippant roll of her eyes. "Just what every woman aspires to, I'm sure."

"Did you expect more?"

"I expected . . ." She caught back her words behind pressed lips and an unsteady breath. "I didn't wish to marry at first, and later, when the duke grew ill, any decision on matrimony was indefinitely postponed."

"Not married, but there was someone . . ." he fished, though maintaining a façade of disinterest was nearly killing him.

She offered him a dark stare. "Does it matter? He died a very long time ago." She returned to her packing, such as it was for someone who'd only unpacked this morning. "Now, can we discuss my departure, or better yet, yours? Sir Dromon's not known for his patience. Any delay might change his mind and this chance for peace would be lost."

"Do you want peace for my sake . . . or his?"

"Peace is peace. We all win." Her ferocity dimmed. "I know you think this is some kind of scheme to lure you back to the holding, but it's not. His Grace has a few weeks left at most. Once he's gone, whatever happens among the clans will happen. I understand that.

But this might be your last chance to make up with your grandfather. Can you really let the opportunity slip through your fingers without even trying?"

Was he a fool to trust her with his life? Was David right that desperation caused him to ignore the danger? Questions continued to dog him, but in the end he focused on the most important; did it matter? Meeryn was his only hope of getting close to Jai Idrish. Vigilance and caution would be his watchwords, but he'd no other choice except to risk it all on this one throw of the dice. And pray he could keep his cock in his pants while he was around her.

"I'll go—"

"You can send me away, shove me off onto your friends, but I'm not leaving London without you and that's final."

"You win."

"I'm just as muleheaded as . . . what did you say?"

"I said I'll go with you to Deepings. I'll sit down with Sir Dromon. I'll make my peace with Grandfather."

Barely had the words left his lips than she flung herself at him. "Gray!" she cried, her arms circling his neck in something akin to a choke hold. "I knew you wouldn't let me down."

Her hug caught him off guard. Her kiss knocked him sideways.

His breathing stopped for that one amazing moment her lips moved soft over his mouth, her arms pulled him close, and her body fit against his like a missing puzzle piece. Then it was over, she was dancing away as if it had never happened, and he was left adrift, alone, and very, very aroused.

What he would give for a fist to the jaw.

# 3

Rain drummed on the coach, seeping in through every crack and crevice, one very irritating drip in the roof forming a puddle at her feet. Mud sucked at the wheels, slowing their pace to a crawl, turning a few days' travel into an ordeal resembling a Greek odyssey. Had it been two days since they'd left London? Three? A month? Meeryn had lost track. She leaned her head back against the seat and closed her eyes, sighed, opened them again to look out on the soggy gray landscape and wish for the hundredth time that horses had wings. At this rate, they might never reach Deepings. Or if they did, they'd be moss-covered and pruny as raisins.

"Why don't you try reading? It might help."

She shot a withering look at Gray, who balanced a writing desk on his lap, somehow managing to scratch a letter without either dribbling the ink or smearing it in impossibly unintelligible lines. "I saw your library," she griped. "Not a book there was less than five hundred years old, didn't smell like curdled milk, or was the least bit interesting."

She waited for a smile that never appeared, but at least amusement glimmered in his eyes and his lips twitched encouragingly. She swallowed, recalling for the hundredth time since departing London, and in excruciating detail, the way those lips felt upon hers. The startled, then ardent, exploration of his mouth, the strength in his arms as he'd drawn her close, the point where cautious became commanding.

What on earth had she been thinking to fling herself at Gray? It was as if another person had taken over her body. A humiliating fool of a person who leapt into men's arms and planted great sloppy kisses on them. She might know a man's touch, but she'd never been a whore.

Thanks be to the Mother, she'd come to her senses in time, playing it as if it had been no more than the act of a heedless, giddy girl. He'd never know how close she came to surrendering to that sweep of unexpected heat pooling in her belly and between her legs. How much his touch still meant after all the lost years between them.

"I apologize for the lack of torrid romances, but this one might pique your curiosity." Gray reached into a satchel at his feet and pulled out an enormous book hinged and clasped in tarnished brass. "It's a collection of stories from King Arthur's reign, written in the sixteenth century by a bandraoi priestess of High Danu."

Pulled back to the present, Meeryn accepted the book with a wrinkle of her nose. This volume possessed the aroma of curdled milk *and* old cheese. Lovely. "Let me guess—the Imnada are depicted as demons who ate babies and deflowered virgins until the valiant Fey-bloods rid the world of their filth in a blaze of righteous glory."

His humor vanished, eyes flat and impenetrable, giving nothing away. "She does a lovely job of describing weather."

"I'll bypass the pleasure if you don't mind." She knew she was being whiny and difficult. She couldn't seem to help herself. She'd not realized how unsettling it would be to see Gray again, or how easily his presence would unlock old childhood dreams from the buried places in her memory.

She turned back to the window and her dreary rain-washed view. A sodden cornfield, a farmer bundled to the eyebrows in mackintosh wading along the verge, a flock of ducks skimming low to land in a farmer's pond. But all the while she remained oh-so-uncomfortably aware of him across from her; the scratch of his pen, the scent of his soap, the stern line of his profile.

Gray had gone away to war starry-eyed and scrawny. He'd come home with an athlete's muscled body and an uncomfortably perceptive gaze. He'd never be handsome in the classical sense; his features taken one at a time were only ordinary—cheekbones high and sharp, a wide mouth and full sensuous lips, intelligent blue eyes beneath swooping dark brows. But all together, they became startling in their intensity, fascinating every eye, drawing all attention. He was a man one ignored with difficulty and dismissed at one's own peril.

And then there was that kiss . . . that dratted kiss . . . It hung between them like a poised sword. Did he think her shameless? Wanton? Barely adequate?

The walls of the carriage seemed to close around her; the air grew thick in her lungs, the damp clung to her skin. Every jut of the coach irritated her. Every scratch of Gray's pen made her grit her teeth. She needed to escape. From Gray. From her reckless thoughts. Lose herself in her aspect where instinct took over and painful regrets and unwanted feelings could be outrun. She straightened with sudden inspiration. "We've been stuck inside for days. What if we instructed the coach to go on without us while we took a quicker mode of travel?"

He followed the track of her gaze. "You want to shift? I doubt mouse would be much faster."

She waved off his sarcasm. "Mouse worked to get me into your house unseen, but I was thinking more of, say"—she tilted a winning smile his direction—"eagle?"

"Ahh, still lording your ability to flux over me, are you? How little has changed in the past ten years."

"Can I help it if I'm unbound by clan aspect and able to assume any form?"

"No, but you don't have to rub it in."

She gave a nod toward the coach door. "So, what say you? Stretch our legs and spread our wings for a few miles?"

Gray's brows lowered, his gaze locked on the scene beyond the glass; though Meeryn had the impression he saw none of it, his thoughts turned far inward. His thumb ran idly up and down the spine of the book he held, his jaw hard with some unknown emotion. "We'll keep to the road and leave the skies to the ducks."

"Gray . . ." she began, but he interrupted with a curt, "It's safer."

"Pryor has guaranteed your safety. No Ossine enforcer will go against his orders."

"Perhaps not." He rolled his cane back and forth between loose fingers. "But I learned through five years of war not to look for trouble. It would find me easily enough without the bother. The same premise holds now. Pryor might seek out a reconciliation, but I don't fool myself into believing he wouldn't be relieved if I conveniently disappeared."

"Then why did you agree to come with me? If you're right, I'd say that's searching out heaps of trouble."

A touch of some expression passed across his face and was gone before she could identify it. Excitement? Desperation? "To make my peace with the duke," he replied. "Isn't that what you wanted?"

She studied him, wishing she might read the truth behind his words, but the ability to see another's thoughts was rare among the Imnada. Not even the immense power of Jai Idrish offered her that gift. "I just can't help wondering . . ."

"What's that?"

"What your real purpose is?"

This time he did smile, a cool humorless twist of his mouth that made her shiver. "Read the book. The answer's clear as day."

"It's as the lady N'thuil spoke, sir. His Grace lies ill and close to death in his chambers at Deepings. They don't expect him to live to the end of the month." Zeb Doule's gaze darted around the crowded smoky tavern as if he expected Ossine enforcers to leap through the windows, swords brandished to skewer him where he stood polishing glasses at the bar.

Gray had hesitated over his decision to meet with the clansman, but he needed information, and Doule, whose brother worked as a groom in the Deepings stables, was a perfect conduit. The more Gray knew about the goings-on at Deepings and the holding, the better he might prepare himself.

He'd waited until almost midnight, when Meeryn would surely be asleep, to sneak out of his room at the posting inn, walk the short distance to this seedy, out-of-the-way tavern, and ask for Doule. The barman had skulked out of the back, his face draining of color when he caught sight of his visitor. It had taken two ales and a cider before he recovered enough to answer Gray's questions without stammering or ducking at every loud noise. Unfortunately, the impulse to tug at his forelock at odd intervals continued to be disconcerting.

"What of Pryor?" Gray sipped at his ale, a rancid brew that reminded him all too much of the sickly viscosity of the Fey draught.

"He's closeted with the duke mostly. But they say he's starting to fret. Looking less dapper than his usual self as if he's worried over happenings. Rumors are flying, and it seems like a power struggle is inevitable. Some say The Skaarsgard plans to ride south from his islands as soon as the duke breathes his last. Others are saying Glynjohns is hungry for the Duke of Morieux's power and he's got ties to the dukedom through his wife." Doule's throat worked nervously, and he hunched closer, his voice dropping an octave until Gray could barely hear him over the din of the tavern's rowdier customers. "Last week, the Ossine trapped three of us in a house in Ashburton. Me and another man got away, but they murdered the families, babes and all, before they strung up the third fellow with a stake through his chest." He used the cloth in his hand to wipe the sweat beading across his brow. "I'd not go to Deepings if I were you. It's too dangerous. The enforcers would snatch you up faster than a fly on a cake. They'll stake you. Stake you and leave you to die in the dirt. I've told my brother to get out but he won't. Says he's got to stay, but it's a risk."

Gray fought back the spasm of fear that rippled up his spine. Ran a finger around the rim of his glass with the same nonchalance he might bring to a night at Almack's or an evening at White's among friends. None would ever see him cringe or flinch or look less than completely confident. None would see him beg—ever again. A vow he'd made in the early days of his exile, when the flesh on his back blistered and broke and blistered again and breathing was an agony to be endured.

"I appreciate the warning, Doule." He tossed his coins on the counter and rose from his stool. "If you hear anything more, send word through the usual channels."

"Aye. As you say."

He'd taken only a few steps before inspiration turned him around. "What have you heard of the new N'thuil?"

The tavernkeeper frowned, as if he was trying to recall any gossip he might have gleaned from his brother's visits. He slowly shook his head. "Only that she's a woman. A lady N'thuil, who'd have thought such a thing would come to pass? Maybe it's true what some say."

"What do some say?"

"That Pryor thinks to control Jai Idrish through the girl." Another long pause as Doule's frown deepened, the shake of his head slower and more deliberate this time, his words seeming to be pulled from him syllable by syllable. "Others say it doesn't matter and the crystal's power is just a faery story. Which do you think it is?"

Gray pulled on his gloves and settled a hat upon his head. "I don't know—yet."

Outside, it drizzled, the waning moon of Berenth lost behind a low layer of thick clouds. He pulled up the collar of his coat, scanning the darkness with a knowing eye. A warm breeze brought with it the stink of the stables and set the trees to dancing. Two drunkards assisted each other home to a rousing chorus of "John Barleycorn." A man took a piss against a tree. A woman's giggles grew breathless when her companion's hand slid into her bodice.

Reassured that he'd not been recognized, Gray set off toward the posting inn, though he still kept to the darkest lanes and loneliest paths, every sense alert for trouble, every mile closer to Deepings tightening already taut muscles. So wrapped up in searching out two-legged trouble, he never saw the dog chained in the timber merchant's lot until he tripped over it.

The brute leapt to its feet, barking and snarling loud enough to raise the dead. Gray eased away, one slow step at a time, never taking his eyes from the dog, sending every calming thought he could muster toward the heavy-jawed, beady-eyed cur. He'd made it as far as a rickety loading porch, stacks of milled boards piled beneath an overhang and out of the weather as they waited to be shipped, when the dog lunged, teeth clamping on Gray's arm.

Pain shot down into his fingers as the dog's jaws tightened. Blood seeped onto his cuffs. He grappled against the muscled weight of the beast, fending off its attempts to tear out his throat. Claws raked bloody gouges across his chest as he fought back. A smash of his fist against the side of the dog's head, another to its snout, and the dog released him with a yelp. Immediately, Gray reached over his head for the edge of the overhang, lifting and rolling himself up onto the roof. It groaned under his weight and he held still, peering down at the dog which stood on hind legs in a frenzy of frustrated barking.

Gray tossed the animal a salute before inching carefully up and onto the main roof of the building. His chest felt like it was on fire and the fingers of his wounded arm had started to tingle, but he wriggled toward the ridge line. Hopefully, the other side of the roof sloped low enough to the street to allow him an easy descent. He made it to the top, pulling himself up the final few feet with his left arm as his right dangled by his side. Not broken, but damned sore. Pausing to catch his breath, his ears pricked and a shiver raced over his skin.

Imnada.

". . . cut out your forked tongue . . . body to the grubs . . ."

". . . carry nothing . . . here to see sister . . . know what you're talking about . . ."

The conversation didn't emanate from the street below but from a narrow alleyway to his left between the timber merchant's offices and storage sheds.

". . . then what is this, *avaklos* scum?"

Gray's gaze narrowed, his hand tightening on the

edge of the roof. *Avaklos*, an Imnada term for any clansman who chose to live within the human world rather
than hide behind the Paling walls. Though always considered odd, in recent years they'd fallen under suspicion
for colluding with Gray and his conspirators. Many had,
but many more had simply been caught within a net that
did not discriminate between guilt and innocence.

". . . who sent you . . . who's the traitor in Deepings . . . answer and I might let you live . . ."

". . . don't know . . . gave me a letter to deliver . . .
all I know . . ."

". . . you lie . . ."

Gray crouched at the ridgeline. His arm screamed
in protest, muscles taut as wires. The blood roared in
his veins, dripping off his fingers. If he sensed their
presence, surely they'd sense his, they'd feel the brush
of Imnada power in the air. His only hope lay in
the fact that both attacker and victim seemed to be
shapechangers. They might assume they sensed each
other and give it no more thought. He might still hold
the element of surprise as an advantage. In a quiver
sparse of arrows, that had to count for something.

". . . please . . . know nothing . . . please . . ."

Gray heard the dull thud of fists on flesh, the
scramble of bodies in a struggle as the Ossine enforcer
dragged his victim farther down the alleyway, where
none might come upon them.

"You say you're in town to visit your sister. Be a
shame if something happened to her, wouldn't it? And
so soon after having that little baby of hers, too."

"She's nothing to do with this."

"Then tell us what we want to know and we'll leave
her be. Simple."

Gray could hear the smug contempt and brazen cruelty in the enforcer's voice. Apparently, not all of the Ossine supported Pryor's attempts at reconciliation. He'd trained them too well, indoctrinated the shamans with the seeds of his hatred for any change in the ancient customs and set them loose upon their own like rabid wolves.

"I . . . I can't . . . it's . . ."

The man was weakening, his voice tired, defeated, his breath wheezy and rasping from the beating he'd already taken. Gray had no time left to weigh options. Besides, every choice left was a bad one. The roof was too steep, and there was nowhere to let himself down. He couldn't go back and challenge the dog again. What did that leave? He knew, even if he didn't like it.

Shimmying free of his coat and his boots, he dragged his breeches off awkwardly with one arm and shucked out of his coat. Calling on the moon's power, he wrapped himself in the magic of his race, bones twisting, muscle transforming. Heat beaded on his brow and slicked his injured chest as his nerves sizzled and his blood pounded in every vein. He spread his wings as the freedom and ecstasy of the shift took over. His face sharpened to a long-bladed beak, lethal as a dagger.

And with a cry carried on the wind, the eagle lifted from his perch, talons extended like razors, and dove for the kill.

Meeryn closed the book with a dusty thump, but she couldn't shake off the tragic tale of Lucan Kingkiller so easily. The Imnada warlord had loved unwisely, allowing the seductress Morgana to convince him to betray his friend and king. To slay Arthur and place her half-blood son Mordred upon the throne. The plan had failed. Mordred was slain at the Battle of Camlann, Morgana escaped, and Lucan had been captured and brutally executed by the Fey-bloods. But it had been the Imnada clans who'd paid the greatest price as the armies of the Other fell upon the shapechanger holdings with savage ferocity, seeking vengeance for their murdered king—slaughtering any who bore the blood of the shifter, scattering those who managed to flee.

Known as the Fealla Mhòr, this war decimated the Imnada. Only Aneavala, the most famous N'thuil after Idrin himself, was able to save the clans from extinction by erecting the Paling mists. But that had been when Jai Idrish still burned with the light of the goddess and the N'thuil was more than a ceremonial functionary.

She was no Aneavala, and she couldn't count on Jai Idrish to save the clans from destruction a second time.

She closed her eyes, hoping to catch a few hours' sleep before sunrise, but the stuffy humid air of her chamber and the unsettling whirl of her somber thoughts kept her from drifting off. She kicked free of the covers, huffing her frustration into the silence. Her nightgown clung to her legs and back and the sheets smelled stale in the heat.

Surrendering, she rose from bed to splash her face and arms with the tepid water from her nightstand ewer. Then crossed to fling open her shutters and open the casement wider to catch any passing breeze that might blow her way. A gentle rain fell, and she leaned into the night, lifting her face to it, sending out the rote verses of a childhood prayer to the Mother whose waning face was hidden from view by the clouds.

That's when she caught movement at the edge of her vision and the buzz of Imnada power burst hot and tingling across her mind. A shape was barely discernible except as a flicker of black upon the dark clouds. As it approached, it revealed itself to be an enormous eagle possessing the elegant sweep of strong wings and a sleek hunter's body with the killing force of a loosed arrow.

*Gray?* Her pathing slid out across the distance like a mental whisper. A focused thread of thought.

No answer.

She frowned. That couldn't be right. This bird veered and lurched as it fought the air currents. It struggled to maintain a steady descent, but with each stroke of its wings it seemed to weaken, one wing beating frantically as the stable roof yawned into view. She squeezed her eyes shut, unable to watch the ugly collision. Opened them again in time to see the eagle skim the shingles by inches before fluttering in a rush of wind and feathers to the ground. Its left wing lay outstretched and limp. *Gray!*

The bird's head swiveled toward her window, its gaze like a blade. *Stay where you are.*

His voice in her head rooted her to the floor.

*What's wrong? Why?* she pathed—when the answer revealed itself as a shadow peeling free of the stable's interior. The buzz of Fey-blood magic ground against her nerves until even her hair hurt. The flash of a blade in the dark chilled her blood. But how did he know the wounded eagle was a shapechanger? Luck? Treachery?

She stared transfixed as the eagle hopped a few steps, attempting to tuck its injured wing against its body. Another awkward step and then it beat at the air in an attempt to take flight, but the wing pinned it earthbound. An easy kill for a Fey-blood with a knife.

She might not be able to guide her people through the Gateway like Idrin or wield the power of the crystal with the ease of Aneavala, but she could kill one skulking bastard bent on murder. She retrieved her stiletto from its sheath beneath her pillow. Conal had made her practice with the weapon until it became an extension of her body and he had warned her to keep it close at hand at all times. He never said why, but she followed his instructions even now, years after his death. The slender knife felt warm in her hand, the grip easy as she took aim, waiting for the perfect shot.

The Fey-blood stalked the eagle, herding Gray toward a low stone wall, but now Meeryn saw that what she'd taken for the gleam of a blade was in fact, the glint off a fine-mesh net. The stranger didn't want to kill Gray. He wanted to capture him.

Her heart plunged into her stomach. She set her jaw, gauging distance and trajectory as she'd been taught. Took a steadying breath and hurled the blade toward the loathsome sorcerer with all her strength.

Years of training paid off. The stiletto found its mark, biting deep into the base of the man's throat. He dropped to his knees before toppling slowly into the mud with a sick thud. She braced herself for a shout, a scream, a witness to shriek a warning to the rest of the sleeping inn, but there was no sound beyond the rain's steady drip and her own rapid breathing. Spinning from the window, she grabbed up her cloak, throwing it around her shoulders before she lifted the latch on her bedchamber door. None moved in the corridors, and the even the lamp at the top of the staircase had burned out.

Quickly she sped down the stairs and through the shadowed taproom. The main door would be bolted and barred, but with luck, a side door or even a window might have been forgotten. She found what she was looking for down a narrow passage from the kitchen. Some lazy servant had turned the key and then left it in the lock. Letting herself out into the yard, she paused a moment to gain her bearings. To her left, a path led to a metal gate and the road. To her right ran the stone wall she'd seen from her window and the dark expanse of the stables beyond.

Even as she pulled her cloak up to cover her head and hurried through the drizzle, a hot starshot wind torched her face while a wild boiling energy pulsed under her skin. She reached the stableyard in time to see the eagle vanished and Gray in its place. He lay unmoving for a moment, the shift from aspect to human leaving him wrung like a sponge. Completely vulnerable. He rolled over onto his back in the mud. Deep bleeding scores raked his muddy chest, and his left arm had been savaged brutally.

Ignoring the muck soaking into her skirts and the dead body sprawled facedown a few feet away, she knelt beside him, hands clenched in her lap. "Are you able to walk? We have to get you inside before someone stumbles on us. Dead bodies have a tendency to beget awkward questions."

Gray rolled up onto an elbow, cradling his injured arm against his chest. His stare moved from Meeryn to the fallen Fey-blood and back again. "More than a few of those questions are mine."

\*     \*     \*

Up the stairs without mishap. Into his bedchamber, none the wiser. By the time he'd pulled on a pair of breeches, washed the mud from his wounds, and sat while Meeryn bandaged his arm, Gray almost believed they might have succeeded in escaping detection altogether. The body would be found, exclaimed over, and carted away by the authorities. Hopefully, if and when they started asking difficult questions, he and Meeryn would be long gone. As for the other body, if it surfaced from the bottom of the river at all, there would be none to identify a faceless, shredded, water-bloated corpse.

"A dog? You were mauled by a dog?" she exclaimed, hands trembling as she wrapped the bandage up and around his shoulder and arm.

"Keep your voice down. Yes, a dog. You know the beast. Sharp teeth, sharp claws, nasty disposition . . . a dog." He winced. "And an enforcer."

She dropped the bandage where it unrolled along the floor and scrambled to retrieve it. "What?" she said, a tremor squeaking her voice.

"Sir Dromon may have offered *me* amnesty, but his Ossine continue to hunt suspected rebels. I stumbled into the middle of a confrontation between an enforcer and a young *avaklos* and decided to even the odds."

"By almost getting yourself killed?"

"That part was accidental. The enforcer was quicker than I thought."

"Or you might have been slower. Did you ever think ambushing a trained killer while suffering blood loss and a six-inch gash in your arm wasn't the smartest idea?"

"The son of a bastard threatened to rape and disembowel the chap's sister before his eyes if he didn't reveal his rebel contacts."

She blanched, fiddling with the frayed hem of the bandage. "No. There must be some mistake."

"The mistake was the enforcer's. The only crime the shapechanger was guilty of was being in the wrong place at the wrong time."

"The enforcers are meant to protect us."

"Once they did, but Dromon has twisted them into his own private army of murderers and thugs. They prowl the countryside unchecked, and their butchery is all too common." He tested his shoulder, flexed his arm, gritting his teeth against the pain. "At least this one won't kill again."

"He's dead?" she asked, casting him a swift sidelong glance as she cleaned up the mess left after her ministrations. It seemed to be taking an awfully long time and involved more than a few clumsy spills and confused shakes of her head.

"We seem to be racking up the bodies, don't we?" He offered her a grim smile. "Now that you've peppered me with questions, it's my turn."

By now, her face bore the pallor of chalk and the trembling in her hands had spread to her body. She clamped her jaw as she pressed her arms across her stomach as if she might be sick. "Are you outraged?"

"As my continued existence rests in your knife-throwing talents, I'll have to claim gratitude rather than outrage."

"Few men would admit to being beholden to a woman for anything, much less survival."

"But it isn't the first time you've saved my life, is it?" he said.

Their eyes met for a brief loaded moment before she flushed and busied herself once more with her tidying, though Gray was almost sure she'd folded that towel at least three times already. Her hair fell forward across her face, shimmering strands of auburn scattered among the lighter honey-gold, hiding all but the curve of one cheek and the determined jab of her chin. She fiddled with a ring on her thumb and he was struck anew at the strength in her slender fingers, and the skill he'd witnessed in the stableyard.

"How did you come to be able to take a man down with a dagger from"—he glanced toward the window—"a good fifty feet? It's an impressive feat . . . for a girl." His smirk had the desired effect. She glared at him in typical Meeryn fashion, followed by a roll of bandages to the head.

"If you must know, Conal taught me."

He didn't have to ask who Conal was. It was clear in the wistful way she spoke his name, the sadness shadowing her gaze as she said it.

She cleared her throat, fiddled with a frayed bit of linen, rolling it round and round between her fingers. "You'd shown me the basic skills, but he refined them. Drills over and over until my muscles memorized every move . . . but it's not the same, is it? Not when it's a real person."

So that was it. No wonder she looked ready to crawl out of her own skin. He knew all too well the racing heart, the clammy sweat, the jumping nerves, and the hollow ache in the gut. "It gets easier. You don't stop caring, but you do stop wanting to throw up your guts and crawl into a hole."

"I don't want it to get easier," she stated, almost angrily.

She swung away to stare blankly into the hearth,

but there was no comforting fire to warm the cold he knew chilled her down to the marrow of her bones, and it wouldn't help anyway. He knew it from experience. Only time would do that.

"I know why I passed on my swordmaster's training to you," he said, hoping to distract her. "Why did he? Don't tell me you threatened to tell his grandfather about secret forays to The Knife and Claw for dicing and drinking with the underfootmen."

A smile tipped her lips as she allowed herself to be drawn back from her brooding thoughts. "Lucky for Conal, I didn't have to resort to blackmail, though it did take all my feminine charms and not a little begging to convince him to train me. He was stubborn as a mule. Said we'd be caught and punished."

Had she loved this man? Did she still? Did Gray care? He could have stayed at Deepings all those years ago. Done the proper thing and married her as all expected he would. None would have faulted him for taking that path or stepping even deeper into his elder brother's shoes, but he'd chosen another way, and that door was long closed.

"What finally changed his mind?"

Her eyes darkened once more with memory. "A shapechanger from the Viyachne in Wales was killed outside Shrewsbury." She paused before continuing. "Conal said the Imnada couldn't count on the enforcers to protect us anymore. That we must protect ourselves."

"He was right. But 'from which side' would be the real question."

"Really?" she replied. "I think after tonight that's been amply answered. Both."

# 4

He finished his last letter despite the pain shooting from his shoulder to his fingers, cramping the muscles, making it difficult to hold the pen. He feared the final paragraph was illegible, his signature a complete loss. By the time he'd shaken free the sand and sealed the pages with wax, pain had given way to tingling numbness and fresh blood streaked his shirtsleeve.

He gingerly stripped off his shirt and unwrapped the bandage with a grimace. The bite wound was ugly but clean, a scent of healing in the pink flesh knitting the edges closed. He'd live—for now.

"You can stop shooting daggers at me from the window, Badb. I know you're there," he said, struggling to rewrap the length of fabric. "And I know you disapprove."

A slender, raven-haired girl stepped farther into the room, her cloak of crow feathers trailing across the floorboards behind her. Beyond that one flowing raiment, she wore nothing else, and Gray was treated to flawless marble-white skin, long slender legs, narrow hips, and small upthrust breasts tipped a dusky rose. Accustomed to her less-than-typical garb and taken up with a bandage that fought all his clumsy attempts at folding, he cast her barely more than a passing glance.

She, on the other hand, sized him up with a flickering burn in her unnatural black eyes, before taking the bandage from him with a sniff of distaste. "I warned you what would happen if you sought to travel this road, shapechanger. Nothing but sorrow can come from returning to your lost home. The past is a dangerous landscape riddled with false dreams and paths that can lead you astray."

"You know as well as I do that my lost home offers me my best chance for survival." He gritted his teeth as she probed at the wound. "Let me guess, Lucan discovered my plan and dispatched you to watch over me."

Lucan Kingkiller—the one person Sir Dromon feared and loathed more than Gray. The ancient Imnada warlord possessed the undiluted strength and cunning of the old clans in every inch of his titan's body. King's confidant, sorceress's lover, savage traitor, and captive of the Fey for thousands of years, Lucan was a man out of time since being freed from his prison three years earlier.

As much an exile as Gray, he'd found a place among the rebels.

But he'd yet to find peace for his sins.

The Fey girl deftly wound the bandage, pinning it in place. "Lucan is wroth with you, shapechanger. You throw all our lives into jeopardy by riding alone into your enemies' camp. Should this girl betray you to Sir Dromon, there will be many who will suffer."

"Should I have brought him with me to guard my back? Who would have guarded his? I couldn't ask that of him. Too many still blame him for the Fealla Mhòr and the massacres that followed. If it's dangerous for me to enter Deepings, it would be certain death for him."

She offered him a contemptuous look. "Enter Deepings? You'll be fortunate if you don't end at the point of a sword by dawn."

Gray rose from his bed to pour a drink. Held another one out for Badb, who wrinkled her nose and swung away in continued agitation. "If Meeryn wanted me dead, she could have let the Fey-blood have me tonight," he argued, "but she didn't."

Badb wheeled around, sharp gaze narrowed, cheeks flushed with anger. "A Fey-blood? Here?"

Gray sipped at his brandy, letting the heat burn life back into his limbs. "No longer. Thanks to a well-aimed knife." He gave a dry humorless snort of laughter and rubbed at the back of his neck in a useless bid to ease the crick in it. "Didn't see that one coming, though not surprised. She always was a terrible hoyden."

"Who killed the assassin is irrelevant. It is the fact that he was here and knew what you were and where you were traveling that is of concern."

"Someone's been talking."

Badb paced the floor, her lip caught between her teeth in a very un-Fey-like expression. "Return to London, son of Idrin. It is the safest course until we know who has exposed your secret and where the danger lies."

"I can't return and you know it."

She stamped her bare foot in frustration. "Then

wait for Lucan . . . or call upon your friends. They would ride with you. They would share your danger."

"I can't ask that of them. Mac and David have done enough already. And they're needed elsewhere. This fight is coming to us whether we're ready or not. And I fear we're not nearly ready enough."

"It's not a sin to ask for help, shapechanger. Or to admit you are not strong enough to succeed unaided."

"Alone means no one else gets hurt."

Badb leveled him with a stare that seemed to strip him down to each individual thought in his head, each drop of blood in his body. He felt her in his mind. Seeing what he did not want her to see, understanding things about him that he barely understood. "Or does alone mean *you* do not get hurt?"

Gray came for Meeryn as dawn pinked the sky. The inn was already awash in confusion over the discovery of a dead body. As the landlord struggled against a tide of frightened staff, inconvenienced guests, and bothersome magistrate's men, Gray ordered his young groom to load their luggage and see that the coach was hitched while he settled their accounts, all with the calm efficiency and arrogant aplomb of a nobleman born. None questioned him. None dare even approach him. Instead they bowed and scraped and fell over themselves in their desire to order all as he wished it. Not until they were safely away did Gray's air of regal superiority slip, and Meeryn detected the most minute cracks in the otherwise bland features. There was a tightness to face and a greenish cast that gave him a washed-out appearance. Deep lines bracketed his mouth, and his eyes lacked their usual icy brilliance.

"How do you feel this morning?"

He lifted his head, shadows hollowing his eyes. "Why do you ask?"

"Because you've got the appearance of someone who's eaten one too many of Mrs. Waverly's mince pies."

"There's a name I've not heard in a long time," he said with a rare softening of his granite expression. "I'm surprised Grandfather hasn't found himself a new cook. Mrs. Waverly was always ghastly. The woman could ruin a boiled egg."

"Yes, but she's familiar. Besides, your grandfather hasn't hired or fired anyone in years. He handed over the running of the household to me when I came of age. I was mistress of his house and hostess for his parties."

"An onerous task."

"I suppose he assumed it would be my role sooner or later so I might as well get used to it."

The greenish hue to his features gave way to pink, a singularly alarming combination of colors. But he rallied and managed to look only slightly ill when he said, "Ollie would have been proud to take you as mate and wife."

She rolled her eyes. "I was eleven when he died. If he thought of me as anything at all, it was more likely as a nuisance and a child." Leaning forward, she offered sotto voce, "Don't panic, but I believe His Grace had you in mind when he began grooming me for the part."

Gray studied his hands, turned the diamond on his finger round and round. His dismay would have been comical if it hadn't been at her expense.

She sat back, smoothing a hand over her skirt. "Now you do look as if you wish to cast up your accounts, but rest easy. That idea is no longer applicable. Nor am I serving these days as anything more than a glorified messenger."

"Surely my grandfather still has need of a hostess and . . ." He seemed to grope for the proper word.

"Housekeeper? Not really. There are no more parties and the duties of maintaining and directing the staff have been given over to Mr. Pym."

"Wasn't he—"

"Sir Dromon's butler? Yes. The Arch Ossine has sprinkled quite a few of his staff among Deepings' servants since your exile. Pym's the latest." Was that disgust at Pryor's insolence she read in his expression, or was he really about to be sick? "Should we stop the carriage? You look a bit green at the gills."

"I've felt better," he admitted, then his gaze darkened, mouth pressed closed. "I've also felt worse." He turned back to the window as the high moors and fertile valleys of Devonshire slid toward the wide, sun-speckled rush of the Tamar.

She let him brood for a few miles before the silence began to ring in her ears. "This isn't the first time it's happened, is it?"

"What?" He glanced over at her with a lift of his brows. "Attacked, you mean?" He shrugged. "A few times—twice in London, once on my estate in Northumberland, and there was a woman in Bath the Ossine hired to lure me in with . . . well, they misjudged my tastes. I like slender brunettes with dark eyes." His keen gaze traveled her face until she wanted to squirm in her seat and the heat rose in her face. Then he added, "Preferably ones who aren't luring me to my doom," which completely killed the moment.

If it had been a moment. Hard to tell. Gray was not exactly the most emotive of people, even at the best of times. The duke had taken care of that over the years. Now to see a smile break that patrician façade was tantamount to a shifting of the earth beneath her feet.

"Not to imply murderous intentions on your part," Gray added smoothly.

"But you do admit that you count me among those women you find attractive?" she goaded, a harpy's smile curling the edges of her mouth.

He cleared his throat. Adjusted the position of his bandaged arm. "If I say yes, I sound a scoundrel. If I say no, I sound a cad. I can't win."

"Maybe I like scoundrels." She wanted to bite her tongue off. What was she doing? Flirting with him? This journey was about reconciling Gray with his grandfather, reconciling Gray with Sir Dromon. It was about establishing herself as a proper and relevant N'thuil. It was not about coy glances and witty banter, and most definitely not about the swirl in her belly that dropped into her sex and ached with a sweet throbbing need.

He cleared his throat again and fiddled once more with his diamond. "As last night's heroics proved. Few proper gentlemen would have taught you those skills."

Meeryn sat back with a snap of her shoulders.

And that . . . brazen hussy . . . was that. She'd been more than put in her place. Détente over. "You're quick to accuse the Ossine of murder, but what of the Feybloods? I believe last night's heroics proved they're a far more serious threat," she snapped.

Gray rubbed a hand over his chin in sheepish thought. "Despite what you think, that was a first, though I suppose it was optimistic to hope the secret of the *afailth luinan* would remain just that."

Few among the clans had believed the ancient cookfire stories describing the miraculous healing properties of Imnada blood. Not until David St. Leger brought Callista Hawthorne back from death with a few drops from his own wrist. The news had spread like fire among the Imnada, but it was the Other's potential reaction that set frazzled nerves on edge and intensified an already explosive situation.

"Did you really think it would be otherwise?" Meeryn asked. "Once the outside world learned of our existence, it was inevitable the oldest legends would be revived and sifted through for fact. And what legend is more tempting than that shapechanger blood offers the drinker immortality?"

He shrugged. "It would have availed him nothing. The power isn't in the blood. It's in the gift."

"How would you know?"

"Professor Gray, remember? Head always stuck in a book." He looked down at his hands again. They lay palm-up in his lap, the crisscross of white scars standing out against the darker tone of his skin. He closed them slowly, hiding the evidence of his accursedness. "What made you decide to act as envoy for Pryor? He might have sent anyone."

"When I heard what he planned, I asked to go. I thought you might listen to me. That you might trust me." She paused. "My mistake."

"It's not *you* I have cause to suspect, Meeryn." The tenor of his voice changed. For a moment, he was the

Gray she remembered; truehearted and steadfast. The blue of his gaze inviting rather than reflecting.

"But you're coming despite your misgivings?"

He put his hands in his pockets. "What kind of leader would I be if I didn't try? I can't ask the men and women who follow me to risk their lives if I'm not willing to risk mine."

"I know Sir Dromon can be self-righteous and manipulative and even cruel at times, but he always has the best interests of the clans at heart. All he does originates in his desire to keep us strong and safe."

"You *really* believe that?"

"If I didn't . . ." She turned to the window, her words trailing off as she studied her own apprehensions for an answer. "I have to believe in him, Gray. He's been the only thing holding the clans together since you were banished."

"Or the one thing tearing us apart . . . depending on your viewpoint."

The conversation faltered and died after that, each lost to their own thoughts. Lunch came and went. Horses were changed. And changed again. The rocky barren uplands gave way to creek-fed glades and deep combes on their way to the western cliffs. Dinner was taken at a snug posting inn outside Camelford. The sun slanted low toward the horizon, the moon high and winking between thin clouds.

They had reached the final leg of their journey. Soon the concealing mists of the Palings would gather around them in an impenetrable wall of silver cloud. Without knowledge of the hidden tracks and byways through the barriers, one might wander lost for hours or days, herded and nudged as if by unseen hands through the heavy fogs and drizzle-spangled vapor. The lucky traveler would find his way beyond the Palings' perimeter, none the wiser to the holding locked within. The unlucky traveler who breached the Imnada's last defense and discovered their secret would never be found at all.

At the Palings' borders, standing like twin sentinels against a dangerous world, were the estates of Deepings, owned by the Duke of Morieux, and Drakelow, the family seat of the Pryors and home of Sir Dromon. For the first time, Meeryn saw those miles of adjoining landscape, not as a buffer to keep the world out, but as a wall to imprison those living within.

"Looks like we have company," Gray remarked a bit too casually.

Meeryn followed the track of his frowning gaze. Two men stepped free of the trees as the coach passed. Another two appeared on the road ahead. All four wore red-tasseled scabbards at their sides and daggers at their hips, and carried pistols in holsters upon their saddles. All four bore the blood of the Imnada and the power of the Ossine.

"Perhaps they're here to escort us. An honor guard for the prodigal heir."

In no way did Gray betray that he might be the least bit worried. She wished she had the same confidence—or the same ability to hide her feelings. Her knees wobbled dangerously and fear slithered up her spine as one of the men ahead signaled the driver to pull up. They creaked to a stop, the driver's shouted question cut off by the crack of a pistol. Meeryn jolted forward as the coach rocked dangerously. She gripped the edge of her seat, her pulse roaring in her ears.

Craning her neck, she saw that the men had surrounded the coach. One gripped the reins of the leader who sidled and backed at the scent of blood. A second prodded the body of the coachman where it lay sprawled in the dirt of the lane.

Gray's eyes glittered with rage. "Shit all."

Of the young groom, there was no sign. Meeryn prayed for his escape. She dropped her hand to the leather sheath strapped against her thigh, the narrow access slit in her skirts artfully concealed by the drape of her gown. Whether she'd have the nerve to use her stiletto again was another matter. The last time had left her with a sour taste in her mouth and a sick snarling of her insides.

One of the men yanked the door open with a grim smile. "Evening, my lord. Had word we might find you traveling this road tonight. Glad I listened to the little bugger squeal before I slit his throat."

Gray regarded Meeryn with a solemn questioning look. "Lady N'thuil? Isn't this where you're supposed to step in and save me?"

The trees seemed to spin as her stomach lifted into her throat. She wanted to be sick. To weep. To bury her stiletto in the enforcer's gut. She drew herself up and directed her most chilling stare at the murderous enforcer. "Lord Halvossa may be *emnil* but he remains His Grace's heir and travels under my protection. Sir Dromon Pryor himself has requested his presence at Deepings."

"I don't care if he's got a solid gold ass and Sir Dromon wants to kiss it. He's a traitor to the clans and deserves a traitor's death. Just like that one there did." He swung around, drew his pistol and fired again at the lifeless body of the coachman. The head exploded in a spray of brains and bone shards.

Meeryn shrank back with a horrified breath. When had the Ossine begun inducting such men into their order? The shamans had always been the scholars and the teachers, the caretakers of the family bloodlines, the interpreters of the Mother's many faces. Austere, perhaps even harsh on occasion, but never malicious or ruthless, and certainly not needlessly savage.

Gray's hands tightened to fists. His stare fell like a hammer blow. "My man had done nothing but seek a better life for his children. Is that a crime in the Ossine's eyes?"

The enforcer drew his self-importance about him like a cloak. "No, but cavorting with traitorous Fey-blood lovers is." He directed his attention to her for the first time as he offered her a half nod, half bow. "Lady N'thuil, I'm sure you think you're doing what's right but the Ossines' directive is clear. I'm to defend and protect my race from all threats. Let one of the boys take you home. I've a job to do, and it's not a sight fit for a woman."

Her fear was forgotten in her outrage. Anything worth doing was worth doing well; be it knifeplay, learning to be a proper duchess, or speaking for the goddess. She'd not asked to be chosen by Jai Idrish, but now that she had been, she refused to be the doormat Sir Dromon and his cohorts all expected. She drew herself up as tall as her sixty-seven inches allowed and looked down her nose at him with all the authority she could muster. "You forget yourself, sir. The Voice and Vessel is not some country goodwife who'll slink back to her mending."

"Kelan," the enforcer barked to the rider standing whey-faced and gore-splattered beside the coachman's headless corpse. "Assist the Voice to her blasted crystal. She can yammer at it all night long if she likes and leave me in peace."

Apparently, she needed to work on that superior take-no-prisoners tone Gray had down pat.

The enforcer yanked Meeryn from the coach, almost sending her tumbling to her knees in the dust of the lane where the young man waited with shifting eyes and obvious discomfort. She used his uncertainty to her advantage and shook him off to stand angry and alert, unwilling to leave Gray alone to face what might come next.

"Come, my lord. Do I need to drag you kicking and screaming?" the brute demanded.

The look Gray offered in return had the enforcer back-stepping, his body bent at the waist in the beginnings of a bow before he realized what he did.

How did Gray do that? She was going to have to ask him to teach her—if they survived.

He stepped from the coach as if he were arriving at Windsor for a royal audience. A cool breeze ruffled his hair while the mellow evening light sparkled the ruby in his neckcloth and emphasized the champagne shine on his exquisite boots. Only the rigidity of his posture and the stormy flicker in his eyes revealed the anger rippling like an undercurrent just beneath his skin. His gaze passed over the scene, pausing briefly on the enforcer Kelan, before settling back on his superior with a contemptuous look of distaste. "Do you have a name?"

"It's Braelin Thorsh. Loyal Ossine enforcer. Defender of the clans. Executioner of traitors."

"I'll stick to Mr. Thorsh," Gray countered. "Easier to remember."

The man scowled. Or rather, his scowl deepened. He was already looking as if he'd eaten nails for breakfast.

"Think you're jolly, don't you? But there's none of your devilish associates to spring to your defense out here," the man crowed. "None to come running when the precious heir to the five clans learns the meaning of pain."

"Ah, but there you're too late, Thorsh. I was already taught the meaning of pain by your superior, a veritable master." Gray's chin jerked up, his face expressionless but for a frightening twist of his lips. "A man far more skilled than you could ever hope to be." He straightened his coat, adjusted his cuffs, one at a time, slowly, methodically. "And I've always been a quick study."

The double-barreled flintlock appeared as if conjured. The enforcer standing at the horses' heads went down like a rag doll. Freed of a restraining arm and frantic at the roar of the pistol and the iron bite of blood filling their nostrils, the horses plunged and reared in terror before taking off at a gallop.

Thorsh jumped to the left of the runaway coach.

Gray shoved Meeryn to the right into the ditch at the road's verge. "Get down. Stay down. Do you hear?" he snarled.

He lifted his pistol and shot again. This time aiming for Thorsh, who was bellowing orders like a drill sergeant. The shot took him high in the left shoulder. He staggered backward as a scarlet blossom erupted across his vest.

"Shit, shit, shit," Gray muttered, tossing the gun aside. "Can't believe I fucking missed."

Meeryn caught a flash of movement from the corner of her eye. "Look out!" she shouted, even as she unthinkingly whipped free her stiletto. The knife buried itself in the shooter's thigh as a bullet sang past Gray's head to splinter a tree behind them.

"Enough!" Thorsh, pale but otherwise defiant, jerked his head at someone just beyond Meeryn's vision. "Come out and face your sentence like a man, de Coursy."

The fourth enforcer. Of course, there had been four at the start. In the confusion, she'd not noticed one's disappearance, but there he was with his arm tight against the neck of the missing groom, a silver blade poised to drive into the boy's heart.

"Do you want to see us stake the lad and send his soul to the grubs?" Thorsh threatened.

Gray's mouth was ringed in white, his face hard and closed. "Let him go. He's committed no crime."

"Hasn't he?" Thorsh strode to the boy, who shrank away with a terrified whimper. He took hold of the collar of the groom's coat and yanked it from his shoulders. The boy cried out. Snot and tears mingled on his chin. Thorsh did the same with the boy's shirt, leaving him bare-chested, ribs heaving as he wept. "No clan mark upon his back nor signum upon his mind. He's an unmarked abomination. A rogue that should have been drowned at birth."

"He's a child."

"Not for much longer. Soon he'll be a corpse."

Gray seemed to consider his options as he stood. A hand opened and closed in agitation. His nostrils flared as he inhaled, lips pursed as he let his breath out in a slow deciding whoosh of air. His gaze fell on Meeryn. "Forgive me," he murmured, at the same time pulling a second pistol from his coat and pointing it at her. "And get up."

Confused, she hesitated.

He cocked his weapon and jerked his hand in an upward motion. "There's little time left, Meeryn."

Her blood froze. Her breath seemed trapped in her lungs. But she did as she was bid.

Gray yanked her back against him. Her arms were pinned useless to her sides, the pistol jammed under her breast. His breath was warm upon the side of her face, but even now he didn't act out of panic or desperation. He remained as calm as if no one's life hung upon a wrong move or an ill-timed gesture. "Let the boy go, or I blow a hole through your precious N'thuil."

Face twisted in a mix of pain and defiance, Thorsh pressed a bloody hand to his shoulder. At Gray's threat, he laughed, his eyes squeezed to slits in an insolent face. "Do it."

"You think I bluff?" Gray called.

"I think no matter which choice you make, I win," Thorsh sneered, drawing a knife from a sheath at his waist. The handle was chased in bronze and carved with the double eagle's head of the Cornish Seriyajj, the blade wrought of pure silver. Light rippled upon its killing edges with a sickening menace. He touched it to the groom's neck, a drop of blood welling behind the point. The boy screamed, his eyes wild.

"You doubt my nerve?" Gray asked.

The pistol's mouth was only an inch from Meeryn's heart. A clean shot would tear her open but she'd be dead before she hit the ground. A fraction off and she'd be gut-shot to linger in agony. She held perfectly still, not even daring to breathe.

Thorsh shrugged. "You doubt mine?"

He pressed harder, dragging it down the boy's throat toward the notch at the base of his neck, leaving a gruesome line of red. The groom thrashed and cried out, but the enforcer who held him cut off his breath until he subsided.

"Enough!" Gray called out, shoving Meeryn away with a curse as if she burned him. "I yield, but let the boy go."

He stepped onto the lane, his palms held out to show he was unarmed.

At a nod from Thorsh, the enforcer released the groom, who sagged at once to his knees with blubbering wails. Grinning his triumph, Thorsh met Gray at the road's crown, his dagger's tip wet with blood. "The lad must mean much for you to exchange your life for his. Do you use him for pillow sport? Perhaps he'd welcome death if the alternative is despoilment."

Gray remained silent, his body taut as a wire, his spine nearly cracking with the strain. Meeryn could feel his rage burning high and bright like a flame—no, an inferno. Thorsh's silver blade whipped out once and twice more, slicing Gray's fine tailored coat to ribbons. "Remove the rest. Show us all your disgrace."

Gray unbuttoned his waistcoat, pulled free his shirt. Both landed upon the road beside his coat. The bandage wound about his arm was stained red while the deep scores from the dog's claws stood out raw and angry against his paler skin. But it was the sight of his bare back that made Meeryn gasp. Not because she hadn't seen the damage before. But those glimpses had been swift and furtive. She had avoided gazing directly upon the physical proof of his exile from the clans. Now there was no escaping the thick, ridged wreckage of scarred flesh where the flames had charred away his clan mark on his grandfather's orders.

"Unmarked rogue. *Emnil*. The sentence for trespass upon clan lands is death." Thorsh drew his sword, the same rippling eerie glow bouncing off the longer heavier silver blade. "May your soul be damned to dark corners and never find the Gateway home."

He lifted the sword high as he prepared to drive it deep. Gray never moved. His golden head remained lifted in challenge, unwilling to bend an inch, even if it might mean his life.

"No! Stop! Please!" she heard herself shout, though pleading gained her nothing.

Thorsh grunted his dismissal of her and lunged, the sword slamming toward Gray's chest.

Meeryn closed her eyes in horror only to have them fly open at a surprised shout from Thorsh as Gray rolled onto his feet with the stolen sword miraculously in his hand, the length of it resting on the back of Thorsh's exposed neck.

None would know what might have happened next, for a shouted halloo and a jangle of harness heralded the arrival of a gleaming black carriage, the crest upon the doors familiar to all assembled.

It drew to a halt. A groom leapt down to open the door, and Sir Dromon Pryor descended in a scented wave of hair oil, cologne, and sweat. He surveyed the tableau before him with smiling excitement as if he regarded a pantomime at Vauxhall. "Welcome to Deepings, my lord. It's good to have you home."


The short carriage ride was completed in a silence thick enough to chew and swallow. Sir Dromon sat beside de Coursy, so close their elbows touched now and then as they hit a rut or bounced through a puddle. So close he could drive a knife through the filthy *emnil*'s heart and be rid of him once and for all. He ignored the impulse. Such crude methods had never been his style. De Coursy's death must be seen as justice, not murder. Barring that, an unfortunate accident might serve as well. He'd erred badly when he'd forced His Grace's hand and had the young lordling exiled. Far better to have kept de Coursy close where he might be used, then subtly guided toward his own destruction.

Sir Dromon sniffed a quick sigh and dismissed past mistakes. The Munro slut had done her work; de Coursy had come running home. All progressed according to his design.

"The N'thuil claimed I would be safe so long as I traveled in her company. I must admit, your enforcer's attack made me doubt her veracity. I'm relieved to see she wasn't as mistaken as I feared."

"It is just as she stated. The N'thuil may offer sanctuary and safe passage to any lost soul she chooses. Mr. Thorsh shamed the order of Ossine by attacking your coach in such a fashion and ignoring Miss Munro's authority. He shall answer for his insubordination, you can be sure of that." He offered de Coursy an obsequious smile. "I'm honored you answered my summons, Lord Halvossa."

"Please, it's Major de Coursy. I don't choose to use that title."

"As you wish, Major. I wasn't certain you would return to a place with such . . . sorrowful memories for you. I'm glad to see you put the good of the clans ahead of your own personal feelings. It shows the true nobility that is so prevalent among your house. A true son of Idrin, you are. His Grace, the duke, would be proud."

"There's a first for everything."

Sir Dromon tittered into his sleeve. "Together, we can find a way through our current troubles. I'm sure of it."

"Fewer of your monsters set loose on the country-side would be a good start."

"Unfortunately, Mr. Thorsh and his ilk are neces-sary in these unstable times. More so, now that we are unsure of the Fey-blood's intent. The clans cannot sit idle while the enemy masses."

De Coursy eyed him like a disease. "Yet they seem more interested in killing shapechangers than in de-fending the Palings against a Fey-blood attack . . . or am I mistaken?"

"All issues to be discussed, all problems to be solved," Sir Dromon said with an accommodating smile.

The coach rolled beneath the arched stone gateway of Deepings outer wall and into the enormous inner yard. Towers punctuated each turning in the thick gray stone fortifications, while straight ahead stood the tall central house, a tangled maze of elegant apartments where the family lived, as well as miles of drafty corridors, twisted stairwells, bustling servant quarters, and dank halls.

De Coursy glanced beyond the glass, his face tightening, his hands drumming on his thigh. Then he turned from the view to address Sir Dromon once more, any nervousness vanished beneath a polished veneer. "My coachman will be given all the proper death rites for one of the clans. I should like you to perform the service personally," he said in a voice that brooked no dissent.

How was it that half-naked and sweat-streaked, he still bore himself with a prideful dignity, as if the world owed him obedience? As if he hadn't been stripped of

place and position, spared only his life? Sir Dromon
gritted his teeth in a grimace of a smile. "Of course.
I've instructed the Ossine to bring the bodies to Deepings for the necessary ceremonies."

"You mean body," Gray corrected. "My groom was
released and sent on his way unharmed, was he not?"

Sir Dromon smiled and nodded. "A slip of the
tongue. I meant to say 'body.' The young boy was
taken by one of Thorsh's men to Haleworthy, where he
might catch the mail coach for London. It was done
just as you ordered."

"Not that I don't trust your men, Sir Dromon, but I
should like confirmation of his safe passage. Have the
enforcer . . . I believe Thorsh called him Kelan . . . have
the young man report to me when he returns."

His not-so-subtle jab wasn't lost on Sir Dromon. It
would seem the snot-nosed prig had grown clever in
the intervening years. "Directly he arrives, my lord."

"It's Major, Sir Dromon. Let's neither of us pretend my title of Lord Halvossa or my presence here at
Deepings is welcome by either of us."

Miss Munro sat through this conversation as
though a poker had been rammed up her arse, her lips
pressed white in a face like a wheel of cheese. Only
her eyes burned with a dangerous light as they rested
upon de Coursy in the seat across from her. That was
good. Whatever happened between them on the journey from London to produce such hostility could only
aid his own plans.

"I've made arrangements to have you placed in the
guest hall," he said.

De Coursy's brows lifted in question. "Won't it be
needed for the Gather elders?"

"The Gather's summer meeting was put off due to His Grace's poor health. We hope he regains his strength and the autumn meeting can proceed as planned. Until then, I have tried to fulfill his duties to the best of my abilities, though I could never hope to replace him in the hearts of the clans."

"Were my old apartments not available?"

Sir Dromon offered a humbling hunch of his shoulders. "I'm afraid I took the liberty of moving my own small household into these rooms. With the duke's illness, it seemed important for me to be on hand at a moment's notice rather than have to travel back and forth to Drakelow each day." He paused. "And of course, we did not expect you back."

"No, of course you didn't. I understand completely," de Coursy replied. "The guest hall will do . . . for now."

Sir Dromon found himself flushing scarlet. He despised himself for his cowardice, though it would serve him for now to have de Coursy thinking he was a cowed subservient. He would only learn differently when it was too late. When the traitor's rebellion lay in ashes around him, his friends dead or driven away, his life balanced in Dromon's careless hands.

De Coursy would beg for mercy. Grovel in the dirt like the lowest grub. Piss his boots and vomit his terror with every slow, methodical pass of the flensing knife.

It would avail him naught as his skin was stripped, his innards pulled from his steaming gut, and his still-beating heart ripped from his broken chest. Buoyed by such cheerful thoughts, Sir Dromon met de Coursy's steely gaze . . . and smiled.

# 5

DEEPINGS, CORNWALL

"His Grace has retired for the night, my lord, and is not to be disturbed for any reason. Sir Dromon's orders are quite strict on that point."

"Does he know I've arrived? That I'm"—he couldn't bring himself to say *home*—"that I'm here?"

"He's been told, my lord."

He'd already tried five times to convince the new Deepings' butler to stop "my lording" him after every sentence. And failed five times. He wasn't sure if this was the man's way of kowtowing to an obvious superior or thumbing his nose at a disowned exile.

"His response?"

Mr. Pym's lips thinned, and he cleared his throat. "His Grace's response was to throw his dinner plate at a footman and curse your black soul to the grubs . . . my lord. He says he has no wish to see you today or any day."

"I see. Thank you, Pym. I suppose if he has the

strength to hurl dinnerware, he's not as close to death as I feared."

The butler made the appropriate noises and bowed his way out.

Gray watched him scuttle down the corridor, doubtless, headed straight to Sir Dromon with news of this conversation. It was safe to assume that every Deepings servant was in Pryor's employ; either bound by loyalty or pressured by fear. It was also safe to assume that, despite Pryor's toadying, the head of the Ossine wanted him dead as much as he always had. So why had he allowed Gray to return to holding lands unmolested, when up until a few months ago, he'd bent every effort to destroy him? What game did the Arch Ossine play?

To take his mind from his endless circle of questions, he surveyed the dark tapestried walls and the ponderous, uncomfortable furniture of his guest hall chambers. His lip curled in a humorless smile. Whatever brutal entertainments Pryor had planned, he'd made his first miscalculation. The guest hall had always been a drab, gloomy, unpleasant place. Almost certainly, a tactic of his grandfather's to keep unwanted visitors to a minimum and the Gather elders from lingering too long. But they didn't know its secret—Gray did.

He passed through a study, a salon, and a small private dining room to his bedchamber. Aside from a tester bed resembling something Henry VIII might have died in, the room held little more than a lumpy wingback chair, a folding officer's desk with a wobbly leg, and an immense wardrobe carved with the de Coursy crest: a double-headed eagle bearing five arrows in its claws. This last piece of ornate furniture took up most of the chamber's northern wall. Beside it, the hearth yawned cold and black with soot from five centuries or more of oak-fed fires, while above it hung a heavy gold-rimmed mirror, the reflection within its speckled depths revealing a lean high-boned face bordering on gaunt, eyes that had seen too much, and a mouth set in a permanent expression of grim resignation. He raked a hand through his hair, straightened his tired shoulders, and ran a finger along the thin slash of red at his throat where Thorsh's blade had left its mark. He looked like nothing more than a dour consumptive. Older than his thirty-one years, bent by pain and battered by injury.

The war had toughened him. The peace that followed had stretched him close to the breaking point. Only determination fired him now. Determination and a sense that all the events since Charleroi—hell since the fateful storm in the Channel had stripped his family from him in one earth-shattering cataclysm— had been leading him to this point and soon he might understand why and what he was supposed to do with this horrible destiny.

But only if he could gain hold of Jai Idrish.

Reaching up, he felt along the mirror's left edge until he found a grooved indentation worked into the gilded frame. He pressed it once, then twice more. A brick at the back of the hearth scraped aside to reveal a narrow cavity—and a key.

He smiled his relief and thanked the Mother that he'd not been summoned here in winter, when the hearth would have been fed a steady diet of logs and the secret panel lost to the flames. He scooped the key from its resting place and opened the wardrobe door. A servant had already unpacked his clothes, but Gray pushed all of them aside and stepped up into the high wooden cupboard. At the very back behind a mountain of coats and shirts and boots and stockings was the flat wooden panel that made up the back of the wardrobe. In the dusty camphor-scented dark, none would notice the tiny inconspicuous keyhole, but Gray knew it was there. He slid the key in and turned. The secret door opened with a puff of dry stale air to reveal a cavernous hole.

He allowed himself a smile of success—it paid to bury oneself in books.

He'd found the secret of the passage in a mildewed journal kept by the third earl of Halvossa, a scholar of history and a skilled warrior. A man who read and wrote extensively when he wasn't hacking people's heads off in battle. He gained a dukedom for his loyalty to one king. He ended on the block for his rebellion against another. But his greatest achievement had been Deepings. From rugged keep and earthen ditches grew a formidable defensive fortress. Only the earl knew what he'd truly been defending; the holding of his clan; the remnants of a race gone into hiding against a dangerous world. The journal had been a catalog of the building process, a daily report of bricks laid, ground broken, workers hired . . . and escape routes should the need arise.

It had not.

Not in the centuries since. Hopefully not in the centuries to come. The knowledge of these bolt-holes had been lost amid the Deepings library, only brought to light by a fifteen-year-old boy in search of a story to lull him to sleep when the nights seemed endless and his thoughts spun like a Catherine wheel.

He stepped into the passage, pausing for a moment until his eyes adjusted to the dark. A faint breeze stirred the air against his face and fluttered the curtains of cobwebs. A dull roar vibrated the stones under his feet where no footprints marred the thick layer of dust and mouse droppings. Ten paces on, the passage became a set of winding stairs that descended hundreds of feet into the cliffs upon which Deepings stood, ending at a trapdoor and a swirling black whirlpool.

All just as he remembered.

The journal claimed that a short swim would empty you onto the beach below the castle. Gray had never had the courage to dive into the impenetrable black water to find out. Just standing at the edge and staring down at the churn of waves would bring on gut-seizing tremors. He'd imagine the punch of icy water closing over his head and the crush of burning lungs as he was spun head over feet by the tugging current. The tears would run, his hands would shake, and he would back away sickened and shamed by his cowardice.

It had been more than ten years since he'd last stood in this spot, but the unreasonable terror still gripped him. He steadied himself, palms sweaty, stomach rolling, and cursed himself for a craven. It would seem the years had hardened him, but old memories still clung like the cobwebs shrouding his clothes and tangling in his hair.

A hundred yards or a hundred miles made no difference. There was not a chance in hell he could leap into that hole and swim the distance to safety.

Escape route? Not bloody likely.

Perhaps Sir Dromon hadn't been so stupid after all.

Perhaps entering Deepings had been the easy part, and it would be leaving that proved to be impossible.

"I hope you've recovered sufficiently, Lady N'thuil. I want to offer my humblest apologies on behalf of the Ossine. I can only hope de Coursy has apologized as well." Sir Dromon fiddled with his pocket watch, running his fingers up and down the gold chain, his thin-lipped, chinless smile giving him a puckish, unnerving look.

"It's of no matter," she said, wishing only for the solace of her own apartments where she might scrub the grime of the road from her skin. The memories of slaughter would not be erased so easily.

"Isn't it?" Sir Dromon challenged, rising from his desk. "He might have killed you had I not come when I did. Rage fills that man. There's no telling what he might do. I only hope I didn't err by inviting him back to Deepings."

"Gray had no choice. The enforcer would have murdered the boy as he'd killed the coachman."

"But to risk your life in such a callous way. If he could not honor your safety as N'thuil, you would think he would at least show respect for a woman in his care. To place you in peril was not the behavior of a gentleman, no matter how he was pushed to the brink."

"What was Mr. Thorsh's excuse? He made it very clear he'd have been more than pleased to see my brains mingling with that of the coachman's on that road. There was neither honor nor respect in his actions nor even a shadow of gentility. The man's a monster."

"In these times, we use the best tool for the job. Thorsh might not have the manners that come with social rank, but he's very good at what he does."

"Killing?"

"I was going to say, protecting the clans from those who would destroy us if given the chance." His purse-lipped, professorial look over his spectacles was meant to set her in her proper place.

She wished she knew where that proper place might be anymore. She felt tugged in too many directions, like flotsam caught in a riptide. The more she struggled, the more she floundered. "I only want to put it behind me and focus on the reason for de Coursy's coming in the first place, putting an end to this growing internal divide. The Imnada can't afford to turn upon each other; not now. Not when—"

"—the Fey-bloods stand upon our very doorstep? But who put them there in the first place? Who went against every law and custom by revealing our existence to out-clans and Fey-bloods?"

"Major de Coursy did what he thought was right." She felt herself retreating in the face of Dromon's argument. Offering excuses for Gray when what she really wanted to do was throttle him for such a thoughtless stunt. When push came to shove, he'd not pulled the trigger, but that didn't mean the thought hadn't crossed his mind.

"That may be, but the laws were put in place for a reason—to keep us safe, to keep us strong," Sir Dromon said. "Those who subvert them must pay a price for their presumption. Otherwise, they pollute with their lies those who remain loyal to the old teachings."

Logical, reasonable; the voice of rational thought among the clamoring squabbles of petty clan leaders.

Sir Dromon ambled about the room, hands behind his back, a self-satisfied master of his dominion. Now and then he would take up a figurine or a carved box, a bit of china statuary or a painted miniature, stare at it for a loving moment and put it back precisely in its place. A man who appreciated order and exactness above all else. He controlled the bloodline scrolls with the same care and meticulousness. No wonder the idea of half-breeds and out-clan marriages disgusted him. They disrupted his clean, neat, tidy view of the world where there was a place for everything and everything in its place.

"But they're not all lies, are they?" she asked, reminded of the Flannery baby. A muddle of magics that ran counter to everything Sir Dromon stood for.

"What do you mean by that?" He dropped his fob, the flash of the pearl bright in the candle's light. His brows creased, and he smoothed a hand over his shirtfront in flustered agitation.

She must tread carefully here. To accuse the Arch Ossine of an outright falsehood would be dangerous, but a bit of clever manipulation might reveal the answers and leave him thinking her as useless a female as he already did.

She cast her gaze to the floor, offered him a slightly awed look through downcast lashes. "It's just that for centuries we've been told the bloodline scrolls are the only way to maintain the purity and power inherent in the race. That out-clan marriages must be shunned and half-breeds refused clan recognition because they weaken us ... dilute us. Yet, in London ... amid Major de Coursy's associates, the half-breeds I encountered possessed the same purity and strength as any true blood. Perhaps if that's the case then they're as worthy of the clans as any born of the scrolls." She finished with an uncertain, doltish half smile.

His answering expression was one of pedagogical condescension. "It might seem so, my dear, but looks can be deceiving. Opening the way to half-breeds and out-clan marriages would be tantamount to surrendering all we are or ever hope to be. When Aneavala created the Palings to protect us, he set us apart and above. Who are we to turn our backs on what has served us well for so long?"

"But wasn't that during the wars, when the clans fought for our very survival? It's different now." She worked to maintain the bland questioning expression that seemed to be working so effectively.

"Is it?" he answered sharply.

She thought about the Fey-blood who attacked Gray. He'd claimed this was the first time, but who could say if it would be the last? The Fey-bloods were known for their treachery and their hatred of the Imnada. The stories were full of such instances even before the Fealla Mhòr, when the clans were supposed to be at peace. If the *afailth luinan* was known to the Other, they would stop at nothing to possess such a prize, gift or not. Who was right? Dromon with his isolationist fears, or Gray with his desire for détente? She feared the answer would only be known after more violence.

"You defend de Coursy's position even after he behaved so badly," Sir Dromon continued. "He must be quite persuasive to win you over to his cause."

A parry and return thrust, bringing the conversation full circle. Nicely played. She would have to concede and withdraw. "I'm not won over, but I'm willing to see his side and judge the truth for myself."

"That's good and as it should be for a seeker of peace. I, too, look forward to hearing his arguments. Perhaps he can convince me of his rightness and that his actions have not doomed us all. That these Feybloods can be trusted." Sir Dromon sighed deeply, his fingers again running up and down the gold chain hanging from his waistcoat pocket. "I only hope he can be trusted as well."

"What do you mean by that?"

"Why do you suppose he agreed to come back so easily? I know you believe your childhood friendship swayed him or perhaps your more recent feminine charms, but he is no fool. He must understand the risks. What could have driven him to come?"

"I told him the duke was dying. That for the good of the clans and his own peace of mind, he should attempt a reconciliation."

Once more appeared the look of patient disdain that made Meeryn want to scratch his eyes from his head with one good rake of her nails. "That would be a wonderful thing, were it true."

She curled her fingers into her palm and breathed deeply through her nose. "You don't believe him?"

"I know the duke pines for his lost family and de Coursy's exile was a bitter blow, but they were never close, were they? Perhaps it's not love that brought de Coursy back but something darker like"—he leaned close, his voice a hissed whisper—"vengeance."

Meeryn went rigid. "You believe he's here to kill His Grace?"

Sir Dromon gave a noncommittal shrug and a quick fuss of his long white hands. "Don't misunderstand. I don't *believe* anything. I only present facts. The Duke of Morieux exiled his only grandson, watched silently as his signum was stripped and his clan mark was burned from his back. That might make the most honorable of men bitter against their tormentor."

"Gray would never harm the duke."

Sir Dromon scanned the ceiling as if searching for an answer. "And you saw him last . . . ten years ago, was it? Be careful, my dear. I know you and he were very close, but people change. Only hours ago he held a gun to your head and bartered his own life against yours. Does that sound like a man who would not lash out if cornered? Does that sound like a man you can trust?"

"My lord? Are you here?" The voice came distant and muffled through the piles of laundry, but it was loud enough to startle Gray from his reverie. He stepped free of the passage, sliding and locking the panel in place. Ducking out of the wardrobe, he pocketed the key to return to its hole once he'd dealt with this interruption.

It was the young enforcer Kelan. He stood in uncomfortable misery within the study, hands behind his back, legs spread and head high as if he faced a firing squad.

"No need to look so martyred. I haven't mur-

dered anyone in"—Gray tapped his chin in thought—
"well . . . since yesterday." He leaned against a rickety
side table and prayed it didn't collapse beneath him.

"I had no idea Mr. Thorsh meant to murder the
coachman, my lord. It happened so fast. He had his
gun out before I realized. I assumed he would scare
the man, not kill him in cold blood. And then when
you . . . when he pulled you from the coach . . . I know
you didn't want me to reveal myself by interfering,
but . . ."

"But you were afraid you were about to stand as a
helpless witness to my execution."

"I've sworn you my sword, my lord. I couldn't just
watch as all we've fought for ended in a sword stroke."

"I appreciate the loyalty, Kelan, but you're far more
use to me as one of Dromon's enforcers than watching
your back on the run with the rest of us."

"But if you'd misjudged the moment, my lord . . ."

"I'd have ended as a headless corpse and you'd have
been left to explain my sticky end to Captain Flannery."

"Not a conversation I'd relish."

"No, I don't blame you. It's that martial, knight-in-
armor, intensity of his. I think the infantrymen in our
company were more frightened of facing him than any
of Boney's soldiers."

"Yes, sir."

Gray wanted to laugh at Kelan's deference, which
bordered on puppyish adoration. A far cry from the
brash insolence and outright contempt he'd received
from the battle-hardened men in his former military
command, Mac included. But then, he'd been as raw
and green as this earnest young man when he'd arrived

in Lisbon with a desire to prove himself. A high-born prig thinking rank alone would command respect. He had been their commander from the beginning, but it had taken five hard years and three dangerous countries before he could call himself their leader.

"What of my groom? Is he safe?"

"Aye, my lord. I saw to it myself. Mr. Thorsh meant for him to die. I could see that clear enough. The boy could too, and he fell to gibbering for his mam. I took him up rough-like and told Thorsh I'd take care of it myself. He didn't argue. His wound was paining him and he was happy to leave the killing to me. I took the youngling deep into the wood and told him to find his way back to the posting inn. The boy fled as if he'd a pack of hounds on his tail."

"Good. Doule will see to it he reaches London safely." Gray dragged up a chair, dropping into it before he collapsed, his legs suddenly weak, his stomach cramping with pent-up relief. He'd not known how worried he was for the boy until Kelan had reassured him.

David cursed Gray's coldheartedness. Mac admired Gray's resolve. But neither one knew how deep the wounds inflicted were with each life lost to his cause. The ghosts of those he'd killed rarely bothered his sleep. The ghosts of those who'd died fighting for him haunted his dreams until closing his eyes was a punishment to be endured.


The duke's hand was dry and fragile as onion skin. Meeryn clasped it, trying not to notice the way he clung to her as if afraid to let go. In his growing senility, did he fear the darkness as a child might? Or did he truly sense the encroaching shadows of rebellion, unrest, and fear spreading across Deepings' battlements into the heart of the Imnada clans?

Perhaps she imagined the way he held her fingers tightly in his own and the confusion in his eyes. Perhaps it was her own doubts and worries making her uneasy as she kept her vigil.

"I missed you, Meeryn. Pym hovers, and that valet of mine eyes me as if I'm a corpse already."

"I missed you too, Your Grace. But I've a surprise; Gray is here with me. He's back at Deepings."

"Pym told me." He withdrew his hand, eyes narrowed. "Is the boy much changed since his exile?"

*How could he not be after what you did to him?* she thought. Probably not the most tactful of answers. She settled on, "He's grim. Formidable. But I see why men follow him. He carries himself like a . . . a . . ."

"Like a duke," the old man snapped. "But that's not his right. Only a mistake of ill fortune."

"You're wrong. It's been Gray's right since he was fourteen. You'd be proud of the man he's become. Of the Duke of Morieux he would make if given the chance."

His Grace's snort of derision turned to a spate of coughing. Spittle leaked from the corner of his mouth, which he didn't wipe away. His eyes watered with tears as his hands clenched the covers.

Meeryn felt a twisted mix of sympathy, love, and anger. The duke and Gray had been two souls torn apart by one tragic act. If only they'd clung to each other, how much different would both lives have turned out? Would Sir Dromon have been able to squeeze his way into the duke's confidence? Would

Gray have departed Deepings for the army as a last drastic attempt to prove himself worthy? So many futures altered, so many choices unmade, if only . . .

"Sir Dromon says the boy's here to kill me." His Grace leaned in with much wheezing and grunting as Meeryn tried not to notice the odor of stale sweat and urine, the broken veins on his nose, or his crusty chapped lips. "Do you believe that's true?"

"Gray loves you. He'd cut off his right hand before he caused you harm."

"Love? He'd do better to despise me for the trouble I've caused him. I'd respect him more for his hatred than his affection." His Grace cackled. "But mayhap you're right and Pryor worries overmuch. Gray was meant for you, you know. Or rather, you were meant for the heir to the five clans. The bloodlines were correct, the pedigree satisfactory. Idrin's line would have been strengthened by the joining. Our house would have been proud to accept you."

"I know."

"That boy of yours knew it, too. The one who stole your maidenhead and your heart. Knew who and what you were. He thought he could outsmart the Ossine's scrolls and wangle his way into my confidence. The wolves of the Viyachne have always been overly cunning."

Old anger flared hot in Meeryn's face, and she turned away until she could master her expression, but she could not steady the wobble in her voice when she answered him. "You outsmarted yourself, Your Grace. You sent Conal McIlroy away and then you exiled Gray. Now there's no heir and no joining and Idrin's line will end. And I'm left alone."

"You're N'thuil."

She wanted to scream at him how worthless such an honor was these days, when the crystal remained cold and silent and the power of her position was as moldy and worm-riddled as Gray's old books. Instead she plumped His Grace's pillows, straightened his blankets. Poured him a fresh glass of water.

His Grace closed his eyes. He sagged deeper into the bed, his face going lax and dull, his hands uncurled to lie knobby and liver-spotted on the coverlet, the gold of the great ring of his house bright against the pasty white of his flaccid skin. "I stayed until the end," he muttered. "That much I felt I owed him. He can't have expected more than that."

"He's your grandson," she countered. "He expected you, of all people, to help him."

His eyes flashed open, and for a moment, they burned as clear and focused as the eagle he was born to be, and he was once more the feared and respected Duke of Morieux. "He's a murderer. You say he's not come to kill me, but he's already killed the rest of my family. I'm all that's left. He's destroyed everyone who touches him. Everyone who loves him." He grabbed her wrist, his grip crushing her bones with a warrior's strength. "Be careful, Meeryn. Be careful lest he destroy you."

# 6

She sliced through the water, down deeper and deeper where the moonlight never penetrated. The current moved like silk over her seal skin and she spun and curled as she dove, letting it caress her like a lover, letting it ease the weight from her shoulders and calm her frazzled nerves. She'd come into her powers amid the frigid northern ocean surrounding the rocky Orkney outpost, but it had been the warmer Cornish seas where she'd learned to love every surge and swell of the ocean. Endowed with the rare gift of flux and unbound by the aspect of her birth clan, she could shift to any creature, big or small; fly with the eagles of the Seriyajj or hunt the mountains as one of the Welsh Viyachne. But when her thoughts and her form grew tangled and tight, it was the seal of her birth clan, the Nornala, she sought; an aspect of sleek strength and unshrinking confidence.

Ahead, a school of pilchard darted and flashed against the green-black water. She carved into their midst with killer precision, feeding until her stomach no longer ached. She could not say the same about her heart.

Lungs empty, she rose to the surface, scanning the distant shore. Lightning shimmered now and again and the rumble of thunder bounced and echoed against the high cliffs. The lights of Deepings glittered like diamonds beckoning her home, and tired enough for sleep to come, she let them guide her in.

The cliffs rose high above her as she beached herself below the house, the grit of the coarse sand rough against her hide while she let the fire and magic of the shift engulf her. The seal's smooth brown fur became a tumbled mane of honey hair. Flippers and tail changed to long limbs and a woman's curves. She blinked and stretched, her human skin always feeling odd and awkward for a few moments as mind and body adjusted to this new form.

The brush of another's shifter magic against her nakedness brought her head up sharply. The clatter of falling pebbles against the rocks froze her silent as she searched the night for the intruder into her solitude. A quick startled breath caught in her throat. No lurking Ossine enforcer sent to do murder. Instead Gray stood motionless on the cliff path above her, his gaze locked on the horizon, body wired with tension. He'd discarded his coat on a nearby rock and loosened his neckcloth. Sweat glistened in the hollow of his throat and damped his hair to his head.

What on earth brought him to the beach? He hated and feared the water. Had for years.

Lightning lit the skies, illuminating his face, revealing the determination etched in every grim line. The crack of thunder seemed to underscore the anger radiating off him, the effort he took to keep his temper in check. Then he swung around, and, in another bright, blinding flash, the pain in his eyes shone starkly clear. It was an expression gone in an instant. Locked away so thoroughly, he might as well have been carved in stone, but the tremble in his hands betrayed him as did the taut working of his jaw.

"A poor night for a swim," he said, breaking the standoff between them.

"I prefer the sea when it's rough and the currents are wild. Normally, I enjoy it for the challenge. To-night it mirrored my mood."

His gaze traveled over her naked body with slow de-liberation, a long sensual stare that started at her toes, skimming up her bare legs to pause just long enough for her insides to flutter, before trailing over the flat of her stomach, lingering upon her tingling breasts and the long strands of her hair dripping over her shoulders.

At last, he settled upon her face. The dark intensity in his eyes reminded her of the ocean's caress sliding against her body, leaving pleasure and excitement in its wake. She felt no embarrassment in her nudity. The Imnada cared nothing for the social prudishness of the day. The shame came from the sweet ache between her legs and the thrill of anticipation coursing like lava through her veins.

Neither feeling was welcome. Either one could cost her in position and reputation, not to mention the risk to actual life and limb. Now was not the time to go pudding-kneed and jelly-headed over a pair of icy blue eyes and a Grecian god's body. Now was the time to remain pragmatic and focused. Hold to her earlier fury. Hold very tight.

"What are you doing here?" she snapped.

"Looking for you."

"How did you know where to find me?"

He lifted a brow. "You always swam when you were angry or upset. I assumed you'd be both tonight—mainly at me. Am I right?"

"I ought to be." Hoping to put distance and layers between them, she grabbed up the bag she'd left on the shingle with her clothes neatly folded inside. Shook out a chemise and pulled it on, tying the ribbons at her throat with virginal precision. "I ought to bash you over the head with one of those rocks over there for pulling such a trick."

"It was a chance I had to take." His expression hardened, and he turned back to peer out over the sea. "It won't happen again."

She was reminded of the duke's warning as she drew on a skirt, its hem sodden where her bag had lain half in a puddle. "No, of course it won't. You've seen how little it will avail you. I'm not the bargaining chip you were hoping for."

"You're N'thuil. Your body should be sacrosanct. Your authority as great as Morieux's."

The blouse she donned was soft, comfortable, and two years out of fashion. Since the duke's illness, she'd not had her annual trip to London to shop for new clothes. "'Should' is the crucial word in that sentence. You know as well as I do how little real power the position of N'thuil wields anymore. Look at Tidwell, he was barely more than Dromon's puppet. I'm less than that. Chosen by accident, I'm seen as a fraud and a laughingstock. I thought if I could broker a reconciliation between Pryor and yourself, if I could offer the

clans some hope that a new and more deadly Fealla
Mhòr isn't on the horizon, if I could be a N'thuil like
Anaveala or . . . or . . ." She shook her head. "Castles in
the air, all of them. I can't even keep you from being
almost murdered a mile outside Deepings' gates."

She'd not worn shoes, so her toes peeked from beneath her skirt and her hair still hung loose in salty
tails. In fact, she looked no better than a peddler's ur-
chin, but at least she no longer felt exposed to Gray's
soul-peeling stare and the dance of anticipation puck-
ering her skin. Then the air grew charged with electricity and the hair at the back of her neck rose. He
locked his gaze on hers as lightning struck cold and
white around them and thunder split the night with a
vicious crack. She stood rooted to the ground as heat
washed over her like a cresting wave, singed her skin,
wobbled her knees. She felt herself swaying toward
him and took a protective step back in response.

Somewhere in this conversation, she'd lost her
fingertip grip on that protective anger. If she weren't
careful, she could tumble, and it was a very long way
down.

Gray seemed to sense her misgivings. His lip
twitched in something coming close to amusement,
and he bent to take up a handful of stones, casting
each one into the waves. One . . . two . . . three . . . The
fourth he held in his hand, rolling it over and over between thumb and forefinger. "If Jai Idrish chose you,
it had a purpose."

"That's what I thought too, at first. Now I just think
it has a really nasty sense of humor."

"Perhaps it waits for the right time to reveal itself."

"What possible better right time could there be?

Factions split and split again, the Gather elders argue and dally and do nothing, the duke slides closer to death, and you . . ."

His eyes seemed to glow with an unearthly light in his dark face, achingly blue and sharp as drawn steel. "I chose the world beyond the Palings as my proper place and paid for it with all but my very life."

"If you'd only stayed . . . if you'd only understood my . . ." Her stomach flip-flopped uncomfortably, and she tightened her arms around her bag as if, left to their own devices, they might unconsciously reach out to him. "It doesn't matter now."

How many hours had she spent staring out over the ocean after he'd left for the army? Far too many. How many angry letters had she begun, only to tear them up? All but one. But that one had been enough—the damage was done. Words were written that could not be taken back.

He'd responded with one short note of apology, then nothing.

The years slid by, and she had wrapped herself in the business of the holding, and gave no more than a cursory thought to the sweet boy of her youth. Only sometimes, when summer storms battered the castle and she heard the tolling of the rescue bell farther down the rocky coast, did her mind turn to Gray with regret for what she'd written. Only sometimes, when she entered the dim musty Deepings library, did her eyes turn instinctively toward the empty chair in the corner as if she might see him sitting there with a book open in his lap. Only in the darkest watches of the night did she sometimes wonder if Gray's mind ever turned to her with the same unanswered questions.

Wind kicked up ahead of the storm. Rain pattered the rocks and speckled the water. She started up the beach, Gray trailing behind. "You won't tell anyone you found me here, will you?" she asked.

"They don't know?"

"His Grace doesn't like me to leave the house at night. He's grown cautious and overprotective. My relationship with Conal only made it worse. The duke spent too many years living in London. He sees me as the human world sees me; a weak, vulnerable female who needs to be protected. He's forgotten things are different among our kind."

The path was a narrow switchback, rocky and lined with great patches of broom that bent in the increasing wind. Gray put a hand out to help her. She clutched her bag tighter and continued on. Once inside Deepings, he would turn left for the path to the dreary guest quarters. She would cross the rose garden, slip through the music room, and return to her bedchamber. Surely she could make it that far without losing control, without touching the narrow slice of skin at the base of his throat or breathing the masculine sandalwood scents in the folds of his shirt. Surely she could hold tight to her righteous indignation for just a little longer.

"Yet he allowed you to travel to London on your own and back in the unchaperoned company of a gentleman."

"His Grace didn't allow it. That was Sir Dromon's idea. He knew you'd be suspicious of any emissary from the clans. He thought I might succeed in persuading you where another might . . ."

"End with a knife in their gut?"

"Something like that."

"A wise assumption on his part."

As if to punctuate his words, the storm broke above them in a gusting wind and torrents of cold needling rain. It slashed at them, pelting their faces, driven hard off the salty wind-whipped ocean.

"Quick! Before we're soaked through." Meeryn dodged the rocks as she scrambled up the cliff path toward the house.

This time when Gray reached for her, she took his hand, and together they raced for cover. She shoved against the door in the westernmost cliff tower, the hinges scraping against the force of her shoulder, the wind scurrying old leaves into the corners of the room.

Gray slapped his wet hair from his face and shook the water from his coat to puddle on the floor, but he did not let go of her hand. Instead his fingers twined with hers, his skin hot, his eyes hotter. "I'd forgotten about this way into the castle. I suppose I thought it must be full of enforcer troops preparing for war upon the Fey-bloods or at least locked tight against stray intruders."

"We wouldn't have the troops to fill these old barracks if every clanswoman had ten younglings in rapid succession. And as for the lock, what's the point of being chatelaine if you can't have a few spare keys made for emergencies?" she babbled, very aware of the way his hand fit against hers, the scorching heat of his soldier's body, and the bone-melting look in his steel-blue eyes. This was where she said her farewells and went her very separate way. This was the moment . . . no, *this* was the moment . . . no, most definitely this *was* the moment . . .

He ran his fingers along the wainscoting, pausing over a chipped piece of trim. "Our initials are still here," he said with pleasant surprise.

Meeryn peered closer to see the barely visible gouged lines that made up MM and GD, souvenirs of happier days. Ran her own hand over the faint traces of friendship remaining.

"Do you remember the night we carved these? It was right before you left for the Orkneys to visit your cousins. I have vague recollections of purloined gin, a corncob pipe, and"—he frowned as if searching his memory—"a smutty song about the parson's daughter."

She swallowed and nodded. "I remember."

What had been impossible to forget was the embarrassment when her drunken boldness had resulted in . . . nothing. Not a kiss. Not a cuddle. Gray had retreated into sober silence and the merriment had petered out to an awkward, uncomfortable silence.

Much like this one.

He dropped his gaze to their joined hands. "I know you blame me for leaving, Meeryn, but I couldn't stay. The memories rode too close to the surface here. I had to get out before they crushed me completely."

"Your family's death was not your fault, Gray. It was a tragic accident. There was nothing you could do." So much for light chitchat, though she should have known this conversation would come soon or late. Gray couldn't come back without those old painful ghosts rising to meet him.

"My head knows that. My heart—and the duke—are harder to convince."

"He's frail. He doesn't know what he says."

"What was his excuse when I was fourteen?" he murmured, his stare lengthened as if lost in the past. "Or when I was twenty-nine?"

"He had no choice. He had to follow the laws."

"He stood aside and did nothing, Meeryn. He watched . . . he let them take me apart from the inside out . . ."

What had Sir Dromon implied? That Gray returned to Deepings, not to forge a peace, but to destroy His Grace. She wouldn't believe it. He'd lived to please the old man, had loved him fiercely even when all it got him was a cold rebuff and a closed door. Meeryn had watched it all, hating each cruel cut of the duke's tongue and stinging lash of his hard blue eyes. Hating the way Gray changed with each confrontation. Little by little, hardly perceptible to anyone who didn't know him as she did, but she noticed. It reminded her of the cliffs below the holdings after each passing storm as more of the soft earth was worn away to reveal the unforgiving granite beneath.

Was this what the Duke of Morieux had ultimately wrought? A ruthless weapon to be turned upon the clans?

The moments ticked by, her heart thudded faster and faster, but her desire to flee was being fast overwhelmed by a greater desire and escape was the last thing she wanted.

"The worst part . . . the part that keeps me awake . . . his eyes never left my face . . . not once the whole time. It was as if . . . as if he wanted to witness my ultimate humiliation."

"Gray," she whispered at the heartrending pain in his voice.

She sensed his intent in the moment before he kissed her and knew she should stop him with a firm hand to his chest and a dismissive turn of her head. Instead she clasped his wet shirt in her fist and pulled him closer. Tilted her chin to meet his lips, parting to let his tongue slide within, plundering her mouth, stealing her breath.

The moment she was waiting for slipped by, and she never even noticed.

The air was cold, but the heat from his body burned away the chill, seared her skin. She wanted to drown in his kiss, melt into his touch. He pushed her gently against the wall, the stones rough against her back, his arms braced to either side of her head as he took his fill of her, his mouth brandy sweet and smoky smooth.

He lifted his head, eyes pale as glass and hard as ice. He dragged her hair over her shoulder, his lips curving teasingly over the sensitive edge of her ear before tracing a shivery path down her neck. One hand palmed a breast through her clinging wet blouse, her nipple pebbling against the teasing pass of his thumb, her sex instinctively tingling and tightening. His other hand reached for her skirt, lifting and rucking it around her waist. She felt his short sharp breaths against her cheek and saw the hunger in his flint-hard gaze.

"Meeryn, I need . . ." he groaned.

What? What did he need? To escape his grief? To reclaim her love? To murder the duke? Her questions flamed to ash as his touch, his kiss, his scent, and his taste blasted their way through her consciousness and she'd no thought but closer, harder, sweeter, slower. She dragged his sopping-wet shirt over his head to reveal a chiseled rippled abdomen, corded muscular arms, and enough golden skin to cause her body to flush and her insides to twist. The ugly marks of the dog's attack remained, though faded now as his enhanced Imnada healing took over. Pale slashes, pink flesh. She traced each mark upon his body as if confirming he was real . . . this was real . . .

"We shouldn't," she murmured, her mind quickly turning to mush.

"You're still angry," he replied between kisses that stole her breath.

"And you're not thinking straight . . ."

"Definitely not."

Thunder shook the tower—or was that her pulse roaring in her ears? Lightning flickered silver-white against the darkness, bathing Gray in its brilliance, etching shadows along every inflexible angle, hollowing his deep-set eyes, flickering like fire in his dangerous gaze.

"And the roof leaks." She gasped and jumped as he nibbled a spot just behind her ear, her stomach clenching into a knot, her sex throbbing with raw desire.

"We're already wet," he whispered, his lips against her face, his breath soft on her cheek.

"And . . . I . . . and . . . that is we . . ."

"Shut up, Meeryn."

"All right," she conceded, happy to let her body have its wanton way.

He dropped to his knees before her, kissing his way from the backs of her thighs to her hips and then her waist, taking his agonizing time as he devoured in delicious inches. She clung to him, bones melting, heart racing as a swirling, coiling pleasure built within her center and tremors burst up through her until she gasped. Her reaction goaded him to offer more, and Meeryn arched into his fingers as he brushed the hair between her legs. Groaned as he probed the moist heat of her mound, stroking the nub half-hidden there. He bent to take her in his mouth, tickling and sucking her sensitive flesh. She jerked against him, shuddering with each teasing pass, tension building as she writhed against him, seeking the hard thrust that never came, the violent furious collision that hovered just out of reach.

Closer she drew toward the spiraling center, her body plucked tight, the storm outside mirroring the tumbling crescendo. She cried out, knees buckling, head spinning. The world became a dizzying collage of emotion and sensation, jumbled and spun till she had no way of knowing which way was up, where he ended and she began. He caught her as she fell into his arms and they knelt forehead to forehead upon the stone floor, each fighting to catch their breath.

The wind howled and rain drummed upon the narrow windows, a wall thickening between them with every passing minute neither spoke nor moved. Water plopped on the floor beside them in a steady beat that matched her slowing heart. She'd no desire to move or speak, no desire to break the dream she wrapped round herself as he held her.

Gray recovered first. He cupped the soft weight of one breast, his thumb sliding provocatively over her nipple, his lips barely tasting the sweat-salty skin before he pulled her blouse up to cover her, then straightened her sleeves, pushed her hair back over her shoulders. Small moves to tidy her, to erase the past minutes as if they'd never been. She allowed it, but each distancing move brought a new lump to her throat.

"That shouldn't have occurred," he said.

"Why not? Because we're unwed? Because I'm N'thuil? Because you're . . ."

"I'm nothing, Meeryn. Society calls me the Ghost Earl. A horrid nickname, but that's what I am. Dead to you. Dead to the clans. As much a wraith as . . ." He dropped his gaze to the stones they knelt upon.

"As your parents and Ollie. I understand." She collected herself bit by bit, until she knew she could ask the question that needed to be asked and not fall apart at the answer. "What do you need, Gray?" she finally asked, her voice soft but strong. "What really brought you back to Deepings?"

He sucked in a sharp gasp that might have been pain or shock or both, even as the burning heat of his body seemed to cool and solidify to unyielding marble. The light winked out of a face wiped clean of expression, the inches separating them suddenly yawning wide as a chasm.

"To live . . . or to die . . . it depends on you."

Half-two. It was time. Satisfied, Gray snapped his pocket watch closed. The house would be sleeping by now. Servants long since abed. Shadows thick and concealing. Gray slipped out a side door in the guest hall. Should anyone challenge him, he would produce the cheroot from his pocket and explain his prowl as sleeplessness mixed with nostalgia. No one did.

Emerging onto the long, sloping lawn, his eagle's gaze swept west to east, before settling upon the Crystal Tower, the sanctum of Jai Idrish. Four stories high and built all of milky-white stone, the tall, graceful tower stood out like a blaze of light amid the bleak fortresslike gray of the rest of Deepings' curtain wall and the cloud-riven night sky above.

He checked for any signs of movement, any patrolling guard or skulking servant. He'd spent years in similar situations, noting French forces, surveying unfamiliar battle terrain, moving ahead of an army that relied on his information for victory. But he'd done it from the air; a distant clinical observer. Tonight, he wore the skin of the human and his war had shrunk to a one-on-one fight for personal survival.

Crouched and moving swiftly through the dark, he approached the door to the tower. The hairs at the back of his neck lifted as magic crawled over his skin and prickled against his brain like needles. A large crow settled on the grass a few paces away, watching him with eyes shiny as jet beads.

"I wondered when you might turn up again." The bird hopped beside Gray as he made his way toward the arched doorway letting into the tower. "Any word on who might have spilled our secrets to the Other?"

A shimmer of rainbow color exploded up from the bird in a column of dancing light. From the midst, Badb emerged in a swirl of feathers, her eyes snapping with anger. "No, though it is clear someone is speaking out of turn. The Other are uncertain and still reel from their own internal strife. It would not be difficult to unite them against a common enemy. You must hope whoever sparks these latest rumors is not bent on causing more than mischief."

"You have no idea who it might be?"

"No."

"So I can't stop it."

"No."

"Then it's a problem for another day."

"You would ignore an impending crisis to play at kiss-me-quick with a woman? Was the taste of her quim so pleasurable, you would forget who you are and what you seek to do, shapechanger?"

He swung around, anger almost, but not quite, causing him to forget with whom he spoke. Badb was an ally, not a friend. She could also be a terrible enemy if she chose. His fists fell useless to his side. He breathed a deep steady breath. "I know exactly what I seek to do and unless you're here to help, you can fly back to Lucan and tell him all's well and I'm not dead yet."

"*Yet* is right. This is madness. Worse than madness since you walk into the mouth of the beast knowing exactly what you do."

"Meeryn is N'thuil. She can help. If anyone understands the powers of Jai Idrish, it is she."

"Or she can betray you to your doom."

"My doom is set if I don't make the attempt, though. Jai Idrish . . . Meeryn . . . they're my only hope."

"You still believe this unnatural instrument is the key to your freedom? It is not of this world nor a source of Fey magic. What makes you think it will be able to lift the curse upon you and your friends?"

"The old writings talk of its power. Ferontes alone states that—"

Badb waved off his words with a snort of disgust. "A blowhard who enjoyed hearing the sound of his own voice and barely said anything worth hearing. What would he know?"

Here was a reminder, if Gray needed one, that the young woman in front of him was as foreign to this world as Idrin's crystal sphere. She was true Fey. Being immortal, she'd lived through the Lost Days, when the walls between the mortal realm and the summer kingdom of Ynys Avalenn had yet to rise, when magic shimmered in the very air and to be born with the gift of sorcery or the power to shift was a privilege. King Arthur had been the last great king of the Other, the linchpin holding together all three races. With his murder, that fragile peace had unraveled like a skein of string. The Fey retreated behind their walls, most of the Imnada were rounded up and killed, and the Other hid their magic from a new and suspicious world.

Badb had seen it all and, unfortunately, held opinions about it all as well.

"The man didn't have the sense the gods gave a housefly, but he could blabber on for hours as if he knew the answers to life."

"Do you have any better ideas?"

She cast him a squelching look.

"I didn't think so," he said, pushing open the heavy oaken door.

The room they entered was black as pitch, no windows to pierce the Stygian gloom on the ground floor and only narrow arrow slits in the next two stories. Only the glimmer of her pale skin lit their passage up the twisting stairwell.

"And if Sir Dromon has his guards waiting to ambush you?" she asked.

"Does he?"

"You're so prepared to trust a woman you barely

remember—" She tossed her cap of curls with a sneer of contempt. "I'll let you find out on your own."

"Then stand aside so I might pass."

She huffed, her feathers a ruffle of indignation. "Foolish shapechanger."

They climbed the rest of the stairs in silence, the darkness fading to gray as they rounded the last landing and entered the topmost chamber. Four enormous stained glass windows, each depicting a diffcrent face of the Mother Goddess, were set within each wall of the sanctuary: the east and the maiden's waxing moon of Piryeth; the south depicting the full moon of Silmith when the Mother's light and the Imnada's power were at their height; the aged crone's moon of waning Berenth looked toward the bleak western moors. Only the fourth, north-facing window was empty of the Mother's beauty. Instead a collage of blacks and grays symbolized the cloaked and faceless figure of Mordoroth and the night of no moon when the Mother fled the skies completely.

Cushioned benches were set beneath the windows. Once, streams of petitioners might have waited for an audience with the N'thuil. Now dust clung in the crannies of the dark carved wood, and the cushions bore a disused, forgotten appearance as if few trod the steep flights of stairs anymore to seek answers. The Voice and Vessel of the Mother had little to do these days but polish the sphere and attend the Gather as the goddess's reprcscntative.

The beauty of the windows, the graceful vaulting of the arched ceiling, and the ornate engravings of beasts and birds that ran the perimeter of the room combined to catch the eye and snatch the breath, but it was the crystal sphere resting upon a silver dais that pulled the gaze to the center of the chamber. It shimmered from within; each rough-hewn facet burning with a different milky shade from gossamer silver through deep creamy blue.

Gray paused for a moment at the threshold, drinking in the scene. An unsettling ache pressed beneath his rib cage, and his fingers curled under to dig into his palms until his breath moved easily in his lungs once more. He felt Jai Idrish's immense power running beneath his feet, thickening the air, pushing the blood through his veins. The heart of the beast within him felt it too and woke from the deepest parts of his soul. The urge to stretch free of his human form and take to the skies tightened its grip on him until he must lean a shoulder against the wall and wait for the dizziness and desire to pass.

"This thing is not of any world I know. Nor of any world the Fey have knowledge of. I do not trust it." Badb's voice sounded in his ears as if from a great distance.

"Jai Idrish has kept the Imnada safe for millennia beyond counting. It's the conduit to the goddess herself and the sentinel standing at the gateway to our ancestors."

"Doors are only as good as they are strong or as long as the guard set to watch them remains vigilant. Can you guarantee this sphere of Idrin is both strong and protected?" Before he could answer her, Badb's head tilted to one side, her bright eyes locked on some unseen vision. "Someone comes, shapechanger."

A breeze swirled up from the stairwell as the door below was opened. "It's Meeryn."

He turned back to find the girl vanished and the crow winging toward the rafters, her voice drifting across the surface of his mind. *I do not like it. Not at all. What you seek to do has not been done, what you seek to undo cannot be undone except by death. The scholars are blind and the mages see but glimpses. And there are darker things hidden within this crystal than a goddess, no matter they shine like her moon."*

"I have to try to wake Jai Idrish. It's the only way to break the curse," he called out to the circling bird just before it winked out of sight in a blink of Fey magic, leaving its warning to scrape the insides of his skull

*Yes, but what if it is something else entirely that you wake? What then?*

"It happened on the eve of Waterloo."

"A battle?"

"A slaughter."

Meeryn noticed with an emotion close to chagrin that Gray held himself carefully apart from her, as if even the slightest brushing of her muslin against his leather might open them both to a return of their uncontrollable heat. He might be right. Just recalling his skillful touch and hot mouth was enough to send shivers of delight up her spine and make her wet with desire. A reaction she'd not expected; Conal had been gentle, Gray was overpowering. Conal had been considerate, Gray took what he wanted. Conal had offered her soft words and tender emotion, Gray offered nothing beyond the friction of their bodies and the dazzling inferno it spawned.

She had wanted the love she'd found with Conal.

She'd not wanted this thunderous raging conflagration she found in Gray's arms, but she knew if
he reached for her again she would respond. It was
blasted humiliating.

It thrilled her to her toes.

She pulled her mind from the gutter and focused
on the sphere resting on its carved stone plinth—no,
not resting, mocking. Jai Idrish had teased her with a
hint of its power, whispering to her, guiding her here
with unseen hands as if nudging her forward to her
chosen role. And when she had woken gasping and
frightened, it had glowed with a light that blinded the
circle of angry Ossine, bursting out from the tower
with the brilliance of ten thousand lighthouse lamps.

That had been two months ago. Two long, silent,
frustrating, months.

". . . Adam's pathing nearly ripped my brain apart.
A mental scream of anguish like claws raking the inside of my skull. Somehow the sorcerer d'Espe knew
what Adam was, he forced the shift upon him. Adam
had no choice and it nearly drove him mad."

The echoes of pain in Gray's voice pulled Meeryn
back to the conversation. She shuddered, imagining
the horror of being compelled to assume her aspect.
The twisting of her nature to something ugly and terrible. Then she pictured it happening day after day,
night after night, in a never-ending agonizing cycle.
That had been Gray's fate . . . his curse, his life for the
last two years.

The destruction of his clan mark and signum in
one violent shredding of mind and charring of flesh
had been a horror, but the bending of his powers to
another's will must have been the worst anguish of all.

"Adam lost control, lashed out against the Fey-blood magic as he'd been taught from the cradle. It was over by the time the three of us arrived, the bodies a slashed and mangled mess. He'd killed the entire household to protect our secret."

"If only Adam had made certain d'Espe was dead, none of this would have happened. He never would have cursed you and the others. You'd never have been declared *emnil* and cast out of the clans. We would . . ." She dropped her eyes to her lap, noting the way her nails dug into her skirt, the racing of her pulse beneath the skin of he wrists. "Our lives would have turned out differently."

"Would they? Or would you have rebelled against marriage to a man you'd not seen in years?" He touched her chin, forcing her gaze to his. Shadows pooled beneath his eyes, his lean, hard-angled face almost gaunt in the light of a single taper. "There's only sorrow in wishing for a past that's long gone or a turning in the path not taken. I have to look to the future now. My future. The clans' future."

Was that a future that included her? Did she want it to? No. She'd found passion with a man once. She'd also found heartbreak, sorrow, and loss. Best to stick to loneliness and be safe.

Safe worked.

Safe didn't hurt.

"It's taken me two long years, but freedom is finally within sight."

She regarded the four scratched and dented disks spread between them. Were these really the fabled Fey-wrought disks that had imprisoned a kingslayer? They looked as if they'd been banging around in someone's pocket with their loose change and a decade's worth of lint.

"You think the combined power of the Gylferion and Jai Idrish will break the curse?"

"It's more than a thought," he answered defensively before shrugging. "And less than a certainty."

"Either way, where did you manage to find these? They've been lost for centuries—centuries upon centuries. Most assume they're just a shaman's stories to while away a cold winter's evening."

"I'm hoping it was destiny that brought them together again, though Mac believes it was dumb luck, and David is sure I've been conned out of a fortune for a blacksmith's forgeries."

"I might have to side with St. Leger on this one," she said, touching the chipped disk of bronze with a tentative forefinger. She expected a tingle, a jolt, a whisper on the wind. She merely sneezed.

"I've studied the texts and spoken with every scholar of ancient magics I could find. The theory is sound. If the vicious collision of warring magics spawned the curse, the same such collision should reverse it." His tone clearly indicated this was not the first time he'd argued his position and it wouldn't be the last. "The Gylferion were created by the Fey but it was Imnada blood spilled to complete their final tempering. Only in that way were they able to entrap the warlord Lucan for his crimes."

"But what has Jai Idrish to do with it?"

"We've got the fuse. Now we need the spark."

"You were a soldier. You must know what happens when a spark hits a shell. It breeds destruction."

"It will work."

"Jai Idrish has been silent for generations. Why should it wake for you now?"

"It's not going to wake for me. It's going to wake for *you*. The crystal is the heart of Imnada power and you are the heart of the crystal."

Was this her chance to make a difference? To be N'thuil in deed as well as word?

If Gray broke the Fey-blood's curse, the cause of his exile would be lifted as well. There would be no impediment to his reclaiming his place as heir. He would be welcomed back into the clans. The in-fighting and backstabbing and factional warfare would cease and the Imnada could face this new uncertain future with hope and a single will.

Her name would be written in the annals alongside those of Idrin the Traveler and Aneavala of the Palings, Yolethe the Hammer, who built the Crystal Tower, and Eurimesis Nine Spoons, who kept his people fed during famine and plague.

She would be Meeryn the Peacemaker. Or maybe Meeryn of the Wise Words. Or perhaps . . . Her eyes fell once more upon the crystal orb, its surface reflecting her face back at her a million times, and her confidence faltered. Who was she fooling? Meeryn the Sapskull was more like it.

"I'm a charlatan and a failure. Jai Idrish hasn't done anything but sit there and laugh at my pathetic attempts."

"Not tonight. Tonight we rattle the goddess from her sleep and make her pay attention."

She laughed. "You're mad enough to almost make me believe."

He leaned forward, eyes alight with excitement.

His breath soft on her cheek, his scent crisp and soapy and completely male. The night, the flickering candle, the soft confidences conspired against her. Safe was boring. Safe was her life to this point. Safe would not allow for a repeat of her exhilarating, stomach-turning, shout-it-to-the-skies, orgasmic pinnacle.

"That's a start," he murmured.

Her lashes fluttered across her cheeks, her lips parted, her arms braced against the seat, pulse racing.

"I timed our visit to fall between guard watches. If we're to slip out as easily as we slipped in, we'd better get started."

Hardly the declaration of yearning she'd been anticipating. She lifted her head to see him standing, eyes ablaze, body thrumming with nervous energy. "How do you know the watch's schedule?" she asked.

But he was already placing one disk at each compass point; bronze to the maiden's east and copper to the Mother's south. To the west of Berenth's crone he set the gold disk, and finally, he lay the silver disk of Morderoth beneath the north-facing window, where darkness hung thickest.

"The rest is up to you . . . and Jai Idrish," he said, pulling her to her feet and toward the waiting crystal.

Dare she try? She glanced over at Gray, who stood legs braced, shoulders squared, and head up. As if he faced an enemy or his last chance at escape from certain death. The bigger question was, dare she refuse?

Meeryn tried to relax. She rolled her shoulders, flexed her fingers, and closed her eyes. Not because she needed to, but because it kept her focus on the sphere and not on the man hovering behind her left shoulder like a storm cloud.

Stretching her mind, she let the outer world fall away as she sought a connection to the crystal's heart, the core of its being. She probed deep within the empty expanse of nothing beyond and between her physical senses; searching for a gleam, a whisper, a presence beyond her own turbulent thoughts. Some hint that Jai Idrish hovered at the edge of wakefulness, waiting only for someone to nudge it to life. But all was dark and cold and empty.

By now, her brain seemed shaved thin as paper, her mind fraying. A painful throbbing started at her temples, spasming down into her spine. She tried retreating, but shadows followed after her, the empty soulless infinity pouring through the holes she'd made in her mental search. She scrabbled to mend the rifts, but for each wound she repaired, ten more opened after her. Her ribs seemed to tighten, crushing her lungs, tightening around her heart. She couldn't breathe. She couldn't move. She tried opening her eyes, screaming for help, but there were only the endless terrifying shadows rolling and curling toward her like a stormy ocean surf. She felt herself drowning, the crush of the shadows too much, snapping bones, sucking the last breath from her shredded lungs, she felt the last gasp of air leave her when . . .

A powerful slap to the side of her head knocked her to the floor, where she scraped her knees and slammed her left cheekbone into the edge of Jai Idrish's altar. The shadows evaporated, driven away by the very tactile explosion of ear-ringing, jaw-bruising pain. At least all the shadows evaporated but one, which leaned concernedly over her, "Are you all right?"

She glanced up through a tangled fall of hair, her

combs lost in the far corners of the room from the force of Gray's so-called rescue. "That remains to be seen."

He stepped back and held out a hand, which she took, only because she didn't think she could make it to her feet without assistance. Otherwise she would have ignored it, but she couldn't trust herself at this moment. She had the insane urge to throw herself in his arms and never let go. Doubtless a side effect of the knock to the head and lack of oxygen. It certainly wasn't the memory of his hands on less proper parts of her making her stomach roll ominously and the room go all dizzy.

"You don't look all right," he said, examining her.

"I felt it, Gray. I bonded with the crystal. Just for a moment and a tenuous link at best, but I did it . . . Jai Idrish's power lives despite its silence." The room steadied, his hand fell away, and she brushed her skirts in a fruitless attempt to brush away the dust. Noticed the blood speckling the fabric. Felt her mouth.

"You've cut yourself." He pulled a handkerchief from his pocket and dabbed her cheek. She winced and tried to step away but he followed. "Hold still. You're smearing it all over your face."

Through the throbbing in her cheek, the throbbing in her head, and the throbbing between her legs, a dim thought surfaced. "Did it work? Did we break the curse?"

His gaze slid past hers to rest for a moment on Jai Idrish. Then his shoulder dipped in a shrug of surrender, his face hard with despair. "No."

\*          \*          \*

He stood at his window, staring out across the courtyard to the lights of the main house. Counted three
from the left and four up from the ground floor. There
would be his grandfather's apartments. The arched
window to the left of the ivy creeping over the stone
balcony would be his bedchamber. He would be sleeping now. They would all be sleeping now. All but Gray.

He slept little. A few hours here or there. Brandy
helped, but his personality didn't allow him to imbibe
to unconsciousness. Not even tonight, when drinking
himself senseless would have been more than justified.
Instead he fingered the four disks, shuffling them and
reshuffling them in infinite designs that meant nothing while his mind spun endlessly in pointless circles.

Bits of tin . . . a blacksmith's forgeries . . .

Failure had always lurked in the back of his mind.
He wasn't so naive that he didn't understand the odds
against his success, nor so deaf that he didn't hear the
persistent whispers hinting at his demise by the end of
the year. Why, then, did he feel powerless and broken,
unable to settle on contingencies, incapable of plan-
ning for what came next?

His hand hovered above the silver disk of Krylesos
Pryth.

Perhaps therein lay his answer.

He *had* planned. For a moment, he'd glimpsed a
future beyond the curse; a life unchained from the
Fey-blood's black magic. A startled revelation lifting
him high only to drop him to the ground as reality
smashed him flat.

Meeryn's kiss . . . Meeryn's touch . . . the scent of
her in his nose . . . the taste of her on his tongue . . . the
memory of her urgent moans in his ears . . .

He had failed. The curse remained. There would be no chance for more than these few precious hours, this short gift of days, fraught as they were with danger.

Gray stripped down until the breeze puckered the skin across his bare back, though it did little to cool the simmering rage twisting his innards and reddening his vision. He felt the first stirrings of the shift, his body hungering to hurt someone as he was hurt, to experience the sweet release of a predator's quick deadly strike, and feel life bleed out between his fingers. An ignoble sentiment, but the totality of all he'd lost tonight shredded his honor with a flogging's agony.

The power of the Imnada took him over. Wind swept over his wings. His razored beak opened on a cry of fury and anguish both. He lifted off to circle the skies above Deepings, where an old man slept, a cunning man plotted, and an extraordinary woman dreamed.

He'd returned home prepared to face his ghosts.

He just hadn't realized he might still be in love with one.

# 7

Meeryn spent the following morning searching for Gray. Not because she thought he might do something foolish, but . . . well, all right, maybe because she thought he might do something foolish. Her last sight of him before he disappeared from the tower had not inspired confidence. His pallor was bleached as bone, deep grooves cut into his face, eyes hard as stones and drained of every emotion but fury. She'd tried to console him, but he'd returned a brusque, twisted smile that sent fear slithering into the pit of her stomach. What would his fury drive him to do? How desperate had he become? And if he decided death was all that was left for him, would he decide to take his grandfather down with him as Sir Dromon speculated?

She refused to believe it. Gray might not be the boy of her childhood memories, but he was no murderer. Still, she couldn't shake the idea that he was fast reaching some final point of no return; a crossed line from which there was no withdrawing.

She looked for Gray in the guest hall, wandering the

chilly, carpeted corridors and poking her head into the empty, disused rooms. It had been years since Deepings had needed to open this part of the house to support the train of functionaries and servants accompanying the Gather elders. It showed in the Holland-covered furniture, stacks of packing crates and straw-stuffed barrels, and the sour air of neglect hanging in the dusty air. In her search, she came across a pair of maidservants hoisting away an empty bath and a basket of dripping towels, a footman with a newly cleaned suit of clothes, and an Ossine enforcer, known by the red-tasseled cord hanging from his stitched leather scabbard. His gaze slid from her face to the floor as he rounded the corner outside Gray's rooms and slipped out a side door to the yard beyond. It wasn't until he was gone that she realized he was the young man from the attack on the road outside the holding.

Fear fluttering her insides, she hurried the rest of the way to Gray's rooms, but there was no one within. The place was empty but for an enormous black crow resting on a windowsill, its eyes sharp, its long beak sharper. "Do you know where he's gone?" she asked.

The crow preened its glossy feathers and took off with a squawk.

"Now I've really lost my head, if I've sunk to talking to myself," Meeryn muttered.

She looked for Gray on the battlements, where the wind tore her breath away and whipped her skirts against her legs. The sea stretched out to the west like pewter satin, a ship sailed hull-up, north toward the Bristol inlet. To the south and east lay the estate's wide landscaped parkland, meadowed hills spotted with small farmsteads, and creek-fed valleys where the trees rose old and close from a carpet of moss and fern. She couldn't see the swirling ebb and flow of the Palings from here, but she knew they were out there just beyond the edge of her vision. Since she was chosen, she'd been able to sense them even if she couldn't see them, and she knew their strength failed week by week, year by year. How long would their waning power protect the clans? How long until the Fey-bloods crossed holding lands unchecked by the warded mists?

Questions she'd been asked over and over in the two months she'd been N'thuil. Questions for which she'd had no answer.

Last night, for the first time since she'd come to her senses with her hands upon the crystal and the angry eyes of the Arch Ossine upon her, she'd felt the sphere rouse from its slumber. She'd sensed a presence beyond her own, a great eye opening, a powerful mind ticking over. Had Gray been the cause? Had Jai Idrish stirred to welcome home the last son of Idrin? Had her ascension to N'thuil been a small part of its greater plan, and did that plan include Gray? If so, then why hadn't it lifted the curse laid upon him? Was it because it chose not to? Or because it couldn't?

A crow lit on the balustrade beside her, regarding Meeryn with cocked head and outspread feathers. The same crow, she was sure of it. Not Imnada. She felt no hint of shifter magic. Instead the tingly rush of Fey power buzzed and burned over her skin and twisted her guts to knots. On any other morning, she'd have raised the alarm and summoned Sir Dromon's enforcers to deal with an intruder so close to the center of Imnada power. But her questions raised too many doubts. Gray's crash back into her life churned up too many uncertainties.

"You must be worried about him, too," she ventured.

The crow hopped a few paces toward her, pecking at the stones.

"I let him down, didn't I? I let them all down," Meeryn said, scanning the woods and fields as if seeing them for the first time. "Jai Idrish isn't sleeping. It's dying . . . like Gray is dying. Like the Imnada are dying."

The crow squawked as it took off from the balustrade in a flutter of wings to soar out over the ocean, a black speck against the silver green of the sea.

Finally, Meeryn looked for Gray in the library amid stacks of old parchments and musty leather-bound volumes, glossy rosewood étagères and glass-fronted cabinets containing pottery from Greece, glassware from Rome, and statuary from Mesopotamia and the Far East. A map desk held unrolled charts of the continents, the oceans, and the heavens, held down by bits of rock, a paperweight, a box of old coins. A narrow door in the east wall led into a smaller room, a darker room, a room kept locked and only one man possessed the key. A room lined with shelves upon which rested the entire Imnada race written out by thousands of different hands over thousands of years, lines connecting the past to the future and each clan member to the next in an elaborate web.

Each separate clan had its own Ossine shaman who maintained their scrolls, marking each birth, death, and marriage. But the Arch Ossine collected and maintained all of them. His was the final word in all unions between the greater houses and his influence was felt down to the least of the traveling shamans with their bags of medicinal herbs and their supply of cookfire stories.

This afternoon the door stood open, a light flickering in the room housing the bloodline scrolls. Voices rose and fell in a quiet murmur of conspiracy, shadows slanting long and jagged across the carpeted library floor.

". . . all in readiness? No slip-ups . . . end this now . . ."

"Aye . . . over before nightfall . . . as you ordered, sir . . ."

The high tenor she recognized as the Arch Ossine, but it was the deeper, gruffer voice that sent a shiver of cold memory splashing over her shoulders—the enforcer Thorsh.

She backed away a silent footstep at a time, freezing when the door swung farther open and a figure emerged with a rustle of dry paper and a fastidious cough into his handkerchief. "Lady N'thuil? Are you in need of assistance?" Sir Dromon asked.

"I'm looking for Major de Coursy. He's not been seen since last night."

"No? I do hope nothing's happened to him. It would be quite an embarrassment after I specifically invited him here under a flag of truce."

Suspicion chilled her skin. "What could happen to him here among his own people?"

"But are they his own people? There are those who don't agree with my negotiations, nor do they trust the Major is here for the purpose of peace. Some might take matters into their own hands and damn the consequences."

"You mean like Mr. Thorsh here?"

The enforcer stepped from the room behind the Arch Ossine, his eyes alight with malicious pleasure, an ivory toothpick tight between his browned teeth. "Good afternoon, Lady N'thuil. Hope you bear no hard feelings about the other day. I knew the man wouldn't really shoot you, though. Knew it was all a bluff."

"Did you?" she answered coldly. "Forgive my skepticism."

He laughed, rolling his toothpick around his mouth.

"What is Mr. Thorsh doing here? The man nearly killed the duke's heir and myself," she said sharply to Sir Dromon.

"He saved you from the duke's heir, you mean," Pryor simpered. "Had it not been for his quick thinking, de Coursy would have shot you in cold blood."

"And if not for Thorsh's brazen attack on the coachman, de Coursy would have had no cause to threaten anyone. You assured me he would be punished for his actions."

"You sound more and more like one of de Coursy's sympathizers. Should I be concerned, Lady N'thuil?"

Should *she*?

She had always known Sir Dromon for a man of skilled oratory and subtle machinations. It's what had made him so invaluable during the duke's illness as tensions rose among the clans and whispers of Feyblood brutality were first heard. But who had started those whispers? Who had encouraged those tensions? Old uncertainties blended with new fears, and she took a step back as if distancing herself from the Arch Ossine and his plans.

"Perhaps I was wrong to use one so . . . ah . . . close

to our idealistic young heir to convince him of my good intentions," he continued. "As a woman, you're too easily swayed by a handsome face and a charmer's tongue."

Thorsh stepped forward with a greasy smile and a gaze that made her want to go to her chambers and scrub. "'Specially when he's probably putting that tongue in her—"

Sir Dromon held up a hand. "Thank you, Mr. Thorsh. We don't need to belabor the analysis."

"I'm willing to concede that de Coursy might have a point," she argued. "Neither my femininity nor his face has anything to do with the facts of the matter."

She'd given up any pretense of being the eager, questioning student as soon as Dromon insinuated that her support might be rooted in desire. She might desire Gray—all right, fine—the word "might" didn't enter into it. She longed for Gray with a wanton hunger that startled her down to her toes and made her want to slide her hands then her lips over every inch of his warrior's body. But that had nothing to do with her quickly mounting doubts about Sir Dromon's sincerity or the clans' continuing seclusion.

"And what would those facts be, my lady?" the Arch Ossine asked, a new harshness in his tone. He'd obviously given up the pretense of playing obliging, indulgent schoolmaster as well.

At least they knew where each stood now.

She folded her arms over her chest. "That no matter how many people we kill, there's no way to erase the Fey-bloods knowledge of us. The Imnada must deal with the world as it is, not how we wish it to be, and with our numbers dwindling and the Palings weakening in strength, perhaps it's time to look for a new path."

"Fine words, if misguided. But you're young, Lady N'thuil. Unrealistic. Forgive me if I say, even a little naive." His pale eyes narrowed, his face splotchy with checked emotion. "If we're weak it's because men like de Coursy corrupt us from within. They spread their lies where the feeble-minded sup them up with spoons. Mr. Thorsh has just told me of a groom caught sending messages to his brother in aid of the rebels. Luckily, the damage was limited and the threat eliminated."

She gasped. "You've killed him without a trial or any hearing before the Gather? Was His Grace told?"

"He is feverish and shouldn't be troubled. It's up to me to hold the line against the Fey-bloods; a sacred trust I take on willingly. And sometimes we must do things against our principles for the sake of our security. If you question my methods, perhaps it's because secretly you side with the Imnada's enemies." He stepped close, his lips curled in an ugly sneer. "Perhaps the rot has traveled closer to the core than I could ever imagine."

"You overstep your bounds, sir," she answered with a tone that could cut steel.

A glint of dark emotion burned in his eyes, and for the first time she was witness as his fastidious demeanor slipped to reveal a frightening mania. "As do you, my lady."

Her suspicions blossomed into certainty. Sir Dromon may speak of peace and reconciliation, but his words were as false as his simpering clerkish façade. He wore the mantle of Imnada defender, but he just might be their greatest threat.

\*     \*     \*

A footman woke Gray as dawn broke over the sea. His grandfather had agreed to see him. He should make himself ready for an audience as soon as he could dress and appear in His Grace's chambers.

Now it was after ten and he'd been kicking his heels for hours, awaiting his summons like a bloody village tradesman. He paced the small salon for the hundredth time, coming to rest in front of the family portrait holding pride of place over the mantel. Father standing proud in front of Deepings' main gates. Mother seated, her smile almost angelic as she gazed out at the world. Leaning against her chair stood his elder brother, Oliver, tall and golden with eyes blue as sapphires. In her lap lay Gray swaddled in the bonnet and gown of a newborn. The idyll had not lasted. Gray was the only one left.

"There you are. I've been searching everywhere." Meeryn burst into the room, skirts whipped about her legs, face alive with relief. No hint of discomfiture in her manner. No trace of awkwardness as she took his hand.

He wished he could say the same. This was Meeryn, pigtails and pinafores. Shared laughter and shared confidences. She'd saved him from drowning, then she'd saved him from himself when relief from his grief and guilt had lain one deep cut of the knife away. There was nowhere to hide with her, no corner of his soul she'd not touched . . . a horrifying thought.

"I was told Grandfather agreed to see me. I'm beginning to think it's merely a ploy to humiliate me one final time. Do you suppose he'll order me to recite the five statutes of Gunthar the Just or prove my mastery with smallsword and rapier?"

"If your little demonstration on the road is any indication, His Grace should be more than satisfied in your battle prowess, but you can't stay to show him. You need to leave Deepings."

"Aren't you the one who twisted my arm to get me to come?"

"Yes, and now I'm the one shoving you back out the door before it's too late. Pryor isn't interested in peace or talking or bringing an end to the bloodletting."

"Of course he isn't. It's easier to control through fear, and what do the clans fear more than a war with the Fey-bloods?"

She frowned. "You knew all this and you came anyway."

He glanced once more at the portrait, a family at the edge of a precipice. They just didn't know it yet. "You know why I came, Meeryn."

"I feel like such a gullible fool."

"You believed Sir Dromon. You're not the only one sucked in by his pose of selfless devotion to his people. He's perfected it over a lifetime."

"Or did I want to believe him because it gave me a reason to go to London and find you?"

Awkward had become untenable. "Meeryn . . . about last night . . . we—"

"Don't," she interrupted.

"Don't what?"

She flung up her arms in a tired gesture of surrender. "Don't say what you're trying desperately not to say."

"And what's that?"

"That last night was a horrible mistake brought on by overwrought emotions and an atmosphere crackling with raw energy. That lightning does funny things to a person. That it gets under the skin and makes you feel alive and wild and a little reckless."

"Who needs oysters when a storm is brewing?" he offered, only half in jest.

"Something like that."

He cupped her cheek, caressed the line of her jaw. A strong face, a keen look in the eye. No, Jai Idrish had not been careless with its choice. She neither flinched nor stepped closer at his skimming touch. Instead she held his gaze, her expression altogether too perceptive.

"Meeryn, I don't want to hurt you," he said.

"You behave as if I'm looking for a ring and a rose-covered cottage for two." She gave a quick scoffing laugh. "I'm not. And had I wanted you to stop last night, Gray, you would have. I may be a powerless N'thuil, but I'm not a helpless woman."

"No, but you were never that, were you?" he replied quietly.

"My lord? His Grace is ready to see you, but you mustn't stay long. Sir Dromon advises against any strain . . . his heart is very weak . . ."

Gray could have kissed his grandfather's valet for interrupting this less than graceful attempt at rationalization, especially since he had no idea what he might say. How do you explain to someone that they made you too vulnerable, knew you too well? That your past together made a future together impossible?

She grabbed his arm, fear back in her eyes. "Gray, you have to listen to me. You have to leave before it's too late."

"Stay or go, I'm just as dead unless I can break the curse. And my best chance to do that is here at Deepings."

"You're mad."

"No, just very desperate."

Feeling Meeryn's gaze boring into his back, Gray followed the valet, hating the all-too-familiar sweaty palms and dry throat that accompanied every encounter with his grandfather. He was no longer an intimidated adolescent. He refused to cringe as he did then.

"I'll be right outside should you need anything, my lord," the servant added with a scraping obsequiousness belied by the hostile gleam in his eyes.

Listening to every word exchanged, more like. Not that it mattered to Gray. There was nothing he intended to say that would warrant more than a contemptible snigger from Pryor. With the dawn, Gray's rage had crept back into the corners where it remained locked away, a fuse he refused to light for fear it would consume him. The duke couldn't help him now—as he hadn't helped him then.

Once again, Gray was very much on his own.

His first impression as he stepped across the threshold into his grandfather's bedchamber was that he'd been thrust into a furnace. Despite the sultry summer weather, fires blazed in the enormous hearth, braziers had been set on either side of his bed, and the handle of a warming pan stuck lopsided from underneath a mountain of blankets and quilts and pillows. Within this heated nest, a face peered out at the world. As a younger man he'd been ruggedly handsome with eyes like chips of stone; now the Duke of Morieux's face had grown flaccid and soft, almost doughy, as if his personality had been sucked away by the illness killing him. His hair had thinned to a few white wisps across a forehead mottled with age spots and moles, and his fingers gripping the bedclothes were knobbed and gnarled, trembling slightly.

"I didn't believe it when I heard you'd come back." His voice, though raspy, possessed the same irascible bluster it always had. Oddly, Gray was relieved to see that not everything had changed. "I didn't think you'd have the guts."

"I came to make peace, Grandfather. With Sir Dromon . . . with you . . . with myself, I suppose."

"That's Mceryn's doing. Bah!" he spat. "She always has been a willful chit of a girl. This N'thuil business has only gone to her head. A good girl for all that, though. She'd have made a grand duchess." He coughed into his handkerchief, blood spotting the linen, his face purpling with effort, tears welling in his milky eyes. "The scrolls agreed, but it was all for naught. All to dust."

"Plans change, Grandfather. It's up to us to change with them."

His Grace struggled to sit up, his expression fierce, his breathing labored. "A lot of pretty talk is all that is. But if it helps you to sleep at night with a clear conscience, so be it."

"Do you refer to the Fey-blood's curse and the taint to my line"—he drew a steady breath—"or is it older and more painful crimes I'm still being punished for?"

His grandfather eyed him with a hard stare. "You blame me for what the Ossine did to you. Blame me for your exile. Probably want to kill me."

Gray clenched his teeth and said nothing.

"No need to deny it . . . I see it in your face." He drew back the covers, pulled open his nightshirt. His ribs stood out against the sunken cave of his chest. "Go on, if you dare . . . you'll be doing us both a favor."

Gray swallowed, but there was no moisture in his mouth, and his throat seemed to close around an immovable stone he couldn't choke down. He curled his fingers into his palms and rested them loosely upon his thighs.

"Knew you couldn't. You're weak . . . no use to me . . . no use to the clans," his grandfather continued. "And the rest of them dead. No bodies to burn. No rites to mark their passing but my own weeping. I've none left but the girl."

He broke down, his face crumpling into ugly sobs, which turned to coughing once again as he struggled to inhale. Gray had to turn away, but not before he pulled the blankets close around the old man's shoulders, wiped the tears from his cheeks, and kissed the duke upon his forehead.

"That's where you're wrong, Grandfather," he said softly. "Where you've always been wrong."

He rose to leave when His Grace grabbed his hand, gaze fierce and red with tears. "Meeryn's all I have left, Gray. Don't hurt her as you've hurt me." And just as suddenly as he'd taken his hand, he released it and closed his eyes.

Gray turned away when a harsh rattling indrawn breath swung him back around. The duke's face had gone from chalk white to deathly blue, his lips purple, his eyes bulging as he struggled for air. He slumped against his pillows, his hands clawing at his throat.

"Grandfather!" Gray bent over him, pulling him upright, banging him on his back to loosen the phlegm.

The door slammed open, the duke's valet, a footman, and the butler Pym rushing to his grandfather's side.

"Hold him!"

"He's murdering His Grace!"

"He's gone mad!"

Gray froze as Thorsh and another flat-nosed enforcer stepped into the room. Flat-Nose dropped Gray to his knees with a fist to the gut, while Thorsh stood grim-faced over him, a silver-bladed knife cold against his throat. The touch of the metal against his skin plucked his nerves raw and crawled like ants into his brain.

"Come to finish what you started?" Gray hissed through a jaw clamped against the rage torching his insides.

Thorsh bent close to whisper in his ear. "All in good time, my lord. But not before we pull every last name from your black traitor's heart."

Gray drew a calming breath . . . and sprang. His hand curled over Thorsh's, dragging the blade from his neck as he slammed a fist into his nose, cartilage and bone grinding to pulp under the force of his blow. Blood spraying from his broken face, Thorsh screamed and dropped his weapon, which Gray scooped up, crouched and waiting. Flat-Nose drew his pistol, but Gray was too quick. One shot went wide, the other skimmed his cheek as he lunged to his left. If he could make it to the window, they were four floors up, there would be time . . . he could shift before he hit the ground . . . he knew he could . . .

Seeing what Gray planned, Thorsh threw himself at Gray's feet. Gray tripped as he yanked off his jacket, his waistcoat, his shirt, but he made it to the ledge, threw open the casement, drawing on the Mother's power, unchaining his aspect, sending it roaring through his veins as he assumed the form of eagle.

He lunged for the freedom of the air, spread his arms. His head exploded with a skull-crushing pain that sent pinwheels and starbursts blasting across his vision. He dropped like a stone, the earth rushing up to meet him. All went black.

A bell tolled slow and sonorous, marking out the years of the Duke's life. Meeryn felt the vibrations in her chest as she flung her cloak on the bed with a muttered oath. Vented the rest of her frustration with a kick to her heavy valise, a footstool, and the wall. The last left her with sore toes and scuffed half boots, but at least she no longer felt as if she were about to spontaneously explode into a million tiny pieces.

The old Duke of Morieux had died this afternoon.

The new Duke of Morieux would die a week from today.

Sir Dromon had been inconsolable in his grief, feverish in his triumph, and adamant in his refusal to allow the N'thuil to speak to the condemned prisoner.

She didn't believe for a minute the allegations against Gray. This was a trap laid and baited by the Arch Ossine, and, naive girl that she was, she'd lured Gray toward the guns like the best of beaters. Damn it, she wouldn't let him die. She wouldn't let the clans destroy themselves in a war of brother on brother.

Already she felt an uneasy tension tightening faces and fists. Men with shuttered gazes whispering in corners. Women with anxious expressions watching from doorways. A few had even come to her as N'thuil, seeking answers, begging intercession with the Mother. She'd sent them away with nothing but platitudes and empty promises. They'd murmured their thanks and departed, but disappointment and frustration darkened their expressions. How did they think she felt? She'd come so close . . . she'd unlocked the vast immensity of Jai Idrish. Of course, it had been for less time than it took to draw an unsteady breath and even that had nearly been enough to peel her mind from her body and drown her in darkness, but surely a little more practice . . . she swallowed . . . a lot more practice and she could finally bring the crystal to wakefulness.

She could break the curse.

She could save Gray.

First, she just needed to . . . well . . . save Gray.

She stared up at the sky from her window as if the Mother Goddess herself might write a solution upon the clouds. She gripped the casement, eyes burning, power pulsing beneath her skin. As N'thuil, her power was limited. But as Imnada, she possessed the cleverness of the wolf and the strength of the panther, the agility of the lynx and the independence of the eagle.

She laughed.

And yet it just might be the meekness of the mouse that would win the day.

She ripped free of her gown, buttons flying to all corners. Stepped out of her petticoats and unlaced her stays. Stockings and slippers, gone. Naked, she wrapped the magic around her, weaving it to her specifications. The soul of the shifter welled up through her like a creeping tide, submerging her in the warp and weft of muscle and bone, tissue and tendon.

The world grew around her as the power of the moon took hold, and soon she was looking up at the windows stretching endlessly toward a distant ceiling. Her claws sank into a carpet lush as a manicured lawn, a dropped thimble high as her shoulder.

Whiskers twitching, she headed for a crack in the corner trim. From there, she traveled down through salons and drawing rooms, galleries and antechambers, past kitchens and basements and the lowest root cellars. Here, catacombs ran deep beneath the castle. Dank, rancid, and smoky from the light off a few greasy torches, they were the last resting place for prisoners of the Imnada. Bereft of the moon's light, they lived in cramped foul cells with only the drip of water and the scurry of rats to keep them company.

She would find Gray among the dismal refuse housed in these ancient tunnels. And, once having found him, she would free him. She would become an outlaw to her people—a rebel.

Is this what the duke had foreseen in his final hours?

Is this what Jai Idrish had chosen her to do?

Was Gray leading her toward destruction? Or the clans to deliverance?

One way to find out and no margin for mistakes. No coming home if she failed.

# 8

Cruder men would have killed him, but Pryor's enforcers had been masters at their craft. No part of Gray's body had been spared. Not an inch of him didn't ache. And each breath he drew was a victory. But he still lived . . . which scared him completely shitless.

It only meant that Sir Dromon had more painful plans for him in store.

He lay where he'd fallen, cataloging each bruise and break, from the bloody gash in his forehead to his swollen and puffy face to his cracked ribs and snapped wrist. Nothing fatal except his masculine pride. Could he count that as a positive? Or was that stretching the hopeful optimism, even for him? He'd forgotten about the lower roof below his grandfather's rooms. Had he plunged four stories, he'd be dead and his problems over. Instead he'd plunged one and been ignominiously hauled down here to await his fate.

Muscles screamed in protest as he rose in careful increments to his knees . . . then his feet. Bursts of blinding pain shot straight to his brain with every shuffling step, but he slowly made a meticulous hand-over-hand inspection of his cell, hampered only by the chain anchoring him to the wall, the silver manacle clamped around his good wrist sapping the little strength left to him.

"Hello?" a thin, tired voice called out. "Is someone there?"

Taking the weight from the wrenched tendons in his right leg, Gray rested against the door, lifting his face to the metal grate, where a salty breeze alleviated the stomach-knotting reek of sweat, mildew, and shit. "A fellow prisoner. Who are you?"

He was met with a silence lasting long enough that he worried he'd begun hallucinating.

"We're alone. The Ossine have gone. There's nothing to be afraid of."

More silence, but this time he sensed the held breath and the tensed body. This was no hallucination. The Ossine held another down here.

"My name is Gray . . . Gray de Coursy," he volunteered, hoping to ease the stranger's fears. "What's yours?"

The breath was expelled with the barest gasp. "Lord Halvossa?"

Not a boy's adolescent timbre, but not yet a man's deeper tones. Somewhere in between . . . eighteen? Nineteen? What could the Ossine want with a youngling barely come into his power? He reached out with his mind, hoping a hint of clan signum or rank might offer a clue. What he found—added to what he didn't find—was more than enough to satisfy his curiosity. The power of the clans was evident in the shape and weight of his consciousness, the animal's primal instinct entwined with the polished surface of the human. But beyond that, Gray sensed nothing. No clan mark or signum. The boy was rogue.

None within the clans to speak for him. No one without who would know what had happened to him once he'd been lost within the confusion of Palings mist.

"So now you know who I am. Care to return the favor?" Gray asked.

Another long cautious silence before Gray heard a faint rustle of straw and a clink of chains on chains. "My name is Jamie."

"How long have you been held down here, Jamie?"

"What . . . what month is it, my lord?"

"August."

The following wait seemed to last forever, a whispered rush of words beneath the boy's breath. Did he pray? Did he count? "Are you certain?"

"How long, Jamie?"

"Six months, my lord. I've not seen the sky in six months." And then he wept.

Where were the blasted keys? Mccryn gave a rodent huff of exasperation as she scurried back along the top of the cabinet. Surely they'd be locked away in here. This was the only spot fit for storage of anything in this horrid place. She rummaged once more through the bits of leftover chain links, snaps with broken ends, a coil of knotted rope, a bent ankle cuff in iron and two in silver. She made sure to avoid these, though just being this close to the poisonous metal made her head spin and her stomach rise into her throat. No sign of keys.

She squeezed between two loose dove joints and dropped into the bottom of the cabinet onto a pile of smelly laundry; a ripped shirt, another with a frightening rust-colored stain across the back spreading outward from a burnt edged tear, three mismatched socks, one shoe with half a buckle. No breeches and no keys.

She pushed through a nibbled hole obviously made by some earlier mousy visitor and found . . . success—of a sort. Pegs and pegs of keys, but which one belonged to which cell? She'd have to try them all. Laborious but not impossible. Retracing her path, she emerged at the top of the dusty cabinet and peered over the edge. The small guardroom was as horrible and depressing as the rest of the catacombs, the only advantage over the prisoner cells that she could see being the tentative flicker of an oil lamp set on a table beside a chessboard, the pieces ready for a fresh match. Of Ossine, she saw no sign but for a tin cup of cider and a button. The place appeared deserted.

Suspicious, but she'd not look a gift horse in the mouth. Who knew when they might return? Racing down the side of the cabinet, she leapt for a chair back, scurried across the table, and dropped to the floor. Drew once more on the moon's power and her own inner magic to shed one skin for another—mouse for human.

She sighed and stretched her arms over her head, loosening the coiled knot of nervous twitchy muscles. Mouse was one of her more useful aspects, but she hated the accompanying rodent jitters. Opening the cabinet's upper doors, she snatched up the stained shirt with a wrinkle of her nose and slid it over her head to fall almost to her knees. Next, she unlatched the bottom doors, running a hand back and forth over the pegs before grabbing as many as she could drop into her outspread shirt.

Set and still blessing her good luck, Meeryn hurried out of the guardroom. The tunnels stretched away into the dark, a gutter running down the center aisle filled with something green and smelly that oozed between the toes.

"Gray," she whispered to the dripping silence.

Nothing, though she felt as if dead things watched her from the crooks and crannies and breathing seemed loud in the deafening quiet of this forgotten place.

*Gray, I'm here to rescue you*, she pathed, reaching with her mind for some hint of where he might be hidden.

A voice burst against her brain like the slam of a door. *Rescue me? Are you barking mad or simply stupid as a bag of anvils? Get the hell out of here now.*

So much for gratitude. She followed his pathing, picking her way over the greasy, slippery stones, splashing through puddles of what she really hoped was water, before coming to rest in front of a narrow wooden door with a barred grate just above eye level, though if she stood on tiptoe . . . "Are you in there? Are you all right?"

"I'm in here. 'All right' is a relative term. I'm not dead."

Grasping the ends of her shirt in one hand, she fished out a key with the other. Fitted it into the lock and turned. "Dromon plans to solve that as soon as possible." And a second. "He's accused you of murdering the duke." A third. "Mr. Pym, the duke's valet, a footman, and the two enforcers are prepared to back up his story. The Gather's been called." A fourth, or was that the second again? "They should be here in a week to pass sentence and witness your execution."

"I expect an I-told-you-so is in order," he answered, his sense of humor apparently undamaged.

"Plenty of time for that later. Now we need to get you out of here."

"We? This isn't a game, Meeryn, and the title of N'thuil won't save you if they find you here."

By now, she couldn't tell which keys she'd tried and which she hadn't. Her feet were going numb on the frozen stones and she knew every second's delay was a second for the Ossine to return in force. "I can't sit by and let them punish you for something that wasn't your fault. Not this time."

He said nothing for a long moment as she fumbled with three more keys, dropping them one after the other with a clatter onto the floor.

"I looked for you that day, even knowing you were in the Orkneys," he said quietly. "I kept hoping I'd spot you in the crowd. Then I prayed I wouldn't."

"I couldn't face it . . . or you . . . so I ran. I'm not running this time. At least, not away. That is, not away from you. Rather, this time it's *with* you. If you'll have me." She shut her mouth to keep from babbling and concentrated on her pile of keys.

Finally, a turn, a click, and the door swung open.

Gray sat curled in a corner where the soiled straw had been piled to form a makeshift nest. His face had fared badly, his body worse. The earlier gashes in his shoulder and arm had reopened, blood leaking onto his chest. He blinked up at her, a hand shielding his eyes from the shuttered lamplight. "I return to my original point, you're barking mad."

She knelt beside him, a hand on his arm. "Quick, before they come back. The way is clear."

"I appreciate the attempt, but you need to go— now." He narrowed his gaze. "What on earth are you wearing?"

"The latest London fashion in menswear. Now, do you want to just sit here and let Sir Dromon drive a stake through you and bury you like a grub in the dirt, or do you want to escape to fight another day?"

"Is that a rhetorical question?"

"Can you walk?" She felt his legs; still attached, no protruding bones.

"Not far." He held up his left arm. One end of a short chain was attached to the wall. The other held a silver cuff locked around his blackened and bloody wrist. She recoiled, the sour taste of bile in her mouth. Purple streaks crept their way up his arm to his elbow and his fingers curled like talons into his palm. "Don't suppose you brought *that* key with you, did you?" he asked.

A figure loomed like a specter in the doorway, his tasseled scabbard banging against his leg, a key dangling from his fingers. "She didn't, my lord. But I did."

"You can't stay now that your cover is blown, Kelan, so take Jamie and ride for the village of Sidnam. I'll meet you there as soon as I can."

"I'm to stay with you, my lord," Kelan answered. "Those are my orders."

"And who gave you those orders?"

The enforcer shifted uncomfortably from foot to foot, his gaze darting everywhere but at the huddled pile of bone and rags standing shaky and wide-eyed beside Meeryn.

"That's what I thought, but Lucan's not here. I am, and I'm telling you to take the boy and ride." Gray glanced down the tunnel. A torch sputtered and died. Their own breathing echoed back to them, harsh and quick, but no voices were raised in alarm. There was no clink of drawn steel or crunch of boot heels. "How hard did you hit them?"

Kelan grinned. "Hard enough, my lord. They'll not wake until dawn at the earliest and even then they'll be hard pressed to point both eyes in the same direction."

Gray didn't like the setup. In fact, the whole thing stank as foully as the rancid gutters, but he'd no choice left to him. Escape now, or be cleaved head to crotch and his innards fed to the grubs next week. "Jamie can barely walk. He needs help if he's to make it away without being recaptured."

"Begging your pardon, sir, but you don't look much better."

Gray couldn't argue that point. He knew he must look a wreck, his wrist throbbed, and every inhalation was accompanied by a woozy pinwheeling of his vision. He leaned against the wall to keep himself from slumping down beside it. "That may be, but I've got some unfinished business."

"I can help, my lord. Let the girl take the lad. I'll stay behind with you."

"That *girl* is still Lady N'thuil to you," Meeryn interjected.

Gray shoved off the wall with only a slight lightening in his head. "No, she's coming with me."

"I don't know, my lord," Kelan hedged.

"You don't have to know, you have to follow orders. Lucan will snarl, but he'll not eat you for breakfast. I'll be right behind."

"Lord Halvossa . . . I mean Your Grace . . . that is . . ."

Gray winced, the pain too raw, his grandfather's death still unreal. Still just words. "Damn it, Kelan. Don't call me that."

"Yes, Major." Chastened, he hoisted Jamie up, supporting him under one arm. "Take care of yourself. Two may be down, but an entire nest of Ossine wait above. Sir Dromon won't let you go easily."

"If we don't arrive by morning or the countryside is too dangerous, you know where to go."

Kelan gave another curt nod before he led Jamie farther down the black tunnel away from the guardroom, their shuffling footsteps dying away but for the occasional slosh of water on stone.

"Where are we going?" Meeryn whispered into the sudden silence as they headed in the opposite direction.

"I'm retrieving the Gylferion and getting the hell out of Deepings. You're going back to your chambers and praying none learn of your foolishness."

She stiffened as if he'd slapped her. "If you think you're leaving me behind, you're a bigger fool than I took you for, Gray de Coursy."

Oh, to be saddled with a biddable woman. He closed his eyes, hoping to stave off the worst of the black spots crowding the edges of his vision, but it only served to focus his attention on the grinding stabbing pain in his wrist. "This isn't a childish lark,

Meeryn. It's not a swipe of Cook's pastries or a toad in your governess's bed."

"Do you honestly think I don't understand the circumstances? I do have a brain in my head. But you can't do this without me. You need me."

"That was last night," he growled cruelly, frustration banding his shoulders, impatience knotting his muscles. "You mistake necessity for expediency."

If her eyes could shoot sparks, he'd have gone up in flames. "If you're trying to anger me, you're succeeding."

"I'm attempting to save your damned life," he answered, trying not to remember the silken flesh of her thighs, the taste of her on his tongue, the way she shuddered against his mouth when she came. What he wouldn't give for a long submersion in an icy pool or a fresh whack to the head to knock in some sense.

"Fine," she said, "you don't need me, but you need Jai Idrish. It amounts to the same thing."

They reached the guardroom. Empty, though they came across two bodies in the passage just beyond, and another in a side chamber. Gray knelt, feeling for a pulse. "They're still breathing." He yanked a knife from the sheath of one of the downed Ossine.

Meeryn grabbed his wrist. "No."

"I have to. Alive, these men remain a danger and a potential threat, a spear pointed at my back."

"And if you kill them now, how much better will you be than Sir Dromon and his thugs?" She touched the sickly purple streaks inching their way up his arm toward his heart, her fingers passing lightly over the ugly jagged gash on his shoulder, the horrible bruising across his rib cage. Her touch raised gooseflesh across his skin, and he shivered, though not with cold.

"I'll be alive," he answered.

"And as guilty of murder as they are."

He drew in a shaky breath. Blew it out in a huff of surrender. "So much for McIlroy's lessons in swordplay."

"Conal taught me how to fight an armed assailant. Not how to kill a defenseless victim."

"It's them or me, Meeryn. I fight to survive."

"But if survival turns you into something ugly and unfeeling, is it really survival?"

"If I make it out of here in one piece, I'll let you know."

She stared on him for a long uncomfortable moment, as if reading the hidden corners of his soul. Just before he humiliated himself by squirming under her disappointed forthright gaze, she bent to the waist of the closest guard, pulling loose his belt.

"What the bloody hell are you doing now?"

"I might draw the line at assassination, but I've never balked at simple thievery." She held out her arms, the overlarge shirt she wore riding high on her sleek thighs.

"Right," Gray answered.

After wrestling one unconscious guard free of his clothing, Gray bound and gagged them both, and if he knotted the ropes a bit tight or shoved the gags a bit farther down their throats than necessary, Meeryn didn't quibble. But she did cast him a swift uncertain glance when he took her hand.

"It's black as pitch down here. I don't want to lose you," he explained.

She snatched a candle from the guardroom and lifted it high to illuminate the black passage beyond. "Me . . . or Jai Idrish?"

He chose discretion over valor and kept his mouth firmly shut. Instead he pulled her along, turning down a narrow, low-ceilinged corridor, ducking to keep from scraping his head.

"Shouldn't we be headed for the surface?" she asked. "This passage is taking us deeper into the cliffs."

"Bring that candle closer and you'll see." Gray scanned the dripping slimy stones, running his fingers along the seams of the roughened granite slabs.

"What are you doing?"

He traced the notched circular outline of a stone with a finger, dug away the surrounding grout until the shape stood out. "This is it." He pushed and the block sank into the wall. A door grated open with noise to wake the dead. A slithery curl of dead air snuffed their candle, tossing them into darkness. "Quick. Inside."

He felt Meeryn move closer, her hip brushing his leg, her fingers tightening. "Mother of All, what is this place?"

The corridor they left had been dark, the passage they entered was as if someone had tossed a blanket over their heads and dropped them into a tar bog. Cobwebs clung to their faces and arms, the air dry and still as if it had not been breathed in a thousand years. "The Imnada built them throughout Deepings in case of attack."

"Find this in one of your books, Professor Gray?"

"I told you that's where the answers are. This passage leads to a lower storeroom. From there, we can skirt the kitchens. You can slip up the servant stairs to your chambers."

The floor descended for another hundred yards before beginning a slow but steady ascent. Gray shuffled his way forward in the complete blindness of the tunnel, leading Meeryn by the hand.

"And then what?" she asked, even her whisper seeming loud in the crushing silence. "Pretend nothing happened? Morieux is dead. He was the last tenuous thread holding Sir Dromon back from taking over completely. The clans are without a leader until you return and take your place."

"I'm dying, Meeryn. I'll be dead within the year unless I can lift the curse and break my dependence on the draught. When that happens, the clans will be no better off than they are now."

If the silence had been crushing before, it now thickened, solid as the earthen walls surrounding them. He could hear his heart beat, the rattle in his breathing, the grind of his bones with every footstep. He tensed, waiting for her sympathy or, worse, her pity. He wanted neither.

"You can only break the curse with my help . . . Jai Idrish's help. Together we work out what we did wrong. We try again. We figure it out together just like I told you we would."

"*We* do nothing. *I*—"

"Oh!" Meeryn stumbled and tripped onto her knees. "Drat! Who on earth would leave a pile of rubbish in the middle of the floor?"

Gray knelt, a hand out. "Not rubbish—bones. Here's the skull." He picked it up, only to have it crumble under his fingers.

"The question remains with only a slight adjustment—who . . . and why . . . ?"

"Perhaps the poor devil lost his way."

"Or perhaps Sir Dromon knows about these passages and our skeleton was unfortunate enough to run into an Ossine."

"No, he's been down here for centuries."

They continued, quieter now, huddled together. Gray pulled her close, her cheek soft under his lips. "We're close," he whispered.

He felt along the wall for the rounded panel that marked the end of the passage. Pressed it, feeling the rush of wind chill the cold sweat on his face and shoulders as they stepped into an empty storeroom, long since abandoned as Deepings population and prominence declined.

"Go back to your rooms, Meeryn. Lock yourself in and don't come out. No matter what you hear or see, do you understand? If anyone asks, you've been there all night. You know nothing."

Her chin jutted in challenge, body braced for a fight. "If Sir Dromon captures you, he won't wait for a proper grandiose execution as an example for those who cross him. A quick blade to the gut will serve him just as well. He can weave any tale he wants afterward."

Arguments Gray had already played over in his mind as he lay in a stinking pile of straw with his body one raw nerve. He gave Meeryn the same answer he'd repeated to himself in the bitter watches of his despair until he almost believed it. "I can take care of myself."

Her gaze was hard and clear as diamonds. "You forget, Gray. So can I."

Gray must have taken a pounding to the head if he thought she was going to slink back to her rooms like a frightened little girl. Instead Meeryn slipped back down the stairs to the laundry and the drying yard beyond. Sheets billowed like ghosts in the salty breeze while enormous wooden racks waited empty for tomorrow's washing. She snatched up a canvas bag hanging from a peg on the wall, slinging it over her shoulder as she headed through the wooden gate and out onto the lawn. No question. No hesitation.

An owl called from the park, sending her heart leaping into her throat. Movement at the corner of her eye had her diving for the bushes until she realized the long sinuous shape was merely a kitchen cat on the prowl.

So there might be *some* very slight hesitation, but nothing a stern talking-to and a few deep breaths wouldn't fix.

Thus fortified, she moved swiftly and softly over the grass, hugging the hedges and buildings as she raced for the Crystal Tower. It rose shimmering above her, moonlight shining through the high windows to create eerie dancing shadows as if someone moved within the topmost sanctuary. Whispers hovered on the breeze, lifting the hairs on her arms with their sibilant hissing words in a language she'd never heard and didn't understand.

Sir Dromon? A phalanx of lurking Ossine? Someone . . . or something . . . else?

Her heart drummed in her chest as she crept up the stairs, testing her weight upon each step, waiting for the inevitable shout to halt, stop, cease, and desist. None challenged her, no one leapt from the dark with swords drawn, and the sanctuary was empty save for Jai Idrish upon its altar.

Gray might think the great crystal slept on, unmoved by the magic of the Gylferion, but she knew better. She'd sensed the stirrings of power, felt the world drop away in those swift frightening moments. Excitement, terror . . . hope.

Sucking in a steadying breath, she laid her hands upon Jai Idrish. Immediately, a jolt of energy sizzled up her arms, curling and slipping over her brain like the undulations of the seas. A voice spoke to her with the same clarity as a pathing, or was it three voices speaking as one? A hundred voices. A million. All of them blending and separating, one taking over from another as they repeated a string of unknown words— chanted prayer, relentless command.

"*Afeitha eineia tharthei. Afeitha eineia tharthei. Afeitha eineia N'thuil noractha tharthei.*"

Her eyes watered as the dark opened up before her in a twisting spiral of unending black, the voices rising and falling in a hypnotic cadence. She couldn't breathe, couldn't move. The crystal vibrated beneath her fingers. The world dropped out from under her bare feet, the sweep and streak of stars moved past her in a dizzying spiral of color and light.

*It's in the blood!*

A new fourth voice smashed through the drone of the other three like the blast of a gun. Wait—Meeryn tore her hands free of the crystal—that *was* a gun! A shot rang out. Then another. The sounds of running feet and men's voices raised in crisp command bounced off the high walls of Deepings.

Gray's escape had been discovered.

Trying not to dwell on the number of sacrilegious desecrations she was committing by stealing the Im-nada's most sacred object, she gritted her teeth against the gut-snarling knot and the seeking, searching voices, and snatched the crystal from its altar, stuffed it into her sack, and raced for the stairs.

Lantern light flashed along the eastern ramparts and down into the kitchen yard. Riders streamed out the main gate, while from the roof of the armory, eagles took flight one after the other to wheel away into the night. Calling reinforcements? Searching the countryside beyond the Palings?

Carrying the disks of the Gylferion, Gray wouldn't be able to shift, and on foot, he'd not make it a mile before he was brought down.

In the chaos, none noticed her serpentining her way from pillar to post. *Where are you, Gray?* she pathed, even her mental shout breathless and slightly frantic. *Have you got the disks?*

*The library. Have to . . .*

*What? What do you have to do?*

He didn't answer. What the hell stunt was he pulling? He was supposed to be in the damned guest hall. He was supposed to be getting the hell out of Deepings. What was there in the library worth—she skidded to a halt, her feet sliding across the hall's parqueted floor, nearly colliding with a suit of armor and two Ossine.

Sir Dromon stepped off the stairs, still in dressing gown and nightcap, his face purple with frustrated rage. "Find de Coursy. The duke's murderer cannot be allowed to escape justice. His crimes cannot go unpunished."

"Aye, sir. The house is being searched room by room. He'll not get away."

"Send word to the Gather elders. In case they have ideas of taking him in, I want them to fully understand the penalties dealt to those who harbor fugitives." He noticed her, his eyes taking in her strange attire, his lips ringed in white, his eyes like coals as he continued barking orders. "If they are not with us in this, they are as guilty of treason as he is and will suffer his same fate."

This was the clearest threat yet to the elders' authority. Would they bow to the Arch Ossine and his army or would they finally fight back? Would she?

Stepping free of the shadows, she lifted her head. "His proper title is Duke of Morieux."

Sir Dromon's expression cleared and a small twisted smile curled the edge of his mouth. "So it is and as worthless a title as N'thuil these days." He snapped his fingers. "Mr. Thorsh, apprehend our misguided little sparrow before she makes any more trouble."

Meeryn hadn't seen the Ossine until he stepped around Sir Dromon, his bullish shoulders wide as ox yokes, his furry knuckles resting on his hips. His face was bruised and battered, his smile still as vicious. "My pleasure, sir. Knew the crystal was wrong when it chose her. A chit of a girl brings naught but trouble."

She backed away, her hand clamping the sack to her side, the crystal banging against her thigh. "You know he's innocent. His Grace died, but it wasn't at Gray's hands. We can still salvage a peace between us. Stop this now before anyone else gets hurt."

"Like you?" Sir Dromon snarled. "Mr. Thorsh! Now!"

Hands grabbed her from behind, pinning her arms to her sides. She screamed and kicked as she was dragged backward into the library. She managed to smash her heel into her attacker's shin. Wiggled an elbow free enough to slam it into his stomach.

Gray responded with a grunt of pain, shoving her away to slam and lock the door. "Next time I'll let Thorsh have you."

"You scared me to death. You might have warned me."

"I was too busy trying not to get skewered."

She'd thought he'd looked bad before. She'd not realized how much the darkness of the catacombs had hidden. Gone was the nobleman's polished austerity. This was a savage fighter with nothing to lose, the burning intensity in his gaze and the raw power in his frame sucking the air from the room and the breath from her lungs. The trembling in her knees and the fluttering in her chest that he evoked was akin to the effect that touching Jai Idrish had on her—as if a new and amazing world hovered just out of reach. She just needed to be strong enough, clever enough, hold on long enough . . .

Hammer blows bulged the door as Thorsh and the Ossine struggled to break in. She caught the click of a cocked hammer a second before Gray threw her to the floor, just as the lock blew out in a shower of deadly splinters.

"Now what?"

Cradling his damaged arm to his side, he pulled her back to her feet with the other and yanked her onward, plunging through unguarded doors leading into a salon, an adjoining drawing room, an antechamber, a gallery. Room after room, up stairs, down passages. One step ahead of their pursuers. They finally emerged onto the ramparts, racing along the narrow stone wall walk. A stitch cramped her side and her bones wobbled like jelly, but she kept up, the bag slapping her thigh, the crystal seeming to grow heavier with each step.

"We can head for the cliff tower," she suggested.

"It's too far. This way."

An Ossine stepped from an archway in front of them, pistol raised. Gray lunged to his right as the gun erupted with a spout of flame and the bullet smashed the wall beside them. He answered the man's shot with one of his own from a pistol whipped from his pocket. The man crumpled to the ground and they were past, Gray tossing the weapon aside as he stepped over the body.

"Not murder," he gasped. "Self-defense."

"I'm not arguing." She grimaced and on they raced toward the guest hall.

Once there, Gray passed through the rooms, intent and unswerving.

"You were almost clear away. What on earth sent you to the library?"

"Answers." He held a parcel wrapped in heavy oil-cloth.

They finally came to rest in a set of musty chambers. Gray locked the door, but that would only serve them for so long. He crossed to a heavy armoire, fumbling with the doors as he sought to open them one-handed.

"Let me." She pulled the doors open.

Instead of retrieving something from within, he stepped up inside the wardrobe, turned to motion her on behind him.

"We're hiding in a closet?" she asked, trying not to sound as panicked as she felt. She refused to give Gray the satisfaction. "What is this? A sadistic game of sardines?"

"No, it's the way out."

\*        \*        \*

All right, so he might have been a bit optimistic when he announced their imminent escape. What had seemed like an inspired idea at the time had become a panic-drenched nightmare. Black water swirled below him. Sucking and slapping at the rickety ladder. A cold infinite crushing mass waiting to push him under, roll him over, pull him down.

"Gray, we have to go."

He took a shuddering breath. He could feel his heart pounding wildly under the hand cradled to his chest. "Perhaps the cliff tower might have been a better option after all."

"It's too late now. They've got us pinned in here."

"Right. Give me a moment."

"We don't have any more moments."

He tore his eyes from the water. Meeryn had stripped out of the dirty shirt and stolen breeches. Her hair tumbled loose and honey-blonde over her shoulders to drape and curl over the curve of her breasts, and he was struck—yet again—at the toned perfection of her golden body. It was like watching the sea, one minute all silken, graceful movement, the next tempestuous, storm-tossed ferocity. He needed tidal maps and depth charts to understand all her hidden, secret facets.

"I'll be right here, Gray. I won't let you drown. Trust me."

"Right," he said with a bracing cheerfulness he didn't feel. "Of course you won't. You didn't the last time, did you?"

"No," she answered gently. "I didn't." She bent and

grabbed a sack, holding it out to him. "Don't lose it. My clothes are in there."

He opened the bag, and his heart lurched uncomfortably in his chest. "Shit in hell! You stole Jai Idrish?"

"I'm the Voice and the Vessel. It belongs to me just as I belong to it. You can't steal a part of yourself." She tried for confident, but Gray heard the uncertain wobble in her voice.

"Tell that to the Ossine."

"If we don't hurry, I'll have to."

"Right," he muttered to himself, channeling David St. Leger's smug, sneering tone. "Buck up, Gray. Pull your shit together, grow some short hairs, and don't be such a bloody great coward."

David would never balk at getting his feet wet. He'd plunge in headfirst and worry over consequences like not breathing later. Mac might run a checklist of possible outcomes over in his head, but then he'd grit his teeth and do what needed to be done. Flannery the soldier. St. Leger the lunatic.

Gray had led them for five years. Could he honestly call himself a leader if he faltered now? And what of Meeryn who'd given up all she'd known to join him on this quixotic quest?

He couldn't let her down. He couldn't let her suffer for his sins.

He leaned over the edge, terror squeezing his chest, crushing the breath from his lungs. He couldn't swallow. He couldn't move. Faces appeared in the swirl of water, Mother's dark hair streaming like seaweed around her bone-white face, Father's expression accusing as he rose and sank under the crush of water, and his brother . . . Ollie . . . vacant staring sockets, a mouth gaping in a horrible smile of welcome. He reached with a skeletal hand . . .

"Gray!" Meeryn's voice stole into his mind over the pounding of the ocean and the pounding of his heart. "Jump!"

A hand shoved him between the shoulders, sending him headlong into the water. The cold hit like a punch to the stomach as he went under. Down and down he sank, one arm out to feel his way through the narrow underwater tunnel, another wrapped tight around the sack bearing Jai Idrish, the Gylferion, and the oilcloth-wrapped package. Lungs screamed as he propelled himself through the icy current, trying not to imagine the walls closing in, the water bearing down. The outward tide pulled him with every surge and drag closer to the sea. He clutched the bag, counting the beats of his heart, the panic a living slithering horrible agony coiling itself tighter and tighter until his cracked ribs split, salt water throbbing in every open wound.

Suddenly the walls fell away to open water, and now the wash and churn of the ocean pushed and spun him. Something bumped him. A fin curled against his leg. A sleek skin buoyed him upward, but the weight of the bag continued to pull him down. He was fourteen again. Storm raging, sails and lines twined round his ankles as the little boat broke and sank in the raging hurricane winds.

He kicked for the surface, but a wave shoved him under, another one smashed over his head. He dropped once more, moonlight a pinprick above him. He opened his mouth to call for help, arms flailing for his father. He would pull him from the water with a laugh and a smack on the back. Mother would wrap him in a blanket and Ollie would chide him for being a sniveling coward. But no hand reached for his, no laughter followed or comforting maternal arms, only the rush of sea water crushing his lungs, filling them until they burned and collapsed.

The seal brushed by him, slid underneath him, lending him its strength and its weightless skill against the ripping currents and tides pulling him northward toward the offshore rocks and the jagged shoals lying just beneath the churning surface. He tried pathing, but his mind seemed to have turned inward, no thought escaping, not even a whispered plea for forgiveness.

*Gray! It wasn't your fault. You didn't kill them.*

He closed his eyes and as the slithering coil of rope tightened around his chest and grief and guilt overwhelmed him, he let the deep claim him and the darkness swallow him whole.

# 9

Toe-nibbling waves woke Meeryn from a nightmare in which she watched, frozen, as an endless shadow rolled toward her, blotting out the sun, stripping the world bare. She gasped, blinking away the sand crusted at the corners of her eyes, brushing away the strands of sea grass twined round her ankles. No ominous Armageddon. Just a lonely beach, high fog-shrouded cliffs, and a man lying stretched out beside her, one hand gripping a waterlogged sack.

His face was turned from her. All she could see was a long slice of cheekbone, the defined edge of his jaw-line, an arched brow drawn low. Salt had dried across his back, the stretched and puckered skin a sickening reminder of the horrors he'd already suffered at Sir Dromon's hands. She tried imagining what it had felt like to stand within the Deepings hall amid a circle of impassive faces as flames tore at her flesh and claws shredded her mind. She shrank from the thought as her gut clenched and vomit rose in her throat.

She brushed sand from his shoulders, the muscles

hard, the flesh warm. Imagined laying her lips to taste his salt-tightened skin, exploring the contours of his hard muscular body with slow sweet deliberation. He would wake with a smile, pull her against him, his mouth finding hers, and they would come together in the hazy dawn with naught but the sorrowful sound of the ocean to accompany their harried breathing. Or, more likely, he would roll away with an unfeeling flash of his blue eyes and she'd be left with only sand running soft between her fingers.

With a harsh bark of angry laughter, she rose and ran into the water, diving into the surf with a jolt to shake herself free of both sensual dream and shadowy nightmare. Worked free the last remaining kinks left over from shifting seal to human. As one of the Orkney Nornala, the skin of the seal came easier than any other aspect, but it still took a good stretching to restore the easy fluidity of one shape for another. Surfacing, she swept her hair from her face. Scanned the beach.

Gray was gone.

She waded ashore, snatching up the borrowed shirt and stolen breeches she'd laid out to dry last night. Stiff, scratchy, and smelling of fish, they were wearable if not exactly the height of fashion.

Just before she shouted his name, Gray rounded a jumbled pile of boulders, hair slicked back, water dripping down his neck. "Where are we?"

She tried to contain her relief. Not that she thought he'd abandoned her here, but . . . all right, she had thought that. It would be just like Gray to assume he was being noble when in fact he was just being pigheaded. She scanned the cliffs, though the fog hid any landmarks. The ocean rolled flat and gray, horizon lost in the swirling cloud enfolding them. "North. Perhaps as far as Duckpoole. It's hard to say."

"Free of the Palings if not out of danger." His bruises had faded to an ugly green collage, and the worrying purple streaks originating at his wrist where the silver manacle had bound him had receded, but he continued to hold his injured arm close to his body, his posture careful as if every movement jarred aching bones. "We need to scavenge mounts. Make our way east and south. Kelan will be waiting."

"Then what?"

But he'd already turned away to walk back up the beach.

She hastened to follow, snatching up the bag as she passed it lying at the tide line. "I'm sorry, Gray . . . about your grandfather."

He pulled up short, staring down at her with a cool look of detachment. "Are you? I suppose it's good someone's sad to see the bastard go."

"You don't mean that."

His laugh was strained, his eyes angry. "Don't I?"

"No, you don't. I know you better than that. I know you cared for him despite everything. I know you"— she took a deep breath—"that you loved him."

"You don't know shit about me, Meeryn." By now, he was striding up a narrow, rocky path away from the water. She had to run to keep up, but when she caught him, she grabbed him and whipped him around to a standstill. His eyes were bright with old anger and new grief.

"Fine. I don't know anything about you. You're a stranger. You're a riddle and an enigma and a puzzle, but I do know that you're the new Duke of Morieux, Gray. The title is yours."

"Damn the bloody title," he snarled. "I never wanted it. People thought I was jealous of Ollie. He was so accomplished, so . . . amazing . . . but it wasn't true. He deserved to be heir. He deserved to live."

"Of course he did. No one wanted him to die. It was a tragic accident. But it happened, and now you're the duke whether you will it or not."

His anger faded, though the grief remained. Gray and his grandfather had never been close; they were too similar, though neither one would ever have admitted it. They both possessed the same magnetic charisma, the same powerful aura of command. Unfortunately, they also shared a mulish obstinacy and a prideful arrogance they wore like armor. Tragedy had solidified that glossy imperviousness. The curse had imprisoned Gray with no hope of escape. Let no one in and no one would know how much you hurt.

"I've always wondered; why did you save me that day? Why not Ollie?" he asked, emotion leached from his voice. "He was the one chosen for you by the Ossine, the one you were supposed to marry."

His gaze seemed to peel away her defenses even as he hid his own thoughts behind an unreadable expression. "Supposed to inherit. Supposed to marry. Life is messy, Gray. People die. People leave. . . ." She turned away lest she reveal more of her heart than was wise. Gave a careless shrug. "I didn't choose one over the other. By the time I found the boat's wreckage, you were the only one left alive. That's all."

"Would you have married him if he'd lived? Would you have done as the Ossine and Grandfather commanded?"

When had he moved so close? When had the air

grown so warm and breathing grown so hard? She swallowed, but a lump clogged her throat. Prickles danced along her skin that had nothing to do with the drying salt. A fluttering excitement began in her stomach. "Imnada law states we must marry the mate chosen for us by the Ossine."

"It also states that an *emnil* is dead to the clans, out-clan marriages result in a loss of Imnada power, and we must destroy any who discover our existence."

"We do this to keep the clans strong, our people safe." Why did she feel as if she were parroting Sir Dromon? And why did that feeling make her queasy?

"What if strength lay in revealing ourselves instead of hiding behind walls, and safety could be found in love rather than duty?"

"I would say you were mad to imagine such a fantasy. But that it might just be a fantasy worth fighting for."

"Is that why you broke ranks with Sir Dromon and freed me? Is that why you saved me . . . again?"

What did he want her to admit? That she'd gone against a lifetime of teaching because she'd finally come to the realization that Sir Dromon's version of security was as calamitous to the Imnada as any Fey-blood assault? That she wanted to prove herself to all those people who doubted her worth as N'thuil and all those souls who came to beg the sphere's intercession despite their dwindling faith? That she couldn't stand by and see the clans' last chance for healing tied down and staked in a public execution?

Or that she'd begun to fear that the clans' last chance for healing was her last chance as well?

"The future you offer scares me to death, but I begin to fear the alternative more."

"Do you?" His words were barely more than a breath upon her cheek. "I always knew you were a rebel at heart."

She felt her body swaying against her will, felt her bones melting and the blood pouring hot through her veins. Every nerve sizzled in anticipation. He hovered above her, over her, his eyes boring into hers, his body so close she had but to reach a hand to pull him toward her. But he never moved, never came any closer. Why did he hold back? What stayed his hand when his eyes gave his desire away? She wished she were brave enough to ask. She wished she were brave enough to hear his answer.

Instead she was left with a choice—frustration or brazenness.

Her hand threaded his hair, her heart skipped a beat, and she kissed him.

His mouth tasted salty while his tongue slid hot between her lips, teasing, tempting, dragging her deeper, offering her everything. Time seemed to stretch as his mouth moved over hers in a slow delicious dance, breath mingling, eyes darkening, passion mounting.

Her vision narrowed to the sharp-edged solemnity of his face, the arching sweep of his brows, the old scar at his temple and the new gash on his forehead, the smudges of exhaustion and the jump of tension. She closed her eyes, letting the weight of her desire drag her under. Her bones turned to ash. Her limbs gave way. She fell hard with a whimper of desire.

He jerked away with a groan of pain.

Not exactly the reaction she was looking for.

So much for brazenness.

\*     \*     \*

"Are you certain your wrist is all right? I can tighten the splint. It shouldn't look like that, should it? Or bend in quite that way?" Meeryn wrinkled her nose.

"I'll heal." He clamped his jaw and tightened his hands on the reins of his "borrowed" horse. He didn't need Meeryn drawing any more attention to the fact he felt like a damned fool for shrieking like a girl and nearly fainting dead at her bloody feet. At least the agony in his wrist kept him from dwelling on the ass he'd made of himself—again.

How was she able to burrow her way beneath every defense until he lost control like an adolescent boy faced with his first bedsport? How was she able to wring such confessions from him when he'd barely acknowledged these truths to himself? Ollie was a name he rarely spoke. A face he barely remembered. But his brother's life had forever shadowed everything Gray was just as his death had forever tainted it. Meeryn was one of the few who knew how much he'd loved his brother and one of the few who knew how much he'd grieved for him.

"Gray, are you certain we're traveling in the right direction? I think we passed that tree twice already."

Her question drew him back to the present. He looked up and, indeed, the tall spruce with the crooked trunk stood at the same fork in the road it had stood the last time they'd ridden this way. He turned his horse's head to the left and followed the uphill track away from a distant church spire and the comforting village rooftops and farm fields. "Aren't we meeting Kelan in Sidnam? That's miles south of here."

"We're taking the long way."

She jogged her bony gray mare up beside him, hair a wild tangle beneath her kerchief, her dark eyes like two black wells in her pale face. She had to be exhausted and unused to such effort, but she continued to sit her horse well, despite the long hours in the saddle and her purloined kirtle and apron, which rode up her thighs with every rough bone-jarring stride. "You mean the wrong way," she muttered.

"Do you want to take over?" he snapped, anger at himself shortening an already frayed temper.

"No, I'm just pointing out that—" With a moan, she slumped forward on her mare's neck, eyes rolled back in her head.

"Meeryn, what's wrong?" He kicked free of his stirrups and slithered to the ground, catching her as she slid down her horse's shoulder into his arms, gritting his teeth as his wrist took and held her weight. "Meeryn? Can you hear me?"

She spoke not a word, but her eyes remained wide and staring and her lips moved as if she fought to answer. He bent his ear close, caught only a hitch of breath and a murmured, *"Katarth theorta . . ."*

He carried her to the grass, hands shaking as he laid her down. Had she been shot? It couldn't be. He'd have heard the cock of a pistol or a musket, seen the slice of a shadow made by a crouching shooter or the flash off a barrel. He'd spent too many years watching his back and surveying his surroundings to be lulled into complaisance. And there wasn't any blood. No wound anywhere on her, not even a graze.

A shudder spasmed her body. She dragged in a ragged breath, chest heaving as if her lungs struggled to work. Her gaze found and locked on his eyes, face ashen, fingers dug into the dirt. "Dromon . . . he's discovered Jai Idrish is missing."

"How do you know?"

Tremors continued to ripple through her body and she hung her head, her fingers trembling. "He told me."

"Sir Dromon?"

"No." She lifted her head and her eyes held a new and terrible knowledge. "It was Idrin."


Meeryn caught sight of Gray as a wheeling speck upon the clouds and again as an arrow unleashed upon a target, the scream of his prey signaling success. They would eat tonight.

Cupping Jai Idrish in her palms, she stared into the flames of the small cookfire they'd risked, its thin white smoke dispersed by a steady breeze. Human figures and animal aspects twisted and writhed within the flames as the pressure built in her head and the crystal sang of distant stars and invisible galaxies and the frantic flight of a race on the verge of extinction. The Imnada had suffered more than once at the hands of dangerous enemies; the Fealla Mhòr had only been the most recent catastrophe.

Could she focus this new power, or would it always be a wild unpredictable tumble of images and ideas jumbling her brain?

Muffled footsteps and the scent of game heralded Gray's arrival. She returned Jai Idrish to her bag as he appeared from amid the trees, carrying two bloody hares already skinned and dressed. "You're awake. How do you feel?" he asked.

"Coddled." She grimaced her irritation. "I'm not an invalid and perfectly capable of sitting a horse."

"You fell off—twice. You're fortunate the beast is lethargic bordering on insensate or you'd be recovering from more than a ghostly visitation."

"It wasn't a ghost. It was Jai Idrish that spoke to me."

"With Idrin's voice."

"Yes . . . no . . . I can't explain it exactly." She tapped her forehead in frustration.

"So it would seem." He knelt to the fire, setting the hares to cook. "We'll stay here and rest until you're feeling better."

"I *am* better, and the Ossine will find us if we linger."

"Not if we're careful."

He tested the sizzling meat, pulling chunks off as they cooked, offering them to Meeryn. She didn't think she was hungry until she began to eat, then she found herself burning fingers and tongue as she devoured the hare's sweet gamey flavor, washed it down with the tepid water from a nearby stream. Night fell, and the fire threw long shadows across the ground, hollowed the stark lines of Gray's face, and burnished his skin a golden bronze. He leaned against the trunk of an ash, a stalk of grass between his teeth, eyes gleaming gold beneath half-lowered lids.

"Better?"

She licked the grease from her fingers. "Much."

His gaze swept to the bag at her hip. "Has Idrin's ghost offered any more words of warning, or are we on our own again?"

"I told you . . . it wasn't his ghost who spoke to me.

Or rather, it was, but he was only one thread amid a web of a million such, the spirits of every N'thuil stretching back to the beginning, all joined within the crystal."

"They're imprisoned within Jai Idrish?"

"They *are* Jai Idrish." Faces moved behind her eyelids, a string of men and women lost to time but forever a part of her as N'thuil. Daunting, yes, but also exhilarating. "We had it wrong. Jai Idrish isn't our link to the Mother Goddess. It's our link to the past going back to the very beginning. Every N'thuil adds his voice to the whole in an unbroken stream of information. Every N'thuil is able to draw on that store of knowledge when it's needed."

"So why has it been silent for so long?"

"Perhaps in our complacency, we forgot how to access the power within its heart. Perhaps it sensed we had no need of its wisdom and so simply stopped listening. I don't know. All I know is that something"— she paused to stare him down—"has caused it to take an interest in us again. Something has caused it to hear me in a way it hasn't listened to a N'thuil since our grandfather's grandfather's day."

"Then you can work the magic that will bring the Gylferion to life. I wasn't wrong."

A whisper of a thought passed fleeting and was gone. Something important she should remember. She grasped for the words but they drifted high and thin as the smoke of the cookfire and were lost. "I think I can. I don't know. I haven't tried to control or guide its power. It just seems to happen. Like falling through a door you never knew was there."

"Falling is a start."

She bit her lip, tasting blood along with juicy fat from the meat. "I don't think Jai Idrish is the answer to the curse, Gray. Or not all of it. The Fey-blood's magic is too strong and there's too much of darkness and evil in its casting."

"Did Idrin tell you that, too?"

"Gray . . ."

He sat up, tossed away his stalk of grass. "I won't believe it. No magic is immutable."

He rose from his seat, his pose of quiet contemplation vanished in a white-hot impatience. The soft gleam in his gaze became a conflagration. His aristocratic features and liquid grace burned away to reveal a warrior's stance and a warrior's will. The eagle moved under his skin, fighting to escape the manners of man, battling to rend and slash and tear its taloned way out of his chest and take flight . . . not to flee his destiny but to remake it.


Dawn was barely a smudge of light in the eastern sky when Meeryn rose from her makeshift bed, traded her frock for the breeches and shirt she'd worn out of Deepings. The horses snuffled and stamped, but a soft pat on their noses and a scratch behind their ears settled them before they woke Gray. He remained a lump at the far side of the smoldering fire, head upon his arm, dark lashes like shadows upon his cheeks. Just as well. Every time she'd woken during the long uncomfortable night, he'd been seated across from her, a brooding figure, eyes locked on the dying flames.

She paused to take up one of the knives they'd stolen along with the horses. A plain serviceable farmer's tool, but sharp. It would work as well as any other.

The path she followed ended in a small meadow. Dewy grass dragged at her legs and already she felt the day's heat in the perspiration damping her back and trickling down her neck. But, as she'd been trained, she located her target—a young birch, its trunk long and narrow. Paced out the distance, as the sky turned from a dark cloudy pearl to a creamy steely blue and the night breeze died.

The blade felt right in her hand, the weight well balanced. She squared her shoulders, and on an exhalation of breath, let fly with a turn of her elbow and a flick of her wrist. The blade buried itself where she'd intended; in the crook of trunk and lowest branch. The second throw was the same, as was the third. Each effort grew easier as her muscles fell into a practiced groove, her movements fluid as a dancer's. Only at the last did the rhythm of her actions falter. A prickle between her shoulder blades that was not caused by the hot sun set the knife flying wide of the tree to land with a thud in the bushes.

"I didn't mean to distract you." Gray scrubbed a hand through his tousled hair, his shirt open to reveal a golden triangle of skin.

She curled her fingers into her palm to prevent her from reaching out to touch the pulse beating steady at the base of his throat. Instead she made a great show of stalking into the undergrowth in search of the lost weapon. "I thought I should take the time . . . just in case."

"I hope it doesn't come to that."

"Hope doesn't mean much these days, though,

does it?" she answered, aiming and delivering the knife blade dead center.

Only now and again did her eyes flick to where he leaned against a nearby tree, arms folded across his chest. His wrist was bandaged, deep purple bruising replacing the ominous black streaks from wrist to elbow. His posture remained slightly crooked, his features slightly strained, but despite looking like a pugilist's punching sack, he still managed to exude an unruffled elegance as if he'd just emerged from his London club. The feral savagery of last night had been smothered until only the opaque aristocratic exterior remained.

"That's all well and good if your target is rooted to the ground, but what happens when you meet up with a foe a bit less herbaceous?" he asked with enough of a superior tone to set her teeth on edge.

She stalked to the birch and pulled the blade free. "That Fey-blood at the posting inn was moving. I don't recall you complaining over my aim then."

"He was almost fifty feet away and unaware of your presence."

She returned to her spot and let the blade fly once more, this time with a bit more force behind the throw. "His failure—not mine."

"And if you'd missed or he'd counterattacked?"

"But I didn't miss, and he could hardly have climbed two stories to come after me." She retrieved the blade, took up position again, hands gripping the knife a bit tighter, teeth grinding a bit harder, breathing a bit more shallow as she fought her temper. Was he really questioning her skills? Was he really critiquing her ability?

"Don't plant your feet," he suggested, "and perhaps if you relax your stance a bit . . ."

"Honestly, Gray," she snapped. "I'm not an idiot. Conal taught me—"

"I'm well aware of everything Conal taught you, Meeryn." His eyes flashed to hers. "Now show me."

What the hell did he mean by that, the bloody, infuriating, smug bastard? She let the blade sing from her fingers with every ounce of strength at her command. And gasped in alarm as he stepped forward into its path, his face blank of expression, lips hard and ringed in white.

"Gray! Look out!" Her blood ran cold, and she unconsciously looked away, hands over her eyes.

"I could have died a thousand different ways over the course of the last week." His words were a mix of exasperation and amusement. "Did you really think I'd end it all on the point of your dagger?"

She turned back, peeking through the gaps in her fingers, to see his hand fisted around the blade's handle. "Did you just do what I think you did?"

He flipped the knife end over end, catching it once more, a smile dancing in his eyes. "A circus trick I learned in the military. Not very useful, though it does tend to make people tread more carefully around you."

He handed her the knife and drew his own. "Did Conal show you"—he lunged, dagger sliding forward as if he aimed for her heart—"this?"

She sprang out of the way, a hand up to block the thrust of his arm. "Yesterday you were trying to wrap me in cotton like an invalid. Now you're trying to murder me. Why the change of attitude?"

He thrust again, giving her only a second to dodge

the blade and parry with her own. "A night to reflect."

She barely fought off his third blow, the blades screeching one against the other, her fingers numb at the force of his attack. They broke apart, she breathing heavily, he dancing about like a marionette. His fourth was a dirty twisting move that had her on her knees. She managed to squirt away but only because she ripped free, part of her shirt coming away in his hand. He grinned. "McIlroy didn't teach you that one? What sort of professor was he?"

That did it. She scrambled back to her feet, face burning, determination locking her jaw. Gray wanted a fight? So be it. She'd give him a bloody fight. To hell with his bruises and his broken wrist.

She attacked with renewed energy and a honed ferocity. Now he was the one on the defensive, dancing in and out as he dodged her assault. Blades met and parted. She caught him a blow to the jaw, another to the ribs. His smile tightened, but he never surrendered or eased up on her. His breathing became heavy as his teasing died away. Now sweat beaded his temples and glued his shirt to his muscled chest. His gaze lost its brightness, his expression as grim as she knew her own must be.

Her arm ached all the way to her shoulder and her legs shook with the effort to stay one step ahead, one step above. Her hair fell from its bun to fly about her shoulders, and the shirt she'd swiped from the soldier at Deepings had at least two provocative tears. But she refused to give him the satisfaction. Knowing Gray, she'd never hear the end of it. She backed him slowly across the clearing, then just as he lunged, she threw a leg out in a move proven to take him down in a tumble of arms and legs.

Off-balance, he stumbled, lurching forward, his blade spinning away into the grass.

She smiled her success, opened her mouth to shout her victory, and found herself on the turf amid the wildflowers with the air punched from her lungs, her body pinned by the weight of his on top of her, her stolen blade resting against her throat.

"Surrender?" he asked softly.

She blinked up at him, lungs burning to fill. Unable to do anything but nod.

He tossed away the knife but did not move from where he knelt above. His eyes burned as they traveled her from head to foot, and now her lack of oxygen had nothing to do with the blow to her back but with the squeeze of her heart. Her torn shirt offered him more than a passing view of her breasts, though his gaze didn't linger there for long. Instead he focused back upon her eyes, the blue of his gaze burning like ice and fire both.

His face filled her vision, the sweeping arch of his dark brows, the flop of hair across his forehead, the chiseled angle of his razor cheekbones. She wanted to touch him, to feel his lips upon hers, to curl her legs around his waist and have him bury himself inside her. It was a raw, visceral need that quivered her insides like jelly and made her sex clench in anticipation.

"I was wrong, Meeryn," he said, his eyes never once leaving her face.

"Were you?" she managed to respond on a sharp panting intake of air. She swallowed a moan as his weight between her legs intensified, the evidence of his arousal nestled against her slit. Sensation spiraled inward until every breath shot a delicious throb from

her crotch to her brain. He would take her here . . .
now . . . under the wide sky in a field of flowers. What
could be better? What could be more right?

An expression passed over his face, so quickly it
was gone before she understood its significance. Only
when he rolled off her and up onto his knees did she
come to her shaky unsettled senses.

"McIlroy did a good job in my stead," he said,
gravel roughing his deep voice, his gaze impenetrable.
"Better, actually. I'm a dreadful teacher. I've not the
patience it takes to explain what I do, only that I do it."

Her knees shook, her stomach turned in a thousand knotted circles and she'd a desire to take up the
knife she'd dropped and plunge it right into his cold,
unfeeling heart. "Yet he was a lot like you in many
ways."

He lifted his brows in question.

"He had the same build, the same blue eyes"—she
scrambled to her feet, snatching up her blade with
now trembling fingers—"and he ran away when it got
too hard to stay, just like you."

The cottage sat off the main road in a twisting alley
running between the back of the tavern stables and
a brewery. Nothing to set it apart from its equally
nondescript neighbors. Same mossy slate roof, same
forbidding granite façade, even the muddy earthen
paths leading to battered boot-scarred doors matched
in almost every detail. The shapechanger had worked
hard to blend into his surroundings until none would
suspect that the barman bore a secret. Head down and
mouth shut; that was how he'd tried to live his life—

until Gray and his group had enlisted him to their cause.

It had cost him his life.

The fly-riddled corpse lay by a door leading to the yard beyond. Blood and offal spattered walls and floor and ceiling, congealed under the mangled limbs and nearly severed head. He hadn't just been killed. He'd been eviscerated . . . and then—Gray swallowed back the vomit chewing its way up his throat—gnawed on. Were the enforcers feasting on those they killed now? Was this a warning to those who remained loyal to the rightful heir?

"Gray? Over here."

Meeryn summoned him to a small lean-to opening onto the kitchen. Another body, this one hanging by the neck from a rope knotted round a high beam. The face purple and black, but still recognizable as the young groom Kelan had set free. Greasy gray entrails spilled from his ripped stomach, a splintered end of bone protruded from his left leg.

"Do you think Kelan and Jamie rode straight into the massacre?" she asked, a hand covering her mouth, her expression a shade of pea green.

"I haven't found any bodies but the two. Let's assume that means they passed through before this occurred or after the Ossine had left."

He returned to the front room, where Doule's battered corpse lay in pieces like an accusation on the floor. Gray closed his eyes and pinched the bridge of his nose, hoping to stave off the pounding in his head. Exhaustion dogged him like a shadow. He moved in a fog, faculties dimmed, sickness a mere shaky breath and trembling hand away.

Meeryn's revelations about Jai Idrish rang in his head, but it was the memory of the longing in her eyes and the tremoring anticipation in her limbs that built the pressure in his chest until he could barely breathe around the immovable boulder lodged against his heart. He could have sated his greedy hunger. Found his climax and rolled away, unmoved by anything more than physical gratification.

But this was Meeryn. And he knew that if he ever surrendered to the staggering demands of his body, there would be no winning his way back. He would be lost to the force of his feelings. She would pay the price for his weakness.

"Who is he?" She stood behind him, chalk white but for two high spots of color on her cheeks. He tried not to flinch away from her proximity.

"His name was Zeb Doule. His brother worked in the stables at Deepings."

"That must have been Caleb. Sir Dromon said he'd discovered one of the grooms had been sending messages to the rebels. He had him killed," Meeryn said, her eyes clouded with sorrow.

"You knew him?"

"I tried to know everyone who worked to keep the estate going. As the duke grew less interested in the running of things, I took over many of the day-to-day tasks. That is, until Sir Dromon insinuated himself into the household. He didn't appreciate my interference."

Gray searched the room. No letters. No journals or pages that might lead to others in the group. Not even a scrap in the blackened hearth, though a pile of ash was evidence of a recent burning. "Bugger all, I have no idea whether Doule destroyed everything he received or if the Ossine found it when they tore the place apart. We could be riding straight into a trap."

"Is that what upsets you? Not that these men were killed but that they might have left a few stray pages lying about?"

His skin crawled with unspent tension, his knotted muscles twitched. "What upsets me is that their deaths put others in jeopardy. That we'll have to find a new informant within Deepings willing to pass information out through the proper channels." A flash of color caught the corner of his eye. He bent, shoving a hand under an overturned chair. Pulled free a shard of rose-colored glass, a bit of notched edge still intact—Doule's *krythos*, dropped and crushed during the brief futile struggle. Gray put it in his pocket, his headache moving into his neck and down his spine into his shoulders.

"Is that all they were to you? Sources of information?" Meeryn asked, shrill anger hardening her words. "Spies for your conspirators?"

"They were soldiers under my command."

"I think your years in the army have made you forget where soldiers come from. They don't spring from the ground like dragon's teeth." A storm brewed in her expression. Just what he didn't need right now when his self-control hung by the thinnest of threads. "Here's some information for you; Caleb was barely seventeen. He wanted to move to London and find work in the city, but he'd an elderly mother and with his brother gone from the holding, there was none to support her but him. Now she's lost them both. They had lives and people who depended on them and hopes for the future. They weren't just pieces to be moved about a board at your whim."

The thread snapped with an audible twang. "Do you think I don't know that?"

"I think you forget as you're strategizing your next move and mapping out this great new world of yours. As you lose yourself to the slaughter and the secrets."

A haze reddened his vision. Aching muscles vibrated painfully as if plucked by an invisible hand. Guilt loosened the boulder until the words came pouring out. "Aren't you the one who's been carping at me about my duty to the clans since you arrived unannounced in my bedchamber?"

"Yes, but . . ."

"What do you think that means? That I serve as some pointless figurehead who'll tell the Imnada that the world is bright when in fact it's burning? That may be your job as N'thuil. It's not mine."

The storm in her eyes became a full-blown cyclone. Hands on hips, chin up and braced for battle. "At least I took on a responsibility. You fled it. You're still fleeing it. Did you think I didn't notice that no one calls you Lord Halvossa, even though it's your title? It has been since you were fourteen."

"Fled it? Two years ago I was bloody well stripped of everything, nearly including my mind. My fucking title was the only thing they couldn't take from me when they ripped away mark and signum. But it was a label I gained by a fluke of chance. The rank of major I earned. If Sir Dromon wants a damned war, he shall have it. But he'd better understand, this isn't my first back-to-the-wall fight-or-die battle. The Arch Ossine won't be allowed to hide in the shadows while others do his butchering and his dying for him."

"You say Sir Dromon hides behind his army of Ossine, Gray." Meeryn's gaze settled once more on the corpse already bloating in the summer heat, her expression grim. "I begin to wonder if you're really any different?"

Sleep. She'd heard of it. As fleeting and mysterious as the mythical unicorn, it had something to do with closing one's eyes, relaxing one's muscles and, if she wasn't completely mistaken, it happened while one was lying horizontal, preferably not under a leaky ceiling and out of any irritating drafts. It certainly had nothing to do with chop-gaited, swayback horses, hours of dragging dullness punctuated by moments of sheer terror, all conducted under a sky that poured endless buckets of rain down on her head, except for those rare moments when it gusted those same buckets sideways into her face.

As the sun sank toward the horizon and they skirted one more village for the less comfortable track uphill across a high boulder-strewn down, she bit her tongue just before she caught herself whining a petulant "Are we there yet?" to the unyielding, broad-shouldered back ahead of her.

It wouldn't have helped. He hadn't spoken to her for the last twenty miles, not since his curt "Get the hell down and don't move." Almost warm and cuddly compared to the icy silence of the rest of this hellish journey.

It was probably the silence that saved her—or the

exhaustion. The pattering rush of falling rainwater from a bush announced the ambush just as Meeryn slumped forward across her horse's withers half-asleep and the explosion of a musket shot sent a bullet buzzing past her ear like a hornet. This time she was the one shouting "Get down!" and sliding from her saddle for the cover of a low stone wall.

Gray was there before her; a blur of uncoiling tension. He dragged her deeper behind the wall where the brambles scratched at her draggle-tailed gown and caught in her hair. Another blast rang out, dark smoke and chattering birds rising in a cloud from the wood. The bullet bit into a tree not a foot from Gray's heart.

Footsteps and a drone of conversation signaled the presence of more than one enforcer. Dear Mother of All, if they were surrounded, they may as well surrender now. Gray was chalky with illness, his body aflame with more than typical Imnada heat, and exhaustion dragged at her like anchor chains.

"Wait." Gray laid a hand on her arm.

Before she could stop him, he slid away through the brush and the saplings lining the wall, barely making a ripple of sound. He was long and lean and deadly, and she was reminded of a snake moving slowly through the grass toward two unsuspecting mice. Not exactly a description normally associated with Ossine enforcers, but then she'd never seen such focused control, every precise motion as Gray slunk toward the far corner of the wall designed for the surprise kill. It was beautiful and frightening to behold, this transformation from the Gray she knew to a remorseless bloodthirsty stranger. Like two sides of the same coin. Only the face on both was as impassive and grim as death.

Two shots gone wide, the enforcers had obviously chosen to wait them out. With the horses scattered and little cover beyond the wall and the scraggly wood beyond, it was a simple matter of patience on their part.

Meeryn had never been patient. She chewed on a fingernail, her heart thudding like a drum until it felt as if it might explode.

By now Gray was lost from sight, not even a breeze-tossed grass blade to signal his trail. Encroaching dusk threw the landscape into a shifting pattern of light and dark, masking movement and camouflaging intent. The air seemed charged, the tension crackling as the moments dragged on with no sound but the swish of the wind and the rustle of the trees.

Then all erupted into chaos.

Gray rose from his cover in a graceful flow of eye, body, and throwing arm. His dagger sliced the air with a killing sing of steel to strike the enforcer in the space between his ribs and over his heart.

Blood welled around the quivering handle as he fell, the second enforcer up and attacking before his associate hit the ground. The man dashed for Gray, hatchet raised, hair and eyes wild, a blood-curdling yell tearing from his foaming lips.

Her breath caught in her throat. Her feet remained rooted to the ground. Her mind reeled off at a million miles an hour; every reckless thought, every shuttered glance, every beloved face, every wish she'd ever wished . . .

*Gray!* she pathed in a mental scream of warning.

He turned and threw his arm up just as the man made his final lunging thrust, and they met with a force to rattle the breath from her lungs, going down in a spinning tangle of arms and legs. The enforcer's hatchet ended lost in the wild overgrown hedge beside the wall. Gray rose from the mud, face streaked black and clothes caked with sticky goo, but his eyes remained glacier cold and sharp as jagged glass as blood trickled from the corner of his mouth.

Loosed from her paralyzing fear, Meeryn ran for the hedge, kneeling to feel her way past the thorns and needling branches for the hatchet. She was useless without it. No match for the maddened masculine brawn of the Ossine's deadliest. Fingers stretched, she searched . . . nothing.

"Murdererous whoreson bastard!" the enforcer shrieked, staggering to his feet. He might have been temporarily unarmed, but he bore a thick wrestler's body and his stance revealed obvious fighting skill. "I'll cut your damned heart out."

He closed in a bull rush that sent Gray lurching backward into the wall with bone-crushing force. He grunted as the breath was driven out of his lungs, his face a ghastly white beneath the mud, but his eyes gleaming almost iridescent blue.

Cut out his heart . . . of course, the second Ossine. He remained where he'd fallen, ominously still but for the blood pumping from the wound in his chest. The dagger lay in his limp hand, his strength used up in the fight to yank it loose.

Meeryn snatched it up with a hasty glance at the downed enforcer, just long enough to notice the fuzz browning his upper lip, the dark curls brushing his homespun collar. And his boots, they were . . . old. Cracked. A farmer's boots, not the soft-footed well-oiled soldier's garb. No knife at his waist, no red-tasseled scabbard, just a rusty musket and a billhook tucked in his belt.

"*Avaklos* will prove our loyalty once and for all. Do what Dromon's men could not."

The shout dragged her from the horrible truth. She spun in time to see Gray drop the man to the turf in a brutal attack that would have snapped a normal human's spine. His face was a mask of unrelenting concentration, but she could see he tired. His moves came slower, his reactions dulled by fatigue . . . and something else . . .

Shadows lengthened as the sun dropped beneath the horizon, bathing the glen in a blue and silver twilight. A hot wind stung her face. Gray screamed and staggered, his face stark and stretched tight as bone, his eyes burning with an icy fire. Flames seemed to ripple over his body, bathing him in an eerie phantasmal glow.

He dropped to his knees, doubled over, hands to his face as the wind and the flames wrapped him within their shrinking cocoon. Mother of All, he was shifting from man to aspect against his will. She watched as he fought the agony of it, muscles in his neck standing out as he refused the scream ripping its way up his throat.

His attacker shrank from the power, eyes wide with horror. "The black curse takes him over."

It was true. The Fey-blood's black spell was changing Gray, twisting him, stripping his soul bare for the world to see. Fey-blood magic curdled her insides and needled her brain. She wanted to be sick, her stomach rolling at the convergence of so much corrupted power.

Recovered from his initial shock, the man attacked with redoubled intent, striking with boots and fists, his fear and anger making him oblivious to anything but dealing death, his muttered curses emphasizing every blow. He never noticed Meeryn until the dagger slid through coat, waistcoat, and shirt to the vulnerable flesh just above his kidneys.

The knife made him pause, but whatever he saw in her face must have terrified him. "Don't make me drive it home," she said, her tone cold, her body colder. She forced her hand and her voice to steady. "It's a messy, painful end."

"You'd not dare," he muttered harshly through lips drawn back from his yellowed teeth in a grimace of rage.

"I was told once it grew easier every time."

He bent away from her blade, his hands opening and closing, his shoulders hunched. Then, just as she drew a shaky breath, he lashed out. His fist came up in a swift lunge meant to take her hard in the face. And just like that, she slid the blade deep, blood gushing hot over her hands as he fell in a ragged retching heap.

"You killed me," he called, tears blubbering down his fat cheeks.

"No, I saved *him*—again." She turned to Gray, but he was gone. All that was left was a bundle of clothes, a crush of matted grass and broken branches, and an eagle beating the air with great golden wings, heading east. When she looked back at the man, he lay quiet, eyes staring in his blue-lipped face, hands reaching for her as if he sought her help in his final moments. Not an enforcer. Not an Ossine whose death she could justify as a battle-scarred killer of innocents. This man had been a farmer, a clansman whose only crime had been believing the Arch Ossine's lies.

"What have I done?" She dropped the knife, seized by a horrible despair, sweat washing cold over her back, up her legs, making her knees buckle until she fell to the earth, tossing the knife away as if it burned her.

"You saved the last son of Idrin and the last hope for your people."

She came from out of nowhere, a girl of no more than eighteen or nineteen years, yet her gaze held timeless wisdom. She seemed to float across the grass, her cloak of crow feathers barely covering the milky shine of her skin, her lustrous dark curls framing a narrow elfin face. The sizzling sting of Fey magic pulsed the very air and made breathing difficult.

"You were at Deepings—the crow on Gray's ledge, the one watching me atop the battlements," Meeryn said.

"I am called Badb; a Fey of the Summer Kingdom once upon a time, though now I walk with duller company in a world infected by ordinary. Are you ordinary, Lady N'thuil?"

"I'm not a murderess, if that's what you mean. I don't kill people."

"What of the Fey-born at the inn? Or does he not count among your casualties?"

"He was . . . that is . . ."

"He was the enemy." The girl bent her gaze to the dead man at her feet, gave it a shove with one delicate slender foot. "As was this one."

"No," Meeryn answered sharply. "He was of the clans. An *avaklos*, yes, but he acted out of loyalty to the Imnada."

"He threatened de Coursy. That made him an enemy." The girl tossed her head, her cap of curls catching the dim moonlight, eyes fathomless. "Sir Dromon has been clever. He spread the word that our young heir murdered the Duke of Morieux. In this way the Arch Ossine wishes to salt the battlefield with fresh soldiers to his cause."

Meeryn shook her head, unable to erase the memory of her hand pushing the blade deep, the tear of tendon and muscle as it passed through him, the scrape of the blade against a vertebra or rib. His fading sobs as he bled out into the grass. This was not the thrill of her duel with Gray. There was no wild excitement as her blood sang in her veins, no leap of her heart as she scored a hit or parried a thrust. This was gruesome and ugly in its brutish savagery. She wiped her sleeve over her face, swallowed the bile and the disgust.

The Fey girl stepped closer, her cloak a ruffle of black on black shadows, her small white teeth bared. "You begged for this skill, Lady N'thuil. Did you think there would be no price to pay? That the ability to take a life was an idle pastime like sewing a seam or painting a watercolor? Your people stand at the brink of a war that will desecrate them, beyond anything your enemies might do to you. Gray is the link that will marry past to future—if he survives."

"If Sir Dromon's lies have spread throughout the clans, nowhere will be safe."

"There remain a few refuges. He flies to one now, a friend who will shelter him."

"Where has he gone?"

Badb smiled enigmatically. "The eagle will fly to see his swan."

# 10

MARNWOOD, DEVONSHIRE

Lips, warm, soft, and teasingly skillful, roused him from a nightmare of howling storms and billowing black seas. A gaze, golden as the sunrise, lit with pleasure as he opened his eyes, blinking up at his visitor in shock. And a stench like maggoty rancid meat mixed with Limburger cheese nearly had him retching in a corner.

"Wake up, sleepyhead." Her smile held bold amusement and more than a little mischief as she wafted the draught beneath his nose. "You've nearly slept the day away."

His heart lurched in his chest while his stomach turned ominously. Not the woman he'd been expecting. Not even close. He pushed himself up on the pillows, muscles groaning with stiffness, and his head foggy with more than exhaustion. "Where's Meeryn?"

He glanced around at the sparse whitewashed chamber as if she might be hiding behind a piece of furniture, except that there was no furniture, other than a bed, a chair, a battered washstand. A servant's garret rather than the royal suite. Rain drummed against the window, throwing blurry patterns across the walls. No surprise. It had been raining almost nonstop since they left the coast.

A hand on her hip, Lady Delia faced him down. "I should be insulted that the first sentence out of your mouth is a question about another woman." She huffed dramatically. "But if you must know, your exalted N'thuil is perfectly safe. Arrived in company this morning with everyone's favorite overbearing faery . . . and two dead bodies. Ugh!" She shuddered.

"Two dead . . . ? Do you mean . . ."

"Don't ask. If it were me, I'd have left them to rot, but Miss Munro seems to think they deserve better." She placed the cup on the washstand. Drew a silver-bladed knife from a pocket in her apron and laid it beside the cup. "You're fortunate we had the needed supplies in stores. All but for . . . you know." She wrinkled her nose.

"All too well." Gritting his teeth, he drew back the quilt, sat up, and put his feet on the floor. The room wobbled, and blue and silver flames licked at the edges of his vision. His skin crawled as if stretched too tight over his bones and the beast sank its razor beak into his brain, talons raking his lungs until it hurt to breathe. It was later in the afternoon than he thought.

"There was barely enough for a day's dose . . . perhaps two if you're cautious," Lady Delia explained.

"That will see me through until I return to London."

"Is that your plan? I thought resurrection lay in Cornwall."

"I brought it with me."

He stood, pausing as the room settled, then padded across the floor to the washstand. Delia followed his every move with arched brows and an appraising stare as if comparing the lover he'd been with the wreck of a man he'd become. Not that he cared overmuch what she saw or what she surmised. Their time together had been brief, both of them fully aware it was an arrangement built on expediency and loneliness. A way to forget for a few hours. A way to remember without weeping.

He took up the knife with a quick hiss of indrawn breath. Spread his left palm, drawing the blade across in a quick parting slice. Blood welled behind the cut. A tip of his hand and the drops slid into the cup of gelatinous phlegm. He tried not to think too hard as he swirled the elixir, put the cup to his lips, and downed it in one swallow. The draught, along with his stomach lining, sought to claw its way back up his throat. He shoved it down with a few swallows. Rested head bowed until the worst passed and the agony of the curse subsided.

"Better?" Delia asked.

"Than what?"

She laughed. "Fair point. But you're breathing, standing, and more or less coherent, so I'll term the whole a success."

He took up a towel, closed his hand to a fist around it until the bleeding stopped. Returned to his bed where fresh clothes had been laid for him. A little large and not the first stare of fashion, but clean.

As he dressed, she continued to regard him with a sly curve to her mouth that never boded well. "A little bird tells me you've inherited a dukedom."

"By English law, I'm a duke. By Imnada law, I'm as outcast as ever."

"Yes, the tale going round is that you're guilty of patricide. Or in your case grand patricide." She waved away the accusation as if it were a pesky fly not worthy of her attention. "Sir Dromon's a boob. Anyone who knows you knows such a story is laughable."

"That's just it. They don't know me. I left at twenty-one for the army and returned to a sentencing and exile. I'm a stranger to most of them. Sir Dromon could tell them I ate babies for breakfast and puppies for lunch and they'd believe him. The men who attacked us certainly did."

He pulled a shirt over his head, recalling Meeryn's accusations at the cottage. Her words had struck a little too close to home. Had he compensated for past weaknesses by armoring himself in callous indifference and calling it strength? Had he lost the use of his heart when he'd lost his clan mark? And was that what this recent horrible pain was in the left side of his chest? Had it come to life again upon the auspicious arrival of a little brown mouse?

"It's not the first time you've been struck with a complication in your plans," Delia countered.

A case in point standing right in front of him, Lady Delia was the definition of complication and synonymous with trouble. Always had been. She was the unexploded shell, the burning fuse. One wrong move, and who knew what chaos would follow. It's what made her so dangerous to enemies and friends alike.

"What happened to Calais?" he asked stupidly, drawing on a pair of breeches one slow leg at a time.

Lady Delia laughed. "Nothing, as far as I know. Why?"

"Aren't you supposed to be there?"

"I was. Unfortunately, just before I embarked, I discovered certain people might be waiting for me; people I'd rather avoid. With London lost to me and the ports guarded, I had one remaining choice—dismal in the extreme, but I soldier on as cheerfully as I can."

"Where *is* Estelle?"

"My tiresome crank of a sister was not happy to see me, but she couldn't very well kick me out of my own home, much as she'd have liked to. Our uncle left the house to both of us; the sly, conniving bastard."

"Let me guess, Ramsay convinced her you should stay."

"Actually, that luscious slice of man cake is away from Marnwood at the moment. No idea when he'll return. Probably why Estelle reluctantly agreed. If her husband had been here, I'd have been shown the door and given a boot besides."

"She doesn't trust you."

"I said she was tiresome. I never said she was stupid." Delia took a slow seductive turn about the room, letting her figure speak for itself, now and then casting him sidelong glances from lowered lashes. Her hand caressed the curve of the washbasin, slid provocatively along the chair rail, trailed with delicious eroticism along the headboard of the bed.

Had she always been so obvious, or was he seeing her differently now that he was comparing her to another woman; just as fierce and equally as bold? But Meeryn would never play for his attention. She was as bluntly candid as Delia was cleverly subtle. She offered him painful honesty but expected no less from him in return. And perhaps that in part was what held him back; for real honesty brought with it an agony as excruciating as the pain the curse delivered.

"Doule is dead, as is his brother," he said, ignoring her invitation. "The Ossine discovered them."

Delia's face dimmed. "I know. I'm sorry."

"This fight is tearing the clans apart. Brother against brother. Father against son. I sometimes wonder if it's worth it. Am I doing this for them . . . or me?"

She brushed the hair from his forehead, a slight frown marring her otherwise serene features. "You're tired. Rest. Regroup. Enjoy Estelle's dubious hospitality. You'll see things better in the morning."

They both heard the footsteps at the same moment. Their heads swiveled to the door in unison, their bodies tensed with the same anticipation. Delia was quicker. She leaned forward, offering him full view of both perfect breasts. Tipped his chin up and kissed him just as the door opened.

Meeryn stood on the threshold, mouth agape, gaze moving from shock to smolder in the blink of an eye.

Delia broke away with a cat-in-the-cream smile. "Did you need something, my dear?"

The heat off Meeryn's body was enough to char bones to ashes, but her expression, once mastered, was bland as milk. "Nothing at all," she answered in a voice calm as the eye of a hurricane.

Gray closed his eyes on a defeated sigh. Shit.


They had placed the makeshift pyre far from the house in an old wooded copse where weather-worn trees twisted in the wind and the rocks pushed grasping fingers up toward a gray sky. The road wound far to the east, crossing the new bridge outside the village. Foot travelers never came this way. The wood was said to be haunted by the spirit of a dead child, though the only hostile ghoul stalking this afternoon was Badb, who sat atop a nearby tree preening her feathers and croaking criticisms like a persnickety schoolmarm.

Meeryn ignored the crow's ugly chatter and concentrated on the two bodies laid out before her. She had no names to offer the ancestors. But she'd gathered up the few personal items she'd found in their pockets, and these she'd wrapped in scraps of silk and placed beside them.

Meeryn was no Ossine. What she did, she did from memory. She prayed that the Mother Goddess would understand if she made a small error or forgot bits of the funeral chant. First she traced the runes at head and foot, the sign of the Mother, the sign of Morderoth's empty sky. Then, dipping her finger in a bowl of wood burnt down to ash, she drew the death sign on each forehead, the spirit sign on each chest, and the sign of the Gateway on each palm.

Finally, calling on the ancestors to open the door between this world and the distant paradise where the souls of the dead *avaklos* would join their clan and kin forever after, she shoved the burning torch into the dry tinder stacked and arranged around the bodies. Flames licked up through the rickety platform and smoke curled like wraiths over the dead men.

This was the second time in a few days that she'd had to speed the dead through the Gateway, the second time in a few days she'd had to watch flames reach for the sky, spirits rising with the thick choking black smoke. She prayed there would be no need for a third.

Badb flapped her great black wings, croaking her dismay.

"If all you're going to do is squawk, do it elsewhere. I'm not interested."

Badb gave one final harrumphing caw and took off from her perch to circle the smoke as it wafted up to be lost within the low clouds.

"I think you offended her."

"I wasn't talking to her."

Gray approached to stand beside her, but she kept her eyes on the burning pyre, resin snapping, heat burning her face, sweat trickling down her rigid spine.

"I came to join you as witness to their passing."

"Then more witnessing and less chattering." She gripped her skirts, the fabric anchoring her in the present lest her memory wander back to the sickening give of flesh, the smell of blood and piss and loosened bowels, the rattle of the man's dying breath.

"You did what you had to do, Meeryn. You took a life to save a life."

"So I was told, but does that make it right?" she asked.

"It might help you sleep."

"How do you know I'm not sleeping?"

"Because I still remember the first man I killed."

"But the *avaklos* wasn't my first. There was the man at the inn . . ."

"A kill from a distance is not the same. I don't know why, but when you're close enough to smell your enemy's fear and feel his dying shudder, it becomes part of you. He's no longer an anonymous stranger. He's real. His death is your death."

She looked at him for the first time since he'd come. His face held a grim resignation, illness, injury, grief, and determination branded onto his features as once his clan mark had branded his back. "You said the more you kill, the easier it gets. That you learn not to care. That it's all about survival. That's what you said. But is that true? Or do you try to convince yourself of your indifference in order to feel better? Or to feel nothing at all?"

"I kill because I've been left with no choice. If I stay my hand, I run the risk of having another lifted against someone I care about. Someone I love."

She'd accused him of disregarding the men who followed him, but perhaps the truth was that he cared too much . . . that he'd always cared too much. His grandfather had thought his compassion a weakness. Meeryn believed it just might be Gray's greatest strength. If he let it be.

"You were prepared to murder those Ossine in the catacombs. Without hesitation. Without remorse."

"Without hesitation, yes. But always with remorse," he replied.

By now the pyre was engulfed, the bodies lost to the roaring conflagration, sparks floating and rising in the air, dancing on the steady breeze. Spirits called to a home lost at the beginning of time.

He drew an uneven breath, and she tensed, knowing what was coming. "Lady Delia enjoys tossing oil on a fire to see what happens."

Her eyes stung and watered from the intense heat. They most certainly did not ache with unshed tears for the sneaking rat bastard beside her. She wiped her face with the back of her hand. "Things burn. People get hurt. That's what happens."

"Or people finally start to see what's been staring them in the face all along."

He clasped her tear-streaked hand, and together they said farewell to warriors fallen in a war that had grown more violent and far more personal than Meeryn had ever imagined.

Marnwood's drawing room was lovely, with pale green walls, white trim, rich elegant furniture and priceless works of art. A far cry from the rest of the house, which gave the impression of being one strong wind from collapse. All right, perhaps she exaggerated, but there was definitely a sense that money was scarce and the household diminished.

Their hostess, Lady Estelle Ramsay, ran the place with few servants and a forthright capability that brooked no nonsense. To look at her slender body and gentle face, one would never imagine she could harbor such pragmatic industriousness, but in the two days Meeryn had been in residence, she'd found Lady Estelle nailing down a loose floorboard in the dining room, bringing in the wash, and weeding the kitchen garden. Not exactly the duties of a gently bred earl's daughter, but she undertook them without complaint and with a proficiency gained over many years.

This was someone who knew what she wanted and went after it without worrying over repercussions. Apparently a trait she shared with her sister Lady Delia Swann, though this seemed to be all the sisters shared.

Estelle was tall and possessed an unfashionable athleticism, while Delia was petite and bore an ethereal vagueness. Estelle's white-blond hair and freckled cheeks gave her the appearance of a hoydenish farm girl; Delia's hair was golden as ripened barley and her pert face and creamy complexion gave her a sweet kittenish quality. And while Estelle was safely and happily married, Delia was little better than a dcmi-rep, her string of lovers as long as Meeryn's arm. One would have been hard put to realize they were related, much less twins. Until they opened their mouths, that is. Then the constant bickering and inside sniping gave them away.

It made Meeryn almost happy she'd never had the dubious pleasure of a sibling.

This morning, Marnwood's elegant drawing room with its pristine woodwork and fashionable air of dignified aristocracy had become a militaristic war room with a map spread on the rosewood table alongside a packet of correspondence. The sisters too had taken a battle footing, though it was hard to tell whether they were more interested in fighting the enemy or each other. They spent the time either glaring at each other, pointedly ignoring each other, or in overt argument.

Gray stood at a window with a view of the carriage drive, jaw taut, eyes hard. It was like watching Wellington at work as he guided the discussion with a no-nonsense attitude, skillfully moving the conversation along despite the squabbles. Now and then his eyes sought hers, and she was struck with the same skin-prickling anticipation she felt when the wind freshened with the scent of rain and low black-bellied clouds flickered with lightning as they pushed their way across the whitecapped sea. Something had

changed between them in the wood as they watched
the flames grow and then die. Too early to tell where
it might lead, too young not to be killed by an errant
chill or a clumsy misstep.

"Has there been any word of Kelan and the boy?"
Gray asked.

"Not yet, but he's a competent soldier," Estelle answered. "He'll find his way through."

Meeryn recalled her last sight of the earnest young
enforcer and his broken charge. Gray's lips pressed
together, deep grooves biting into the edges of his
mouth. No doubt he was remembering as well and
giving the pair up for lost.

"I believe I heard our feathered Fey friend talk of
searching for them," Delia said with an airy wave of
her hand. "At least she's gone off somewhere and good
riddance. She gives me the willies with those eyes that
see right through you."

"She'd have to scrub after such a probing of your
filthy mind," Estelle snapped.

"Have we heard from Lord Deane on Skye?" Gray
asked, heading off another argument.

Even in the wilds of Cornwall, Meeryn had heard
of the powerful Earl of Deane. It was said he had the
ear of the Prince Regent himself, though his influence
at court had been sorely tried by his marriage to an
actress off the London stage. But not all Lord Deane's
power was based in wealth and patronage. He bore the
blood of the Fey in his veins and the magic of their
realm lay at his command. A valuable ally when their
worlds teetered on the brink.

"As far as we know, he's still in talks with the Amhas-
draoi," Estelle answered like the good aide-de-camp

she seemed to be. "Unfortunately, St. Leger's recent visit to the fortress at Dunsgathaic didn't exactly leave a good first impression. I believe irresponsible, dangerous, and devious scoundrel were the most commonly used words used to describe him."

"He sounds positively delectable," Delia purred. "I wonder how I let him slip through my fingers." She tapped one manicured finger to her lips. "Perhaps there's still hope."

"He's married."

"Even better. They're the easiest to seduce, my dear," Delia said with a pointed look toward her sister.

Estelle glared but refused to rise to the bait. Smart woman. It was obvious Delia ached for a catfight. "Word from Lord Carteret's holding in the north is that the clan leader is uninterested in pursuing a bid for Morieux's throne. But he's also uninterested in pushing out Dromon's Ossine."

Gray nodded. "Makes sense. He's old and his son and heir is young, barely out of shortcoats. There's nothing to gain and everything to lose should he back the wrong side in this. He'll wait and watch and announce his loyalties to whomever comes out on top."

"And then there's . . . ah . . the news from London"—Lady Estelle cleared her throat, clearly uncomfortable—"another murder of a shapechanger."

"It won't be the last while the Ossine hunt those whose loyalty is suspected."

"True, but . . . ah . . . this Imnada was murdered by a Fey-blood."

Meeryn felt her breath catch in her throat. This was a painful reminder that while Gray may have surrounded himself with Other who spoke of peace between the races, there were factions who wanted only Imnada deaths and Imnada blood.

Gray's head came up, every sense alert. "What happened?"

"We don't know. All we have are sketchy reports. Nothing we can verify. That's where Jack's gone. To see what more he can learn."

Delia rose in a lazy sinuous spectacle of shapely limbs and tossed smiles. "I hope my brother in law doesn't fall foul of his former cronies. It could get ugly."

Estelle stiffened, crumpling the letter in a tight fist. "Jack's a big boy, and Nelson Skaytes is dead."

Delia's smile held all the warmth of a cobra. "But there are plenty of his wretched gang left to offer payback." She drew a line across her throat. "He might be walking into a trap."

Estelle paled, her gaze narrow, her lips pressed white. "You'd like that, wouldn't you?"

"You're my sister. I want your happiness. If a base-born criminal is what brings it, fine. Just don't say I didn't warn you when it comes crashing down around your ears."

The woman was completely shameless. Meeryn imagined shifting to a tiger aspect and biting the pretty little trollop's head clean off. She met Estelle's eyes and knew her hostess was having similar violent thoughts.

Lady Estelle drew a deep breath and forced her gaze and her attention from her sister and back to the letters in front of her. Pulled the last one free and held it out to Gray. "This one arrived from Captain Flannery. The Ossine have ransacked your house in Audley Street. Torn it apart nearly down to the bare joists. They were there for more than murder."

"They search for Jai Idrish," Gray said, shooting Meeryn a look.

"The sphere is useless to Sir Dromon without me to guide the power," she replied.

"True, but the enforcer Thorsh was right—with your death, the crystal would search for another to bond with. And this time Dromon would make certain the N'thuil was one of his choosing."

"Then I suppose I'll just have to stay alive, won't I?"

"Easier said than done," Estelle commented. "By all evidence, Sir Dromon has given up any subtlety or pretense of defense. He's on the attack, and he's called on every Ossine enforcer he can muster to drive us into a corner."

A sudden horrible thought occurred to Meeryn, and she sat up, stomach knotting. "Are Captain Flannery and his wife safe? What of their son . . . surely the Ossine wouldn't . . . I mean, he's just a baby . . ."

"They would kill him if they found him," Gray answered. "He's a half-breed unmarked rogue. To Sir Dromon, he's an abomination and a threat to Imnada purity. By his way of thinking, the boy's death cleanses the clans of a weak link. He refuses to acknowledge that the chain itself is dwindling."

"The family is safe. For now," Estelle reassured them. "But it's just one more indication that we're falling back on every front. If the Fey-bloods are moving against the Imnada, it will be the final nail in the coffin of our hopes for peace. Sir Dromon will have all the ammunition he needs to persuade the clans to retreat behind the Palings. Any who oppose him will be outnumbered and silenced . . . starting with you."

Meeryn sat up. Then she stood up. "Unless Gray

assumes the Duke of Morieux's throne and takes his rightful place as ruler of the five clans."

Delia rolled her eyes, casting Meeryn a look as if she were a rather addlepated child. "Is that all he has to do? Why didn't we think of that before? Assume the throne, Gray. That is, if they let you within ten miles of the place before they stake you as *emnil* and feast on your carcass."

By now, the idea had taken root and none of Delia's sarcasm would shake it. Meeryn knew the answer. It was there right in front of them if only they would see it. "He wouldn't be *emnil* if he broke the curse."

That gained their attention, though with various shades of interest ranging from incredulity to indulgence.

"You said it yourself, Gray, in the catacombs. Until you break the curse, none of this matters. Not the clans or peace between the races. You'll be dead within six months and we'll be right back where we started."

Delia shot Gray a quizzical look which he ignored.

"The curse is the answer to everything. Once your bloodline is restored, your sentence of exile would be overturned by the Gather. You could take your place as Morieux."

"You think Sir Dromon will just let that happen?" Delia snapped.

"No, he'll do everything in his power to stop it. But once Gray is duke in fact as well as name, there's nothing Sir Dromon can do to him or any of his followers."

"She might have a point . . ." Estelle hedged.

Deila's laughter was brittle and ugly. "On the top of her head, perhaps. But it's madness to think Gray will break the curse before Dromon breaks him."

Gray shook his head, gaze locked on some distant inner thought. "I have the Gylferion. I have Jai Idrish."

Lady Delia sniffed. "Four useless hunks of metal and an old rock."

Meeryn bristled. "Jai Idrish is more than an old rock."

"Is it? Then prove it. Break the damned curse. Save his bloody life before the black magic tears him apart bit by excruciating bit."

"I would if I could," Meeryn said quietly.

"My point exactly. You're as useless as your rock."

"Delia . . ." Gray cautioned.

But the woman had stood up in a fluster of furious skirts and black looks. "Excuse me. I have better things to do than talk pointless blather about a future as bleak as this dreary house in the middle of nowhere."

She stormed out of the room, for once no sashay, no saunter, not even a backward glance to see the kind of effect she might be having on her audience.

"Is she right, Gray? Is it hopeless?" Estelle asked, breaking into the jagged silence left in her sister's wake.

"You underrate my motivation," he replied.

"No, I see all the pieces and I worry. Just as Delia does." She turned her gaze to Meeryn, questions clouding her clear golden-brown eyes. "Can Miss Munro really help you, or have you only brought more trouble down on your head with her defection and the stone's theft?"

Gray bowed his head, hands clenched. "Meeryn just might be the only one who can help me."

"Break the curse?"

"That too," he said gently.

*        *        *

He heard her before he saw her; the rustle of leaves, the snap of a twig, a mucky slosh followed by a muffled oath. She wasn't exactly subtle, but she was intrepid. He stared up at the setting moon for strength. Down into the pool where the moon's mirror image floated amid the water lilies.

She broke through the underbrush into the glade, twigs in her hair, a smudge down one cheek. Skirts trailing mud. "Found you."

"Didn't know I was lost."

She ducked under a branch, pushing the leaves out of her way as she stepped across the grass. "Only hiding. I don't blame you. I'd not be surprised if our hostesses started shelling each other with dinner rolls."

She glanced up at the moon, her face an alabaster disk against the dark. Night sounds surrounded them, the scrabble of small creatures emerging, the hoot of an owl in the far wood. Moths brushed by him, their wings soft as a whisper.

"Did you mean what you said earlier?" Meeryn asked, kneeling to trail her hand in the water. The moon fractured and dissolved.

"I say a lot of things. According to David and Mac, I'm very good at long-winded speeches and self-righteous declarations."

She glanced over her shoulder at him. "You do have a knack for sounding a bit Henry the Fifth from time to time. But I was referring to the bit about my helping you."

"Break the curse?"

She rose, shaking out her skirts. "Among other things."

He breathed in the humid scents of summer; the dripping foliage, the pungent fragrance of moss and fern, the brackish odors off the still water of the pond. A long-ago conversation came back to him—he amended that—argument was more like it. David St. Leger always tended to bring out the priggish worst in Gray. It was as if he had to counter St. Leger's reckless irresponsibility by being doubly staid and three times as dull.

They'd been arguing about women. Come to think on it, most arguments with David tended to be about women. Before his improbable marriage to Callista, David had sought any female with the proper parts to forget the wreckage of his life for a few blissful hours. Gray had wanted more, yet known that way was lost to him as long as he lived under the Fey-blood's spell. Now perhaps he stood on the edge of breaking free of the curse's chains. If that was so, his last argument was no longer valid. He would have to face his fears . . . if he dared.

"His Grace warned me about you," Meeryn said, her voice overloud against the country silence.

"'That I'd pull you into my war willing or not?" He snapped off a twig, stirred the water to create a miniature whirlpool. The ripples pushed outward across the surface to break and lap at the far edges before gliding back to him.

"Perhaps in part. But I think he realized how much I missed you when you left for the army all those years ago. Perhaps he worried your return would reawaken old affections. Make me vulnerable to old heartbreak."

He reached the stick farther but never struck bottom. No telling how far down it went. How dangerous the depths. "We were friends, Meeryn. Nursery play-mates."

"You were twenty-one. I was seventeen. I'd hardly call us babes in the cradle."

He let the stick go. It fell with a soft splash, lazing away across the pond like a slow snake. "But we never . . . I never . . ."

"No, you never did, did you? I always wondered why. None would have faulted us. We were promised. Ossine-blessed. It would have been as natural as the ocean's tides, but you always kept your distance. You were never anything less than the perfect gentleman."

"Were you looking for a rake who'd steal your maidenhead? Did you find it with McIlroy?"

He felt her tense, saw the lines crease her brow. "Conal was handsome and charming, and I was passionate and angry. It made for a combustible combination. But I knew it couldn't last. The Ossine had already chosen my destined mate and it wasn't the second cousin to Owen Glynjohns, no matter how well connected he was nor how secure his future." She held his gaze, her expression one of resignation. "Nor how much he cared for me. When your grandfather sent him away, I was sad, but not surprised."

"The duke should have let you have your husband. He'd have been dandling younglings on his knees. He'd have had a new family to replace the one he lost."

"And you'd have been let off the hook. Freed from the chain you thought was wrapped round you like an anchor."

"That's madness." He snapped off another stick, but this one fought back. It broke with a jagged spray of splinters, one catching him below the eye. He felt the sting and the drip of hot crimson down his cheek.

"Is it? Or is it that you couldn't take what wasn't yours by right, Gray? Not your brother's title. Not your brother's intended. That's why you left without saying good-bye. That's why you stayed away so long. And that's why you won't look at me now. I'd always thought it was that stupid, foolish letter I wrote you. But it wasn't, was it? You'd already made up your mind to avoid Deepings . . . and me. The army was just a convenient escape."

He said nothing. There was nothing he could say.

"Look at me, Gray. Ollie is dead. He's gone. So, look at me."

He kept his eyes upon the glade.

"Look at me, damn it!"

He swung around to face her. She leaned against the bole of an old tree, its trunk misshapen, its branches spread low and wide like open arms. Like a ghost, she gleamed lithe and white in the gloom of the glade's shadows, her hair spilling free of its pins, her feet bare of their slippers.

"Did you mean what you said tonight," she repeated. "Can I help you?"

He couldn't tear his gaze from her as she stepped toward him, the moon's soft glow haloing her in silver, throwing stars into her dark eyes. He saw her chest rise and fall and knew she was not as cool and collected as she wanted to seem. He scented the rush of blood to the surface of her skin. Felt her desire.

She lifted a hand, wiping the cut on his cheek with the soft pad of her thumb. "Do you need me?"

He clasped her wrist, feeling the race of her pulse, seeing the darkening of her eyes as she moistened her lips, uncertain but not afraid. He leaned down, his lips against her neck, the taste of her like wine. "Yes."

The woods were quiet and dark, as was the house. Entering through an unlocked door into a small parlor, they held each other's hands as they crept through silent rooms muffling their laughter and jumping at shadows. Meeryn felt fifteen again. Sure that she and Gray would be discovered any moment and sent to their beds without supper for sneaking out to the barns to drink stolen brandy and smoke cheroots.

Up the creaking stairs, past a corridor of closed doors. His hand in hers was rough and strong, his expression grim as if every floorboard were a potential enemy. At the gallery, she paused. If she were fifteen, this was where she'd wait for . . . what? She hadn't known at the time. Only that her body yearned for something only Gray could give her. Her skin would tingle, her heart would beat loud as a drum beneath her ribs, and she'd feel an aching pull between her legs. She would watch him, expectant, afraid, then disappointed as he slid free of her with a last fading grin and perhaps a brotherly peck on the cheek.

"Second thoughts?" he whispered now, brows furrowed, confusion flickering in his bright gaze.

Drawn back to the present, she shook her head and smiled as he drew her toward him for a long, deep, toe-curling kiss.

"I can't offer cheroots, but I do have brandy," he said as if reading her thoughts. He guided her up the stairs to the attics and his whitewashed garret far from attentive ears or nosy neighbors.

The room was small and sparse, making the bed loom large as a ship of the line. Gray poured her a drink which burned all the way down. Another which made her woozy and warm. She noticed absently that he merely sipped at his, swirling the liquid round and round just as he'd watched the water in the glade, curling back in upon itself in an endless set of ripples.

She took the glass from his hand. Stepped close so that their bodies touched, her breasts pressed against his chest, her chin tipped to meet his gaze. He stood, arms at his side, pupils black as sin surrounded by glacier-blue irises. An expression of mingled desire and determination so obvious it made her want to laugh—or weep.

She touched the scar at the edge of his mouth. First with her fingertips, then with her lips. "It frightens me to think what might have happened had I been even a few minutes later."

"I'm not sure which shocked me more, the fact that you stopped me or the fact that a thirteen-year-old girl had a right cross strong enough to fell an ox." He closed his hand around hers, drawing it gently away from a reminder of an old shame, slanting his gaze from her face to the window and the shadows beyond the glass.

"Killing yourself wouldn't have brought them back, Gray," she said. "It wouldn't have changed the past."

"It would have ended the pain and the guilt. Penance for my sins." His eyes burned, but no tears blurred his vision. No useless weeping or pointless sobs, though he shuddered with more than the breeze on his damp flesh.

"Your only sin was being fourteen and impatient for a promised birthday excursion."

"I know that now."

"Do you? I wonder." She traced the brittle lines of his face, the tight seam of his mouth, the hard edge of his jaw. "Your grandfather refused to let them go. You refuse to acknowledge they ever existed. Neither way seems to have brought anything but grief."

He drew a breath into his lungs, clearing away the ache. Turned his shaky sigh into shaky laughter. "Trust me, Meeryn. No more knives."

She lifted a brow in question as she traced a fingernail over the silver scars on his palm.

"A different case entirely," he said, closing his fingers around the evidence of his deadly addiction. "That knife saves me."

"And kills you at the same time."

His lips curved in an acknowledgment if not a smile.

She cupped his face in her hands, forcing him to look at her. "Listen to me, Gray. You can't forgo your life to atone for Ollie's death. You can't simply ignore the truth about who you are and about . . . about what we meant to each other because of a tragedy that happened almost twenty years ago."

He placed his hands to either side of hers, palms roughened by work and by battle, a pulse beat in his neck, his jaw tightened under her touch.

"And now that I've got you treed and trapped, I refuse to let you escape me so easily a second time," she added. "I've waited a long time for this, thank you very much."

"So have I."

This time he bent down and kissed her. A stomach-plunging kiss that exploded through her like lightning. She melted into him as if their bodies had fused, no part of her wanted space or air or inches to separate them. Just before she must breathe or faint from suffocation, he backed up a step, leaving her body chilled, though sweat dewed her skin. He reached around her to unclasp the buttons of her gown . . . one . . . two . . . three . . . she shivered at each inch of skin he exposed. Each kiss he dropped behind her ear, the base of her throat, her collarbone, until her bodice and his lips ended at her waist, skirts sliding off over her hips to puddle on the floor. He stood once more, cupping her breasts, the pad of his thumb running over the sensitive flesh, budding her nipples until they ached. His kiss was sweet and tasted of the brandy they'd drunk and he smelled wild of the glade and the summer heat and the masculine scent of his golden skin.

She skimmed his coat from his shoulders, pulled free his neckcloth, started on his waistcoat when he turned her so that she stood facing the bed. She braced her arms against the bedpost as his breath fell warm on her neck and her shoulders, his cock nestled against her rear. She gasped, moving into the feel of him, but he held her away, his fingers deftly unlacing her corset. She had never realized how erotic being undressed could be. It was like being unwrapped a delicious inch at a time. Every sensation heightened, every moment increased to a seismic shift. The slide of the loosened cord, his fingers against her back, the ripple of pleasure up her spine and into her scalp, the small gasps escaping her lips, the roaring of blood in her ears—all worked together to push her temperature higher. She felt her face go hot, her body ignite, her sex contract in a sweet throbbing pain.

The corset ended atop the gown, followed quickly by the chemise. Gray took his time as he traced the crescent of her clan mark, his hand slipping up over her shoulder as he followed the curling tattooed spiral of the N'thuil. Sweat sheened her skin and she shivered as he licked it from her neck. He lapped down the column of her spine, his tongue gliding long and curving sweeps of desire down over her buttocks, his hands coming around to touch her breasts, skim her ribs, brush the hair between her legs before his fingers plunged deep.

She gasped, arching against him. Flames erupted along her nerves. She gripped the bedpost, knuckles white as she dropped her head back against his chest, her hair loosened to spill around them both. *Clothes . . . damn clothes . . . take them off . . . NOW . . .*

He chuckled. *I love a woman who knows what she wants*, he pathed, straight from his mind to hers on a ribbon of steamy thought. His sultry, deep voice acted like molten honey melting along her already boneless limbs. She could ride that voice all the way to damnation.

The scrish of fabric and the rising scent of man, and the air grew hot as a furnace. He stood behind her, body like an inferno. Nothing between them but their own ghosts. He nuzzled her as he cupped her close, his erection sending jolts of wild electricity along every frazzled nerve ending. She wanted him inside her, wanted him deep and fast and hard. She let him know with a shift and wiggle of her hips that left him panting.

He obliged, bending her over the bed, taking her from behind, thrusting until she moaned his name. Until the animal inside her writhed, biting and clawing to escape. She felt claws and fangs extend, felt blood boil in a wild lava flow that pooled deep in her knotted stomach. His teeth grazed her shoulder, sank into her skin. He thrust harder, every push weakening her knees, weakening her hold on the human part of herself.

Her heart stopped. Her breathing stopped. She paused at the topmost swing of the pendulum before exploding outward along rivers of fire. She was falling, knees buckling, body tumbling, pleasure something she could touch and feel.

He dragged her onto the bed, rolled her onto her back, and paused above her. Now the glacier blue was swallowed by the black of desire. He was as much animal as she. The spirit of the Imnada burned like a flame under his skin. He spread her legs and took her again. Watching her, face intense and unblinking as an eagle's. His predator stare moved over her like the killing edge of a sword, searching for weakness, tempting her with its danger.

She smiled, feeling a wickedness she never knew lived inside her. She wrapped her legs around his waist, tilting her hips to bring him deeper, the friction winding her tight as a watch spring or the cock of a pistol. They found a rhythm of escape, of desire, of need, of lust. He groaned her name as she arched once more, and he spilled himself inside her. A thrust and then another, and she was with him, driven up then crushed beneath the same cresting wave.

Aftershocks sizzled through her, giddy reminders of her climax, and she held him close as her brain was poured back into her lifeless, spent body.

They lay quiet for a long time until finally, when she could move again and her limbs stopped wobbling and her head stopped spinning, she kissed him, her hand splayed over his chest where she might feel his heart like the steady beat of a drum. "I should go before anyone wakes."

"And if I don't want you to leave?" His arm tightened around her.

"Gray . . ."

"Right. Proprieties must be met. We're not on holding lands anymore and this world is unforgiving of such lapses."

"That's not what I meant."

He skimmed his knuckles up and down her rib cage, sending new shivers along her spine. "Then stay at least until dawn, when I know . . ." He looked to the window where the dark crouched close. "Stay until the sun comes up."

She sensed his uneasiness and nodded.

Gray's body moved beneath hers, just that slight brushing of skin on skin enough to set new fires where the old ones still smoldered. His gaze lit with something alive and mysterious as if he meant to speak. But the voice erupting like a volcano in her head was that of Badb, shrill with anxiety and alarm.

*He is here! He needs help! He needs you!*


He was twice as formidable and three times as frightening as Meeryn could ever have imagined. It was as if a page from Gray's moldy history had taken human form. Lucan Kingkiller, the Traitor Lord, radiated power and strength and wisdom in equal measures, but it was the sadness she saw in his eyes that kept her from shrinking into a corner in abject awe. He might be a legend sprung from her darkest nightmares. He was still a man who'd suffered loss and agony enough to turn most people to jabbering idiots. Yet he stood proud and tall and untouched by madness.

At least she hoped he was sane.

Blood-streaked and vibrating with unspent rage, it was difficult to determine.

"I found the boy high in a tree hidden among the branches. He must have climbed there, hoping the fight would pass him by. There was no sign of Kelan."

Gray ran tired hands down his face before plowing them into his hair. And for a moment, the sadness in his eyes matched those of the ancient war leader Lucan. "They wouldn't have been merciful to an Ossine caught in such treachery."

"No," Lucan replied.

Meeryn offered a silent prayer to the Mother for the repose of the young enforcer's soul.

"A party of Ossine backtracked, and I was forced to flee with the lad. They thought they had us cornered south of Okehampton but I drew them onto the moors and sprang their trap. None are left to report back to Su Dromon. The Gateway swings wide tonight."

The way he explained bloodshed and battle was like listening to a recounting of grain prices or the latest rainfall predictions. The gore and the violence, the blood and the horror fell between the syllables, but Meeryn felt them tremor the air just the same. He spoke none of it. He felt it all.

Badb moved from the corner where she'd settled like a black wraith amid the gloom. "And how do you think you would have fared had the Ossine captured you? The boy wasn't worth your life, Lucan. He wasn't worth the enforcer's life," Badb complained, her cloak of feathers a restless cloud around her white face, black eyes shot with anger.

"For once, I agree with Badb. It was needless risk for little reward," Lady Delia said, managing to look coquettishly beautiful even dragged from her bed at two in the morning.

Lucan offered her a tired smile. "Yet, how do we know who will play the greatest role in this story unfolding? A kingkiller . . . or a ragged broken boy?"

Badb sniffed, displeasure evident. With a shimmering sparkle and a furl of feathers, the girl was gone; all that remained was the Fey's magic lifting the hair at the back of Meeryn's neck and along her arms. The Fey's answer tingled uncomfortably across the surface of Meeryn's mind. *The answer's in the blood.*

"Should you go after her?" Gray asked.

"It's best to let her be for now. No matter how long she has lived within this world, we must remember she is not of it. And to her, the emotions bound up in our existence are difficult to comprehend."

"Or just maybe, she's lived so many eternities in this world, emotion is all she understands," Lady Delia suggested with an arch look toward Lucan. "What do you suppose she did for all those centuries you were lost in the prison of the void between realms? A thousand years of going without is bound to tie anyone in knots."

"Delia," Gray warned.

"Yes, Major?" She sat back, her robe sliding free to expose one long leg and the curve of her hip. Her gaze passed between Gray and Meeryn with a knowing lift of her brows and cynical twist of her lips. "As I was saying, going without can tie anyone in knots."

Meeryn refused the blush stealing to her face. She would not be ashamed, and she would not show this harpy of a woman she cared what she bloody well thought.

Thank the Mother of All, Lady Estelle bustled into the drawing room and the moment passed, though Meeryn caught a continuing look of both consternation and irritation on Delia's face. Another fuse lit, another bomb tossed. But who would suffer the most when the unavoidable explosion occurred?

"He's sleeping." Still dressed in wrapper and nightgown with her hair in a loose plait over her shoulder, Lady Estelle wiped her hands on a towel, face pale but satisfied. "Imprisonment has left him weak, but he's young. That should count in his favor."

"Does anyone know who he is?" Meeryn heard herself ask. "Or if he has family we should write to?"

"I do," Gray said wearily. "His name's Jamie Wallace. His father's Imnada. His mother's human."

"An out-clan marriage."

"A loving marriage. He left home last winter, and wasn't heard from again. His father came to me for help but there was little I could offer him but hypotheses."

"Sir Dromon had him imprisoned all this time?"

"His insignificance worked both for him and against him. As an unmarked rogue, he was nothing to the Ossine. Not even worth killing. They must have tossed him into the catacombs assuming he might give them information and when he didn't . . ."

"They left him to rot." Shivers hunched her shoulders. An hour spent in those catacombs had been too much time. Imagining Jamie's horror at being sent down there to die brought tears to her eyes.

"He bears the power of the Imnada," Lucan's voice was deep and gruff as if unused to speaking. A thousand plus years alone would make anyone tight-lipped. "Like the Flannery's baby, he's one of us no matter his lack of mark or signum."

Gray leaned against a table, boots crossed at the ankle. Arms crossed at the chest. "He's stronger in some respects, for he bears new blood carried through his mother. Young Declan is the same. This is what the Imnada lost when we retreated behind our walls. This is the legacy of generations in hiding."

"We all used to look like *him*?" Meeryn asked skeptically with a sideways glance at the dark Goliath standing in the corner.

Lucan's face softened. "Even in my time, I was considered a bit beyond the ordinary. But it is true what de Coursy claims, the Imnada clans lose much when they cut off the outside. Even one who considers himself the most pure of blood probably has an out-clan ancestor somewhere in his roots. The walls had yet to be built when I led the clans. Fey, Other, Imnada, human, all moved within each other's lives."

"Until the massacres of the Fealla Mhòr," Meeryn said.

His eyes clouded. His softness vanished back into a granite indomitability. "Aye. Until the Fealla Mhòr. That's when the peace unraveled and the world shattered. I would give all to restore what I tore apart."

"Penance for your sins," Meeryn muttered under her breath.

Gray turned toward her. Her legs nearly buckled under the weight of his spearpoint stare and her skin prickled with icy goose bumps until she had to look away.

It was then she noticed Lady Delia watching them—or rather watching Gray—her arms wrapped tight around her body as if warding off a chill, though the house was stifling even in the cool of predawn. The self-satisfied expression was gone and her golden eyes dimmed with some unknowable emotion. "Then again, there are some sins no amount of atonement can wipe clean," she said.

Lucan opened his bloodied fists, dropping his hands to his sides in surrender. "No, those we must simply endure."

# 11

"Can you really read this?" Meeryn studied the soggy, ink-smeared parchment spread on the table between them. Turned it upside down. Cocked her head to the left . . . to the right. Squinted at it. "It's just squiggles and lines."

Gray pulled the parchment from her with a sideways cut of his eyes and a smirk. "So is English when you come right down to it."

She sniffed. "Don't be obtuse. Just answer the question."

"Grandfather slipped up. He hired a weapons master to drill me in small arms who also happened to be a scholar of dead languages. This one was dead, buried, and forgotten. I learned how to shoot the spot off a target at twenty paces and to read and write ancient Carspethic."

"Lucky you," she said with a grimace.

The late-morning sun beat through the dusty windows, throwing golden squares across the table, sculpting the bones of Gray's face into sharp relief.

The swoop of his dark brows drawn in concentration, the smudge of ink alongside his nose, the curve of his sensual lips as he felt her stare.

"Did you come to gawk or do you have a reason for being here?" he asked without looking up from the pages of scribbled notes.

"I came to inform you that Lady Estelle says Jamie's awake and eating. He still resembles a walking bag of bones, but the corpsish overtones are definitely receding."

The muscle tightening his jaw jumped, and he closed his eyes for a brief moment.

"He's yet to speak of Kelan or . . . or what happened up on the moors," she continued.

"What of his months in the catacombs? Or the questions put to him by Dromon's enforcers?"

"I wouldn't dare ask. Would you?"

She didn't fail to notice the way he rubbed at his bandaged wrist nor the fading marks of his own imprisonment. "No."

She continued to watch as he worked, head bent over the page, a hand plowed into his thick hair. A hand that last night had touched her in ways she'd never been touched. Conal had been a considerate lover. Like the sea beneath a calm sky and a thousand stars; the slide of easy currents over her skin and the deep's sweet whispers in her ears. Gray was a lightning-shot, thunder-clouded tempest where one didn't know down from up and swirling tides and screaming winds threatened to smash her against the rocks or drag her down into the deepest ocean chasms.

Conal had been easy to love.

Loving Gray scared her to death.

"Anything else?" he asked, placing his pencil down, the notes in both English and ancient line and squiggle so much gibberish to her uneducated eyes.

She'd begged Gray to pass on his training in swordfighting and gunplay. Dead languages and ancient scholarship had never been her cup of tea. Another reason her choice for N'thuil made no sense. If Jai Idrish was the sum of Imnada wisdom from the beginning of time, what on earth could she add? How to best grip a dirk in your off hand? How to load and fire a flintlock?

She wished Idrin might speak to her again; reassure her that the crystal had not made a horrible mistake. Then she immediately rescinded the wish. She couldn't be sure she'd find Idrin at the other end of the sickening tumble into the blinding light at the crystal's heart. She might end among the stalking oily shadows instead. No way to tell. No way to control it.

She brushed aside her thoughts with a shudder. Met Gray's clear blue eyes with the fear firmly locked away. "He's . . . ah . . . very tall."

He pressed his lips together in an apparent attempt to keep from laughing. "I assume you're referring to Lucan, not Jamie."

She took up his pencil, rolling it between her fingers. "I'd heard rumors of his . . . return, of course, but really who expects to bump into the bogeyman in a Devonshire drawing room? It's disconcerting."

"How do you think he feels? The world he knew is gone. The world he's living in reviles him as a traitor and a murderer. Not exactly a fond homecoming."

"Yet you and he are . . . friends . . . comrades . . . it just seems so . . . that is, Sir Dromon accused you, but I never really believed it."

"You believed a legend came to life but not that I might put aside a thousand years of prejudice to find out the truth behind the monster. Is that it?"

"His is the hand behind the Fealla Mhòr."

Gray's amusement vanished behind a veneer of weary defeat, as if he'd had this same argument more times than he could count. "His is the hand that saved young Jamie Wallace and David St. Leger before him."

"Two lives against a slaughter of entire villages and holdings?"

"He doesn't ask for your forgiveness, Meeryn. He doesn't forgive himself. But he's no more a monster than we are."

He took back his pencil with a decisive this-discussion-is-over manner. Began scrubbing through earlier translations and rewriting them with much chewing of the pencil end and hard, painful stares at the page as if forcing the words to come.

"Why didn't you steal the entire book? Wouldn't it have been easier than trying to piece together these bits out of context?"

Gray shrugged. "Sir Dromon would have noticed the absence and questioned it. He might look like a clerk in a shop, but he's still a shaman of the Ossine. He's spent his entire life studying Imnada wisdom and practicing all our oldest ways. He knows Jai Idrish is in my possession. If he discovers I hold the Gylferion as well, it won't take him long to put the pieces together and know exactly what I plan."

"So, what does it say, Professor?"

His gaze flicked to hers and back down. "It's part of a chart outlining the properties of each disk; bronze, copper, silver, and gold. This bit down here describes

the maker of these disks; a Fey by the name of Golethmenes. He forged the Gylferion to bind Lucan
within the abyss of between for all eternity. A suitable
punishment, it was thought, for the man who betrayed
Arthur to his death."

"But Fey-blood magic doesn't work on Imnada. It
never has."

"Golethmenes made it work. I'm hoping that between this page and what I have in my own library, I'll
be able to shed some light on how and why it didn't
work when we tried it."

The fear was back, and this time there was no pre-
venting the shudder. It rolled down her spine into her
belly, where it curled ominously. "But your library is
in London . . . in a million pieces."

"A minor complication."

"And the Fey-bloods on the prowl? The Ossine enforcers searching for you? You'll be heading straight
into their waiting arms if you return to London. An
easy target."

"It can't be avoided. Marnwood is a short-term refuge at best. I can't hide away here forever."

She opened her mouth to protest, swallowed her
words at the unwavering glare from across the table.

"Even if I had all the answers in front of me, I'd still
need to travel to Town. In another day or two, I'll be
out of the draught. Without it, no amount of struggle
will prevent me from shifting at sundown and sunrise. And as the draught wanes in my system, I'll grow
weaker, sicker, less able to defeat Sir Dromon. Time is
everything."

She clamped her hands in her lap, over the hollow

frightened place in her gut. Clenched her jaw. Offered him a devil-may-care smile. "When do we leave?"

He laughed. "You're not coming. You're safe here at Marnwood and Estelle has said she would be glad of the company while Jack's away."

"Lady Delia less so."

"It will only be for a few days. A week or two at most."

"You rode away last time and stayed gone for ten years. How do I know you'll keep your word?"

"I need Jai Idrish."

She gritted her teeth on her look of complacency. "Of course."

He reached for her hand with a quick devilish grin. "I need Jai Idrish, Meeryn; I want you."


The book she found among Marnwood's less than stellar collection was thin, smelled more of printer's ink than old cheese, and . . . glory to the Mother . . . contained illustrations. Not hasty sketches but beautiful renderings done by a fine artist's hand. Curled into a reading nook set within a window, the light spilled across the pages and what had been a frightening bogeyman's tale when read in the quiet creepiness of the posting inn became a child's faery story. Yet, the facts remained sadly and inevitably the same no matter the state of the volume or the state of her mind; Lucan Kingkiller betrayed Arthur, conspired in his murder, and died upon the field of battle at Camlann.

Gray had told her the reasons for his alliance with the Fey-bloods could be found in the books with which he surrounded himself. All she found were tales of destruction, death, and demonization.

"You don't look hard enough."

She broke from her page-flipping to find the subject of her scholarship standing at a nearby window, staring out upon the park, hands behind his back—Lucan Kingkiller, the Traitor Lord, scourge of the five clans, himself.

She bit back an oath at being startled from her reading; few people could sneak up on her unawares. But the follow-up epithet over the man's obvious spying on her thoughts slipped out, a muttered "bloody hellfire."

It had been said that the ancients possessed the power to read as well as path. If this was an example of its use, she was very relieved it was a skill long lost to them.

He glanced over at her before returning to his study of the parkland beyond the glass. The room seemed suddenly smaller, the silence thicker, her mind afire with questions; the most all-consuming being . . .

"Why?" he said, his voice raspy but resonant, as if used to shouting over the ring of battle. "That's what you really want to know. Why did I betray my friend, and my king?" His gaze remained on the park, posture relaxed though hardly at ease. He didn't seem like a man who lounged about much. Perhaps a thousand and more years trapped in the hell of the Fey's between taught you to stay alert. "The people who wrote those stories believe I did it for love, that I was infatuated with Morgana's beauty, and perhaps I was for a time. She could be quite . . . persuasive."

"Sounds familiar," Meeryn grumbled under her breath.

His gaze slid toward her once more, but his expression never wavered. "It wasn't for Morgana, despite her obvious charms. I did it for the clans."

She sat up, untucking her legs, the finger smashed in the book going blue with the force of her grip on the binding. Now *she* was on edge.

Lucan continued as if he didn't notice her sharp interest or the way she caught her bottom lip between her teeth. But she knew he noticed. He saw everything; one could just tell. "There was peace between our peoples, but we were not *at* peace. Tensions ran high, and the constant mistrust kept true unity from flowering. We were so much alike, and yet we couldn't see past our differences. Mordred was a half-breed child of Imnada and Fey-blood. A ruler who might join Other and Imnada at the highest level. Something Arthur with all his talk of harmony could never do. He was too much a creature of the true Fey, and there has never been love between shapechangers and faery folk."

Hearing the most ancient fables treated like gossip around the village well was disconcerting to say the least. Arthur, Morgana, Mordred . . . Lucan . . . they were characters in a legend, not men and women who felt and acted like the people she knew and loved. The shamans spoke these names with respect, and, in some cases, loathing. Lucan spoke of them as if he were chatting about his neighbors.

"Mordred was a treacherous despot," she argued. "The stories all say so."

"He was a spoiled, selfish boy. And as you yourself just pointed out, the Fey-blood stories describing the Imnada as monsters and demons are wrong. Why shouldn't the stories the shapechangers told of the Fey-bloods be just as inaccurate?"

She didn't have an immediate answer for that one, though she was sure she'd come up with the perfect rejoinder about an hour from now.

"Mordred won the throne but he lost the kingdom," Lucan added sadly.

She sat up. "*You* won him the throne."

He bowed his head, not in shame, though she noted a tightening of his jaw, but as if he were lost in dark memories. A look she'd seen cross Gray's face more than once. A pensive, remorseful expression. "I did, and in so doing, I loosed an evil upon the world. My ideas of a greater peace became a nightmare of bloody war."

"Are you saying Gray is repeating your failure? That the Fey-bloods will never accept us?"

"If I believed that, I would not be aiding him. No, my failure came from arrogance and pride. I believed that I could impose peace between Fey-blood and shapechanger from above. That I, through Mordred, could decree it so and it would happen. De Coursy seeks to channel a groundswell and ride it to a new and real alliance. Look around you at Captain Flannery and his human bride; St. Leger married to a young Fey-blood. Jamie Wallace and the Flannery's son are half-breeds with powers as great as any marked Imnada of the clans. Lady Estelle and Lady Delia are Fey-bloods, young Kelan and the Doule brothers marked members of their clan and holdings—all of them bound by one cause. That is hope, Lady N'thuil. That is the future."

"And if the curse takes Gray? Will that future unravel?"

Lucan turned toward her, his gaze solemn. "Gray did not start this movement, but his position as heir to the five clans has forced him to the head of it. Should he die, it is likely our best chance for peace will die with him."

Lifting his head from his notes, Gray rubbed the space between his brows, the back of his neck, stretched the kinks until he cracked, but still the tension banded his body; a tightening grip he couldn't shake. Despite the dwindling afternoon sun, heat smothered the house, the air stifling as a wet blanket, the atmosphere charged like a held breath. For so many people in residence, it was oddly silent. He'd seen no one since Meeryn tried to press lunch on him. Heard no one since Estelle and Delia passed in the corridor, voices raised in argument.

He stood up, the rush of his rising causing blue and silver light to pinwheel across his vision. He staggered, banging his hip against the table, jarring the disks, the silver spinning away to the floor with a thud. Squeezing his eyes shut, he steadied himself until the episode passed, but it was a warning, as if he needed one, that his hours dwindled. Perhaps tonight he'd be safe. Perhaps even tomorrow, but there would be a time . . . very soon . . . when the curse would roar up from the dark horrible corner of his soul and take him over.

A life spent learning control—schooling features, masking hurts, refusing pain—had been obliterated in a cataclysmic hellfire of Fey-blood sorcery. He could no more control the shift than he could stop his lungs from filling or his heart from beating. A prisoner of the very power that made him Imnada.

"Lord Halvossa? Are you all right?"

Gray started to refuse the title as he'd always done, then looked up and saw Jamie Wallace watching him from the doorway. The long mellow afternoon light only managed to make the boy look worse, his face barely more than skin stretched tight over his skull, his body gaunt, shoulders hunched. But his eyes burned with a light that had been absent in the catacombs and his chin bore a new and defiant jut.

Gray squared his shoulders and offered a soldier's game smile in return. "What are you doing out of bed?"

"I was tired of resting, and I . . . I needed to see the sky." Color pinked Jamie's emaciated white cheeks. "You wouldn't understand."

"I understand more than you know about freedom and the lack of it." Gray gathered up the disks. Bent to pick up the dropped one, faltering as the curse flickered and died once more at the edges of his vision.

Jamie continued to watch him uneasily. "It's the curse, isn't it? You suffer the way Adam did. He said there were four of you."

Adam Kinloch; the sword stroke severing Gray's life into a before and after. The hand of hope when hope had all but vanished. Adam had died almost two years ago, cruelly and needlessly at the hands of a murderous Other bent on vengeance, but his discovery had started the three left alive on a quixotic quest that resembled a bad anecdote. A Fey, a shapechanger, and a dead kingslayer steal a girl and a stone. . . .

"I forgot you knew Adam," Gray said as they walked together through the quiet house.

"He spent a lot of time at my da's farm. I liked him.

He treated me like an adult. He spoke to me about things my da wouldn't."

Glass doors led out onto a wide stone terrace where weeds poked through the cracks in the bricks and a rose twined its wild way up over the wall in a profusion of blossoms and droning bees. Jamie lifted his face to the sun and drew in a deep breath, letting it out slowly. When he turned back to Gray, his face bore less the look of an escaped prisoner and more of the naive adolescent boy he'd been before his captivity.

"Adam spoke to you about the clans?" Gray asked.

"Some. Mostly it was about the war. Stories of bloody battles and midnight raids, and sneaking past pickets, and the pretty Spanish girls in the villages you passed through." He grinned. "Ma didn't like those stories."

"What did he tell you of the curse?"

Jamie swallowed, his face solemn. "Not much. But I saw what it did to him. And I helped him gather what he needed. All of us children did. It was like a great scavenger hunt." He kicked at the base of the stone baluster, shoulders hunched, eyes down. "Adam told me once that it was all his fault. That he was responsible for the four of you being cast out of the clans."

Guilt. Responsibility. Those two words drove so much of what one did in life. Shaped so much of what one became. Gray stared out across the overgrown lawns toward the distant belt of trees. Reached out for Meeryn with the slightest of mental touches. He felt her answering path as a breeze on his cheek and was surprised how reassuring her presence was. She'd always been the missing piece. Ten years hadn't changed that.

"Lord Halvossa? Are you certain you're feeling well?"

Lord Halvossa—it had been his father's title and would have been Ollie's when the time came. But they had died. The earldom had fallen to Gray, who had felt the guilt but refused the responsibility . . . until now.

"I'm sorry, I meant to say Your Grace," Jamie fumbled. "Kelan told me about . . . that is . . . that your grandfather the Duke . . ."

Gray plucked one of the roses, twirling the stem between his fingers, the scent saturating the drowsy air. "I've sent word to your parents. Not where you are, but that you're alive and safe."

Jamie's gaze slid away. "They'll never forgive me for running off. Da warned me . . . Captain Flannery, too. They said I'd never make it through the Palings in one piece. But . . ." He shook his head. "I thought . . ."

"You wanted to understand where you came from . . . what you were . . ." Gray said, watching a bee hover close to the plucked bloom.

"Father told such stories about the Imnada. On one hand he made the holdings hidden behind the mists sound like this amazing paradise, and on the other he was always carping on about the dangers of surrendering to our animal aspect. We weren't to speak of the clans, we weren't to use the power within us, we weren't to tell anyone, we weren't to care that he was asking us to be something we weren't, to cut off the best part of ourselves."

The bee landed, creeping among the riffled petals in search of food before departing for greener pastures. "You're unmarked, Jamie. A rogue with neither signum nor clan mark to protect you. Your father knew you'd be hunted down and killed if the Ossine suspected your powers."

"But surely I'm not the first half-breed. The Imnada must know we're out here."

"I'm sure they do. The enforcers defend and protect the clans from all threats."

Jamie's gaze flicked to his. "Including from people like us?"

Gray tossed away the flower, catching sight of the crisscross of scars on his palm. "Especially from people like you." He ran a thumb over the spiderweb of knife cuts, barely a place on his hand untouched by the silver blade. "No, Jamie. You and your siblings are not the first half-breeds. There are graveyards full of those who came before."

Jamie ran a hand over the balustrade, hair flopped forward to cover his eyes. "Funny, but I felt as if all those months . . . all those times they dragged me before Sir Dromon and asked me questions about the rebels . . . all that time, Sir Dromon was more scared of me than I was of him."

"He is scared. But his fear is what makes him dangerous."

"Kelan said the Arch Ossine would never let you live long enough to take over leadership of the clans. That we were fighting a rearguard action and it was only a matter of time."

Gray closed his hand around his scars, but he could still feel them like a ghost pain, a threat of what awaited him if he didn't break the curse. Then he reached out one last time to feel the bright glow of Meeryn's happiness, the promise of what could be. "Kelan was right about that."

*          *          *

They lay side by side upon the soft turf beside the murky pool, hands clasped, bodies cooling. Savoring the last fading echoes of pleasure dancing through her sluggish limbs, Meeryn stared up through the trees at the fragments of night sky. A star glimmered, unchallenged by the moon which had set an hour ago. A soft splash broke the quiet as a frog entered the water.

A perfect idea. She rose from the soft bower they'd made among the ferns, to dip her toes into the chilly pool. Stretched her arms over her head and launched herself like a knife into the water. The cold snatched her breath away, but by the time she surfaced, the shock had become a delicious caress. Gray rolled up on an elbow to watch her, his eyes seeming to burn like blue fire in the dark. She sensed his smile even though she couldn't see it.

"Join me?"

His smile faded. "Probably not the best of ideas."

She swam to the edge, then hoisted herself back upon the bank beside him. He rolled up to sit, his thigh lying warm against her own. So close she could feel his ragged breathing and the new tension ratcheting his shoulders. "You used to swim like a fish. They couldn't keep you out of the water."

"That was a long time ago."

"It's like riding a horse. Once you learn, you never forget."

"That's the problem, though, isn't it? The not forgetting."

"Someone once told me not to dwell on a past that's long gone. To look to the future."

"Wise words. But it's not always so easy to do what we know we should, is it? There's no way to know what that right path is until we take it and then it's too late."

"Is this the right path?" She said it and immediately wished the world would swallow her whole. A fool's question with no good answer. It was like asking him if she were too fat or if the dress she wore made her look like a sack of potatoes. Of course, he'd say what she wanted to hear. That's what smart lovers did.

"Honestly? I don't know."

Maybe he wasn't as smart as she thought.

"But it's the path I've chosen," he continued solemnly. "And right now, it feels damn near perfect."

He slid his hand into hers, his touch shooting sparks through her insides until she felt as if she glowed. She leaned her head on his shoulder as he put an arm around her waist.

She smiled into the dark, memories unearthed from a deep place where she'd held them tight. "Remember the cove we found that we promised to keep secret from everyone?"

"Until we realized Ollie had known about it for years?" He stared down into the rippling water. "I remember."

"I was sure you'd told. I wouldn't talk to you for a week."

"It was closer to a month."

He was quiet for so long after that she thought she'd put her foot in it. The topic of Ollie was still tender to the touch. Gray might have allowed himself to be swayed by his desire, but his guilt remained like an old battle wound, twinges felt whenever it was jarred too cruelly.

"I have a confession to make, Meeryn," Gray said softly.

She held her breath, an unexpected shiver overtaking her despite the humid night air.

"I . . . ah . . ."—he stared up into the trees, down into the water, everywhere but at her face—"I *did* tell Ollie about that cove."

Her head snapped up and she shook off his arm. "You bastard. You scared me to death."

He laughed, the shadows lifted from his eyes and his voice. "Had you going, didn't I?"

If he'd seen her answering smile, he'd have fled. But he was too busy feeling proud of himself for nearly stopping her heart. So when she grabbed his hand and half-leaned, half-shoved against him, he had nowhere to go but in.

They landed together, the water closing over her head, his hand still in hers. She felt his grip tighten in a spasm of panic, felt his first flailing kicks. He ripped his hand from hers as his body descended. Now it was her turn to panic. What had she done? As far as she knew, Gray hadn't voluntarily gone into the water since the shipwreck. He was probably terrified, frozen with horror.

She dove, seeking him amid the dark murky gloom of the pool. Felt for the churning stir he would make in the otherwise calm water. *Gray! Where are you?*

By now, her lungs were screaming for air. Her feet still hadn't touched the bottom, while her arms reached and felt nothing beyond tangled strands of duckweed and frogbit. She surfaced with a strong scissor kick, bursting free with an anxious gasp, to find him treading water a few feet away, the water slapped from his grinning face.

"Are you mad? Was that your idea of a sick joke?" she growled, furious and frightened at the same time. Foolish tears formed at the corners of her eyes, and a lump choked off her words. Just as well. She couldn't trust herself to speak without tearing him tooth and claw.

His grin vanished as he crossed the distance separating them with a few able strokes. "I'm sorry. I didn't mean to frighten you." He curled an arm around her waist, legs tangled with hers as they buoyed them both up. "I was afraid I'd plant you a facer with one of my more awkward flounderings." He traced her eyebrow and down around the curve of her cheek with one finger. "Coming to the breakfast table with a black eye might beg a few awkward questions."

He lowered his mouth to hers, pond water sliding to mingle with the teasing heat of his tongue. She answered by wrapping her legs around his waist and lowering herself onto his shaft with a hiss of pleasure as both water and skin caressed her throbbing sex.

"Are you trying to drown us both?" he said, voice raspy with arousal as she withdrew, only to plunge down once more in a wriggling, hip-tilting exploration of this new and interesting manner of lovemaking.

They went under still locked together. He shoveled them up with one powerful churn of his arm. Toward the shore with a second sweep as his other hand cupped her rear. She felt when his feet gained a foothold upon the pond's sloping floor. The dreamy curvette of cool water and slow sweetness increased in tempo and vigor to a powerful, frenzied thrusting as he took her deep. Her body welcomed the demanding crush of his body, desire building at the point where they joined before hitting a crescendo as he drove into her, her name whispered over and over like a prayer.

Afterward, they lay back upon the soft carpet of grasses, neither one finding the will to break from this intimate interlude. She knew why she lingered. To return to the house was to return to the fear and the uncertainty. Out here, among the pinprick stars and the velvet night sky, she could forget what the dawn might hold. Gray sought to bury the past, but with no idea how many days might be left to them, she wanted to hold tight to it with both fists.

"You're right, Meeryn" he said, eyes closed in drowsy contemplation. "Once you know, you never forget. And fortunately that goes for the good memories, too."

Sir Dromon stood before the Gather elders, hands behind his back. He was not on trial, nothing of the sort. In fact, he had brought them here; Lord Carteret; Glynjohns from Wales; and The Skaarsgard, who watched from the corner, arms folded over his chest, feet up in a brazen display of disregard for the seriousness of this meeting. Only Sir Desmond Flannery had yet to arrive in answer to his summons.

They had come for the Duke's funeral. They had stayed because Sir Dromon wished them to stay. He wanted them to witness de Coursy's punishment. It would be a good life lesson to see what happened to one who sought to defy Imnada law—his gaze flicked to The Skaarsgard—so brazenly.

The Orkney clan leader noted the Ossine guarding

each doorway to the salon where they had gathered. His lips curled disdainfully. "Do you expect Halvossa to come barging in pistols blazing and army at his heels?"

"I expect his head on a plate in less than a week. My enforcers have guaranteed it."

"You don't fear repercussions?"

"Sympathy for a murderer and a thief?"

The Skaarsgard lifted his brows in mild surprise. "Loyalty to the proper duke and heir to the throne."

"He's *emnil*. Stripped of his rights. Poisoned by Fey magic."

"Yet you invited him to Deepings under a flag of truce."

"I sought a way clear of this quagmire of killing and bloodshed. I was repaid with treachery of the most fiendish kind." He nodded toward one of the Ossine, excitement rising to a fever pitch. This was the moment, the point at which defiance collapsed. "Not once," he proclaimed, "but twice by those in whom I placed my trust."

The door opened. Mr. Thorsh entered, dragging a body behind him, a trail of blood smearing the newly waxed floor, soaking into the salon's Turkey carpet. The men leapt to their feet in unison. The Skaarsgard's smirk wiped clean off his face, replaced with a white look of shock.

"Gareth!" Owen Glynjohns lurched toward the battered, nearly unrecognizable body pooling scarlet beneath it. "What have you done to my son?"

Sir Dromon stroked his chin, his lips quivering with distaste. "I've rooted out another head to this hydra. Gareth Glynjohns was found to be in alliance with de Coursy and his traitorous clansmen. He was dealt with as we deal with all traitors to the Imnada. A stake to the heart."

The usually clever and quick-witted Glynjohns now cradled his son to his chest, his keening like nails on a slate, his body collapsed like a bladder emptied of air. Sir Dromon wrinkled his nose. Such effusive displays disgusted him. They reeked of sentiment and overwrought passion. Neither emotion served a purpose. Detachment from these weaknesses led to clarity and a clear path.

"Treason is a matter for the full Gather to review." The Skaarsgard's eyes glittered. "You are not the leader of us yet, Pryor. You do not act on your own authority."

"Wrong, my reckless Nornish seal. I've led you for years. It's just taken me this long to ascend my throne and take my place among the Imnada kings of old."

"The Gather will never allow it."

"The Gather is a farce. Four preening coxcombs, an old dottering fool, and a voiceless N'thuil without the power the Mother gave a goose. I've kept your clans safe while you played at ruling. I'm the one who protected your peace, and I'm the one who has defended your borders despite the Palings' weaknesses. The Fey-bloods beat at our gates. Do you think they'll be content to treat us as friends? Or do you think they will drain us of our blood before they hack us apart for their amusement? The Fealla Mhòr comes anew, and my Ossine will meet them in battle. Them and any who stand with them . . . including treacherous clansmen." He spat on Glynjohns's corpse. "And the one you believe is the rightful ruler of us all."

"You wouldn't dare."

"I would and I have." At his signal, the Ossine stepped closer about the men. "Escort these men to the guest hall. Offer them all conveniences, but they are not to leave. And they are not to path."

"You would take our *krythos*?"

"Would you rather I take your son, Lord Carteret? Or your daughter, Skaarsgard? All it requires is a word from me . . . or a wrong word from you."

Lord Carteret blustered while Skaarsgard merely met Sir Dromon's gaze with one as steady and as determined. "De Coursy will return. And when he does—"

"De Coursy is as good as dead. If the Ossine don't kill him, the curse will. I have it on the best authority."

"Whose?"

"Someone who's always available to the highest bidder."

# 12

Meeryn floated on her back, the cool water lapping softly around her, buoying her up. Her hair spread out in a trailing wave to tangle with the grasses, and now and then a tiny fish would inspect her toes. Afternoon sun filtered through the canopy of leaves, dappling the pool in greenish light. She closed her eyes, hoping to calm her thoughts enough to take stock of her situation. But the fear that left her ice cold and knotted tight in her chest wouldn't leave her. Not even in this oasis where the world felt a million miles away.

Despite her best intentions, the sun still rose and set, the days moved on, and events closed around them. Meeryn couldn't hide from the coming trouble. It seemed to close in from all sides. The best they might hope for was to delay it for a little while.

"I hope I'm not interrupting, but what a perfect place for a private heart-to-heart."

The world had just landed on the banks beside her with a thud. Meeryn opened her eyes to see Lady

Delia watching her from her seat upon a fallen log, gaze narrowed in catlike expectancy.

"I'd almost forgotten about this place. It's gone a bit brackish and green these days." Delia dipped her hand in the water and shivered. "Ugh, but still just as cold."

Meeryn trod water, droplets sliding fresh down her cheeks like tears. "Is there something you needed, Lady Delia?"

"I thought we might have a cozy chat, just you and me."

"Cozy" was not an adjective that sprang to mind when dealing with Lady Delia Swann. Cunning, clever, sinister, subtle; these were far better words to pin to this blond goddess. But Meeryn wasn't surprised she'd been followed. She had a feeling Delia would seek her out sooner or later.

As with all unpleasantnesses, best to get it over with quickly. Meeryn swam to the shore, climbed out onto the bank. Water sluiced off her body, puddling at her feet. Cold rivulets dribbled off the ends of her hair and down her back.

Lady Delia's brows arched in approval. "The Imnada got one thing right—they aren't ashamed of their own bodies."

"The eagle doesn't hide his feathers nor the seal her fins. It is who they are."

Lady Delia flashed her a toothy smile as she arranged her skirts to drape more artlessly. "How philosophical of you. But forgive me if I feel it seems a tad ironic for a race that hides its very existence."

Meeryn snatched up the chemise and gown she'd left hanging from a nearby branch. "Only after *your* people left us no choice but secrecy or slaughter."

Lady Delia flicked an imaginary piece of dirt from her bodice, gazing up at Meeryn through her lashes. "Did you think we could allow our king's murder to go unavenged?"

"Babes at the breast? Mothers and daughters cowering in corners? Boys put to the sword as their fathers looked on? They weren't soldiers on a battlefield. They were innocents slaughtered."

"Does one kill only the rat that steals the grain? Or does one seek out and kill the entire nest of vermin?"

Meeryn scooped the undergarment over her head to fall clinging against her wet skin. "Interesting comparison for one who professes to side with those seeking peace." Her gown followed, which she buttoned with fumbling fingers, noting absently that while Delia's outfit made her look graceful as a Grecian statue, Meeryn's borrowed wardrobe made her feel frumpy as a spinster aunt, tight across the chest, narrow in the waist, and at least six inches too short.

"I don't choose sides. It hampers my options. I assist Gray because he amuses me. And because . . ." She gave a halfhearted shrug and a wave of her hand.

"Because you care for him."

Delia stiffened, her smile slipping. "Actually, I was going to say because he pays me well to do so."

"Someone whose loyalty is bought with coin, can be bought again."

"Did I say Gray bought me with coin, Miss Munro?" she said, gliding her hand down her body to illustrate her point, as if Meeryn needed to have the rest spelled out for her in big letters and small words.

She ignored this obvious attempt to goad her into an argument and instead twisted the water from her hair, hastily pinning it atop her head, her manner as cool as a queen's. Two could play at this little game. Meeryn was not the shy retiring miss this woman expected. "If you're looking for prey to bat between your paws, Lady Delia, look elsewhere. I'm not in the mood."

The courtesan lifted her chin, gaze clear of artifice or animosity. "Did you mistake my good manners for subtlety? Oh no, my dear, I'm not looking to play at anything. I'm here to warn you."

"Warn me? Or warn me off?"

"Perhaps a bit of both. He *is* a delectable creature, after all, and I haven't quite tired of him yet." She waved an airy hand. "But a word of caution before you fall headlong in love with our tragic hero. Gray might offer his body. He does not offer his heart. I'm not sure he even has one, come to think on it. It's why we were so perfect together once upon a time. We had white-hot passion, and that was more than enough for both of us. We wanted nothing else. We needed nothing else." She spun a leaf between her fingers. "I can see how you'd hope for more. The tale is an affecting one: our fair hero returns to slay the dragon and sweep the fair damsel off her feet. But the hero doesn't always win his faery story ending, does he? Sometimes he dies. Sometimes the damsel ends up alone." Her face hardened, the leaf shredded in her lap.

"You don't believe Gray will break the curse and win back his throne?"

"I don't think he'll survive beyond the end of the year. And there's nothing he—or anyone—can do about it."

"Gray believes he'll succeed."

"Does he? Or does he tell you what you want to hear? Why alienate someone who might come in handy down the road, if you know what I mean?"

"He wouldn't lie to me about that."

"No? Then perhaps he's lying to himself."

Gray sensed the moment the sun dropped below the horizon. His skin crawled and his stomach clenched. His muscles constricted and his eyes blazed with a blue and silver fire as his body struggled against the draught. He clamped his jaw and gripped the arms of his chair until the spasms passed. A few moments that felt like a few hours.

"It grows worse. I can see you struggle."

"I leave for London before dawn. Lucan reports the roads are clear. If I'm careful and fast, I can be there by sundown tomorrow."

Arms encircled his chest as Meeryn came up behind him, leaning over his shoulder to kiss his cheek. His groin tightened with anticipation and the smell of her perfume. "Take me with you," she replied.

"It's too dangerous."

"You've said yourself you need Jai Idrish to break the curse. I *am* Jai Idrish. You can't succeed without me."

"And I can't risk your death while I struggle to work out what I'm doing wrong."

He pushed his work away and passed a tired hand over his face. Hours he'd spent reviewing the pages he'd stolen from the Deepings library, but they were scattered and useless without the weight of his own research to guide him further. His eyes fell on each disk in turn, gold, silver, bronze, and copper. Four keys that unlocked a hole in the very fabric of reality. Four objects borne of Fey magic and Imnada power. He arranged them at the compass points; north, south, east, west; maiden, mother, crone, and specter. Rearranged them into a line, edges touching. Stacked them one on top of the other.

"What am I missing? What is staring me in the face that I cannot see?"

"It wouldn't be the first time you were blind to the obvious," she said, coming around to bump him with her hip as she cast him a long-suffering sideways glance.

Leaning over the table, she tilted her head regarding the disks and the scattered pages. Turned to look on him. Turned back to the table, lip caught between her teeth. She lifted off the gold disk and set it on the table. Followed by the bronze and the copper. The silver she handled with care as she pushed it into position. "Four disks to represent the four faces of the Mother," she muttered.

Something Jamie said niggled at him even as she spoke. They'd been talking about Adam and the curse. Jamie had said . . .

"Four disks could represent the four seasons or the four elements or the four points of the compass . . ." Meeryn suggested.

"He said there were four of you. That was Jamie's comment when he spoke of Adam's work on the draught," he muttered to himself. "Of course! They represent us. Four disks. Four men. That's why it didn't work, Meeryn. We have to work the spell together."

"But you can't. Adam's . . ." Her words trailed off

into an uncomfortable silence. She shook her head, eyes dark in a face gone white as chalk.

He leaned back, careful lest the slightest movement double him over. He touched each disk before placing his hands in front of him. Smooth and untroubled, barely a flicker behind his half-lidded eyed . . . a howling yawning horror squeezing off his breath, raking his innards until he felt torn inside. "Yes, I know. He's dead."


Meeryn was given a reprieve from having to offer either a comfortless reassurance or an overwrought denial. Lady Estelle entered just then with news of a letter come from her husband in London and the two departed. Gray was as colorless and expressionless as if he already lay in his grave, his stare distant, his manner exact, his posture frozen.

She touched his sleeve as he passed her and their eyes met briefly. "This is not the end," she murmured with a quiet intimacy.

His shoulders stiffened, hands to fists at his side. He paused as if he might answer, but Lady Estelle turned still speaking of couriers and travel times and Gray nodded, continuing on silently around a corner, and was gone.

Meeryn knew her words sounded trite and ridiculous under the circumstances. Adam was dead. The four who together found themselves bound by the Fey-blood's spell could never be reunited to break it. For Gray, this must seem exactly like the end. And who was she to offer him different?

The answer came back to her like a slap to the

head, and she straightened with renewed determination. She was the bloody N'thuil, that's who. She had the sum of Imnada wisdom at her fingertips. If she couldn't find an answer, there was no answer to be found.

Fleeing to her rooms, Meeryn grabbed up the hold-all where she'd stowed Jai Idrish upon their arrival. The sphere spilled into her hand, the weight of it seeming greater than before, the milky light gleaming within every facet of its surface seeming to shine with a prism's colors. She placed the orb on a desk in her room, propped up by a perfume bottle, a box of hairpins, and a ladies' magazine to keep it from rolling onto the floor. Hardly dignified, but altogether serviceable. She placed her palms upon its surface. Cleared her mind.

"Three pearls from my bodice and two from my hem are missing." Lady Delia stomped down the hall. "The bloody laundresses are robbing me blind."

A door slammed.

Meeryn silently wished the woman to the devil as she sought to focus her mind once more and try again.

"Jamie is trying to sleep. Would you please take your fit of vapors somewhere else? I hear the Far Antipodes are lovely this time of year," Lady Estelle hissed as she hurried to intercept her sister.

Raised voices and slammed doors and more grumbling followed until Meeryn finally surrendered. Taking up Jai Idrish, she retuned it to the hold-all, and took everything with her as she left the house for calmer parts—like the Far Antipodes.

She paused at the bottom of the terrace steps.

The hidden wooded glade would do perfectly.

The walk across the park stretched her legs and soothed her heart. By the time she reached the ferny clearing and the lily-covered pool, she was breathing hard but the stitch in her side had taken the place of the ache beneath her ribs.

An oak had fallen, its roots pulled up through the soft earth in a knot of reaching twisted limbs. One such tangle was a perfect receptacle for the sphere. A thrush called from the bushes. Another sang high in the ash trees, shaking the branches as it hopped. Frogs chirruped along the banks of the pool or splashed amid the ferns. But no sisterly squabbling. No crow's contemptuous cackle.

She was alone.

Once more she placed her hands upon the sphere's roughened crystalline surface. Once more she sought to empty her mind of everything but the question tearing at her heart, though this proved harder than she imagined. Gray's face swam before her, the futility of his final gesture, the helpless rage burning in his bright eyes.

She opened her mind as she might when seeking to path, searching for the connection that would link her to Jai Idrish and the wisdom of the ancients. For a time, nothing happened. Her arms and shoulders grew sore; her fingers grew stiff and her knees ached where she knelt upon the loamy earth. Her eyes burned as she stared unblinking into the crystal's center, where the light coalesced like an altar flame. Jai Idrish remained cold and silent. The ancients fled as if they'd never been.

She wanted to cry. Tears leaked from the edges of her eyes to trickle salty into her mouth. She wanted to scream at the sphere; a useless rock. And she a useless Voice. Perhaps Lady Delia was right. Perhaps Gray lied to himself. Perhaps there was no way to break the curse. The Fey-blood sorcerer had done his work too well.

Just as she started to pull her hands away, the light within the crystal flickered and expanded. It blew outward like a ripping curling tidal surge, dragging her under as it receded, pulling her far from shore to the deepest places where light never shown. She was no longer in the glade or even in the world she knew.

She felt no ground beneath her feet, heard no call of birds or whispering breeze. She was suspended within an infinite darkness surrounded by the specks of distant stars, great spiraling clouds of glittering dust and the boil of brilliant suns brighter than the one that shone above her every day. She searched farther, seeing the planets like points upon a map. The space between like a great ocean with depths and currents and shoals and hidden rocks. And just at the edge of her vision, an infinite stretch of horizon banded by a great rolling cloud of shadow, black and ominous as a cyclone. Eating the distance between them, swallowing the specks of stars, gobbling the blue planets, blotting everything out forever.

". . . *naxos nreothma lioxnahal . . . dark angels aloft . . . naxos briothmeh ionuhath . . . katarth theorta . . .*"

The shadow seemed to boil and roll with new life. It grew in size. As if it suddenly noticed her existence, it turned its immense energy in her direction. Defenseless, she watched it approach like an enormous wave, with the force of the entire universe behind it.

And, like the seal of her clan, she used every bit of guile and strength to slide clear of its crushing attack. Driving ahead of it, sliding away from it. Moving through the darkness before the shadow, diving down, curling up. She tired, her heart raced, she screamed for Idrin or Aneavala or any one of the thousands who'd come before to help her. Just as the shadow must overtake her, she felt herself falling, her vision burst with the brightness of an exploding star, and she was back in the dim leafy glade, the crystal empty of life but for the tiny flickering gleam of light at its heart.

"Hold this tight, my lady. It will help to anchor you among the living." Lucan cupped her fingers around a small jagged stone. The edges bit into her fingers but the pain was welcome after her time trapped in the dark heart of the stone.

"Not trapped at all," he answered. "You were freed like none can be free but those who allow Jai Idrish to fill them with its power."

She really wished he wouldn't snatch her thoughts without asking. Surely there were protocols about that sort of intrusion. Perhaps he didn't even realize he did it, like the boot trampling a hill of ants. They were so small and insignificant, the boot never even noticed them.

"My apologies, Lady N'thuil. I'm still unused to the lack of mental barriers among the Imnada of today. It is a lack that leaves me a bit like . . . a boot, I'm afraid. But you are no ant."

Heat crept into her cheeks. "I suppose if I'm being filled with power, I'm closer kin to a cup."

He offered a thin smile. "Did you not wonder why you are called Voice *and* Vessel? You speak for all those who have passed before you, but you are also the sharpened spearpoint upon which Jai Idrish directs all its power. You are both weapon and wisdom in one divine."

She knelt to splash water on her face, disregarding the ruin of her gown. The cold cleared away the foggy drunken feeling left from her time connected to the sphere.

"Did Jai Idrish offer you the answers you sought?"

"I don't know. There was a shadow coming toward me." She stood up, but her legs wobbled and she had to lean against the dead oak for balance. "No stars. No light. No life within it. But I have no idea what it means. Was it a real seeing? A metaphor?"

Lucan's face hardened, his already forbidding features growing bleaker. "I am not N'thuil. And I do not know how Jai Idrish offers its knowledge. If you saw a shadow, you must interpret it as you see best."

"But I wasn't trained to interpret. The crystal's not spoken to us in centuries. It's slept until none living remembers how it works or what it does. I wasn't even supposed to be N'thuil. It was a mistake."

"There are no mistakes."

"A great darkness is coming that threatens the Imnada. But I don't know what it means. Is Jai Idrish telling me to beware Sir Dromon, or the Fey-bloods, or . . ." A shadow fell over her, chilling her heated skin, lifting the hairs at the back of her neck.

"Or me," Gray answered for her.

"It's not a battlement, but it does have a lovely view."

Gray turned his gaze from a study of the far horizon to the woman standing just this side of a nearby chimney, skirts trailing in the dust, face smudged with a bit of mud from the gutter. She approached, hesitating only slightly upon seeing the silver-bladed knife lying beside him, an empty cup at his elbow, bandage wrapped round his hand.

"To have the resiliency of youth," he said.

Meeryn followed his gaze to where Jamie walked amid the gardens in company with Lady Estelle. She kept close to his side, but only once did her hand reach toward him and only once did he pause to catch his breath aside a long low stone bench.

"He owes you his life," Meeryn said,

"I hope I didn't save him only to be slaughtered at a later date."

"It won't end that way, Gray. It can't."

He closed his hand more tightly around the wadded handkerchief. The draught worked as it should for now, but he sensed its weakness increasing. He felt the choking evil of the curse as it wrapped its way around his spirit, twisting tighter until he couldn't move, until he couldn't fight. Until his body became his worst enemy. It wouldn't be long now. He had thought six months; he might have three. "You disbelieve Jai Idrish?" he asked.

"No, I believe in you." She settled on the roof ledge beside him. He felt a smile tug at his mouth as he watched her unease, the way she gripped the gutter as she glanced uncomfortably at the shrubbery below before fixing her stare on the distant pair.

"You're safe enough. I'll not let you fall."

She jerked her chin up, her face a mask of gritty determination. "Forgive me if I'd rather not test that theory."

His smile widened, though his words were meant in all seriousness. "You already have."

She nodded as she caught his meaning. "And you've been true to your word so I suppose I have nothing to fear."

She sounded so certain, but he knew her doubts remained. Of course they did. Hell, he doubted himself when the clock struck three in an empty house and he felt the ghosts thicken. Daylight banished them but they always returned in the dark. Much like the curse in that regard.

"Sir Dromon wants to erase all knowledge of the Imnada from the face of the earth. He wants to return to the days when we were thought a sweet faery tale. Those days are past, Meeryn. There are too many who know our secret. The Ossine can't kill them all."

"Do you worry what will happen when the walls come down and we're faced by our greatest enemies?"

"Of course. But I worry more over what will happen if we bury our heads in the sand and do nothing."

She stared out over the treetops, to the blue hills and the haze of sky beyond. "Jai Idrish showed me a darkness without end, a world without light. There was nothing but emptiness forever. Is that what this rebellion is risking? Or is that what we're fighting?"

"Forget the crystal's heart for a moment. What does *your* heart tell you?"

She smiled. "It's telling me I'm a fool to doubt you. But then again, my heart's never been the best guide. It told me once I should dye my hair raven black and it ended a horrid shade of green."

He laughed. "I remember when you did that. The duke was horror-struck."

"Not half so much as I was. It took six months to grow out and a year to recover from the humiliation."

"If it's any consolation, I prefer your hair color just the way it is. It suits you."

She grinned. "Not too light. Not too dark. Not too straight. Not too curly. I've resigned myself to ordinary."

"You couldn't be that if you tried."

Jamie and Estelle followed a path from the garden into the park, the boy's strength returning and his white-eyed nightmarish panic receding under their hostess's care. They disappeared near a grove of pines, and Gray was left without a focus for his gaze, a distraction from Meeryn's unnerving presence. There were things he wanted to say to her but reticence had been his watchword too long. Besides, there was little to be gained by offering her his heart when in a few short months it would cease beating. She would be alone . . . he would have left her again.

No, best to keep silent. To keep still. To deaden his feelings as he'd always done. But it was harder now. Returning to Deepings had created the first cracks in his granite façade. Meeryn had been the slow incessant drip of water forcing her way into the dead places where nothing had lived but ghosts and regret. She offered him his past back. Then she offered him her love.

She felt no such reserve. She took his good hand in her own, threading her fingers with his, their shoulders brushed, her thigh warm beside his as she leaned against him. "You're strong, Gray. Far stronger than your grandfather ever realized, but you can't carry the world on your shoulders. Sometimes you have to admit you need help. Sometimes opening yourself up to hurt is the only way to gain love."

"And if it's too late?"

"It's never too late."

Her lips touched his, her breath soft in his mouth as he opened to take her deeper, to own her in a long desperate kiss of claiming. He cupped the back of her head in his good hand, smelled the windswept freshness of her hair and the salt of her skin. She was lush against him, a feast for his senses. He caressed her breasts through her gown, felt the gasping catch of an inhalation, heard the sigh as she surrendered to his touch. He leaned her back against the chimney as she skimmed her hands down his chest, freeing his waistcoat, sliding up under his shirt. He shivered. Groaned her name as she circled a nipple with her fingertips.

Arousal dragged the blood straight to his groin. He wanted to be inside her, to feel her tight hot muscles close around him, to taste the slick wetness between her legs, to hear her cry his name as she found her release. He wanted to feel this rocketing runaway desire so that when the end did come, he would remember what he had and what it felt like and how close he had almost come.

"You won't let me fall, Gray. I'll not let you drown."

He smiled as his fingers found the bud between her legs and she jolted and arched against him. He strained against his breeches, wanted her straddling him, wanted her riding him. She fumbled with the buttons on his breeches.

The first gunshot broke them apart, breathing as heavily as sprinters. The second brought them lunging to their feet. But it was the wolves erupting from

the treeline that had Gray stuffing his shirttails in as
he headed for the stairs. "Fuck all, they've found us!"


Blood leaking from her shoulder, Lady Estelle stood
over the dead man, following the stealthy movements
of the enormous black panther stalking her. On the
ground in front of her, the severed head of the young
enforcer Kelan stared up at her with sightless eyes. No
way to tell what other information besides Gray's loca-
tion he might have given up before he was slaughtered.

"Run, Jamie. Get out of here now," she hissed as the
young half-breed crouched behind her, his face pale
but set. His body shuddered as the power overtook
him.

Meeryn stood at the edge of the garden wall. She
didn't need to touch the enforcer's mind to discover
clan or signum. The panther's savaged right ear was
identifier enough. *Leave them alone, Wesh,* she pathed.

The panther froze, swinging his catty green gaze
her direction. Lips drew back from long white fangs,
claws extended in anticipation of a fresh kill. Meeryn
stepped from the shadows, sensing the shapechanger's
shock and dismay as his gaze traveled the length and
breadth of her aspect. She stretched wide her mouth,
allowing a glimpse of her own gleaming teeth, flicked
the tip of her orange and black striped tail in pensive
deliberation. A deep threatening growl rumbled up
her throat. *Leave them and leave Marnwood,* the tiger
warned. *And I might let you live.*

*You might assume a fearsome aspect, woman,* Wesh
sneered. *You're still a pampered kitten where it counts.*

With the enforcer's attention on Meeryn, Lady

Estelle dashed for the dubious safety of the house. Of Jamie, Meeryn saw no sign, but for the fleeting brown tail of a lynx disappearing into the shrubs. Where were the others? She'd not seen Gray since the chaos of the Ossine's arrival. He'd charged down the stairs ahead of her, his shouts lost amid the pounding of her heart and the roaring in her ears. She'd chosen to face the threat rather than hide praying on her knees behind a locked door. A threat that sized her up from ten feet away, his long muscular body a ripple of black, ears pressed close to his head, eyes alive with hate.

*You've not the guts to kill me, you treacherous cunt. I'll rip your throat out then I'll fuck your dead body, beast and man,* he snarled.

*Nice language. Do you eat with that—*

He sprang, a move designed to throw her back on her hind legs and on the defensive. Caught off guard, she might have retreated, but prepared for such a move, she beat him off, her enormous paws enough to swat the smaller panther away. He skidded over the ground on his side with a screech of defiance.

*Care to try again?* she growled, uncertainty hiding behind bold-faced bravado.

Wesh came at her again, sizing her up before launching himself at her, claws reaching to rake her throat, her chest, her ribs. She knocked his blows aside, her massive size giving her an advantage when skill failed her. She might wear the temporary skin of a tiger, but the enforcer bore the true soul and the fighting ability of the panther. He drove under her guard, lunging for her throat. She scrambled to counter his attack, but only managed to deflect his blow, not avoid it. His teeth sank into her skin, his claws raking her side. She screamed her rage and her pain, as she shook him off, but circling, she knew she had only so much time before he wore her down and the advantage fell his way. He drove again, but this time she connected with a bone-crushing blow of her own, her fangs crushing down on his skull.

He struggled, but her hold was too strong. She felt him thrash as she clamped down, felt his body jerk and spasm as he sought to escape. A slamming blow dropped her to her haunches, but she refused to loose her hold. Instead she tightened her grip, feeling blood slide down her throat, the iron tang of it dancing hot and greasy on her tongue.

The panther growled and twisted, but even these movements grew less violent, death throes as his skull splintered and cracked under the monumental pressure of her tiger jaws.

Pain sizzled up her leg and into her spine. She screamed and let go, whipping around to face this new foe. The pistol's muzzle was a black hole staring her right between the eyes. She heard the roar of the gun, saw the blinding, singeing flash, and the dark dragged her under.


It missed her. For the love of the Mother, please let it have missed her. Throwing his rifle away, Gray ran toward the hot whirl of light and wind as tiger gave way to woman. Meeryn's skin shone white as marble against the pool of spreading scarlet beneath her. Her honey-blonde hair spilled around her, matted and sticky.

One enforcer lay half beneath her, his naked body

shredded, his head a pulpy unrecognizable mess. The second lay sprawled beside her, a hole blown through his back where Gray's shot had torn into him, his spent pistol a few feet away from his outstretched hand.

"Meeryn, forgive me," Gray whispered, his breath trapped in his lungs.

*Time's run out, my treasonous friend.*

The hair at the back of Gray's neck prickled and his skin crawled. He drew a knife from his waist as he swung slowly around.

There were four of them. Great shaggy wolves of the Viyachne, eyes narrowed in vicious savagery. They closed around him, mouths pulled back in grimaces of triumph. One stepped forward, eyes alight with a dark fire. *The Arch Ossine will reward us well for this day's work.*

The words slithered like ice over Gray's fevered brain. "I'm not dead yet," he spat.

The wolf lunged at the same moment Gray flung his knife. The blade buried itself in the animal's gut. It dropped, writhing in agony. One down . . . three to go.

He fought to reach his feet, body braced for their attack when an enormous shadow blotted out the sun and a bear tore into the pack of hunters, tossing animals aside like tavern spillikins.

*Go, de Coursy.* Lucan's path scraped the inside of Gray's head with a voice hard as nails.

"To hell with that. I can't leave Meeryn," he countered.

*It is too late for her. Save yourself.*

Gray wanted to throw up, to scream. His eyes burned. His face was tight and hot with rage and anguish. He looked to the house. None moved behind the windows. No shouts of alarm or cries for help. No way to know if anyone yet lived. Estelle, Delia, Jamie . . . they might all be dead. Would he have to face Estelle's new husband and offer his condolences? Would he have to send word to Jamie's grieving parents that the son he'd saved he'd then killed? How many would die because of him?

No more if he could help it. He'd too much blood on his hands, too much weight upon his conscience. Sir Dromon was the key. There would be no concessions, no conversations, no peace until the man was dead. That would be Gray's final legacy. He might not offer the Imnada a peace. But he could offer those who survived a chance for peace.

And he would be the bait to lure the snake.

Lips curled in a tight hysterical smile, Gray scrambled in search of a weapon to replace the lost knife. Yanked at the dead enforcer's sword that was trapped beneath him. His movements caught the attention of an enormous black wolf, its muzzle tipped in white. Blood dripped from its jaws and spattered its thick fur. It approached slowly, warily, cutting Gray clear of Lucan's protection, stalking him toward the garden wall where he would have nowhere to run.

"It doesn't have to be this way." Gray slid a hand along the edge of the sword.

*Your death or ours, Fey lover,* the wolf growled deep in its throat.

"These people are not your enemies."

*But you are, fucking whoreson bastard.*

An explosion sounded from the house. He lost his sword as a slashing burn spun Gray to the ground just as the wolf lunged. Who the hell was firing at him?

Had he miscounted? Was there another enforcer on the loose? Shit all!

He threw up his throbbing bloody arm in the last moment before the animal fell on him, driving him into the ground. Branches snapped under the crush of weight, jagged broken pieces of dead wood scraping along his ribs and digging into his shoulders. The wolf snarled and struck, teeth inches from Gray's throat. A claw raked his chest. Another slashed at his stomach.

The beast within him bore up under the onslaught. The cool killer instinct of the predator focused his mind and controlled his muscles. For every move the wolf made, he was there ahead of him. For every slice of his claws or close of his jaws on Gray's body, he was able to grapple himself free. Lungs filled and emptied, blood pushed through his arteries and veins, his movements as natural and effortless as a heartbeat. But neither his otherworldly strength nor his battle-hardened body would sustain him for much longer.

Gray reached for the sword, his fingers just grazing the pommel before it was knocked from his grasp. Instead his hand fell on a short splintered branch, which he gripped in a tight shaking fist. The wolf evaded his weakening grip and sank his teeth into Gray's forearm. He screamed and with strength born now of desperation, he drove the branch up into the wolf's belly.

The animal yelped, blood spilling hot over Gray's face and chest. He drove it in deeper, turning the makeshift weapon, forcing the animal off him. It collapsed in a chaos of death throes, Gray barely dodging the maddened animal's final spasms.

Muscles shaking and stomach churning, he sucked in gasping lungfuls of air, afraid to return from the cold empty place where he felt nothing and cared for no one. Where anguish fled and sorrow was a memory. Blood leaked from a half dozen wounds, but he was unaware of any sensation even close to pain. Tears burned his eyes and his throat closed around a tight knot.

As the hot charring wind of shifter magic engulfed the dead wolf, Gray rose stumbling to his feet. He was back at Deepings on the day when his world had been stripped from him in fire and agony. Once again searching for a face he both desired and feared to find.

Lucan stood at the portico steps. He wore the shape of a man, nude, blood-soaked, but whole. Two men lay dead upon the gravel; one almost ripped in half, the second pulsing blood from a gaping wound in his side.

Delia was at the front door, a musket in her arms.

Then his eye fell upon Estelle laying a blanket over the naked body of a woman.

"Don't," he croaked, his voice hoarse and cracking as he stumbled, half ran toward them. "Don't . . . please . . . don't cover her up," he begged.

He collapsed onto his knees, hands and fingernails caked, chest heaving. His fingers shook as he took the blanket from her. Pushed the heavy fall of hair from her face.

"She's not dead, Gray."

He blinked at her, not understanding her words around the pounding in his chest,

"She's alive. Some ugly bruises and the blade caught her in the leg, but the bullet missed her. A crease on her cheek that might leave a nasty scar but otherwise she's fine."

He shook his head, his hands shaking. His body twitching with nerves shattered and unglued.

"Look for yourself," she said gently.

He bent close enough he felt the soft sough of her breath against his cheek, the warmth of her skin under his caress. "Meeryn, *bereth n'hai*. My heart," he said, kissing her. "I'll not let you fall."

A smile curved the very edge of her mouth. "I'll not let you drown," she whispered.

His eyes stung as he blinked back tears. His shoulders shook with the sobs that ached up his chest and into his throat. And for the first in a very long time, he wept.

# 13

He sat on the edge of his bed, his *krythos* lying in the flat of his scarred palm. He'd not used the far-sending disk since before his exile, not even drawn it from his pocket in over a year, but he'd carried it always, unable to smash this last connection to his race. The smoky obsidian of the glass caught and refracted the light from his candle. The power locked within the *krythos* tingled up his arm into his brain. It would do as he asked ... if he dared use it. Sir Dromon might sense his amplifying draw upon the disk to increase the reach of his pathing. If he were paying attention, the Arch Ossine would feel it like the plucking of one thread among a web of such. He might even follow the tentative vibrations to their source and know what Gray planned.

That was all to the better.

Gray loosed the fetters on his mind, his thoughts unfurling with the strength and speed of a stooping hawk. The world dropped away as he sought out those who would answer his call. They might question him but they would do as he asked, knowing it might be their last chance.

Mac's Irish lilt was gruff and gravel-coated with sleep. *I've sent Bianca away to safety. She understands what's coming and is prepared.*

*Are you?* Gray asked, thinking of Mac's child. Declan was barely a month old; should Dromon win this war, the boy would be lucky to survive the purge of half-breeds that would follow. There would be no mercy shown. No pity offered. Dromon's version of safety for the Imnada would wreak a trail of death and destruction as vast as the Fealla Mhòr itself.

Mac's thoughts were as grim as his words. *It's a fight we've been preparing for since the Fey-blood cast his black magic.*

*And if it fails?*

*Then we meet our end in battle, as soldiers should. I prefer that over an illness that takes me slowly until I can't leave my bed.*

David responded with his usual brand of irritating sarcasm. *So Dromon hasn't used your guts for garters yet? Guess I owe Muc fifty quid.*

*You can refuse if you choose, David. I'd not hold it against you. Callista's magic and your courage have won you your freedom from the curse. What I ask is more than a risk.*

*And leave the two of you to face Dromon and his hordes alone? Not on your life. Do you know how many hours I've spent imagining his messy and painful demise? I want to be there to shove a sword up the bastard's ass, blow a hole through his prissy face, and dance on his dead body.*

Gray could almost see the steely gray of David's

wicked eyes light with murderous glee. St. Leger could try the patience of a saint and play the scoundrel better than anyone, but a wolf's heart beat beneath his polished exterior and a wolf's strength would be needed if they had any hope of victory.

Messages delivered, Gray fell back into himself with a lurching drop as if he'd taken to the skies without wings. His stomach rose into his chest, his throat closed on a rush of breath, and the power of the *krythos* sizzled in his head like a burst of cannon fire.

He opened his palm to find that a jagged crack like a lightning strike had sliced the face of the far-sending disk; its dark surface roiled with a storm cloud's dying ferocity. Blood welled from a cut on his hand where the serrated edge of the disk had cut into the flesh beneath his lifeline. A voice seemed to echo from within his head; a last cynical comment from David or had someone else usurped the dying power of his broken *krythos* to speak to him?

*It's in the blood.*

She woke during the night, feeling the presence of another in the room with her. A black shape against the dim shadows. He leaned back in a chair, neck tilted at an awkward angle against a pillow shoved behind his head. His arms were folded over his chest, and his long legs stretched in front of him. She smiled, wincing only slightly at the pain in her cheek. "Is that as uncomfortable as it looks?"

"Worse."

"I don't need watching over as if I'm on my death-bed. That is, unless there's something you're not tell-ing me." She rolled over, hissing as she shifted the weight onto her leg. The stab wound had been deep but clean. It was the silver the blade had been dipped in that posed the greatest risk. She'd seen the ugly purple streaks creeping outward from the stitched edges. She'd felt the sickness as the silver's venom slid through her bloodstream. "Mostly fine."

"I know I needn't watch over you. I wanted to. It makes me feel less useless."

"I can't imagine anyone considering you useless."

"You didn't see me . . . you were unconscious when . . ." He opened his hands in a gesture of surren-der. "Take my word on it—I was exceedingly useless for a long time."

Actually, Lady Estelle had recounted everything to Meeryn in amazed detail. And even now, as she leaned for the tinderbox to light a candle, she could see the reddened puffy eyes and granite set to his face as if he battled still to recapture his lost stoicism.

A fluttery excitement took the place of the unset-tled nausea in her stomach, and she wanted to smile despite the cut on her face, despite the fear and worry weighting her limbs, despite the dark memories lin-gering close around her like wraiths. Gray scattered these emotions like a bracing wind. The solidity of his presence chased the worst of her nightmares away. The memory of his words slid like honey along her weary consciousness. "Did you really speak to me in the tongue of the ancients?"

He scrubbed a hand across the back of his neck. "You noticed that?"

"I did, so there'll be no backtracking now."

"Can I attribute my babbling to overwrought emotions brought on by the chaos of battle?"

"If that's the explanation that helps you sleep at night," she replied, unable to completely mask the smugness in her voice. The flutters expanded into her chest and down into her toes.

He looked grimly to the dark window and then down at the basket of medical supplies resting by her bed. "Little else does." He swung back to meet her eyes, a new ingenuousness to the icy depths. "But tonight I might sleep well and for the whole night through."

She drew back the covers in blatant invitation.

"Meeryn, I can't . . . you're . . ."

"No more battered than you." Her eyes traveled his body as if she might spy the wounds he'd taken.

"A few cuts and bruises. A gash Lucan stitched up for me. I'll be sore as hell tomorrow morning, but for tonight I'm numb to everything but victory." He stood up. "I thought I'd lost you. I thought I'd killed you."

He traced the cut on her cheek with one tentative finger.

She covered his hand with her own. "Now we own matching scars. We're a paired set, like bookends. Break one and the other is completely—"

"Useless," he finished for her with a dry laugh.

"Exactly." She drew him to sit beside her. His body bore a fever's heat and he smelled of battle and soap and brandy and sky. He shuddered at the touch of her hand on his arm. "The draught is losing its power," she said. "Yet you remain . . . human."

"I've taken the last of it. Tomorrow will see me once more trapped by the curse. But tonight . . . I wanted to be with you tonight."

She curled against him so that her head lay upon his chest, his arm around her back. His heart beat strong under her cheek and his slow deep breaths felt relaxed and easy, unlike the usual tension stringing his muscles. "Can you say it again, Gray?"

She felt his heart drum louder and he tightened his hold upon her body. "*Bereth n'hai.* My heart." His voice rumbled under her ear, deep and low and lilting.

She smiled. "Do you know how long I've waited to hear an endearment like that come out of your mouth?"

She was met with silence, though he caressed her hair and kissed her forehead.

"Since I was ten and knew boys were good for more than frog-catching and blind-man's buff."

"I'm still very good at feeling my way," he admitted and snuffed out the candle.


When she woke again, it was to daylight and an empty bed. She stretched, feeling only slightly dizzy and off-kilter. Her leg ached, but it was a healthy ache. She wiggled her toes. They were still attached. A good sign. She'd mend. Actually, it was her cheek that stung like the devil. She touched a finger to the raised pink flesh where the Ossine's bullet had passed like an assassin's kiss. An inch to the right and her brains would have ended all over Lady Estelle's pristine lawn.

The smell of coffee and the promise of the accompanying breakfast drew her from bed. Rising on shaky legs, she tottered across the room to grab up a robe. Splashed water on her face and pulled a comb through her tangles until she looked passable if not presentable. Watery, milky light hollowed her sallow face, and she stood with a distinct hunch to her shoulders and list to her starboard side. Not exactly the elegant stare of fashion. Not even a distant second.

Did she care?

After last night, she could resemble a hag with crooked nose, hairy moles, and a hunchback's lump and she wouldn't bat an eyelash.

She pushed aside the curtain at the window to see a plume of smoke rising above the trees where it caught the wind and smeared thin across the gray cloudy sky. Closing her eyes, she offered up a prayer for the dead. Offered a second for the living. Looked inward, searching for the familiar knot in her stomach and weight in her chest. But there was only a dull sadness like a weather ache. Uncomfortable but survivable. Perhaps Gray had been right; without hesitation but always with remorse.

". . . was a bad idea. I should have known what would happen."

"Always thinking you're stronger than you are. It will kill you in the end. I've told you . . ."

Gray and Lady Delia in conversation. Meeryn's stomach squirmed with more than hunger. How far would the woman go to win Gray back to her side was her first jealous thought. Her second was far darker and more dangerous; how far would Lady Delia go to gain the wealth she craved?

Dismissing her eavesdropping as a wartime necessity, Meeryn placed her ear against the panel.

"How is our Sleeping Beauty this morning?" Delia cooed. "Or perhaps she's both Beauty and the Beast. Best be careful, Gray. Your precious N'thuil could rip your head off and shred you like a cabbage if she chose."

"She's well," came Gray's cool reply. "Thank you for asking."

"A long and satisfying night will do that to a girl. And you always proved most satisfying."

Meeryn could just picture the lightskirt's oozing sexuality as she turned on her charms. She was probably touching Gray's arm, bending close to offer him a glimpse of her perfect powdered cleavage, looking up at him through those dark lashes with great cow eyes.

Her hands curled to fists. Angry heat flushed her cheeks. Beast, was she? Dangerous, was she? A desire to pummel the bitch senseless almost had her ripping the door open to confront her with force enough to knock her teeth down her slender white throat.

"I have a job for you, Delia. Give me a day's head start and then . . ." Meeryn pulled up short, hand on the knob as she strained to hear. Blast it all. What job did Gray have for Lady Delia? What did he plan to do with two days' head start? Whose bloody side was the woman on anyway?

Good sense finally giving way to frustration, she yanked the door open on the quiet tête-à-tête. Scrambled at the last minute to drop into a pose of languorous pleasure, hoping her injured leg didn't give out and send her sprawling at Lady Delia's feet. "There you are, Gray. I'd wondered where you'd run off to."

It wasn't dulcet cooing, but it was the best she could do without notice or practice.

He lifted one skeptical eyebrow, though his eyes gave his amusement away. Lady Delia on the other hand made no bones about her pique, an expression she quickly turned into a catlike smile. But Meeryn noticed it, and her own smile was one of triumph as she slid a hand up Gray's arm.

What she'd overlooked within the dark room and soft bed was more than evident in the raw light of day. Bruises dulled his golden complexion; cuts and scrapes mottled his throat. But it was the uneasy tension coiling his body and the feverish chills she felt him fighting off that had her catching her lip between her teeth with concern. He dropped his arm to his side, offered her a slow unhappy stare, the rebuff like a slap to the face.

Lady Delia shook off the interruption with a tight sniff of distaste before turning her attention to Gray once more and ignoring Meeryn completely. "I'll do as you ask, but are you certain you're not inviting worse? Especially if Sir Dromon knows what you have and why you have it? Are you willing to risk so much on such a hazardous throw of the dice?"

"It's the only way to end this once and for all."

She gave a dramatic sigh of resignation. "Very well. I'll do as you ask, though I think love might have addled your brains."

"It's naught to do with love," he countered.

"Don't lie to yourself, Gray. It's everything to do with it. After all, when you die, it will be the ones left who suffer the punishments meant for you. A traitorous N'thuil will not be treated with mercy. She would be a fine object lesson to the grumbling clans. Nothing like a good fiery staking of a rebel to sway people to your way of thinking. Perhaps this is your last attempt at a noble sacrifice."

"I don't need Gray to sacrifice himself for me. I can handle Pryor," Meeryn argued.

Lady Delia's expression was hard as stone. "We saw how you handled his enforcers, Miss Munro. You're fortunate Gray was there to kill the bastard before he blew your brains out."

"Enough, Delia," Gray said. "Just do as I ask. Payment will be directed to the same account as always."

"Consider it taken care of. My lips are, as always, at your service, my darling." She leaned forward and kissed Gray on the mouth, her hand running up his shirtfront, her stare focused on his reaction.

Meeryn stiffened with rigid fury as Lady Delia stepped back, a smile playing over her porcelain features. "Never let it be said I don't concede gracefully, Miss Munro. I am, after all, an earl's daughter. Poise and refinement were beaten into us at a young and tender age. The field is clear. Enjoy it while it lasts. If Gray's gambled wrong, there might be less time than you think."

"It's no gamble. Dromon will come," he said.

"That's what terrifies me most of all, my darling." This time there was nothing but sorrow in her expression.

"You understand what I'm asking?"

"I *am* able to comprehend words of more than one syllable, Professor Gray."

He grimaced but carried on. If Meeryn was skeptical, she hid it well. There was only quiet confidence in her stern face, the hints of strength he'd glimpsed over these past weeks evident in the determined line of her mouth, the glint in her dark eyes. How had he ever thought he could return to Deepings without returning to her, without sliding back into the well-worn groove of familiarity? Meeryn not only knew his ghosts, she was one; a shade made flesh. A dark, painful memory resurrected and then exorcized. He had tried to make his peace with his grandfather, he had sought redemption for his family's tragedy. He would spend whatever time he had left rediscovering the girl he'd left behind and learning anew the woman he'd come home to.

"Do you think it will work?"

"It's unlikely with only the three of us, but I have to make the attempt. I have to know for certain I've done all I could. And I have to force an end to this war with Dromon once and for all. He would use his hatred of me to exact vengeance on anyone I care about, and his desire to keep the clans isolated from the world as an excuse to make war on his own people."

"But you said you were afraid he would discover you possessed the disks. Now you *want* him to know?"

"I want to draw him out into the open. At Deepings, he held the advantage. But London is my city. I choose the ground I fight on. You once said we hid behind our armies and let others do our killing and our dying for us. I would make this a one-on-one battle, to the death, winner take all."

"And you think Lady Delia can convince him of the need to go to London after you?"

"She can be very persuasive when the money's right and the cause amuses her."

"But trusting her with such a task? She's a provocateur. Willing to feed information to the highest bidder. She said so herself. Who's to say she won't sell you out?"

"I don't pretend to believe Delia's not playing both sides, but that will only mean he'll accept what she says without questioning too closely why she says it."

"So you do trust her?"

"I trust she won't betray me, yes."

Her brow furrowed, her lips drawing tight with anger. "You think lingering affection will stop her from turning you over to Sir Dromon if the price is right? Were you two so in love she would hold back from the wealth he could offer for betraying you?"

"We were never in love."

"But she was your lover." Said simply and without emotion, though he knew what it cost her to do so. He'd felt the same visceral twisting of the knife when he'd imagined Meeryn in the arms of Conal McIlroy.

"Does that shock you?" he asked.

"No. Of course not."

He lifted his brows in skeptical amusement.

"It doesn't shock me, but I don't have to like it," she huffed.

"Would you be unhappy if I admitted a part of me revels in your jealousy?"

"As long as you don't mind me admitting I think your prior taste in women was absolutely rotten."

"Delia and I . . . that is she . . . it's complicated." He plowed a hand through his hair in agitation. A move she noticed with a quirk of her lips.

"It must be, if it's flustered the unflusterable Major de Coursy." She folded her arms over her chest, offering him a go-ahead-and-try-me look.

He inhaled through his nose, exhaled a defeated sigh. He'd told no one, not even Mac or David what he'd known for the last five years. But, should the

unthinkable happen in London, it was best the information didn't die with him.

"Lady Delia has a son."

The blood drained from Meeryn's face, eyes wide,
lips parted. She swallowed once, twice, her throat
working convulsively.

"He's not mine," he hastened to clarify. "The boy is
Ollie's get."

"No," she murmured. "That can't be. Your brother's
dead."

"Yes, but eighteen years ago, Ollie was in London.
Just down from university and ready to take on the
town."

"He didn't . . . he wouldn't . . ." She shook her head,
gaze glassy with confusion as she tried to grasp what
he told her.

"He would and he did. Lady Delia was barely fifteen, but old enough to succumb to Ollie's charms.
The pregnancy was hushed up and the child sent away
to be raised. Ollie died soon after and the matter was
swept under the rug. None knew of the bastard he'd
sired, not even my grandfather, but I found out. Lady
Delia won't tell me where the boy is or even offer me a
name, though I've asked."

"Another son of Idrin. The line won't die when . . ."
She dropped her gaze to her slippers but not before he
saw tears sparkling on her lashes.

Now that she'd ripped open his half-healed scars,
emotions battered him from all sides. Fury. Frustration. Anguish. Anger. He fought them back as best he
could. He could not return to the empty deadness of
the past, but he could not fall to pieces now, with so
much riding on his next move.

"No, my heart, the line won't die when I do. But does he know who he is? What he is? He's almost a man grown. He must have some idea he's different, but does he understand the gift that came with his father's blood? Or does he believe he's a monster, a warped creature of nightmare? And what if the Ossine discover his existence first?"

"That's what Lady Delia meant when she said you don't pay her in coin."

"I pay into a trust set up for his use. That is what her trade in secrets has bought; a future for a son she can't even acknowledge."

"And so she offers the hope of him as a lure to keep you coming back; a way to leash you to her side."

"Perhaps, but I believe she fears more that I'll take him away, and she'll lose the only person on this earth who truly loves her for herself."

# 14

"Beautiful rooms, though not quite what I would have imagined your tastes to be."

Slanting a gaze over his sumptuous chambers, Sir Dromon bared his teeth in what passed for a smile at Lady Delia Swann's compliment. The woman had arrived at the wayside inn just beyond the Palings, offered the proper words to the proper man, and been delivered to Dromon's doorstep with an eye for everything and a smile that boded secrets in his future.

"I selected the furnishings and artwork myself when I moved my household to Deepings upon the late duke's illness. These chambers were quite plain and shabby before. Barely livable."

She ran a manicured hand along a chair back. Picked up a priceless Meissen urn from a nearby table, admired it, then placed it on a cabinet behind her. "I'm surprised you haven't taken over the late duke's apartments now that he's"—she paused as she offered him a significant look—"died."

He hurried to put the object back in its proper place. "Murdered, you mean?"

"Is that the story you offered your clans? How very Machiavellian of you. I suppose they're up in arms chanting for de Coursy's head."

Not as many as he'd hoped, but he'd hardly reveal that to a Fey-blood bitch who traded in the well-worn cave between her legs. She was a tool to be used until the job was complete and then discarded. He had enjoyed using her. He would enjoy discarding her even more. Thorsh was deserving of a treat to keep him loyal. Perhaps the brutish enforcer would find the courtesan to his taste.

"I'm not the Duke of Morieux, nor do I aspire to be. His heir holds the title now. It is his by right."

"The title, yes . . . but not the power. That belongs, as it should, to you—for now. But suppose that were to change? Suppose the new young duke was able to return untainted by the curse that exiled him? Your precious chambers would be for naught. Your precious plans in ruins."

"What is it that you want, Lady Delia? I'm a busy man. You told my secretary you had important information."

"And so I do, Sir Dromon. I would almost say it's priceless."

He winced, settling his pince-nez farther up his nose. "It always is."

She crossed behind where he sat, draping an arm over his shoulder, her lips against his ear as she whispered, "We're old friends, you and I. You understand the game that's played. I tell you what you want to know and you pay me for the pleasure . . . both pleasures if you like." Her tongue flicked out to slide invitingly along his earlobe, her other hand reaching around to rest upon his already stiff cock. He shuddered, his groin tightening as she slowly caressed him through the fabric of his trousers.

Clearing his throat, he leaned forward, opening a bottom drawer and removing a wooden box. With a key from his waistcoat, he unlocked the lid and drew out a leather pouch.

"That should be more than enough for whatever you have to offer."

She took her hand away, leaving him hard and quivering. Hefted the pouch with a satisfied smile. "That will do nicely . . . for a start. But a woman on her own in the world, she has needs that must be met if she's to continue to betray her lover to his enemies."

He pictured that whoreson de Coursy riding the bitch, her golden hair spilling loose of its elegant chignon, her eyes flushed with arousal as she screamed.

Did de Coursy truly believe Lady Delia Swann was loyal to him alone? Did he truly believe the woman loved him? She was like all females; untrustworthy secretive temptations that should be kept to their place, a man's bed, where a good stropping would keep them timid and respectful of their masculine betters.

But de Coursy had always been a romantical milksop, with his head in the clouds. He probably saw her as his maiden; fair, golden, and virginal. He couldn't see the deceit behind those guileless gold-flecked eyes. It's what made the boy such a weak leader, a fool to be swayed by these treacherous Fey-bloods who wanted to lull the clans into complacency so they might destroy them once and for all. The Imnada needed strength and cunning if they were going to survive. They needed someone unafraid to make the hard unpopular choices.

"The same account as we usually use, Lady Delia?" he asked, his cock nearly bursting free of his clothing. His need flushed his face, making him sweat.

She popped the first button on his trousers. "That will do."

Reluctantly, he removed her hand. "Time enough for that when I get what I paid for."

She leaned against his desk. He sought to keep his eyes upon her face but they fell to her breasts, round and pendulous, the nipples showing through the thin fabric. He swallowed and curved his hands around his chair arm to keep them off her body.

She knew his need and smiled again. Oh yes, he'd pay for the privilege but so would she in the end.

"De Coursy is on his way to London."

"Old news, Lady Delia. We know where he's headed and have made arrangements. You shall have to do better than that for the price you've asked."

"And do you know what he takes with him?"

"That too is known to me. The theft of Jai Idrish is a grave insult to the five clans. The trollop who stole it will pay for that treachery. But the sphere will avail him nothing."

"Perhaps not, but the Gylferion just might."

"No." He stood up, shoving the chair back until it toppled on its side. "He can't have found them. They've been lost for centuries. They're legend."

"A legend come to life . . . much like Lucan Kingkiller, the Imnada who helped him gather them together."

Fear splashed cold through him and his dick shriveled like a dried fish. "The Kingkiller rides with de Coursy still?"

"He does."

"Four disks. Four souls. One door." He recited the ancient teaching from memory. "It can't be. It's stories . . . just stories."

"Are you willing to risk the future of the clans over it?"

"No. I am not. You've done me a great service, Lady Delia. You've told me what I need to know. And now you shall have your payment as promised."

He pulled the bell rope behind his desk. The door opened and Mr. Thorsh stepped in, his thick lips pulled back in a feral grin, his gaze resting upon the Swann woman with lascivious excitement. It wouldn't take him long. "Gather your best. We will be leaving for London within the hour."

"You as well, my lord?"

"Developments require my presence on this foray."

If what Lady Delia said was true, and if Lucan Kingkiller was involved, which he didn't doubt, Dromon could not leave this to Thorsh and his soldiers alone. The Gylferion were too valuable to be left in their possession. For all his scholarship, de Coursy was no shaman of the Ossine. He might not yet understand how close he came to breaking the curse upon him. He might not know the forces needed to unlock the keys' true power. But could Dromon take that chance? "Call on those of your company from the Seriyajj. I need their eagles' swiftness."

"Very well, my lord."

"But before you go, Mr. Thorsh, I've a treat for you."

The enforcer's grin widened.

"I've paid good coin. I expect a good show."

The enforcer stepped forward with a nod. Lady Delia's head swiveled between them, alarm only now replacing the smug catty expression from her face. She stood up, backing toward the windows, but they were four stories up and far from where any cries for assistance could be heard. "That's not what was agreed to. I'm no tavern whore to be had by some base soldier."

"No, you're a Fey-blood. The enemy of my people. A witch and a temptress who should be flogged at the cart wheel. How many have taken you? Ten? Twenty? You're as well traveled as the Great North Road, Lady Delia. And I believe you promised me pleasure. Today, my pleasure is to watch Thorsh's pleasure."

The man grabbed her roughly, fisting the collar of her gown and ripping it to her waist. Her breasts spilled free, as large and rosy-tipped as Dromon remembered. Mr. Thorsh pawed her bush with one greedy hand. With the other, he grabbed her hair, pulling her head back as he kissed her deep and hard.

Sir Dromon's hand dove beneath his waistband to fondle his limp staff to rigidity once more.

It was but a moment before the cunt surrendered to Thorsh's brutish assault. She capitulated with a businesslike sigh, her hands falling to her sides as he had his way with her body. The enforcer had her on the floor in minutes, just as Dromon knew he would, her lily-white legs spread wide. She made no move to protest. She understood the business of men and their urges. She might be an earl's daughter, but that only made her quim smell sweeter.

Sir Dromon's hand pumped in rhythm with Thorsh's grunting thrusts.

A pity the Fey-blood bitch didn't scream. But there was time for that. And she'd been paid very well.


London was dour skies, slick cobblestones, and unpleasant faces. Gray passed through the early-morning crowds with barely a flicker of recognition for the noise and the smells and the overwhelming press of humanity hemming them in on all sides, but Meeryn felt her neck swiveling at every new distraction. Her last visit to the metropolis had been brief, her mind preoccupied with retrieving Gray. Before that, she'd made only short annual visits, accompanied by the duke and his household, for a few weeks to shop and perhaps take in the theater or the British Museum. All edifying experiences in the cloistering company of governesses when she was younger and of hatchet-faced companions as she grew older.

This visit was filled with bittersweet excitement. Gray took her hand as they threaded a gap between a rowdy group of apprentices and a butcher in gaiters and spattered apron carrying half a pig over his bloodied shoulders. Both sights to amaze, but Meeryn noticed only the way Gray's fingers fit with hers, the heat traveling up her arm to tingle in her belly, the callused strength of his grip. He glanced over his shoulder, eyes querying her well-being, and she nodded. His answering smile was fleeting, but he tightened his hold on her hand in acknowledgment.

She would have felt nothing but pleasure had it not been for the telltale tremors passing like a current through his muscles and the way his skin stretched sickly and greenish over the bones of his face. It had been two days of hard travel since Marnwood. Three days since he'd taken the last of the draught. Each night had been a hell as he was taken over by the curse to become the eagle of his aspect. Each dawn a tragedy as the scissoring anguish of the Fey-blood's dark magic tore through him once more, leaving him retching and weak, naked upon the ground, man again.

Should Sir Dromon or his Ossine find him this way, it would take little effort to overpower him; no matter how well Gray chose his battleground.

They'd not stopped to refresh or relax in Audley Street upon their arrival in the city. Instead Gray had hired a hackney to carry them as far as St. Anne's Church in Soho. A second to bring them to Holborn. The rest of the way on foot. He'd explained this round-aboutation with a simple "I want the Ossine to find us, but not yet. There are things I must take care of first. People I must speak with."

She wished she'd worn more comfortable half boots.

Precaution had her checking behind every so often, glancing down alleys and side streets. Was that a sinister shadow in that far doorway? Did the gentleman across the street with the brown silk waistcoat watch them a bit too carefully? What of the old woman selling gingerbread, her mop cap covering her dirty curls?

Meeryn tried not to jump at every odd character or startling noise, but it was difficult when there was no way to know from what direction danger might fall on them. Gray was confident that he could evade the Ossine until such time as he chose to reveal himself.

Meeryn did not possess the same self-assurance. She'd resided under the same roof with Sir Dromon since he'd moved in to Deepings to be near the duke. She'd witnessed the man's cunning firsthand, been both an observer and a victim of his insidious, twisted cleverness.

They crossed London Bridge into Southwark and the wide thoroughfares narrowed to crooked lanes and shady alleys. The buildings grew drearier too, soot covered and tightly packed, doors of peeling paint, windows stuffed with rags or gaping empty to the fish-laden breeze. The shop sat in the dim, muddy valley between a great, looming church to the south and the pumps and machinery of the nearby waterworks to the north. A sign hung faded to obscurity over the entryway. She sought to peer through one grime-encrusted window but the interior was as shadowy as the alley they stood in; no way to know what lay beyond the rusted hinges and battered door.

"Are you certain they'll be open so early?"

Gray turned the knob, the door giving way with a screech of defiance. "I'm not sure Ringrose actually sleeps."

Meeryn's eyes widened, her jaw dropped open and she knew she must have made a noise somewhere between shock and amazement. The shop was a musty peddler's dream of cluttered shelves and stuffed drawers. Dusty old books warred for space with jars containing brews of questionable origin labeled in unknown languages, fizzing beakers and bubbling tubes and coils of wire, and in one case, a pickled human head that stared out at her in mild astonishment. Above her, bunches of dried herbs hung from the rafters, creating a tunnel of green, while to either side, a wild profusion of trailing vines and flowering plants covered every surface. The air was a fragrant aroma of spicy, ferny earth, the light a strange greenish glow filtered through the leafy walls. But it was the prickle of Fey magic against her brain and lifting the hairs on her arms that made her stomach knot and her hands clench in uncertain fists.

"What is this place?"

"To the world outside, it's an obscure apothecary's shop. To the Other, it's a thin place; a point where the earth and the Summer Kingdom of the Fey overlap." With the tip of his cane, Gray pushed aside a drooping wide-leafed plant with small yellow flowers. "Ringrose is the proprietor or the gatekeeper, depending on your point of view. He's . . . ah . . . hard to describe. Best if you meet him and make up your own mind."

As if cued from the wings, a muttered curse came from behind the far curtained doorway. "Who's there? Don't they know what time it is? Bloody dawn, that's what. I've barely put aside nightgown and cap and had a proper cup of tea and I'm being hounded by poky-nosed customers. Badb, go see what horrid interlopers have come sneaking about my doorway at such a frightful hour."

The curtain was pulled aside to reveal a little man with a long beard, flowing white hair, and bushy white eyebrows. He was dressed in the manner of a down-at-heels shopkeeper, but Meeryn had the impression he'd be far more at home in wizard's robes and a tall pointed hat. Yet, it was the odd little man's companion that narrowed her gaze and made her breath catch. An enormous crow dove from his shoulder to alight on a nearby shelf, its beady eyes watching them with nothing less than disdainful amusement.

"What is she doing here?" Meeryn blurted.

The man harrumphed, his beard and eyebrows bristling with indignation. "Are we acquainted, madam?"

Gray stepped forward. "No, but you and I are old friends. I need your help, Ringrose."

If the man bristled at Meeryn, he fairly quivered with suppressed emotion at Gray's appearance. His silver eyes went round as saucers and his jaw worked as though he were masticating a particularly tough piece of beef. "You! Haven't we seen the last of your kind yet, shapechanger?"

"I'm out of the supplies I need to create the draught. I need more, or else . . ." His words trailed off into an awkward silence.

Ringrose took up a basket at his elbow, began walking the aisles pulling a leaf here and stem there. "You stick your old spoon in the wall? Don't beat about the bush, young man. It's plain as the nose on my face you're close to death as a chap can be, and still be walking, talking, and"—he cast another indignant look at Meeryn over his shoulder—"swiving." He paused, purple flower in hand, to sniff Gray up and down, nostrils wide, tongue at the edge of his mouth. "You smell of Arawn's realm. Not much yet, but soon enough the door will swing wide."

"Can you help me?"

"Of course I can, shapechanger. Hasn't old Ringrose been there from the beginning? And the beginning of the end? Really, the beginning of the beginning if you count back far enough." He waved them to follow. "Step lively, but be careful of the inventory. I've new items yet to be cataloged and no time to do it while the world rolls topsy-turvy."

Gray followed, but Meeryn hung back, awaiting a chance to confront the crow without an audience. She waited until they passed into the back room and the curtain dropped into place. When she swung around, the shelf was empty, the crow gone. In its place stood the young girl, her cap of black curls framing her narrow impish face. She wrinkled her nose. "Ringrose is right. De Coursy is failing faster than expected. He has little time left."

"Where have you been? We needed you. The Ossine attacked Marnwood."

"Just because I have aligned myself with your cause, Lady N'thuil, do not mistake me for a soldier in your war. I do not fight your battles nor do I follow your orders."

"Then why did you come to Deepings? Why did you help us on the moors when the *avaklos* attacked? Or offer your advice when young Jamie was found?"

Badb seemed to grow more agitated with every hurled question. Her face, already an unnatural pearlescent white, seemed to blanch to the color of bone. Her black snapping eyes shot sparks, and her slender body quivered with unspent rage. "De Coursy is to me just one more generation in an eternity of such. He will live and die and the world will spin on. There is nothing special in this one."

"That's not true. You said yourself he's the last hope for the Imnada. There has to be a reason why you, one of the Fey, help him when the Other who bear the blood of your race seek to murder him."

The door opened, and Lucan entered the shop.

Badb and Meeryn's heads turned in unison, and Meeryn had her answer. It was clear in the expression written all over the other faery's face. "You don't do it for Gray at all. You do it for *him*."

Lucan's dark gaze went opaque, his stern face rigid with an ancient pain. "She does it *because* of me, not for me."

Mac hadn't exaggerated. The Audley Street town house looked as if it had been on the receiving end of a direct artillery strike. Furniture had been toppled and smashed, cushions ripped open, drawers emptied, pictures ripped from their frames. Glass, pottery, and bits of once expensive and exquisite pieces of artwork crunched under his boots. Walls had been hammered, and floorboards pulled up.

Gray passed from room to room in silent study, relieved he had closed the house and sent his staff north to his estate at Addershiels before he'd departed for Deepings. There would be no unexpected grisly discoveries. No repeat of the mutilations at Zeb Doule's small cottage.

He ended his tour in the kitchens, which had somehow remained relatively intact, though not completely without casualties. Ash from the open range lay scattered like a black film across the floor. The fire shovel, poker, and tongs lay in a clutter by the door amid a pile of three saucepans and a bent brass candlestick. The pine worktable had an ominous gash across its already scarred top, while a sack of sugar and two of flour had been stabbed, white powder spilled on the floor beneath an upper shelf.

Meeryn knelt in front of a row of cabinets, her skirts dusted with both ash and flour. "Look, Gray! I've found a crock of oatmeal, a half wheel of cheese, and"—she grinned—"David St. Leger."

David poked his head around a larder door like a jack from a box. "Here's a heel of bread, a jar of olives, and, best of all, cherry wine." He waved a bottle above his head in triumph. "A veritable feast."

"Did anyone see you arrive?" Gray asked.

Arms full, David brought his treasures to the table along with three wineglasses and three plates. "Aside from half your neighborhood, no. It's two in the bloody afternoon. It's not as if I can poof myself in here like a djinn from a bottle. But I've placed our own pickets with orders to sound the alarm should they notice anything suspicious. They know their business and have no love for Sir Dromon."

"What of Callista?"

David drew the cork from the wine, topping every glass. "She's gone north."

"You sent her to her aunt on Skye?"

St. Leger paused a moment before placing the bottle on the table with a plate rattling thump, laughter gone from his eyes. "Sent her? I almost had to crate and mail her to the place. It took a day and a half of persuading, cajoling, threatening, and finally pleading before she agreed to ask for refuge from the old battle-ax. The woman hates me, and she's not too fond of Callista, but they're family. And Dunsgathaic is the safest place to be, with a plague of Ossine descending."

Meeryn stiffened at mention of the name. "Isn't Dunsgathaic the fortress of the Amhas-draoi?"

"It is, and a more grim-faced, humorless bunch you're not likely to find this side of a charnel house," David said, spearing an olive on the tip of his knife.

The brotherhood of Fey-blood warrior-mages were soldiers with no equal and sorcerers with immense power at their command. Even Sir Dromon would think twice before assaulting such a stronghold. Callista would be safe.

Meeryn cut off the usable portions of bread and cheese, placing helpings of each on the plates. Rummaged through a drawer for three forks and a bread knife and returned to the table, righting a stool.

"Who needs Mrs. Waverly?" Gray complimented, tearing into his foraged sandwich.

Meeryn smiled over the rim of her glass. "I doubt even she could ruin bread and cheese."

"Don't be too sure. Remember the time she served Ollie that pudding topped with currants? He had a rash for a week and spent twenty-four hours attached to his chamber pot."

Gray hadn't realized how much he'd lost until he began foraging his mind for lost memories of his brother. His heart still twisted in his chest and occasionally his voice would tremble over a recollection, but each instance grew easier, and Ollie's face grew bright and clear again where it had once been no more than a dark shadow Gray shied away from.

"Who's Ollie?" David asked with a curious tone in his voice.

Gray downed his wine in one gulp, the sandwich caught in his throat. "He was my brother."

David speared another olive. "I didn't know you had a brother."

Meeryn went blankly still as Gray poured another glass from the bottle on the table.

"I mean, I knew you had a brother, but I never knew he had a name. That is, I knew he had a name, just that you and he . . ." David flashed desperate eyes toward Meeryn in a silent plea for help.

Gray rolled his glass around, watching the amber liquid spin. "I don't speak about him much."

"Try at all," David retorted.

Gray shot him an irritated gaze. "He's been gone a long time. There didn't seem to be a point."

Meeryn's gaze clouded, and he noticed that her own wine seemed to be disappearing as swiftly as his. "Do you remember the time he ran off to Plymouth on your grandfather's best hunter and came back with seventy-five pounds he'd won off three sailors in a game of dice?"

Gray felt his mouth twitch upward despite the hard knot in his gut. "Grandfather couldn't decide whether to be angry at his theft or proud of his winnings."

Meeryn laughed. Did anyone else hear how forced it sounded? "What about when he was almost taken up by the press gang in Polperro and had to dress up like a woman to escape?"

Gray laughed. "Mother scolded him for his irresponsibility. Father scolded him for his ugly choice of bonnet."

The stories flowed with the wine and the food, each one more outrageous than the last. David offered a few choice tales from his own sordid past, while Gray reluctantly added a wartime escapade with a donkey, a chicken, and a bag of peppermints. The camaraderie disguised the dread of what was to come. It did not

ease it. All three knew they sought to outrun a coming
storm. All three knew it would swallow them anyway.
There was no outrunning it. Only outlasting it.

David wiped away a tear after Gray's hilarious re-
telling of Ollie's being sent down from university for
setting fire to a dean. "He sounds like my kind of man."

"He was arrogant, prideful, sarcastic, clever,"
Meeryn interrupted, "and just when you thought he
was the most conceited, pigheaded, self-important
know-it-all, he could turn around and do something
incredibly compassionate or kind and you'd forget all
that and want to follow him about like a puppy and
hope he noticed you."

"Sounds like someone else I know," David said
with a sideways glance toward Gray.

She put her glass down, and this time her smile
held real amusement as she studied him like a pinned
bug before announcing, "A little, perhaps."

Gray's spine locked, his shoulders bracing in an in-
stinctual defense. "I'm nothing like Ollie."

She leaned across the table, a hand barely touching
his. Just a skim of her fingers, but enough to make his
chest tighten. She caught and held his gaze. "No, my
heart, you're not like Ollie in any way that matters."

"I think that was supposed to be a compliment,"
he said, trying to laugh off the vising squeeze on his
lungs with a jest.

She didn't take the bait. Instead her hand slid into
his and held on. "You spent a lifetime trying to emu-
late a ghost, Gray. You never realized you'd stepped
out of his shadow long ago."

# 15

Mac arrived with a shake of his greatcoat and a shovel of wet hair off his face. An afternoon storm slanted rain over the rooftops and split the air with window-rattling thunder. The wind pushing east came as a brief respite from the oppressive heat that lay like a dome over the city. If fortune held, the wind would die with nightfall and fog would collect along the city's streets, giving them the advantage of cover should they need it.

"Report?" Gray asked.

"Things are quiet. None's seen hide nor hair of any of Dromon's Ossine. If they're hunting, they're well hidden."

Gray locked the front door behind him. "Oh, they're hunting. I've no doubt about that. Pryor can't allow me to win free of the curse. Not now, with the leadership of the clans in play. He needs me out of the way once and for all."

"But will he really come himself to see it's done?"

"He understands the significance of the Gylferion.

His shaman's training will have ensured it. Not only might they hold the key to the curse, they are priceless and powerful artifacts in their own right. Can you imagine the accomplishment it would be for him to return them to the clans after so many centuries? He would be hailed as a hero; a champion of the Imnada."

"Makes my skin crawl just thinking about it." Mac shuddered.

"So we stop him. And we bring the Gylferion home, curse lifted and lives returned to us."

"You make it sound so easy. Defeat the Ossine, kill Dromon, break a Fey-blood spell, reclaim your throne. Have I left anything out?" Mac shot a pointed look toward Meeryn descending the stairs, a smile of welcome on her face.

Gray frowned and swallowed back his reply. He dare not look ten steps ahead to a future as distant as the moon from the earth. He must stick to the task at hand. Work through the immediate problem of surviving the next twenty-four hours. Fretting over his feelings for Meeryn like an adolescent schoolboy would only get him killed—and her as well.

"No," was his curt reply.

Mac's face tightened while Meeryn's fell, but at least he'd be offered no more leading questions. Time—if he was fortunate—to mend his fences with Meeryn. And if not, better she hate him than mourn for him.

"Good afternoon, Captain Flannery," Meeryn said, passing Gray in an affronted swish of skirts.

Mac offered Meeryn a gentlemanly nod. "Miss Munro. I'm sorry you've been caught up in all this."

She paused on the bottom riser, head lifted, eyes solemn. "I'm not. I've asked myself for the last two months why I was chosen by Jai Idrish to serve as N'thuil. Perhaps this is the crystal's answer."

"To save the clans from Sir Dromon?"

"No, I'm not a warrior. I know that now. But if I can help to lift the curse, then Gray, with your help, can save the clans from Sir Dromon."

Vanished was the hoydenish freckled girl Gray remembered. In her place stood a competent, strong, and very determined woman. Where once there had been frenzied enthusiasm now there was bold and fiery passion, and the reckless bravado of childhood had firmed to an unhesitating courage.

Would she be the same woman if she'd married Ollie, as Grandfather had intended? Or even if she had married Gray and taken up the destiny others had laid for her? He didn't think so. She was a result of choices made and roads taken, not just by her but by others around her. He wouldn't regret the lost years behind them. But he'd damn well fight to keep from losing any more.

She turned her attention to Gray, expression cool as a winter ocean. "While you're meeting with Mac and David, I'm going to double-check the house. Secure the windows. Be sure all the doors are latched and bolted." The scent of her was cool and salty clean. Her eyes gleamed, dark and mysterious as the depths in which she swam as seal. "You have an odd look on your face. Too much wine with lunch?"

"Waxing philosophical."

"Always dangerous."

"In this case . . . long past due," he replied.

"Well, I hope you came to some profound conclusions."

"Ask me again in a week, and I may enlighten you."

"It's a deal, Your Grace." Her voice glided molten and smoky smooth along his bones. The sinuous grace of her slender body as she picked her way through the rubble of the entry hall reminded him of the feline slink of the tiger aspect she'd worn at Marnwood. Proud, bold, and dangerous as hell.

"Uh . . . I'll . . . ah . . . just join David, shall I?" Mac's voice sounded from down a long hazy tunnel.

Gray barely noticed his departure. Hell, he'd barely notice a full frontal assault from half a dozen assassin-trained Ossine at this moment. Hands upon his chest, Meeryn leaned up on her toes, her mouth sliding invitingly warm and soft against his. She paused, looking into his eyes, a mischievous glint in her gaze.

"What?" he asked, almost plaintively.

"Waiting for the moment when your good sense reasserts itself." The light in her face faded. "Or the moment when I gain some."

"Anything?" he asked.

She pursed her lips. "No, I'm singularly impractical and unapologetic."

She kissed him again, a slow, deep passionate kiss that left his senses swimming. Cherry wine had nothing on Meeryn for inducing head spins and hallucinations.

He stepped out of her arms before he forgot himself completely and backed her against a convenient wall, skirts around her waist. "If you're going to be wandering about on your own, take this." He grabbed his dubious gift from a nearby table and knelt to ruck up her skirts.

"Gray!" She flushed crimson. "Even my impracticality has its limits."

He skimmed her leg, his cock hard as a hammer. "I've embarrassed you? I didn't know that was possible."

"That almost sounds like a challenge," she said, offering him a look that could melt steel.

What would he give for fifteen minutes and an empty house? He forced himself to stop his ascent midway up her thigh, though the wicked and extremely excited parts of him wished to continue the climb. Instead he took deep breaths as he buckled the sheath's leather strap around her thigh. Slid the dirk into place, its ebony hilt capped with the de Coursys' double-headed eagle bearing five arrows.

"I know you lost the one Conal gave you. I thought this might take its place."

Color flooded her cheeks. "It's not even my birthday. What do you think? Does it match my eyes?" she asked with a flutter of her lashes.

"Not many women can wear a deadly weapon and carry it off with such panache. You're the one in a million."

He stood, dropping her skirt in place. Offered her the pistol he wore at his belt. "This, you carry. And blow the head off anything that moves."

"What if it's one of you?"

The edge of his mouth quirked in a dark smile. "Then we should have ducked."

She accepted it with a faint lift of her brows. "Not that I don't appreciate the sentiment—I mean, what woman doesn't like to receive her own private arsenal—but if the Ossine want to get in, they will. I'm not the only one with the ability to shift to any form. And this place is riddled with mouseholes."

"Humor me," he said, with one more check of the bolt on the front door before he sent her off with a last kiss, then took a few moments of deep breaths and arctic thoughts to recover.

In the library, Mac and David were waiting for him. David wearing a smirk that always meant trouble; Mac staring at the ceiling as if the answers to life were written among the cornices. Gray chose to ignore them both. He righted an overturned chair. Stooped to pick up a fragment of Wedgwood, a jagged triangle of celadon green with a woman's arm in white, all that was left of the expensive vase that had formerly sat in one corner. He tossed it back on the floor to be lost among the piles of rubble and refuse. "Pryor's desperate."

"Not that you're not well aware but I think it begs repeating; Dromon's going to have a bloody army of Ossine with him," David replied, dropping onto a slightly battered sofa. "Are you prepared for that? For what that might mean?"

"Torture, dismemberment, death, desecration." Mac ticked them off on his fingers.

"And not that I don't love a good disemboweling with some broken bones for good measure," David added, "but I tend to prefer to be on the winning side. We're not exactly . . . ah . . . equal in numbers. You, me, Mac, and . . ." He waved a hand as if searching for an answer.

"Lucan," Gray finished for him.

"Four of us against Dromon's marauding bloodthirsty Ossine. Love those odds. I can see why you don't gamble."

Gray took a seat. His normally organized and immaculate desk had been turned inside out. Folios dumped, drawers pulled out and upended in a blizzard of files and scattered pages. Ledgers ripped open then ripped apart. "Can you think of anyone you'd rather have fighting at your side than the Kingkiller?"

"Ten thousand of Wellington's finest? A hundred of Boney's best?" David wisecracked. "A few dozen street urchins throwing stones? A nasty puppy with a case of the mange?"

Gray began the long task of salvaging what he could from the mess. "Sorry, none were available. You'll have to take what you can get."

"Me and my overactive honorable nobility. It's never done anything but get me into trouble."

"Where *is* Lucan?" Mac asked. He stood at the window facing the street, his feline gaze on the afternoon traffic, his pose one of cautious vigilance. Gray could almost imagine the very tip of the panther shapechanger's tail twitching in catlike watchfulness.

"He said he'd be here. I don't question him too closely."

"Afraid of what you might find out?" David asked.

"Something like that." A ledger of receipts. A book on alchemy. Correspondence from his tailor.

David sat up. "Not to rain on your brilliant plan, General, but even if somehow we manage to win over a company of zealous enforcers happy to stake us out like yesterday's laundry, we're still not free of the curse. You're still not free of the curse." Leave it to David to point out the obvious.

"No, not yet." A book, pages scattered from the broken binding. Another bore a boot print, the words a pulpy mess. A third had been torn to shreds. "But the Gylferion are here. Jai Idrish is here. The two of you are here. It's only a matter of finding the missing piece that brings it all into focus."

"Adam's not missing, Gray. He's dead. And not even Callista's gifts of necromancy can pull him free of death for our purpose," David commented with his usual flippant delivery.

Had Gray not been aggravated, exhausted, uneasy, and slightly feverish, he might have ignored him. But the curse gnawed at the edges of his consciousness like a cancer. He worried for those he'd put in harm's way and grieved for those he'd put in the ground. Too many lives. Too many souls. Too many ghosts to drag him into despair if he weakened for a moment. He slammed a book onto the desktop with force to rattle and sway the chandelier.

"Do you think I don't know that Adam's dead, St. Leger? Do you think somehow I've forgotten the day we lowered him into the ground like a grub rather than releasing him to the wind and the flames in the proper way?"

"I think you've forgotten that it's taken you two years just to gather these dented disks." David's tone carried a sharp whipcrack, reminding Gray that the laughing scoundrel had a dangerous edge. "You can't expect to find every answer in an old book or organize your way to victory. Sometimes you just have to improvise and hope events come right in the end."

"The answer is here. The knowledge is in one of these volumes." Gray rose from his chair and began pulling books off the broken, battered shelves. Those he recognized as valuable, he placed on a table. Others he dismissed, tossing them aside. The pile grew along with his frustration. "I just have to find—"

"What? A sentence that reads, 'To break a Fey-blood curse add one onion, dance around the table in your small clothes, and touch your nose with your tongue'?" David shot back.

"Don't be a blasted idiot." Gray plucked a book up from the topmost stack he'd made. Leafed through the torn pages for something . . . anything . . .

David's shadow fell across the page as Gray leaned against the table. "Are you certain this duel with Sir Dromon you've contrived isn't your way of going out in a blaze of glory rather than a whimper of shriveled weakness?"

Gray opened the next book, scanning the two chapters on Golethmenes. There wasn't much. The author had only the vaguest theories to espouse. He plucked up a third, but the pages were ripped clean away, leaving nothing but a few ragged threads where the binding had frayed.

"Or your way of exacting the vengeance you were denied when your grandfather died?" David continued.

His question pierced Gray's concentration like a swordthrust to the gut. He felt the edges of the leather folio bend under the force of his grip. Gray hadn't killed his grandfather, but he'd imagined his death more times than he could count. "I never wanted vengeance."

"Bullshit," David barked. "You've always wanted it. You may have prettied it up in a noble cause, but come down to it, this has always been about standing over your enemy and driving a sword into his chest and seeing the life drain away. Smiling when he begged for mercy. Watching him writhe in agony like he watched you."

"That's not true."

He no longer saw the words upon the page or the monk's elaborate illuminations. His stare turned inward to a scaffold, a crowd of unsmiling faces, and the rank odors of piss and sweat and vomit as his life was taken from him.

He'd had the opportunity. The old man had invited it. Gray had turned away. Was sparing the duke's life a weakness or a strength? Did it matter? Vengeance might have been his reason for entering into this conspiracy. What drove him now was more than simple retaliation.

"You're wrong, David," he repeated. "And this conversation is over."

"Is that an order, Major?"

"If you want to take it as such," he snarled through clenched teeth.

"You can deny until you're blue in the face, but if you do, you're lying to yourself. It wouldn't be the first time."

He locked his gaze on David's, fists itching to knock the bastard on his ass. "What the hell is that supposed to mean?"

"Why is Meeryn Munro here? She was your ticket to Deepings, you told us. But you're not at Deepings anymore."

"She's N'thuil. I need her to summon the power of Jai Idrish."

"Is that why? Or did you just need her—period?"

His heart clenched and he tossed off an ugly laugh. "London's Lothario is giving me advice on women? That's rich. Mac, are you listening to this?"

"Don't drag *me* into this. I'm minding my own

business. If you two want to beat the stuffing out of each other, go ahead."

"Tempting, but I'll let Dromon's Ossine have first crack." Gray slammed the book closed, took up a restless pacing walk wall to wall and back again. "Fine, so I need her. I might even love her. What the hell am I supposed to do about it?"

"Tell her so?"

"No."

"Why not?"

Gray paused at the hearth, staring into the cavernous mouth. No fire to lose himself in, no warmth to ease the chill along his bones. He plowed both hands through his hair, linked them at the back of his neck. "I can't believe we're having this conversation."

"Why—because it galls you to know I'm right?"

"Even a broken clock is right twice a day."

"This clock says it's time to tell her how you feel . . . before it's too late."

He spun around, gut aching, head pounding. "You make it sound so fucking easy, St. Leger. Find the girl, tumble head over ass, live forever in a little dream cottage for two."

"Do I? Then perhaps you're not as observant as I thought." He slammed his mutilated hand on the tabletop, a finger missing, compliments of ganglord Victor Corey. St. Leger had fought for his life . . . and then he'd fought for Callista's. Death didn't frighten him. He'd been there and done that already.

Silence descended as each party surrendered to a neutral corner. Gray tried to focus, but his thoughts were scattered and restless. His nerves jumping. David had skated too close to too many truths that Gray wasn't ready to confront.

"I can't tell her anything until this is over. It wouldn't be fair when I don't know how this will end. She could be grieving a corpse by the end of the week."

"Hell, she could *be* a corpse by the end of the week."

Mac cleared his throat and gave a subtle shake of his head.

David shrugged and answered with a widening of his eyes. Mac subsided to his role as lookout. "All I'm saying, Gray, is that if you care about Meeryn and she cares about you, there's no time like the present. Tomorrow might be too late."

His parents and Ollie gone without a good-bye. Grandfather dead before Gray had a chance to make his final peace. Would his time with Meeryn end the same way?

"I'll take it under advisement."

David snorted, subsiding back onto the sofa with a disgusted roll of his eyes. "You once told me you wanted more than a quick swiving. Seems to me you've found it. Now the question becomes, what are you going to do about it?"

What indeed?

The rain had passed and now evening light faded toward dusk. The windows in the houses across the street glowed orange and red, as if fires licked from room to room. Heat shimmered up from the street and the few pedestrians out looked wilted by the oppressive humidity. She scanned the corners, the alleys, the rooftops, her nerves scraped raw with waiting, when a startled cough and a shimmer of color at the corner of her eye caught her attention.

She spun, finger on the trigger of her pistol, to find not a merciless Ossine enforcer but the wizened figure of Mr. Ringrose blurring into being. He'd changed from his earlier attire of down-at-heels shopkeeper and now wore the crimson and gold robes of a sorcerer born, a long tasseled cap upon the sparse white hair of his head, and his long beard combed to a brilliant snowy white. Over his shoulder, he bore a leather sack, which he patted as he came into being, as if afraid he might have lost it during his magical travels.

"You nearly had your head taken off," she snapped, still trying to catch her breath and ease back the cocked trigger without blowing a hole in the ceiling, the floor, or Mr. Ringrose. "What are you doing here?"

He sniffed and smoothed a hand down his beard. "I might ask you the same question, impertinent snippet of a girl. Where is de Coursy?"

"Downstairs in what's left of the library." She put the pistol down on a table. Turned it so the barrel pointed away from her. Changed her mind, picked it up, and shoved it in a drawer where she didn't have to look at it.

"Where am I?" He glanced around with a somewhat owlish expression.

"My bedchamber . . . such as it is."

He took in the disheveled room, face growing pink, lips pursing with disapproval. "How did I end here? I was certain my directions were spot-on"—he touched a finger to his lips—"and then I made a left at"—he motioned as he thought out loud—"and then down at . . ."

"I hope your knack with medicines is better than your skill at directions."

He sniffed, his long nose quivering with distaste. "My knack with medicines has never been questioned before, thank you very much."

"Aren't you the one who gave Gray and the others the secret to the draught in the first place?"

"I offered them a few hints. Nothing more."

"And now they sicken when they take it and sicken when they don't."

"It's not my fault the blood of the shapechanger pollutes all magic it touches, turning life to death and death to . . ."

"To a curse they can't control."

He clenched the strap of his satchel. "Does de Coursy want the draught or not? I've things to do and places to be. I do not like to leave the shop too long. There are so many specimens to catalog, so many new items to identify. "

"Of course. I'll take you to him."

Ringrose followed her down the corridor to the main staircase. The banister was lying in pieces on the floor in the main entry hall and three risers had been axed to splintered shreds, but Meeryn circumnavigated the damage, stepping over the broken urns littering the floor and the glass sparkling like diamonds from a fallen shattered chandelier to lift the latch on the library door.

Mac Flannery stood at the mantel, his soldier's stance and sharp features revealing his military bearing better than any red coat or gold braid ever could. David St. Leger leaned against a table, one leg dangling, casually spinning a bronze disk like a top with his scarred and disfigured hand until Gray reached over and snatched it away. "Enough larking about, David. We've work to do."

"Seems to me we've been kicking our heels for hours awaiting . . . oh, that's right . . . our execution."

"You can leave anytime."

"And miss all the fun? Wouldn't hear of it."

"What have you there?" Ringrose said, his voice scraping across the conversation like a bow across an out-of-tune fiddle.

Everyone stopped as one and turned to the new-comers.

"Ringrose. You've come," Gray said, Meeryn noting the relief in his voice even if his expression never changed.

"What have you there? I asked." The sorcerer scurried across the floor, robes flapping about his bony ankles, a finger toying with the end of his beard. "What are you playing with as if it were child's toy? *Anata Asantos! Deux breolmi neophirotha.*"

"What did he say?" David nudged Mac, who shrugged.

"The Gylferion." Ringrose stopped dead at the edge of the table, staring at the disks as if they were the sun, moon, and stars tied up with a pink bow. "You've found them again."

"You know what these things are?" David asked.

Ringrose swung around, eyes crackling with indignation. "Of course. My master and maker himself created the disks of the Gylferion."

"Your master?" Gray asked, his face unnervingly blank of expression. "You mean Golethmenes?"

"He was the greatest of the Fey craftsmen. He

could forge magic from the very elements around him. Bring death with a thought. Create life with . . ." Ringrose worried his hands over and over, his beard quivering, his eyes darting round him in wild fright. "With . . ." He scrubbed at his face. Paced in a circle. "It's in the blood. He said it's in the blood. That's what he told me. That's what I know. More than that I cannot say. More than that I dare not say."

"You're saying you knew the chap who made these?" David asked slowly.

"Knew him, that's right," Ringrose answered. "He created the Gylferion at the behest of the Queen of the Fey, she who was wroth at the shapechanger for young Arthur's death. The boy was her favorite. He was meant to rule. The Kingkiller ended that. He tore all she had worked for asunder. Like a blundering bear through the finest spider's silk."

"How did Golethmenes make them work? How did he use them to imprison Lucan Kingkiller? How did he overcome the Imnada's resistance to Fey magic in order to get the spell to work?" Gray's voice remained carefully neutral. Only Meeryn could know what control it took to hold to such a measured tone.

Ringrose grew more and more agitated, hands opening and closing, shoulders hunched as if he expected a beating should he answer wrong. "Four keys. Four souls. One door. That's what Golethmenes said. That's how he did it."

"We've got the four keys, but what does he mean by . . ."

A new voice answered. "He means just what he says."

For a big man, Lucan Kingkiller was incredibly

quiet. Meeryn nearly jumped out of her skin at the low rumble of his strangely accented voice just behind her ear. His mouth quirked and he offered her a small contrite nod of his head. "I'm sorry, my lady. I did not mean to startle you."

"You didn't. I just . . . I'm not used to people sneaking up on me."

"I would think few things sneak up on you." His gaze passed beyond her to settle on Gray with a dip of his shoulder, his voice pitched so that only she might hear.

She acknowledged his remark with her own half smile. "I'd been waiting a lifetime for that one and it still caught me by surprise."

"Let us hope your wait is soon over."

He strode into the room, his head seeming to scrape the ceiling, his presence charging an already explosive atmosphere. He faced down Mac, David, and Gray, who waited on him, their eyes hard as stones, their faces set. "Four keys"—Lucan recited as he took the gold disk from Gray's hand—"Golethmenes created the four disks using all he knew of the alien powers of the Imnada shapechangers." He picked up the bronze disk. "Four souls. He sacrificed four of the Fey to infuse the keys with the strongest of their magics. Stripped of their inner spirit, there was no way back through the walls to Ynys Avalenn." He picked up the copper disk. "One door."

"A thin place," Gray answered, snatching up the silver disk from the table. "Golethmenes used a thin place to concentrate the energy into one huge cataclysmic force."

"He used Badb, didn't he?" Meeryn stepped forward, a horrible ache low in her stomach.

Lucan turned to her. "Aye, my lady. Badb was lost to the Summer Kingdom. But her imprisonment was my freedom. For she stole the Gylferion in retaliation against those who cast her out. Hounded for her treachery, she spent years and centuries hiding and running, and the disks were scattered and lost. It would be many centuries more before they were unearthed and brought together once more."

"But why are Badb and Ringrose companions if Golethmenes was his master and Badb betrayed the Fey and stole the keys from him? Shouldn't they be enemies?"

"Ringrose is a Realing; a creature spun from magic. He was created by the Fey smith to serve his daughter. Where she went, Ringrose followed. He was protector, adviser, servant, and friend. His service did not end with her exile. He did as he was trained to do."

"You mean to say Badb is Golethemenes's daughter? How could he sacrifice his own flesh and blood?" Meeryn couldn't keep the pain from her voice.

This time Lucan's gaze rested on Gray, with the weight of a thousand and more years behind it. She watched as his face reddened then paled, the bones standing stark against the hollowed skin, his hands curling around the silver disk like talons despite the pain, the blue of his eyes like the heart of an angry sea.

"I suppose he thought he was doing it for the good of his people."


Gray stood at the door, watching Meeryn as she packed her belongings, with a sense of déjà vu as if he were reliving another scene from a previous life.

But this time there was but one thing she carried; a crystal sphere which she stitched into an inside seam of her gown with big clumsy stitches. "I've never enjoyed mending, but now I wish I'd spent more time at the pursuit."

"Your hands are shaking."

She bit off the final thread and poked her needle back on its cushion with a killer stab. "I'd hoped you wouldn't notice."

"Your pulse is racing. Pupils are dilated."

Her brows furrowed with irritation. "I know I'm scared, Gray. I don't need a physician's diagnosis."

"I've never thought of you as being scared of anything. That was always my purview. The cautious one, the timid one, the one who spent his days with his head in a book. You were the bold one who enjoyed skating the edge between naughty and downright wicked. I guess it still holds true."

"Are you afraid of what's coming?"

"No, I'm afraid of what's already here in front of me. I'm terrified. I feel eight again and afraid to sleep without a lamp to chase away the dreams. Or twelve and too frightened to tell my grandfather how the coachman's son thrashed me for a penny. Or twenty-one again and too afraid to . . . to show you how I feel."

She touched his cheek, the scar at the edge of his mouth. "I'm not sure if I enjoy being compared with the bogeyman or a bully, but that last bit . . . I might enjoy that."

He cupped her face, kissing her slowly and deeply, hoping she felt the depth of his need for her in every pass of his lips and teasing flick of his tongue. He took her hand, fingers resting at the underside of her wrist, feeling her pulse skitter ever more rapidly. "I'm told the odds are stacked against me"—he sensed her stiffen in his arms—"but I don't gamble unless I'm certain I'll win."

She lifted her head, eyes black with desire now rather than fear. "Together, we can do this. Jai Idrish will answer to my call. I know it will. And with the Gylferion . . . we're close, Gray. So close I can taste it."

"I wasn't speaking of the curse this time."

Her face softened into a smile so welcoming it made his heart turn over and he knew what David accused him of was true. He didn't just need her . . . he loved her.

He leaned her back upon the bed, his hands threaded in the curling tangle of her warm honey-blonde hair, his thigh resting across her legs. She ran a hand over his face, eyes wide and shining with unshed tears as if she memorized him. "You won't die. I won't allow it."

He chuckled. "The Voice and Vessel has spoken?"

"No, Meeryn Munro has spoken." She lifted her head to take his bottom lip between her teeth. Her tongue plunged within, her body pliant and alive beneath him. "You might have been meek, you were never subservient. When you make up your mind to do something, there's little that stands in your way."

"A few hours or a few days will tell if I can reclaim my place untainted and unchallenged."

She grinned, her hand sliding beneath his shirt to skim the rippled contours of his chest. "I wasn't talking about the curse this time."

He smelled her arousal on her skin, the scent of her desire inflaming him until he ached. But he took his time, skimming her free of her clothing, taking care to offer her every pleasure, every caressing evidence of his own desire. Finally, she lay naked before him, hair loose about her shoulders and down over her breasts to tickle the flat planes of her stomach. But as he bent to taste, she suddenly rocked up on her knees, a devil's grin on her kiss-swollen mouth. "You don't think I'm going to let you stay dressed, do you? It's my turn."

She loosened his neckloth, tossing it away. Kissed the hollow at the base of his throat. Unbuttoned his waistcoat, sliding it from his shoulders as she pressed her body against him, the heat of her like a blast furnace. He reached for her but she took his wrist and held him away.

"If you've waited this long, you can wait a little longer."

She released him to pull his shirt over his head. The breeze danced over his skin, and he closed his eyes to the coolness of it across his hot flesh. Her hands played over his body with a feather's touch, her lips following. She took his nipple in her mouth, teasing it hard. Every drop of blood fled to his cock which was close to exploding. He hissed as she tongued him to the breaking point before moving to the other nipple. Her teeth grazed and nipped, her tongue swirled the sensitive skin until he growled with need. She met his stare, her own black as sin, her lips wet and full.

"Your breeches next, Your Grace."

He kicked off his boots as she shucked him out of his smallclothes. His cock springing free, the tip dewed with his seed. She pushed him down upon the bed, his arms over his head as her eyes traveled with languorous ease over his nudity. She touched each scar, followed by a kiss. Caressed the marred and ugly flesh at his shoulder. Traced each rippled muscle of his abdomen before taking his cock in her hand. He groaned and nearly leapt off the bed.

"I'd prolong the agony, but I don't think you could take much more."

He shook his head as she slid her tongue up the length of his shaft, once twice, her lips circling the head, her breath hot and soft and oh-my-god . . .

He groaned her name, tangled his hands in her hair and dragged her up to kiss her mouth, tasting his seed on her tongue, his other hand feeling the slick heat of her sex. She lifted her hips and sheathed herself onto him, deeper until he felt he must rip her in half. Rocked forward and took more of him. He squeezed his eyes shut, praying he didn't humiliate himself by coming too fast, too soon. She rose and plunged again, hips tilted, face flushed. He rose to meet her, hands holding her waist, making her feel him, slowly, easily. She wanted faster. He'd not give it to her. He would take his time. If he could.

Each thrust curled tighter in his gut, each fluttering spasm of her inner muscles tensed his body like a drawn bow, every inch of him alive and awake. He drove into her once more as she cried out in a shuddering gasp. He exploded inside her as she rode him, drawing out her pleasure and his own, her sex tremoring against his cock, her whimpering gasps against his ear bringing him to climax again.

The shadows lengthened. The curse moved sluggish and slow through his bloodstream. He saw the blue and silver flames crowding his vision. But he pushed these away as he held her. The battle would be joined soon enough. If he could not give the clans a future, perhaps he could offer them another son of Idrin, a boy who would take up the fight he might fail.

"He would be an eagle and strong as his father," she said, sensing his unspoken thoughts.

"He would not be the Duke of Morieux," he replied.

Her tears splashed hot upon his chest. His own stung his blinking eyes. "But he *could* be leader of the five clans. It's in the blood," she whispered.

# 16

―⟨⟩―

It was past midnight when they convened in the foyer. With a few final instructions and a firm handshake for each, Gray sent Flannery, St. Leger, and Lucan into the night, each bearing a disk of the Gylferion.

Meeryn carried Jai Idrish, though she hid it in an inside seam of her gown, hastily stitched closed around the sphere. A bit bulky, but in the dark none would notice the odd drape of her skirts or the way her hand rested gently against her hip. At least that was her hope.

She and Gray lingered behind, making final adjustments to the traps he'd laid and the snares he'd set. Should the Ossine attempt another attack, they would receive more than they bargained for.

He kissed her in the dim light of a last candle. "If Ringrose is right, I can meet Dromon whole and unsullied by Fey-blood magic. He'll have no choice but to accept my ascension."

"He has an army of choices, and they still believe you murdered your grandfather and they still fear you'll destroy the clans through your alliance with Fey-bloods."

"It's the only way, Meeryn."

He was so solid, so warm, so incredibly dear to her. She wanted to hold on to him and not let go. Escape back to their upstairs chamber, lock the door, and forget the world. Then a tremor passed through him, no more than a stiffening of his body and a tightening of his embrace, but it was obvious the curse fought to overcome the draught's protection. That every day, as the draught's effects weakened, the curse grew stronger. What they had hoped were months might be less than that. Weeks before potion and curse together did what Dromon's forces had not been able to do in the last two years—destroy Gray.

She lay her head upon his chest, listening to the steady beat of his heart. "I understand the reasoning. I hate the necessity. And . . . and I'm afraid."

"Of Dromon?"

"Of losing you. Of losing this so soon after I've found it."

He looked as if he wanted to say something, his eyes darkening like clouds slanting across a dark sea, then he pulled her cloak close about her shoulders and kissed her on her forehead and the sun returned to his bright stare.

The heat seemed to press at her from all sides beneath the heavy fabric. "Ugh, nothing worse than wool in the summer," she complained. "Must I wear it?"

"You must. Sir Dromon's enforcers will recognize you if you don't. And there's no saying how many he's salted London with."

She pulled the hood up around her face. "I can

hide my features, but I can't hide my presence. They'll feel me as soon as I pass."

"That's why I've called on assistance to draw off any enforcers who might stray too close. It won't give you much time, but if you need it, he'll see you have the seconds you need to elude them."

"Who?"

A figure stole clear of the alley. A man dressed to blend in, with a face as nondescript as his attire.

"This is Breg."

The old man doffed his cap and offered her a slight gentlemanly bow, his gaze shifting from shadow to shadow in the house as if he spied spooks in every creak and enemies in every flicker of the candle's flame. "Lady N'thuil. It's an honor."

"Please call me Meeryn."

"Not likely. I may have been raised *avaklos* in Whitechapel 'stead of the family's holding in the north, but I know what's due the Voice and Vessel. You'll be treated with the respect what's owed."

"Get her to Ringrose, Breg. Do whatever you have to, but make sure no harm comes to her. Do you understand?"

"You can trust Breg. He'll make sure she turns up right and tight when and where she's needed, my lord . . . I mean, that is . . . Major, sir."

Meeryn turned to Gray. None but she would have noticed the slight shiver that passed under the skin of his face or settled like a mask behind his eyes. "I'm the Duke of Morieux these days, Breg. It's to be Your Grace from now on whether I like it or not."

Breg gave another doff of his cap and a deeper bow. "Aye, sir, as you say, my lord, I mean Your Grace. As you say, but you see"—he peered over his shoulder with an odd shrug and a squint into the alley's dark— "if it were up to me, my lord, but you see . . . they . . ."

Meeryn stiffened, her blood like ice. "Gray. Run! It's the Ossine!"

There were no shots fired or knives hurled, not even a voice raised. Instead the shadows stretched long and lean and cruel up the side of the alley walls. The crackling feel of Imnada like a tug under her breastbone. "There are too many of them. We'll never win our way through."

Gray dragged her into the passage and snuffed the single candle, plunging the room into darkness. "Do just as I said. Go toward the roof. Always toward the roof. If all else fails, take to the air. I'll find you."

With a last kiss and a final squeeze of her hand, he was gone. Black against black. A silent figure moving away into the maze of store rooms and sculleries. She nodded, her fear like a plunge of ice water burning her down to the bone. She raced toward the kitchens, clamping a hand to her side as Jai Idrish banged against her hip.

The door flew open behind her, men spilling into the passage like ants from a hive. Glints off knives. The gleam off pistol butts. At least in the city, they were safe from attack by a pack of wolves or ambush by a panther. Even Dromon would avoid that kind of notice, no matter his desperation in stopping Gray.

"Done what I was told. Done it and no tricks." Breg wept. "I'm not a harm to none. Not a harm to—" There was a muffled shot as if the pistol had been held close against the body as it was fired, a groan quickly cut off, and silence but for the scrape of men's boots and the rasp of men's breathing.

Breg had paid for his betrayal with his life. Meeryn spared a hasty prayer for the little man. She didn't fault him for his treachery. Many far stronger than him had fallen to the Ossine's rougher persuasions.

She pelted through the kitchens, and up the stairs toward the ground floor. Smashed through into the entry hall. Two men stood just inside the front door, eyes white in dark faces. They approached her cautiously as she stood frozen to the spot, luring them closer. Another step. Then another. The twine Gray had stretched across the corridor snapped. The makeshift spring gun fired, sending a plume of choking smoke rolling through the downstairs. One of the men screamed, going down with a blast to the chest. The second man threw himself to the side, but Meeryn was prepared for that. Her dirk ended in his throat. He clung to the handle, mouth opening and closing as blood gushed over his hands.

Gray's orders had been specific. Do not hesitate. Do not falter. She took the stairs for the first floor.

The men behind her hit the entry hall and found their comrades. A new howl of anger met her ears as they followed, now less restrained by silence or deception. A shot splintered the doorjamb three feet to her right. Another exploded a sconce by her head. In the dark, the snaking fuse Gray had set glowed like a single red eye as it ate its way toward the small bag of black powder collected from his store of weapons.

She raced down the corridor and around the corner, where a rush of wind and heat knocked her to her knees, tore the breath from her lungs, the explosion ringing her ears. She lay on her stomach, her heart threatening to tear its way from her chest with the pain of its beating. Moans and groaning whimpers and the charred stench of flesh soured her stomach.

Slowly and painfully she climbed to her feet. Made her way up to the second floor and the third. The determined sounds of pursuit had become the cries of wounded and the death rattles of the dying.

She threaded her way through the cluttered attics. She would hide Jai Idrish here among generations of de Coursy cast-offs. She would shift. She would flee. Gray had told her to take no chances. She was more important than the sphere. Her life meant more to him than his salvation.

How about that trunk? Or perhaps the chest of drawers over there? Did that suit of armor in the corner make a good hiding spot? Or perhaps in plain sight was the best. Lay it in the empty eye socket of that lion skin rug rolled in the corner.

A figure broke free of the boxes and crates. His body was bulky and beefy-shouldered, an expression of triumph on his jowly face. He was dressed oddly, as if his clothing had come from the trunks and crates surrounding him. On anyone else and at any other time, she might have laughed at the odd assortment of shirt, waistcoat, frock coat and knee breeches he wore. She wasn't laughing now.

"You overlooked one detail, Lady N'thuil," Thorsh gloated.

"And what was that, Mr. Thorsh?" she replied in her most arrogant tone of voice as she slid her hand into the hidden pouch sewn within the seam of her dress and fingered the loose threads free. The sphere dropped into her hand. Using her fear as a cover, she backed against an unlidded barrel overflowing with straw to cradle the china or glassware within. She braced herself with one arm as if to steady herself, easing the sphere into the tub, where it sank quietly from view.

He stepped toward her, his commandeered clothing stretching across his wide chest, revealing his hairy knees. "I'm of the Seriyajj, too. And the distance from Cornwall to London is much shorter . . . as the eagle flies."

So intent upon the man in front of her, she never heard the two behind who'd apparently escaped Gray's rough and ready man traps. They gripped her arms. Dragged her nearly off her feet.

"Where's de Coursy?" Thorsh demanded.

She tried controlling the knocking in her knees by locking them together and forced herself to meet him eye to eye as she scrambled to channel the authority of every N'thuil that had come before. Her chin lifted in an attempt at calm disdain. "The Duke of Morieux is gone. I told him to flee while I distracted you. He's more important than I am. You said it yourself. The N'thuil is a useless title."

Thorsh's mouth tightened, his brows low across his broken nose. But the smile that followed caused Meeryn's stomach to drop into her shoes and goose bumps to rise up and down her arms.

He chucked her chin as an elderly uncle might a favorite niece. A sweet gesture, had it not been for the savagery in his pale eyes. "Useless as Voice and Vessel, mayhap, but as bait you're a prize indeed."

\* \* \*

Bent over, hands braced on his thighs as he gulped in precious air, Gray surveyed the results of his scheme. Two dead in the entry hall. Another lying on the staircase where he'd dropped with a knife in his back. That didn't count the two dispatched before they made it past the kitchens or the ones caught by the blast upstairs. He straightened, wincing at the pain in his side. Shrapnel had caught him in the explosion; wood and plaster ripping into the flesh above his hip. He pressed a hand against the wound. Blood leaked through his fingers.

He removed the drawstring bag where he'd placed the silver disk for safekeeping. Dropped it into his left boot. It would be safe there.

"De Coursy? You still here? We've got someone who wants to speak to you."

Gray lifted his head, dread sliding cold and deadly through his gut, as he eased his hand into his pocket for his loaded pistol.

"Miss Munro has been a naughty girl," Thorsh continued. "Sir Dromon will enjoy seeing her punished. He gets off on hearing women scream." He chuckled. "Anybody scream, for that matter. Seen him take a man apart bone by bone just to hear him screech."

Thorsh's smarmy voice set Gray's teeth on edge. His self-satisfied bluster itched Gray's fists. But his words chilled him to the core.

"This is the madman you would have lead the clans?"

"This is a madman that'll make the Fey-bloods tremble in their boots. Skin the hides off a few of those magic-breeders and the rest will see we're not to be trifled with. But first, we'll start with your whore."

Two enforcers half-dragged, half-carried Meeryn

between them, Thorsh leading the gruesome parade dressed as a . . . Gray frowned. What the hell was the man wearing?

No time to worry over that now. The foursome paused at the top of the staircase. Thorsh gave a signal and one of the men pulled a pistol and held it against Meeryn's head. "Surrender or . . . how did you put it"—he tapped a finger to his lips in thought—"that's right . . . or I blow a hole through your precious N'thuil."

Gray's heart thrashed in his chest, his stomach rolled up into his throat, but none of it showed on his granite exterior. "I'm right here. Shoot me and get it over with, but leave her out of this."

Thorsh smiled. "Shoot you? That'd be too easy. Besides, Sir Dromon wants you alive. He wants you to pay for your crimes in the stone circle of the Deepings Hall, but this time, there'll be no escape. You'll die chained to that scaffold."

"Very well, I'll come with you now, but let Meeryn go. This wasn't her fight. I stole her from the holding. Forced her to take Jai Idrish—"

"I heard about that." Thorsh tsked his disappointment and shook his head. "Thought you'd break the Fey-blood's curse, did you? What a crock of nothing. Jai Idrish is as dead as you're gonna be soon. The stone's useless. The N'thuil's useless. The Imnada have to live by our wits and our strength, not some ancient power that doesn't exist anymore."

Gray's hand eased into his pocket, his fingers cocking the pistol. "If it's a crock of nothing, I'll be dead in a few weeks. Why even bother to go to all this trouble when I'm barely a threat?"

"Your death's no trouble at all."

"Feeling's mutual." Gray dragged the pistol free and fired in one swift motion. The enforcer holding the gun to Meeryn's head went down in a spray of skull and brains.

Meeryn dove for the floor, Thorsh crashing with her in a tangle of arms and legs. Gray snatched up a splintered piece of banister, hurling it like a spear toward the second enforcer. The jagged wood ended in his chest and the man fell, gripping the slick bloody wood with astonishment, eyes and face white.

Gray leapt over him as he took the stairs two at a time.

Thorsh scrambled back down the hall, dragging Meeryn with him, using her as a shield. He let fly with a dagger, the point aimed for Gray's heart. There was no time to avoid the blade. No time to think. Gray stepped into the throw, snatching the handle just before it pierced his breast.

"Bloody fucking hell," Thorsh muttered as he dragged Meeryn through a doorway into an upper bedchamber.

Gray pounded up the final stairs after them.

"Don't! It's a trap!" Meeryn shouted.

Too late. He skidded to a halt as the door to the room swung shut, and Thorsh stepped behind him. "Should have listened to her."

The fist to his wounded ribs dropped him to the floor on a bitten-back scream of pain. The slam to his stomach stunned him. The boot to the head he never felt.

She paced the room. Paused to listen. Paced again. No sounds to let her know what was happening elsewhere.

.

Just an ominous silence, a quiet that could mean anything. She had no idea how long she'd been locked in here, clouds obscured the sky and the moon had set hours ago. Was it long enough for Mac and David and the others to come looking for them? Or had Gray instructed them to cut their losses and keep out of the way if plans went sour?

Was she on her own?

She tried jimmying the latch on the door, but she'd no talent for lockpicking, and with her wrists bound with silver-laced cords, she couldn't shift to escape. Besides, she'd be damned if she left Gray behind. They would figure it out together, she'd promised. She wouldn't back out on him now. At least Thorsh hadn't found Jai Idrish. As long as the sphere was safe and she was breathing, there was hope. Slim and fading with every minute that ticked past, but she'd cling to whatever reassurance she could.

She sat on the bed, curling her legs underneath her. The silver sapped her will. It would be easy to surrender to the nausea and the headache and the teeth-chattering fever and just lie down and close her eyes to sleep. No, she had to keep moving, keep thinking. There had to be a way. She rose to continue her restless pacing.

A key turned in the lock, bringing her up short, and the door swung open. She caught her breath and braced for the worst as Mr. Thorsh stepped into the room.

"Ever hear of a whipping boy, Lady N'thuil?" He grinned. "I'll wager de Coursy has. And I'll wager he gives me what I want to keep you from being harmed."

"You're mad."

Thorsh backhanded her. She fell across the bed

with a gasp of pain, ears ringing. She brought her bound hands to her swollen mouth, refusing the tears burning her eyes.

He grabbed her up, pushing her roughly ahead of him out the door, down the corridor. She stumbled on the stairs, nearly falling through the broken banister, but he dragged her up again and marched her on.

A lamp had been lit in the library, a few sconces, and a candle sputtering on the mantel; more than enough light to see Gray, hunched and bleeding, on a chair set close to the desk amid his scattered ruined books. He looked up, an eye swollen shut, his shirt ripped to his waist to reveal deep black and purple bruising. Low on his ribs, he bore an ugly blackened blast wound. "What is she doing here?"

Thorsh drew free a long serrated knife. "See this? You answer a question. I don't hurt her. Simple."

Gray's throat worked as if he fought to speak.

Meeryn gave him a quick shake of her head, her eyes focused on the knife. If she could just . . . her fingers moved as she worked at the rope on her wrists. It wouldn't be easy and would probably end in dismal failure, but she and Gray were out of options.

Thorsh glanced at her, and she offered him a fearful, cowed look. Not hard to conjure. She was fearful . . . in fact, blubbering panic was as close as a heartbeat and a shaky breath away, but falling to the floor and weeping buckets would serve no one. And she refused to give the enforcer the satisfaction.

"Where have you hidden Jai Idrish?" Mr. Thorsh demanded, fingering the blade.

Gray's lips pressed tight, his cold stare hard as stone.

She never felt the sting of Thorsh's knife until the blood welled from the cut to her cheek. She put a hand to her face with a gasp.

Gray's gaze was murderous, every muscle strained as he fought his bonds.

Meeryn shook her head again, inched closer to Thorsh, though every fiber of her being told her to run for the hills. She angled her body slightly, braced herself against the desk. One try . . . she'd only get one try . . .

"Let's try again," Thorsh demanded. "Where's the sphere?"

"Fuck off," Gray growled. His eyes flashed to her in warning.

Another darting blur of Thorsh's arm and Meeryn's upper arm burned with the pass of steel, blood soaking hot into her sleeve.

"You're a slow learner, de Coursy. That or you want me to carve your woman to pieces. This blade was made for me special. Sharp enough to take a man's head off with one lop. I've done it. Twice. The rogues never knew what hit them." Thorsh fingered his knife in a gloating show of force, sliding it past Meeryn as if he might strike.

She gave a quick jerk of her head, and Gray lunged forward, dragging his chair with him. Startled, Thorsh fumbled the knife—the moment Meeryn was looking for.

Pushing off from the desk, she swung her knee up and into Thorsh's groin. He shouted, his hands unconsciously dropping to cradle his balls. She was ready. Her hands flashed out, and snatched the blade free. Drove it up and into his stomach with all the strength in her body.

He roared and batted her away. The knife clattered from her hands.

Blast and damn! She'd not killed him, merely made him very, very angry. Not good. Not good at all.

She slid across the desk, hoping to avoid his bull rush, landed hard on her side, smacking her head on the edge of a fallen cabinet. Her hip throbbed, and white lights danced across her vision.

He snatched up a broken table leg, swinging it above his head as if to club her. His face was contorted into a mask of rage and shock and pain. He drove it down, but she rolled one way. He swung again, and she rolled back, the leg smashing into the wall, a table, papers flurrying around her, the lamp toppled to catch on the books. Flames burst from the spilled oil and the old parchment. Singed her hair and beat white-hot against her skin.

She backed away from the cudgel, came up hard against the wall. Nowhere to go. Thorsh was an enormous shadow above her, backlit by rolling smoke and the flicker of flames in his pale eyes. One hand was clamped to his stomach, where blood spread like a poppy across his front. "Bitch!"

She cringed and squeezed her eyes shut, anticipating the blow she could not avoid. Something heavy fell hard beside her, followed by a softer rolling thud.

"It's over, Meeryn."

Gray's voice. She opened her eyes. He stood above her, one arm held out, ropes loose about his wrists. Thorsh's bloody dagger in the other. Of Mr. Thorsh, there was only a decapitated corpse, his head a few feet away, staring at her with consternation, as if still not quite believing in his own death.

"He was right." Gray tossed the knife on the dead man's chest. "Sharp enough to take a head off with one stroke."

Smoke filled the room, and the flames had caught the downed curtains, licked at the cushions of the chairs. A sound like thunder pummeled her ears as the fire spread.

"You killed him," she murmured.

"It was a team effort. Conal would be proud."

She felt the first shuddering tremors chattering her teeth, the sweat breaking out across her back, and the sick roiling of her stomach. "I couldn't see any other way."

"There was no other way."

She ran her hands down her face, bit her lip and shook her head. "I'm not a soldier, Gray."

"No, but you are a fighter."

# 17

He sat in the closed traveling coach, watching flames light the night sky. Men and women scurried like ants to stem the conflagration before it spread to neighboring houses, while a fire brigade barked orders, their hoses and tools of little use at this point. Thorsh was dead. Dromon had sensed the man's killing, the strand between master and servant severed with brutal finality. Gray and the girl had escaped. That had been conveyed to him by his Ossine, who had trailed the pair deep into London's rookeries where they'd disappeared into the chaos and filth of crooked lanes, dangerous alleys, and foul company.

The enforcers had been stymied, even their heightened abilities useless amid the maze of such an enormous city. The one sent to confess this failing had bowed before his Arch Ossine, apologetic but full of assurances of success sooner or later.

Dromon did not have sooner or later.

De Coursy must not be allowed to bring Jai Idrish and the Gylferion together. He must not be given the opportunity to lift the curse that kept him from his throne.

He turned to his traveling companion with an open, pleasant countenance and hands lifted in surrender. "My dear Lady Delia, I fear the future hangs upon you."

She lifted an arched brow in world-weary ambivalence. "And how would I possibly know where they've gone? London is a large city. They could be anywhere."

"They could be, but they are not. They are heading to the one place where de Coursy believes he can work the magic that will save him. He would not have begun this life-or-death chase if he didn't have its end planned to the last detail. An organized mind, our young duke. A methodical, practical conspirator who does nothing without understanding every implication."

"You sound almost admiring."

"I am. After all, he and I are much alike. We see the whole picture where so many see only the bits and pieces that concern them personally. He sees the future of the clans over generations, as do I."

"Then why do you two war if you're such boon companions?"

"Because what he sees is a false hope, a mirage"— his chin lifted in anger—"a Fey-blood conjuring woven to entice us beyond our borders. But I'm trained in the arts of divination and schooled in the history of our past. I understand the dangers, and I see through the web of lies your people have wrapped about our young lordling."

"The Imnada are not our enemies."

"No? What of these recent murders of Imnada by

your fellow Other? What of the growing call for a re-
newal of the hostilities between us? What of the *afailth
luinan*? Can you tell me the Fey-bloods would not kill
to gain the healing power of our blood?"

She looked away, flames dancing in her golden
eyes. "You paint us with a broad brush."

"I use only the palette your kind has shown me."
He caressed her cheek before cupping her chin and
turning her so that she must look at him. "Where is de
Coursy? Where has he taken the girl?"

She wrenched away. "I don't know. Gray doesn't tell
me everything."

"Only what he wants to be certain I hear, is that it?
He sends his little Fey-blood bird to scatter her secrets
where she will gain the most crumbs. And he pays you
well for that service, doesn't he?"

"I do all right."

"But I pay you as well. In coin and in . . . safety."

"Hardly enough of one and even less of the other
recently. Excuse me if I'm less inclined to offer up
what I know."

"Thorsh was not a rough lover, was he? A bit crude
perhaps, but you're used to such ungentlemanly handling. Your string of lovers is prodigious. Prinny himself is said to have tasted of your fruits."

She pressed her lips together and sought to turn
away.

"But you were not always this way, were you, Lady
Delia? Your first lover, he was all that was gentle and
loving. A charming young man with a golden future."

He smiled when he felt her tense, saw the way her
throat muscles tightened, her jaw clenched. "I barely
remember my first," she replied. "As you're always

so quick to point out, the numbers who have parted my legs are too numerous to hold long in my vague memory."

"Oh, no doubt. But this one was difficult to forget. He offered you his love and then his seed"—he leaned in close, inhaling her fear like a drug—"seed that bore fruit. Your child would be, what . . . seventeen? Eighteen? A young man strong of limb, handsome of face, and bearing the blood and powers of his father."

Her hands gripped her skirts, but the trembling was obvious.

"Where is de Coursy?"

She shook her head. "I don't know."

"As I said, I've paid you both in coin and safety. Not just for yourself but for your son."

"You're bluffing. You might know of his existence, but you have no idea where he is. No one does. Not even Gray." Her chin wobbled, but she thought herself a match for him and so held her tongue.

"That is where you're wrong, my dear." He leaned close enough to smell her perspiration mixed with her perfume. Feel the small hairs at the nape of her neck tickle his nose. He whispered the name of a village in her ear. Sat back with satisfaction to watch the sickening draining of blood from her face and the way her eyes widened in shock before glassing over in surrender.

"Bartholemew Ringrose," she answered dully. "His shop lies in the shadow of London Bridge."

"As always, you are a font of knowledge, my dear."

The upthrust dagger entered just below her heart. She was dead before they rounded the corner and left the flames behind.

\*          \*          \*

Ringrose's shop was dark; no candlelight shone from behind the dirt-smudged glass, no movement in the shadows. The way was clear. Gray avoided the street, instead leading Meeryn through a narrow lane to a muddy fenced yard where weeds sprouted from a crumbling cistern. A family of rats seemed the only ones interested in their passing.

He shoved open the unlatched door and stepped into the narrow back hall of the shop. Angry voices could be heard farther up the passage. "You cannot ask it of him. It is not fair of you. It is not right."

"The Gylferion were created to imprison Lucan within the emptiness of the between. He is bound to their magic and they are bound to his life force. There is no telling what might occur should he be one of the four."

"It's Badb and Ringrose," Meeryn whispered.

Gray stepped into the shabby back room, his eye traveling over the flushed and hostile faces of Lucan, Badb, and Mac. Ringrose hovered in a corner, worrying at his beard with a harassed look upon his sharp features. They swung to meet the two of them, stern expressions melting into relief.

"You made it," Mac said, stepping free of the circle.

"By the skin of our teeth," Gray said, wiping a hand down his blackened face. Behind him, Meeryn shook her skirts, ash dusting the floor.

Mac eyed their sooty, slightly singed features and ash-blackened clothing. "What the hell happened?"

"The Ossine slipped through the lines we set. We managed to escape with Jai Idrish, but the town house is gone, or close to it. By the time we got out of there, a bucket brigade had formed to keep the rest of the street safe from the fire, but my place was engulfed."

"Where's St. Leger?" Badb asked sharply, peering into the darkness of the alley.

"David's here, isn't he?" Gray asked.

Mac shook his head. "When you didn't turn up, he went out looking for you."

"Damn it to hell. You mean that bastard is still out there somewhere? Why didn't you stop him?"

"Have you tried talking David St. Leger out of doing what he wants to do lately? It's not exactly an easy task." Mac rubbed his chin and Gray, for the first time, noticed the bruising across his face.

Gray turned to leave, a hand on the latch. "I'll see what I can find out."

Meeryn stopped him with a hand on his arm. "You can't. We only barely made it here without discovery"—her gaze shifted to his hand pressed hard against his ribs—"and you're hurt."

"I can't leave David."

Badb's gaze passed over the group, her eyes glittering. "Without him, there is no foursome. The curse can't be lifted with only three. Lucan will be safe."

"And they will die," Meeryn snapped.

The door opened and David stepped into the room, out of breath, a bloody score down his cheek, his shoulder wet with blood. "The Ossine are coming. And Dromon's among them."

"How the devil did they know to find us here? Did they track one of us?" Mac snarled.

"Or did someone give us away?" David complained. "I told you sending Lady Delia Swann to pass your messages was a mistake. The woman's got more coils than a snake."

"We can accuse each other later." Gray scanned the back room. Stepped into the passage as he struggled to come up with a plan—any plan. Shoved aside the curtain to gaze into the darkened storefront and the myriad shelves of clutter. He turned back to the knot of anxious bodies crowding behind him. "If there is a later."

Ringrose swept past him, motioning him after with a wave of his hand. "Follow me. Quick . . . quick . . . don't tarry. Don't linger."

"We can't just wander out the front door. There's nowhere to hide, not even amid all that mess."

"You think you're so clever, shapechanger, but your knowledge is a thimbleful compared to the wisdom found within the Summer Kingdom." He shoved the curtain back on its rings.

Where moments before he'd been standing amid the confusion of a dark and shabby apothecary's shop, now white walls rose above him coming together in an enormous vaulted ceiling. Beneath his feet, rose and gold marble gleamed with polish, and tall arched windows draped in scarlet velvet looked out, not on a dingy Southwark street, but on a moonlit scene of aching beauty, a lake shimmering between snow-capped mountains, trees moving in a soft breeze. Fey magic pressed on his skull, beat behind his eyes like a hammer strike until he wanted to be sick. His stomach congealed to a hard curdled knot. He turned, but instead of one narrow passage, four wide corridors branched away into infinity.

"What is this place?"

"Our prison and our sanctuary. A place where worlds come together. A doorway. A thin place."

"Are we safe from Dromon here?"

"No, the Imnada can tear through even the thickest of our magics like knives through canvas, but the conjuring will hold for a time and it will slow him in his tracking. Take the far left tunnel. It will bring you down below the earth where a secret river runs. Follow it, and you will be where the power of our world folds over upon the power of this one. That is where you must call upon your magic and ours, shapechanger, if you wish to lift the curse."

"Let's go," Mac said, pushing through to start down the corridor. Torches burst into flame as he walked farther into the dark. Flickered out as he passed beyond their orbit. He paused. "Anyone?"

David and Lucan followed with Meeryn right behind. Gray hesitated. "If the magic is at risk, so are you."

Ringrose shrugged. "There is risk in all we do, son of the Imnada, son of Idrin, but last I checked, the true Fey were still a match for a few blundering beasts wearing human skins."

"So you'll hide."

"Quiet as the tomb, shapechanger. He'll never know we're here."

Gray smiled and clapped the man's arm in a firm handshake. "Thank you."

"Do not thank us yet. We have led you false once. Who's to say we won't lead you false again?" And with that, Ringrose shimmered into oblivion, pinks darkening to reds, purples into blues, his form fading into a sparkle of dying light.

"What I wouldn't give to do the same," David muttered.

Badb stood close to Lucan, though she did not touch him and her eyes held as much anger as affection. "You'll do this whether I will it or no."

He bowed his head, his face close to hers, his expression holding sorrow and the weight of his imprisonment and hers. "I have endured what I could not atone for, but this is my chance to finally restore what I tore apart. To make right what I destroyed."

"Penance for your sins," Badb muttered and, as if she realized he stood as witness to their last words, she looked toward Gray, her gaze bearing the chest-tearing pain of a sword stroke.

Gray turned away, unable to bear her accusation and her grief. "Let's go. Ringrose and Badb will buy us time. It's up to us to use it well."

"And if they're leading us false?" David asked.

Gray offered a gallow's smile. "Then we end in a hole in the ground either way, don't we?"


"Dank, spidery, filthy catacombs and now dank, spidery, filthy tunnels. It's a rabbit warren down here," Meeryn muttered as they followed the river's winding course.

It had been a slippery, uncomfortable journey. Twice she'd stumbled and scraped her palms, once she'd banged her bruised hip against an outcropping of rock, and worst of all, she'd smacked her head into a particularly low passage of rock, leaving her with starry-eyed vision and a duck-egg-size lump on her skull.

"Let's hope Sir Dromon finds it equally as confounding." Gray pushed aside a drifting strand of spider's silk from the ceiling of the slimy cavern walls.

"At least we have light." The torches had continued on, one after the other, blinking into being up ahead, then winking out as they passed.

"A double-edged sword," Gray said, glancing back over his shoulder.

"I wish we had a few of those, too."

Meeryn glanced behind her then down at the strange tumbling surface of the water flowing past. Much like the conjured palace above them, this river was more than it appeared. The surface shone an incandescent green, from which mist rose like smoke. If that wasn't enough to make her want to avoid it, the smashing anvil inside her skull and nauseous clutching of her innards warned her of the convergence of Fey magic centered within the curling, twisting currents and eddies.

David bent to wash away the blood from his face, but Lucan stopped him. "It's not wise to take of this place. Neither stone from the earth or water from the river. If this is truly a fold between the realms, there is no telling what effect it might have upon us or what we might ignite with our trespass."

"Wouldn't our being down here count as trespass?" David asked in an aggrieved tone of voice.

Lucan shrugged and the two pressed on, David's gash untended, his fears more than stoked, if the doubtful looks he continued to cast at the murky river were any indication.

"Is he right?" she asked Gray. "Are we tempting something worse by using the thin place to break the curse?"

"Can you think of worse? I can't."

She could think of lots worse; the shadows waiting
for her when she stepped into the heart of Jai Idrish;
the sickening jolt of muscle, tendon, and fat parting as her blade sank into Thorsh's gut, the hot spill
of blood on her hands and spattering her face; Gray
palsied with sickness, his face green with fever, his
body curled in on itself as the poison of the draught
devoured him; and finally, the emptiness of her life
should this fail, should she fail.

Gray trusted her to break him free of his curse. He
counted on her.

She could not let him down.

"Do you still hear them behind us?"

Gray paused as he listened, then gave a frustrated
shrug of his shoulders. "I can't hear anything above
the roar of the river."

"I almost wish I heard shouts and the clomp of
boot heels and a few clanging swords for good measure. Better that, than wondering if they're out there
just beyond the light of the last flickering torch."

Gray offered her a half smile but she could tell
his heart wasn't in it. "Knowing Badb, she's got them
chasing their tails, literally and figuratively."

"But even she can't delay them forever."

"No. She can't. They'll come soon or late. It's up to
us to be ready for them when they arrive."

They rounded a corner and found themselves in a
slick-walled cavern, the roof lost in a strange gathering of mist, as if the river's surface had risen to coa-
lesce like a cloud above them. The river itself poured
through the center of the room, in a tumbling rocky
rush, before spilling down beneath an overhang in a
gushing fall to be lost from view. Amid the torrent, on

a small island accessible by a narrow bridge of rock where the cavern's floor had been worn away, stood a tall fingerlike stone. Birds fluttered and animals crawled over the carved granite surface; the interlacing knots and spirals of the Fey wove in and out of every remaining cranny. Upon each of the four sides was inscribed a line of runes, the markings matching the odd gibberish in Gray's ancient text.

"Carspethic."

"Similar, though much older," Gray said softly. "I've never seen such markings."

"So you can't be certain it doesn't say 'Beware, traveler. Touch this and you shrivel up and die'?" David quipped.

"One way to find out." Gray stepped out on the bridge, slick with moisture and a thin sheen of green algae.

"Be careful," Meeryn cautioned. A silly warning. What did careful matter when they were being chased down here like rats into a cellar, curse hanging like a cloud, poisoning a dose away, and Fey magic scraping the insides of her skull like caged animals howling for release? Slipping on a wet rock rated low on the scale of dangers to be overcome.

He held out a hand to her. "We'll place Jai Idrish upon the dolmen."

"Are you certain, Professor Gray?"

"More than a theory, less than a certainty, Lady N'thuil."

She drew in a steadying breath and stepped, balancing her way on the narrow band of rock. A footstep, then another. She stumbled and nearly toppled headfirst into the drink. An arm wrapped protectively around her middle just as her hem dragged along the murky water.

"I think my heart skipped a beat," she said, catching her breath.

"Mine stopped." Gray tightened his arms around her for a moment. He withdrew Jai Idrish from the pocket of his coat, the sphere burning a strange milky yellow, its light flattening out along the roughened walls of the cavern and casting upward into the mists to illuminate each silver droplet. "It wakes, Meeryn. I feel a humming beneath my hands."

He placed it on the dolmen. As sphere touched stone, the light burst outward, bathing them in the same eerie milky glow. Faces hollowed by loss, by battle, by sickness, and by guilt. Without even touching the crystal, she heard the voices whispering in her head, a blur of endless N'thuils sharing their wisdom and their strength. But she also heard the first distant shouts. The scrape of bodies passing quickly through the approaching tunnels.

"Gray!" she said, unable to keep the fear from her voice. But he'd heard them, too. His head was lifted to the sound, the men shuffling restlessly as they touched knives, patted pistol butts, reminded themselves they were not defenseless. They would not go down without a fight.

"Quick! Jai Idrish at the center, the Gylferion at each compass point," she said, repeating what the voices told her.

"And how are we to tell compass points with a mile of earth above us?" David asked, shooting sidelong glances over his shoulder.

"With this." Gray pulled a small round box from

his pocket and flipped back the hinged lid to reveal a hidden compass. "East. *Nivatha Chu. Anada
Asantos.*"

David, holding the bronze disk, crossed to stand
where Gray pointed at the river's edge. Jaw tight, eyes
fixed upon Jai Idrish, he bore an expression of steadfast resignation. He had made his last farewells. He
would live or die with no regrets.

"South. *Anakalo Filios. Anada Asantos.*"

Copper disk in hand, Lucan stood as if he faced an
oncoming army without hope of survival. But it was a
look of peace. Of finality. Of ghosts laid to rest.

The sounds grew louder. The stamp and scrape
of boots. Muttered instructions. No way to tell how
many came. No way to tell if Sir Dromon led them or
if they faced a rabble of cannon fodder sent to flush
them out.

"West. *Pinota Asneeri. Anada Asantos.*"

Mac clenched his gold disk in a tight fist, green-
gold eyes fierce, mouth twisted in a grimace of final
hope. No surrender. He would not succumb. He
would battle to the last breath for the chance to live
free of the Fey-blood's taint.

"And north. *Krylesos Pryth! Anada Asantos.*" Gray
pulled the leather drawstring bag from its place at his
belt, spilling the silver disk into his palm with a hiss
of pain. The poison would be seeping through his fingers and into his bloodstream. With every moment
that the silver was in contact with his skin, it would
be chewing its way through his body and draining his
strength. But he did not wince after that initial gasp.
Instead he left Meeryn's side to cross back over the
bridge and stand at the river's edge to her right, eyes

flickering blue and silver in the crystal's shimmering glow.

"Do it, Meeryn!" he shouted. "Now!"

Gray clutched the silver disk until the edges burned into his skin, his heart near to slamming free of his ribs as Meeryn placed her hands upon the crystal. This was the moment he'd been waiting for since that long-ago summer afternoon at Charleroi when the Fey-blood's dying breath had stolen his own life away.

The shouts grew louder. Two Ossine. Then two more. A pistol cracked the cavern wall above him. David dropped one with a dead-eye shot from his own weapon, his other hand grasping the disk. Mac felled a second.

Sir Dromon stepped into the unearthly light, a hand shielding his eyes. "Stop her! Shoot the girl! She's the one!"

The remaining Ossine trained their weapons on Meeryn, the cocking of their pistols freezing Gray's blood. He flung himself across the slippery, narrow bridge even as he was pulling his own pistol free of its holster, cocking it, and firing in one swift fluid motion. Sir Dromon was blown backward, his body limp as a wrung rag.

Gray's triumph lasted but a moment as the Ossine followed through on their leader's final orders. The first bullet hit Gray in the shoulder, blood spattering Meeryn's gown crimson. He fell against her as the second bullet exploded through his chest. His legs gave out as if his strings had been cut. He fell upon the crystal, the sphere covered with his insides, blood pouring down the side of the dolmen.

*It's in the blood!*

The voice seemed to burst inside his head with the same crushing agony centered in his chest. A rumbling shook dust from the cavern's ceiling and mixed with the billowing mists. Jai Idrish's humming increased until it matched and surpassed the roar of the river. The sickly yellow light exploded crimson and gold, blue and silver. It bounced off the walls, bathed the iridescent river a brilliant blue, and etched a burning white light on the backs of his eyelids.

Weight and momentum carried him onward to tumble headfirst into the river. The water closed over his head, but there was no freezing punch of cold, only a scalding heat centered in his torn and broken chest. He surfaced to hear the sounds of struggle, a woman's sobbing, ragged screams, but the river dragged him under again, and weightless, boneless, and drained of strength, he let it.

He felt himself falling, a spinning twisting piece of flotsam caught in the cascade as the river carried him away. He tried to breathe but his lungs wouldn't work. Pain burst against the back of his head. He gasped once and went under. And the world went black.


A seeming enternity passed as Meeryn knelt on the cavern floor, an arm pressed to her middle, the dolmen casting a shadow over her bowed body. The sphere's light faded as slowly as the power surging through her body. Every now and then, her eyes would travel to the overhanging lip of rock where the river raged through the gap to spill in a froth deep beneath the earth, as if expecting Gray to climb from the edge of the river sopping wet and fuming like a cat tossed into a well.

"Meeryn?" She winced at Mac's touch upon her shoulder. The gentle worry in his voice. "Is all well?"

She lifted her eyes, red-rimmed with weeping. "He hated the water," was all she could muster with another long look at the river as it rushed over the falls and down beneath the cavern's wall.

Mac and David exchanged glances. She knew what they were thinking. That she'd lost her mind. That she was a hysterical female with straw for brains. That she was as useless a N'thuil as Muncy Tidwell with his grotesque belly and pinhead brain.

"Is it over?" she asked, looking around her, seeking to gather her wits and regain her composure. Her heart might be lying in pieces around her, but she was N'thuil. The crystal had chosen her. It had spoken to her as it had not spoken to anyone in centuries. She would not be found wanting after such a gift.

"Aye," Mac said, straightening with a swipe of his brow. "Or just beginning, depending upon your viewpoint. With Sir Dromon dead and Gray . . ." He turned away, his hands fisting at his sides. "The clans could tear themselves apart in their fight for a new leader."

For the first time, she noticed his blood-soaked shirt, his bruised knuckles, the cut upon his chin. St. Leger, too, held himself stiffly as he leaned awkwardly against the dolmen, his blond hair plastered to his head, mist and sweat mingling on his battered face.

The bodies of the Ossine had been laid out as if for burial. She noticed all had death offerings lying upon their chests, above their crossed arms. Sir Dromon, on the other hand, had been hauled to a corner of the cavern and dumped unceremoniously to lie forgotten and unmourned.

"Where's Lucan?" she asked, reassured by the strength in her voice.

*He's gone.* Badb's words burst in Meeryn's head as her body burst into being in fireworks of color, her crow feathers ruffling outward in a surge of feathery black. Her cloak billowed and swirled around her pale young woman's body of pert breasts and narrow hips. Her eyes bore a flat emptiness unlike their usual snapping fire.

"What do you mean, gone?"

The girl tossed the gold disk to the ground at Meeryn's feet. "I mean he has paid for his sins twice over. Freed from a thousand years trapped in the between of nothing, only to be taken once more by the Gylferion's powers that you unleashed. He is gone."

Meeryn took up the disk, fingering the clan mark of the Imnada on the face, the double parallel lines crossed by the diagonal on the back. Gazed at Badb, who stood hunched, hands wrapping her stomach as if she too fought to hold her grief back.

"I'm sorry. I didn't know that would happen."

"He did. And he chose to go through with it anyway. Your people call him Kingkiller and curse his memory. But love drove him to such a madness. As love drove him to this one. Is that a crime? A sin to be endured or atoned for?" Badb searched each face as if trying to understand, but none had an answer for her. She made a jerking motion with her hand as if cutting off any more discussion. "The tunnel will take you out as it brought you in. Be gone from the shop by dawn. Do not come back. It will not be here."

And just like that, the magic of her race congealed around her, pulling her inward as her feathers disappeared in a strange tightening swirl, popping out with a final burst of weary color.

The three of them seemed to hold close as if offering one another the comfort of nearness. She was grateful, for just the act of keeping body and soul together seemed a Herculean task.

"Can you walk?" Mac finally asked, a hand propped beneath her elbow.

"I'm not hurt. Only heartsick," she said, taking one last look around her. The crystal shone dim and cloudy once more, its voices silent. She took it in her hands, feeling the warmth beneath her fingers, the eddying vibrations like a dizzying pulse. Her eyes followed the green mist-shrouded river as it disappeared in a roaring spill over the edge of the cavern floor. "Do you suppose he suffered much?"

Mac followed the track of her gaze. "I would think he was dead upon hitting the water. Neither Ossine missed their mark."

She spat upon Dromon as she passed his lumpish tangled body, bullet-shattered face hidden by the careful drape of an arm. "Nor did Gray. All that bloody training at last paid off."

# 18

DEEPINGS, CORNWALL
FEBRUARY 1818

Sigurd Skaarsgard shuffled the papers on his desk, fiddled with his watch fob, then peered over his spectacles at her. It was a stare meant to intimidate, but she had never been easy to cow, and recent events had only firmed her resolve and her backbone.

"The man comes of good family. The Nornala prosper and the holdings are fat with wealth under his handling of the clan in my absence. The new Arch Ossine supports the cross in bloodlines. Why do you refuse?"

Meeryn sat calm and still, hands folded in her lap, eyes ahead. A pose of careful deliberation on the outside. Within she was howling her frustration and grief. "His focus is solely for the Nornala, as it should be, while you remain at Deepings, cousin. I need a man whose love for all five of the clans allows him to see beyond the acres in front of his nose. The next years will not be easy ones for us."

The Skaarsgard cleared his throat and sat back, arms crossed over his chest. "What you need, Meeryn, is a man who'll look past your growing belly and take you as his mate anyway. Who'll be strong enough to keep you safe from your enemies and your child's enemies. Do you think they don't know whose child you carry? Even the bastard son of de Coursy could be a powerful threat if he grows to manhood. There are men out there who would seek to do you and the babe harm. Some who blame you and de Coursy for the state of the clans and seek vengeance for the death of Sir Dromon. And some who see your interference as carrying us toward a new Fealla Mhòr with the Fey-bloods. We live in dangerous times and you need a powerful protector."

"I know, but Findlaech Orlspath is not the answer."

He's the third candidate in two months. You're not growing any smaller. And the clan's troubles are not growing any easier."

She ran a hand over her stomach. Already the gowns she'd ordered in the autumn were straining against her bulk. Gray's child prospered. She had done what she could. She had accepted Gray's seed. In a few short months, she would have a living memory of their love. A face to look upon where she might see traces of Gray perhaps in the sweep of the child's brows or the hard steel blue of its eyes. That both comforted her and saddened her in equal measure.

"The Gather does what it can, but with the throne empty, the clan leaders squabbling amongst themselves as they seek to solidify their positions, and Idrin's line ended, there is too much uncertainty. You're the only glue we have that can keep us from fracturing further."

The Skaarsgard's criticisms drew her back to the conversation at hand and the concerns of today. Gray had died in the caverns. It was up to those who survived to keep the destiny he envisioned alive . . . if they could.

Mac Flannery and David St. Leger tried to hold the alliance between Fey-blood and Imnada together, but even they found the way difficult and the tensions increasing.

"I will think on it, my lord. And give you my answer tomorrow. Is that time enough?"

He smiled, obviously satisfied he'd convinced her. "You always were a headstrong lass, even as a youngling barely free of your mother's womb, but growing up within the duke's household has taught you cleverness and to keep your own council. Jai Idrish chose wisely when it chose you."

"Did it?" Sometimes she wondered. In the dead of night, when the soft hissing voices tricked her brain and she dreamt of the black unending shadow rising above her like a rogue wave, she feared what she might have unleashed when she freed Gray and the others from the curse.

He stood at the window, staring out on the snow drifting small and white from a wintry gray sky. His chest ached in the cold, every breath was laced with dull pain, but his shoulder seemed much improved. It didn't throb as it had in the weeks and months past, when every bump of his injured arm elicited an unconscious scream of pain that brought tears to his eyes and left him gasping and retching.

He'd not remembered how he'd gained such horrific injuries nor how he'd survived them. The wizened, stooped old woman who tended him spoke little beyond explaining he'd been fished from the river barely alive. How he'd ended in the river in the first place, she could not say . . . or wouldn't. She brought him three meals a day, cleaned his rooms, pressed his clothing, and tended his hurts. Questions, she did not answer. Frankly, she barely spoke at all.

It had been six months since he'd arrived here and he knew only that he was not wholly within the world he spied through his window, though what world he inhabited he could not quite say either. It seemed as real as the cityscape beyond the glass; the bed was soft, the food tasty, and the books smelled of old leather and dusty pages. But there was no way to get from this place to that, not one door that he had found in all his meanderings once he'd gained the use of his legs again and walking didn't involve a crutch and a steadying arm.

Corridors emptied into more corridors and rooms followed rooms, but of doors, he found not a single one. And the windows, when smashed—as he'd tried three weeks ago in a fit of rage—seemed to tear through the veil of both worlds, leaving only a howling darkness.

He had not broken one since. Better to stare out upon a world he recognized and pretend he was living among the men and women he spied going about their lives in the streets below than face the reality of his imprisonment.

But why? What had he done? He rubbed his forehead as if that might bring some recall, but naught but dim shadows met his study; a woman's eyes dark as treacle, a woman's body lithe as a willow reed. Whenever he probed this vision deeper, he came up against an unspeakable madness where terrors lurked and voices called. He did not court these memories often. And recently, not at all. He kept to the pleasant thoughts of the mysterious woman and hoped that whoever she was, she did not grieve overmuch for his loss.

Turning away from the window, he spied the mysterious old maidservant enter his room, a cane in her hand. "This is for you."

At this point, he didn't even question her. Curiosity had succumbed to ennui and he already knew she'd offer him nothing more than the same story of his being dragged from the river and brought here for her to mend as best she could. He knew the tale by heart.

She left as quickly and quietly as she came, leaving him alone with the dubious gift. What on earth did he need with a cane? He'd long since thrown away the crutch. His wounds had been to his upper body, the scars proved that. Still, it was a diversion in a life of few amusements beyond his books and his window.

He took up the cane, ran a thumb over the handle shaped in the form of an eagle's head. Now, why should that evoke a tightening in his chest and a tremble in the hand that held the ebony walking stick? He'd no idea but he gripped the cane like a weapon, the window a target for his sudden and overwhelming rage.

With two hands, he swung the cane like a bat, the glass shattering, shards flying to mingle with the falling snow. But instead of the emptiness of nothing that he'd come to expect, snow swirled in to settle on his shoulders and hair. It stung his face with its icy touch and melted on his lips.

The smells of coal fires and dung, Thames mud and roasted apples, filled his nose. He drew in a breath, ignoring the stabbing pain in his chest; stood watching the dim, smutty winter skyline with new delight and new focus. Somewhere out there was the dark-eyed woman. Somewhere out there someone knew who he was and what he was and why he had come to be here, wounded and lost.

"You need seek no further than me, Your Grace."

He spun, cane in hand, to confront this stranger standing before him. A young woman, her curling mop of black curls and snapping black eyes giving her a lively mischievous air. Dressed in the height of current fashion and carrying herself with all the arrogance of the aristocrat, she must be a duchess—his duchess? For she had addressed him as duke. He frowned, no, the dark eyes did not belong to her. The woman he remembered had eyes soft and dark and gleaming with love. This woman's gaze was keen as a knife blade, though wisdom lurked in those black depths.

"Who are you? And how do you read my thoughts?"

She smiled but it was not a pleasing smile. It held too much malice behind it. "So many questions you have, but which is the most important? For I don't know if I should answer them all."

"Fine. Who am I? That will do for starters. From there, perhaps I'll piece together the rest."

"You might, though it's a tattered life and you may decide to surrender it for a shiny new one more to your liking."

He cast a swift glance to the city, which bustled and moved just feet from where he stood. Turned back to find her staring with that same quirk of an ugly smile.

"You are the Duke of Morieux, though the claimants for that title are clawing each other's throats out since the news of your untimely demise."

He passed a hand over his forehead, but her answers jarred nothing loose.

"Duke is my title. What's my name?"

"Gray Cosantine Trevivian de Coursy."

He frowned with the first stirrings of images, faded and half lost to time, but shimmering into focus with each word she spoke. "What happened to me?" He pressed a hand to his chest and the roughened edges of scars atop scars. "Why am I here?"

"You died . . . almost. Fate lent a gentle shove when it toppled you into that river, my friend. For the headwaters of the Condatus originate within the summer kingdom of Ynys Avalenn. The river flows from that world to this and back again, the currents bearing the power of the Fey."

"It wasn't the Thames?"

"Hardly. The Condatus saved your life. A dunking in the Thames would have likely killed you six ways to Sunday. Well, it's proper to say the river did *most* of the saving. Your own otherworldly strengths assisted. The Imnada are known for their toughness and their ability to heal from hurts no normal human could withstand. It takes much to kill one of the clans."

Clans . . . Imnada . . . Ynys Avalenn . . . piece by piece, his life fitted itself into place within his head.

"Where am I?"

"A place of rest. A place where none of Sir Dromon's more rabid followers can find you should they decide to finish what the Arch Ossine almost succeeded in doing—ending your life. Deepings is in turmoil. It was not safe to take you there."

"This is a prison."

"A sanctuary."

Deepings . . . the Duke of Morieux . . . Sir Dromon Pryor . . . faster they came, jolting into his skull with the force of his cane through the window until the room spun and tilted and he wanted to be sick. Mac Flannery . . . David St. Leger . . . Adam Kinloch . . . the curse that bound them together even as it tore them apart.

He swallowed back the rage tearing at his throat. He wouldn't give her the satisfaction . . . Badb . . . He recognized her now, though she was not as he recalled. The cloak of crow feathers had become a demure gown of deep green velvet seeded with pearls. No skin shone free but the long column of her white throat and her oval face, hard as marble.

"Where is she?" Dark brown eyes . . . lips full and sensuous and curved in an arch smile . . . pride and courage and determination and love . . . he remembered all of it. "Where's Meeryn?"

Badb's smile widened, and this time the pleasure at his discomfort was obvious. "Being courted by every aspiring pretender to your throne. She is truly N'thuil in name and force, and in times such as these, her voice can be a valuable asset to anyone seeking to further his position."

"In other words, the clans claw at one another like rabid dogs."

"The Other will not need to lift a finger to see the eradication of your kind. They do such a convenient job of the task all by themselves."

"What of Lucan? Surely he didn't countenance holding me witless in a cage while the Imnada destroyed each other."

"Lucan is no more." Her voice held grief and rage in equal measure. Badb might have begun her journey to free Lucan out of vengeance, but she had ended it in love with the ancient warlord, no matter how she might deny it.

"Is that why you've kept me here? Trapped me here? Out of anger?"

She swung away, head bowed, hands covering her face. But it was a moment's weakness and then she turned back, her face wiped clean of any revealing emotion. "Lucan believed in your cause. He believed in you. I brought you here because he would have wanted me to do so. I kept you here because to set you free any sooner would have meant your death. You carry the magic of the Fey within you now, it moves within your blood and binds your spirit to its human shell and so you live, but such gifts are not without cost. You lost yourself when your spirit floated free. You spilled your memories when you spilled your blood, and you became a ghost in name as well as reputation when the river took you in its arms."

"So I lifted the curse. My death lifted the spell holding me captive."

"You are free of it. It was all as you predicted, shapechanger—almost. Jai Idrish was indeed the spark needed to light the powers locked within the Gylferion, but you overlooked one important aspect of Golethmenes's original spell."

"Which was?"

"Blood. The most powerful spells call for the most painful sacrifice; so it has always been. The Chevalier d'Espe knew this when he set the curse upon you. It was his blood; fresh, hot and spilled in violence that shaped the dark magic binding you. So it must be your blood spilled in the same way that loosed those chains."

"And Jai Idrish?"

"The N'thuil joined with the crystal, her body made stone, its essence made flesh. All was as you theorized, the power unleashed equal to that drawn from the Fey whose spirits were used in the disks' forging. But what you have woken may not be so easily laid back to rest. There is no knowing what will come of its being used in such a manner and for such a purpose. You have set the first stitch. It remains to be seen what pattern emerges. What decisions your N'thuil makes when the hard choices come."

"Let me go, Badb. Let me step out into my world and leave this refuge behind. Let me find my way back to Meeryn and to the clans. Let me offer my right to rule as the last son of Idrin and hope they accept it."

"But you are not the last son of Idrin, shapechanger," she sniffed, her form already fading within a rainbow of color, the room he stood within paling with every breath he took until barely the outlines of his elegant apartments remained.

"Ollie's son! You know where he is?"

"No, but your own grows quickly within his mother's womb . . . if you dare to claim him," came the scoffing taunt as the last of the magic winked out and he was left in a bare room in an empty house with naught on his back but a ragged shirt, a pair of worn breeches, and dry, cracked leather boots.

He fingered the gold-knobbed cane, the eagle's beak curved like a scimitar under his palm. Lifted his head with a purpose he'd not felt for months. And stepped through the door.

She placed her hands upon the crystal, her mind winging free of her body to dance out along the ribbon of thought where the crystal bade her to come.

The earth fell away until there was naught but a marbled ball set amid a string of jeweled planets. She sought farther, deeper into the expanse, following the sphere's whispers, begging it to wake, calling it from the slumber of centuries.

Now the whispers became hisses, sibilant and persuasive. Dark words and sinister deeds. Seeking her aid. Seeking her strength. The welcoming darkness split by distant golden-white stars and spinning iridescent clouds of light deepened to an empty black vastness where no spark shone, a fearsome rolling wave moving with a typhoon's force toward her. If she remained locked within the crystal's heart, she would be consumed by it. If she broke the connection she had formed, she would have failed Gray.

She sought to outrun the horrible creeping shadow, and when that didn't work, she armored herself behind mental walls she erected with every shuddering breath she took. But it poured past her, finding every chink she failed to stanch, every gap her faltering strength opened up.

With a scream, she ripped her hands free of the crystal and the world righted itself to the cavern, the men, the spraying torrential rush of the river. But the sphere burned on. The light filled the room. It burned her eyes until she had to squint and avert her gaze, and her indrawn gasp of breath hissed through her clenched teeth.

"Gray!" She flung herself up, nearly striking her head against the headboard, gasping her terror and the shock of his loss. Blinked and wiped her face with the back of her nightgown's sleeve. Tears . . . again. She grew tired of rising in the morning with red eyes and damp cheeks.

N'thuil was no longer the useless empty title of the past. Jai Idrish had come alive and was once more a force to be reckoned, its Voice and Vessel, to be treated with deference. Petitioners filled the benches in the Crystal Tower once again. And sleepless nights made for uncomfortably long days.

She couldn't explain the sphere's reawakening after such a long silence, any more than she could explain the reasons it had chosen her to receive its wisdom and speak its secrets, but she had her suspicions, even if she continued to shrink from them.

Her dreams had grown increasingly dark, every night revealing a new tear in the fabric of the universe, bringing the shadows closer, the threat more real. What these images signified she had yet to unravel, but her certainty grew with each dawning of clear skies and jewel-strewn seas, that what the clans had taken for war was, in fact, the calm before the real storm.

She rose, grabbing up her robe, crossing to the window and throwing the casement wide. Her bedchamber was bathed in the glow of Silmith's full moon. The Mother in her full glory cast great purple shadows across the courtyard and lawns while a balmy southern wind blew soft and warm, bringing with it the deep growl of the ocean as it beat against the cliffs below the house.

A temptation she couldn't ignore. A call she welcomed.

With Sir Dromon's death, the number of guards had dwindled, and it was a moment's effort to slip out of her bedchamber and through the quiet house.

The path to the beach was steep and rocky, but the moonlight made going easy and soon she stood at the edge of the sea, toes dug into the sand and pebbles,

the nip of chilly surf against her ankles welcome.
Skimming off her nightclothes, she stared out toward
the horizon where black sky met black water. Drew a
calming breath, letting the wind caress her body like a
lover, letting the growl of the ocean soothe her aching
heart and her troubled thoughts.

Findlaech Orlspath—a name she knew from meet-
ings and clan gatherings. A face she barely remembered
but for the keenness in a pair of soulful brown eyes. Could
she marry him? Did she have a choice? The Skaarsgard
was right in thinking she needed allies. And the Orkneys
were isolated, easy to defend should she have need of a
refuge. The child could grow up relatively safe, out of
the way of clan intrigues and potential threats.

It was a smart choice. A safe choice.

She had tried passion and found heartbreak. She'd
experienced love and found loss.

Just as she'd always known; safe worked.

Safe didn't hurt.

Running into the ocean, she called forth the shift,
losing herself to the power locked inside her. Letting it
take her over as she donned the skin of the seal. Diving under the surface, she pushed with flipper and fin,
seeking release from the ache gnawing at her heart,
hoping to fill the emptiness consuming her with the
ocean's buoying serenity.

By the time she returned to the shore, it was with a
calmer mind and her decision made. She shifted, the
heat flushing her skin pink as she stepped free of the
magic's cocoon. A shadow glided over her like a spear.
She looked up, but saw nothing beyond silver-lined
clouds moving lazily east.

*I hoped I might find you here.*

The words glided over her mind like a lover's touch. A lover all had seen disappear over a waterfall with his chest ripped open. Her heart stuttered, her body crackling with mingled hope and horror. She stood very still, unable to turn around lest she be dreaming, lest this was all some terrible hallucination.

*How did you know where to find me?* she pathed, unable to use her lungs to speak aloud.

"You always swam when you were angry or upset. I assumed you'd be both tonight—mainly at me. Am I right?" That familiar crisp aristocratic tenor, polished to perfection but with just enough of a rasp to send tingles up her spine.

She swallowed, trying to control the dizziness. She was N'thuil. Swooning was out of the question. "I ought to be."

There. She spoke. A little wobbly but hardly as bad as her trembling limbs might indicate.

"Angry enough to refuse to look at me?"

"I'm afraid if I turn around, you'll be gone. A ghost sent to test my determination. Orlspath will make a good husband. A strong reliable mate."

"I would make a better one."

She turned then. Her feet moved. Her body followed. Her eyes swept up to meet the icy blue stare of the man she'd thought dead six months past. The man who'd not just taken her heart but torn it still beating from her chest.

"Are you real?"

The arched brows, the raking dagger cheekbones, the full sensual lips; he was as every dream had conjured him. He stepped from the shelter of the cliff into the light, the moon revealing every line of his lean sculpted naked body and every fresh hideous scar spiderwebbing across the broad planes of his chest.

"As real as this."

"I don't know whether to throw my arms around you or beat you senseless."

"I know which I'd prefer," he answered with a wry twist to his lips.

She reached out to touch the puckered flesh of his chest, tracing the ridges, the uneven seams of newly knit skin. He allowed her study as if he understood her need to reassure herself. He was too warm to be a ghost. Too solid to be a fantasy.

"How dare you come home now?"

He took an uncertain step back, but she couldn't stop. Six months of tamped-down grief erupted all at once. Six months of holding herself and her world together through sheer force of will unraveled with the abruptness of a severed knot.

"I hated you." She could not stop the words or the rush of tears or the shaking that left her crouched upon the sand, hands wrapped about her midsection, hair falling across her face. "I hated you and then I hated myself, but it was the only way I could draw a breath without feeling as if I were inhaling shards of glass, as if my heart were being scissored with every beat." She took a quick shuddery breath. Damn it, she would not let him see her weep. "I said good-bye, Gray. I burned my offerings and said my prayers to the Mother for the safe passage of your soul, and I moved on. Hating you let me do that. It made the pain bearable. It was the only way I could keep living."

Arms collected her like a child, wrapped around her so that she lay nestled against his chest, his heart beating steady beneath her ear, his lungs filling and emptying with human regularity. If she'd possessed the strength, she would have pulled away. Instead she remained curled and shaking in the circle of his embrace, the heat of him saturating her down to the coldest, hardest knots where she'd buried her pain.

"I never meant to stay away so long. I didn't know. Not about you, not about the . . . not about the child. I knew nothing of what went on in the world."

"What do you mean you didn't know?"

"I lost everything when I was taken by the river. I had my life and that was a broken, scattered thing. Only when I recovered my strength did Badb hand me back all I had forgotten—including you."

She should have known the Fey had a hand in this. The marks of their interference lay all over his return, as clear and present as the scars upon Gray's body.

"I can walk away now, Meeryn. None will know. I can stay dead. You can go on as you have done. You can . . . you can go on hating me if that's how it has to be."

He started to withdraw, leaving her cold and alone. Panic snatched away her breath. Her hard-won struggle with hate dissolved and sloughed away. She leapt to her feet, grabbing his wrist, clasping it between her hands hard enough that she felt the tendons tighten and the bump of an old break. "Don't!"

He turned back, his eyes luminous in the light of the full moon.

She didn't let go of his wrist. Instead she pulled him back until he stood before her, and she was surprised to see his shoulders trembling, his throat working as he swallowed back his own emotion.

"Don't leave."

His stare carved into the stone of her heart, but it was his kiss that broke through the last crumbling barriers she'd maintained through six months of anguish. His lips moved over hers, tentative at first, then when she did not pull away, the current running between them grew in power until she must grab his shoulders to keep her knees from giving way and she wanted to melt into his body.

Tears tracked her cheeks, slid hot into her mouth where his tongue danced and plunged. He threaded the long wet fall of her hair, cradled the back of her neck, glided a hand over the swell of her buttock and finally her stomach.

"I need you, Meeryn," he murmured, his breath warm upon her cheek.

"Me or the child I carry?" she only half-teased.

His mouth found hers again and he kissed her like a man drowning. A sensuous, desperate kiss she matched with every slide of his tongue against hers. Her heart still ached, but now with a surging flood of desire and relief.

His hand fell to skim the bulge of her stomach, pausing in wonder as the surface rippled with the baby's movement in her womb. "I need you, my beautiful and powerful N'thuil. I love you." His gaze darkened with desire and a longing that tore her breath away. "I'll beg if you want me to," he said quietly. "I'll fall to my knees before you if that's what it takes."

Joyous laughter dizzied her insides and slid hot and fizzy along her nerves. "You need never beg again, Gray. I'm here for the asking. Now and for always." She leaned close to his ear, her words barely more than a breath. "You're in my blood."

# Glossary of the Imnada

**Afailth luinan.** Also known as the blood cure. According to ancient legend, Imnada blood possesses great healing powers. It's said that a drop can heal most injuries or illness, though few believe the old stories anymore.

**Berenth.** The night of the last quarter moon. This begins the period when the Imnada's powers to shift at will begin to ebb and it becomes both more difficult and more dangerous.

**Bloodline scrolls.** The written history and genealogies created and maintained by the Ossine. These records are used to select mates for the Imnada from the five clans.

**Clan mark.** The crescent symbol tattooed on the upper backs of the male members of the Imnada, signifying their full acceptance into the clan upon their majority. Both males and females are also marked mentally with a signum identifying their clan affiliation and holding.

**Dunsgathaic.** A mighty fortress located on the Isle of Skye in Scotland that encompasses both the military headquarters of the brotherhood of Amhas-draoi and a convent of Sisters of High Danu.

*Emnil.* An exile who has been formally sentenced by the Gather and had his clan mark and signum removed and his name erased from the Ossine's bloodline scrolls. An *emnil* is considered dead to the clan and his life forfeit if he attempts any contact with a clan member or a return to clan lands.

**Enforcer.** The warrior arm of the Ossine whose job it is to track down and eliminate any potential threat to the Imnada.

**Fealla Mhòr.** The Great Betrayal: the betrayal and murder of the last king of Other, Arthur, by the Imnada warlord Lucan. This event triggered a vengeful purge of the Imnada by the Fey-bloods, who had always mistrusted and feared the shapechangers.

**Fey-bloods.** (Slang.) Also known as the Other. Men and women who possess the blood and magical powers of the Fey.

**Gateway.** The door between Earth and the galaxy where the Imnada first originated.

**Gather.** The ruling council of the Imnada, consisting of seven members: the clan leader from each of the five clans, the head of the Ossine, and the Duke of Morieux, who is hereditary leader over the five clans.

**Idrin the Traveler.** Among the first Imnada to come through the Gateway and settle on Earth. He is considered the father of their race and from his seed the five clans sprang.

**Imnada.** A race of shapechangers and telepaths divided into five clans overseen by the ruling Gather. They wield no magical powers, though they are sensitive to its presence and can identify those who possess magic. At first they existed peacefully with the magical race of Other but when the Imnada betrayed King Arthur to his death, they were hunted down in the wars and uprisings that followed. In the ensuing centuries, those who survived grew reclusive and fiercely suspicious of all outsiders to the point that most believe the Imnada no longer exist.

*Krythos.* Also known as a far-seeing disk. A notched glass disk about two and a half inches in diameter. It is used to augment and amplify the Imnada's natural telepathic abilities over long distances.

**Lucan.** Leader of the clans during King Arthur's reign. He conspired with Morgana, the king's half sister, to place her son Mordred upon the throne. His betrayal led to Arthur's murder. He was captured by the Fey for his treachery and imprisoned within the Bear's Stone for all eternity.

**Morderoth.** The night of the new moon, when the shift is impossible for the Imnada.

**Mother Goddess.** The moon from which the Imnada derive their magical powers.

**Ossine.** Shamans and spiritual advisers to the clans, they tend to be the strongest and most powerful of the Imnada. They maintain the bloodline scrolls used for selecting each Imnada mating pair and protect the Imnada from out-clan interference with their armed militia of enforcers.

**Other.** See Fey-blood.

**Out-clan.** Someone who is not a member of the five clans.

**Palings.** Magical mists conjured and maintained by the Ossine of each clan. They are used as a natural force field, disguising and shunting people away from the hidden holdings. In recent years, these warded fields have weakened as the clans' powers have weakened.

**Pathing.** Speaking mind to mind. Imnada can use this telepathy to speak to one another over short distances or when they are in their animal aspect. For longer distances, they use the amplifying power of the *krythos* to connect with each other mentally.

**Realing.** A magical servant bound to a specific person or place.

**Rogue.** An unmarked shapechanger without clan or hold affiliation.

**Signum.** The mental imprint set on every shapechanger's mind at birth by the Ossine. It identifies clan affiliation and rank. Those cast out of the clans have their signa stripped, denoting their outlaw status.

**Silmith.** The night of the full moon, when the shift comes easiest and the powers of the Imnada are at their height.

**Sisters of High Danu.** An order of Other priestesses, also known as *bandraoi*, devoted to a contemplative life in service to the gods.

**Warriors of Scathach (Amhas-draoi).** An Other brotherhood of warrior mages who serve as guardians between the Fey and human worlds.

**Ynys Avalenn.** Also known as the Summer Kingdom, this is the realm of the Fey.

**Youngling.** A child of the Imnada who has not yet reached maturity or been marked.